A CLASH OF KINGS

THE GRAPHIC NOVEL

VOLUME 3

GEORGE R. R. MARTIN

A CLASH OF KINGS

THE GRAPHIC NOVEL

VOLUME 3

ADAPTED BY LANDRY Q. WALKER

ART BY MEL RUBI

COLORS BY IVAN NUNES

LETTERING BY TOM NAPOLITANO

ORIGINAL SERIES COVER ART

BY MIKE S. MILLER AND MEL RUBI

COLORS BY NANJAN JAMBERI AND IVAN NUNES

BANTAM BOOKS · NEW YORK

Copyright © 2021 by WO & Shade LLC

All rights reserved.

Published in the United States by Bantam Books, an imprint of Random House, a division of Penguin Random House LLC, a Penguin Random House Company, New York.

BANTAM BOOKS and the HOUSE colophon are registered trademarks of Penguin Random House LLC.

All characters featured in this book, and the distinctive names and likenesses thereof, and all related indicia are trademarks of George R. R. Martin.

ISBN 978-0-440-42326-3
Ebook ISBN 978-0-593-15970-5

Printed in China on acid-free paper by RR Donnelley Asia Printing Solutions

randomhousebooks.com

9 8 7 6 5 4 3 2 1

Graphic novel interior design by Foltz Design.

Visit us online at www.DYNAMITE.com
Follow us on Twitter @dynamitecomics
Like us on Facebook /Dynamitecomics
Watch us on YouTube /Dynamitecomics
On Tumblr dynamitecomics.tumblr.com

Nick Barrucci, CEO / Publisher
Juan Collado, President / COO
Brandon Dante Primavera, VP of IT and Operations

Joe Rybandt, Executive Editor
Matt Idelson, Senior Editor

Alexis Persson, Creative Director
Rachel Kilbury, Digital Multimedia Associate
Katie Hidalgo, Graphic Designer
Nick Pentz, Graphic Designer

Alan Payne, V.P. of Sales and Marketing
Francis Limcuando, Sales Manager
Vincent Faust, Marketing Coordinator

Jim Kuhoric, Vice President of Product Development
Jay Spence, Director of Product Development
Mariano Nicieza, Director of Research & Development

Amy Jackson, Administrative Coordinator

CONTENTS

A CLASH OF KINGS

THE GRAPHIC NOVEL

VOLUME 3

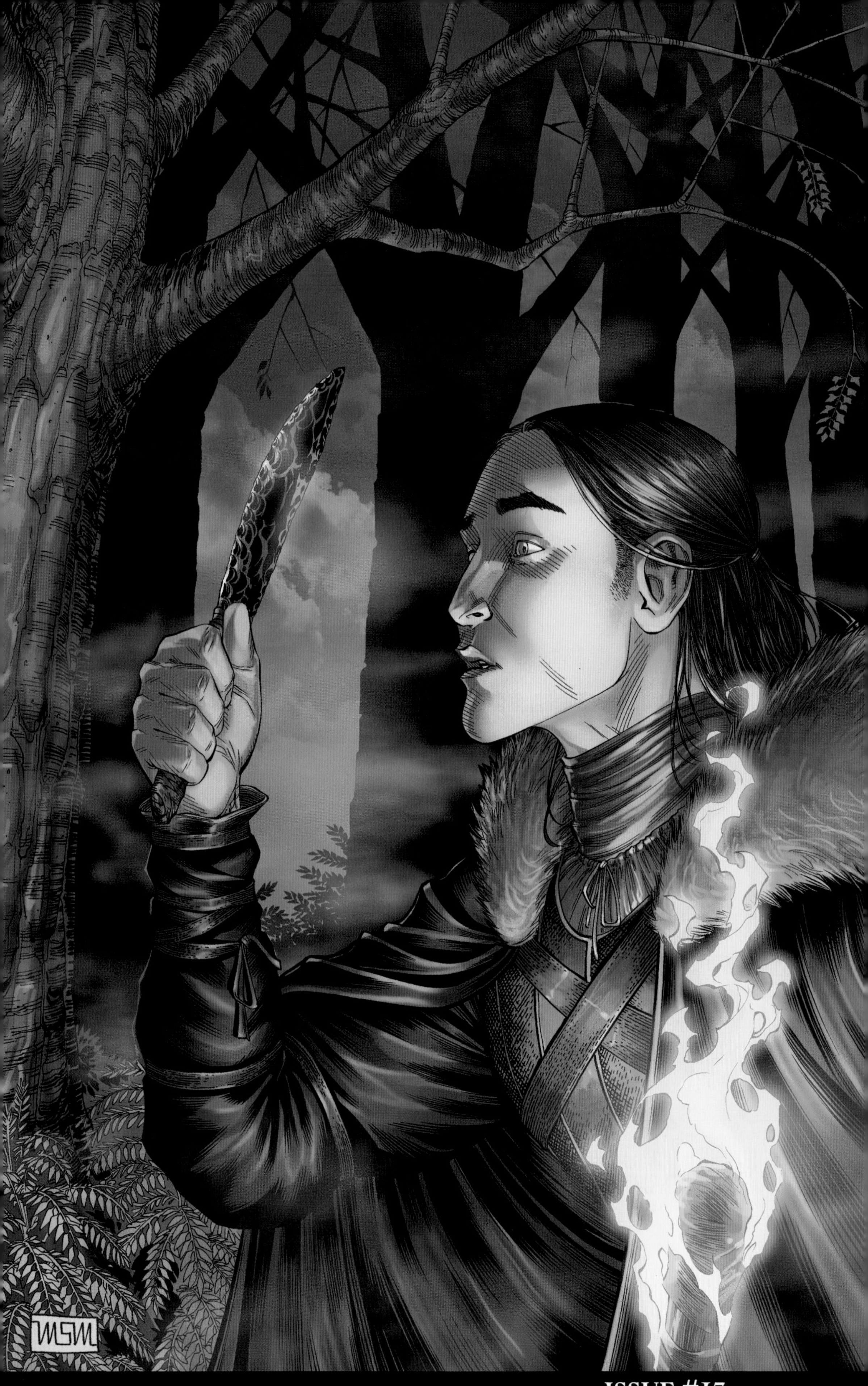

ISSUE #17

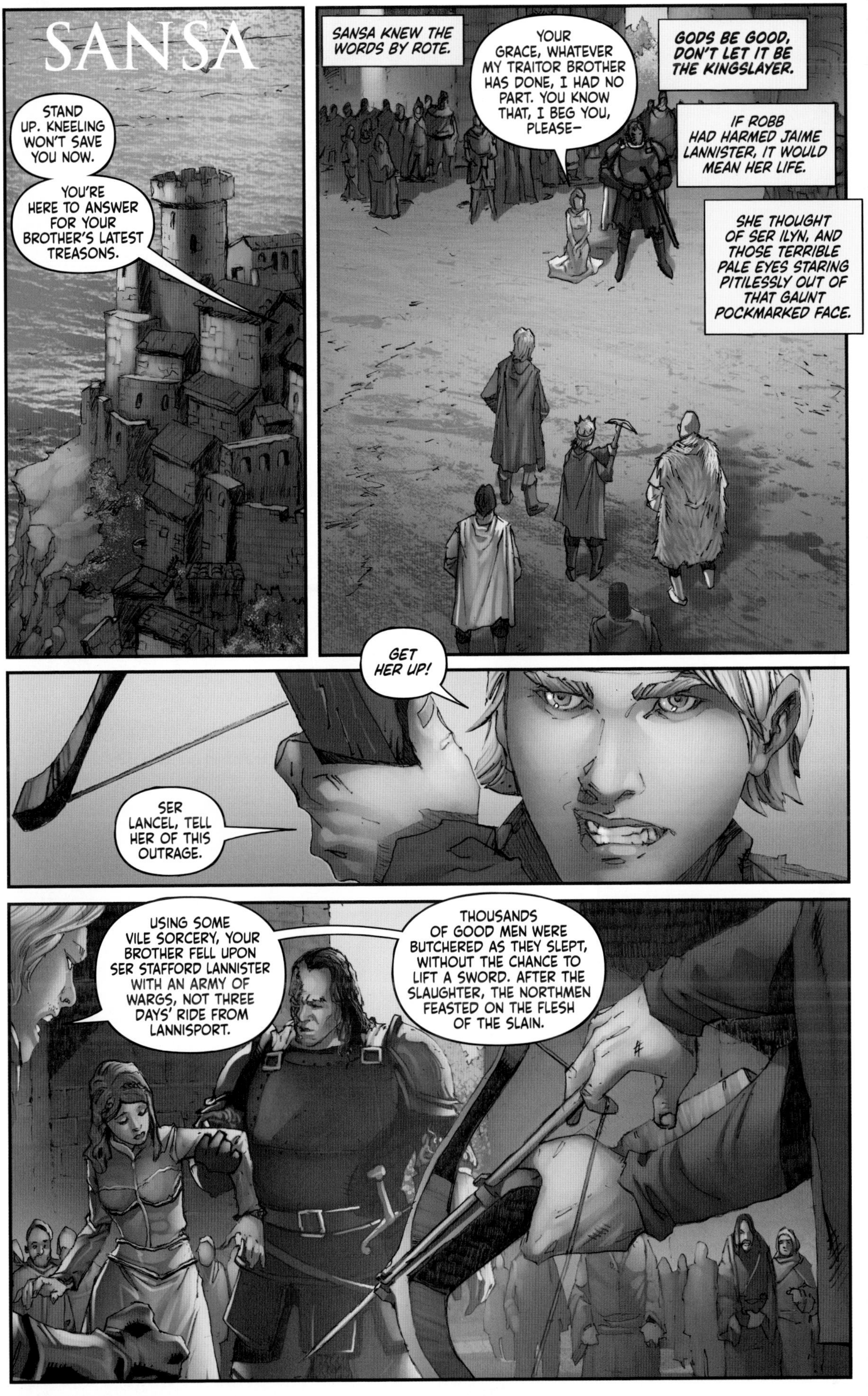
SANSA
STAND UP. KNEELING WON'T SAVE YOU NOW.
YOU'RE HERE TO ANSWER FOR YOUR BROTHER'S LATEST TREASONS.
SANSA KNEW THE WORDS BY ROTE.
YOUR GRACE, WHATEVER MY TRAITOR BROTHER HAS DONE, I HAD NO PART. YOU KNOW THAT, I BEG YOU, PLEASE–
GODS BE GOOD, DON'T LET IT BE THE KINGSLAYER.
IF ROBB HAD HARMED JAIME LANNISTER, IT WOULD MEAN HER LIFE.
SHE THOUGHT OF SER ILYN, AND THOSE TERRIBLE PALE EYES STARING PITILESSLY OUT OF THAT GAUNT POCKMARKED FACE.
GET HER UP!
SER LANCEL, TELL HER OF THIS OUTRAGE.
USING SOME VILE SORCERY, YOUR BROTHER FELL UPON SER STAFFORD LANNISTER WITH AN ARMY OF WARGS, NOT THREE DAYS' RIDE FROM LANNISPORT.
THOUSANDS OF GOOD MEN WERE BUTCHERED AS THEY SLEPT, WITHOUT THE CHANCE TO LIFT A SWORD. AFTER THE SLAUGHTER, THE NORTHMEN FEASTED ON THE FLESH OF THE SLAIN.

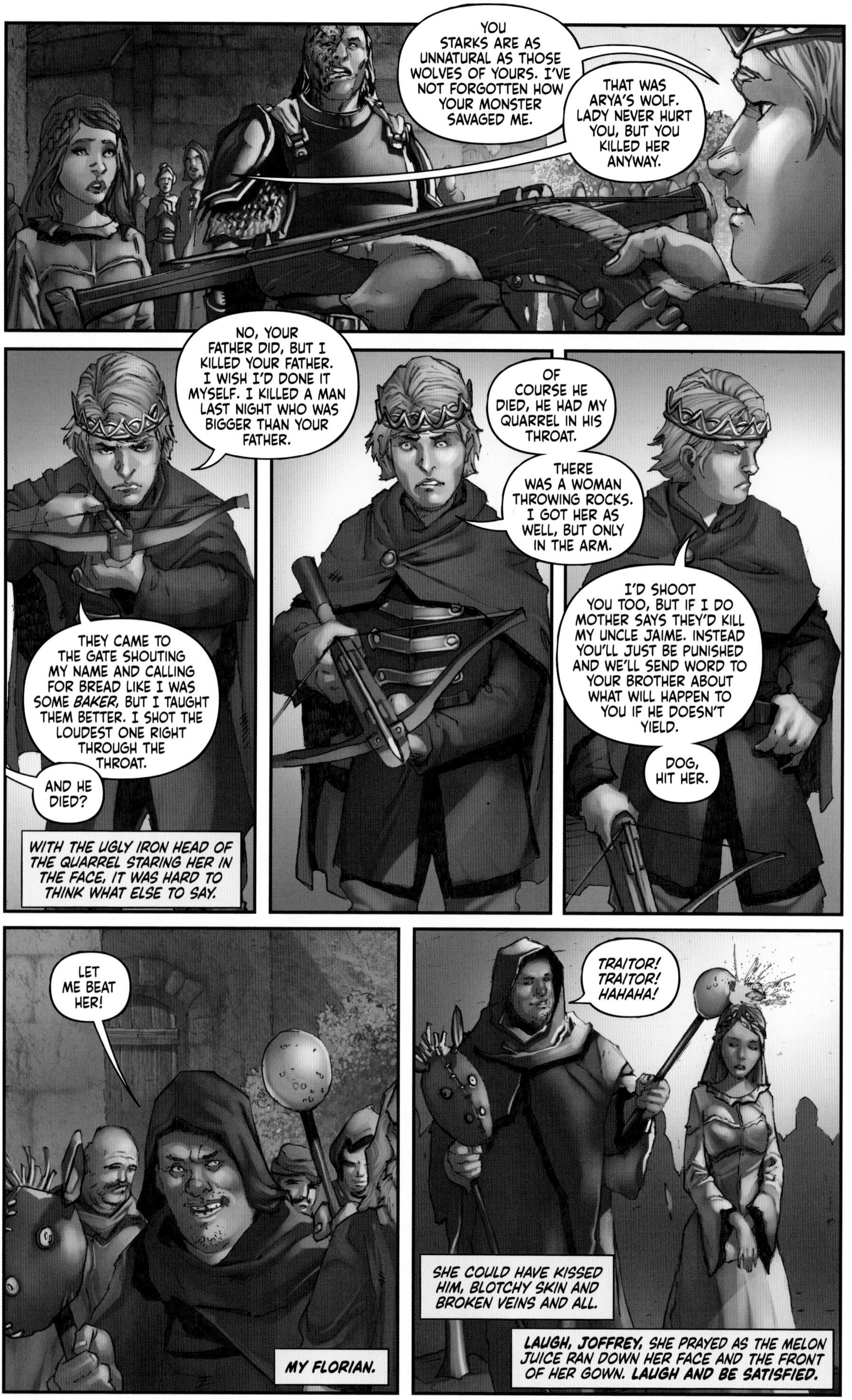
YOU STARKS ARE AS UNNATURAL AS THOSE WOLVES OF YOURS. I'VE NOT FORGOTTEN HOW YOUR MONSTER SAVAGED ME.
THAT WAS ARYA'S WOLF. LADY NEVER HURT YOU, BUT YOU KILLED HER ANYWAY.
NO, YOUR FATHER DID, BUT I KILLED YOUR FATHER. I WISH I'D DONE IT MYSELF. I KILLED A MAN LAST NIGHT WHO WAS BIGGER THAN YOUR FATHER.
THEY CAME TO THE GATE SHOUTING MY NAME AND CALLING FOR BREAD LIKE I WAS SOME *BAKER*, BUT I TAUGHT THEM BETTER. I SHOT THE LOUDEST ONE RIGHT THROUGH THE THROAT.
AND HE DIED?
WITH THE UGLY IRON HEAD OF THE QUARREL STARING HER IN THE FACE, IT WAS HARD TO THINK WHAT ELSE TO SAY.
OF COURSE HE DIED, HE HAD MY QUARREL IN HIS THROAT.
THERE WAS A WOMAN THROWING ROCKS. I GOT HER AS WELL, BUT ONLY IN THE ARM.
I'D SHOOT YOU TOO, BUT IF I DO MOTHER SAYS THEY'D KILL MY UNCLE JAIME. INSTEAD YOU'LL JUST BE PUNISHED AND WE'LL SEND WORD TO YOUR BROTHER ABOUT WHAT WILL HAPPEN TO YOU IF HE DOESN'T YIELD.
DOG, HIT HER.
LET ME BEAT HER!
MY FLORIAN.
TRAITOR! TRAITOR! HAHAHA!
SHE COULD HAVE KISSED HIM, BLOTCHY SKIN AND BROKEN VEINS AND ALL.
LAUGH, JOFFREY, *SHE PRAYED AS THE MELON JUICE RAN DOWN HER FACE AND THE FRONT OF HER GOWN.* ***LAUGH AND BE SATISFIED.***

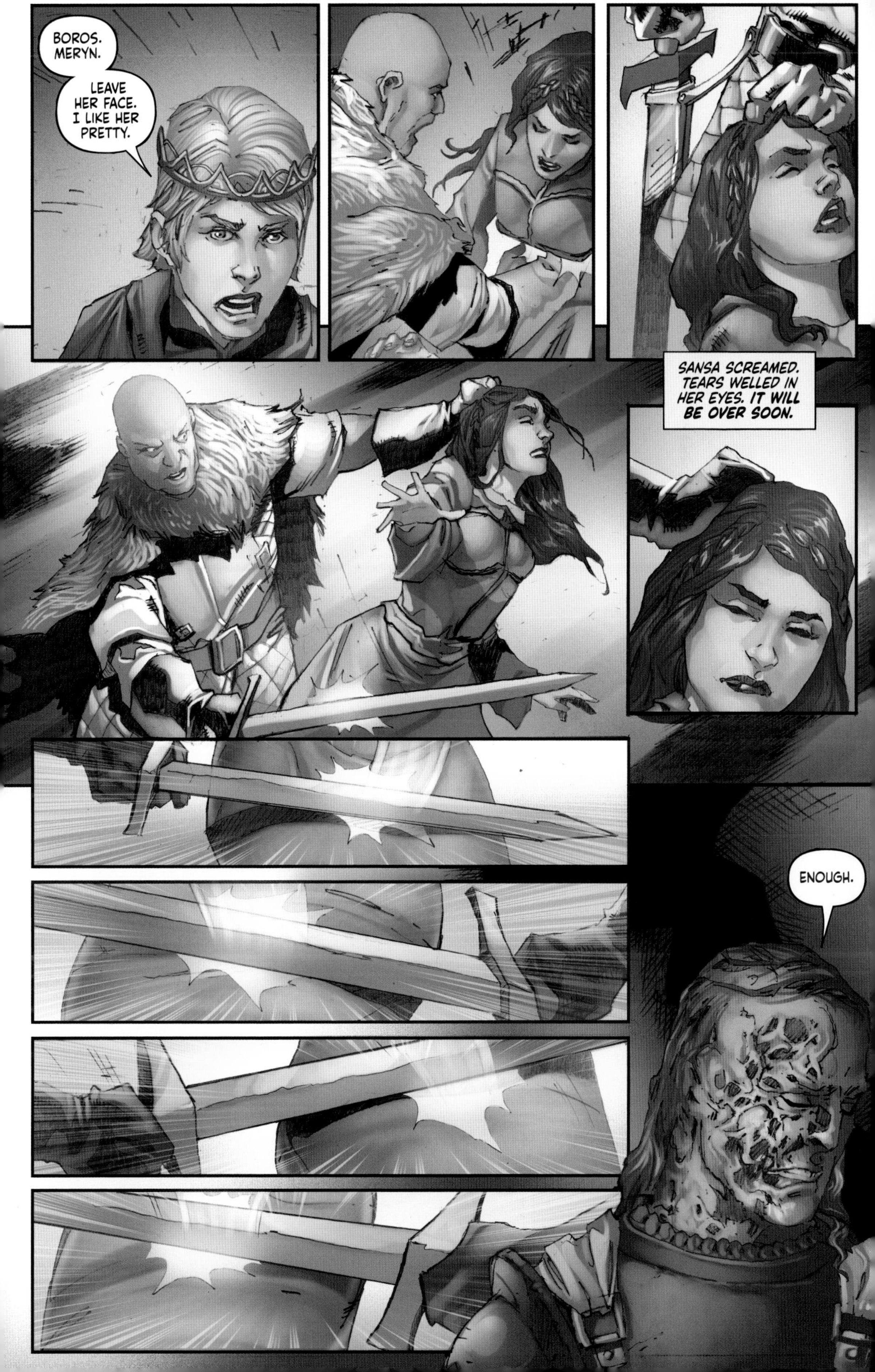
BOROS. MERYN.
LEAVE HER FACE. I LIKE HER PRETTY.
SANSA SCREAMED. TEARS WELLED IN HER EYES. IT WILL BE OVER SOON.
ENOUGH.

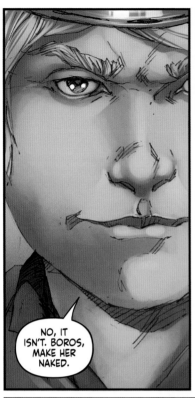

NO, IT ISN'T. BOROS, MAKE HER NAKED.

BEAT HER BLOODY. WE'LL SEE HOW HER BROTHER FANCIES—

WHAT IS THE MEANING OF THIS?

THIS GIRL'S TO BE YOUR QUEEN. HAVE YOU NO REGARD FOR HER HONOR?

I'M PUNISHING HER.

FOR WHAT CRIME? SHE DID NOT FIGHT HER BROTHER'S BATTLE.

SHE HAS THE BLOOD OF A WOLF.

AND YOU HAVE THE WITS OF A GOOSE.

YOU CAN'T TALK TO ME THAT WAY! THE KING CAN DO AS HE LIKES.

AERYS TARGARYEN DID AS HE LIKED. HAS YOUR MOTHER EVER TOLD YOU WHAT HAPPENED TO HIM?

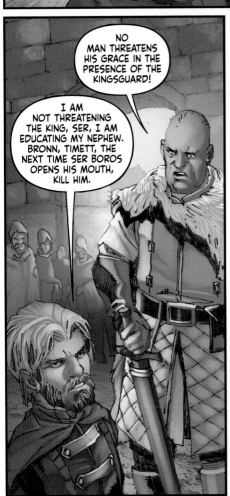

NO MAN THREATENS HIS GRACE IN THE PRESENCE OF THE KINGSGUARD!

I AM NOT THREATENING THE KING, SER, I AM EDUCATING MY NEPHEW. BRONN, TIMETT, THE NEXT TIME SER BOROS OPENS HIS MOUTH, KILL HIM.

NOW *THAT* WAS A THREAT, SER. SEE THE DIFFERENCE?

THE QUEEN WILL HEAR OF THIS!

NO DOUBT SHE WILL. AND WHY WAIT? JOFFREY, SHALL WE SEND FOR YOUR MOTHER?

NOTHING TO SAY, YOUR GRACE? GOOD. LEARN TO USE YOUR EARS MORE AND YOUR MOUTH LESS, OR YOUR REIGN WILL BE SHORTER THAN I AM.

WANTON BRUTALITY IS NO WAY TO WIN YOUR PEOPLE'S LOVE...OR YOUR QUEEN'S.

FEAR IS BETTER THAN LOVE, MOTHER SAYS. *SHE* FEARS ME.

YES, I SEE. A PITY STANNIS AND RENLY AREN'T YOUNG GIRLS AS WELL. BRONN, TIMETT, BRING HER.

SANSA MOVED AS IF IN A DREAM.

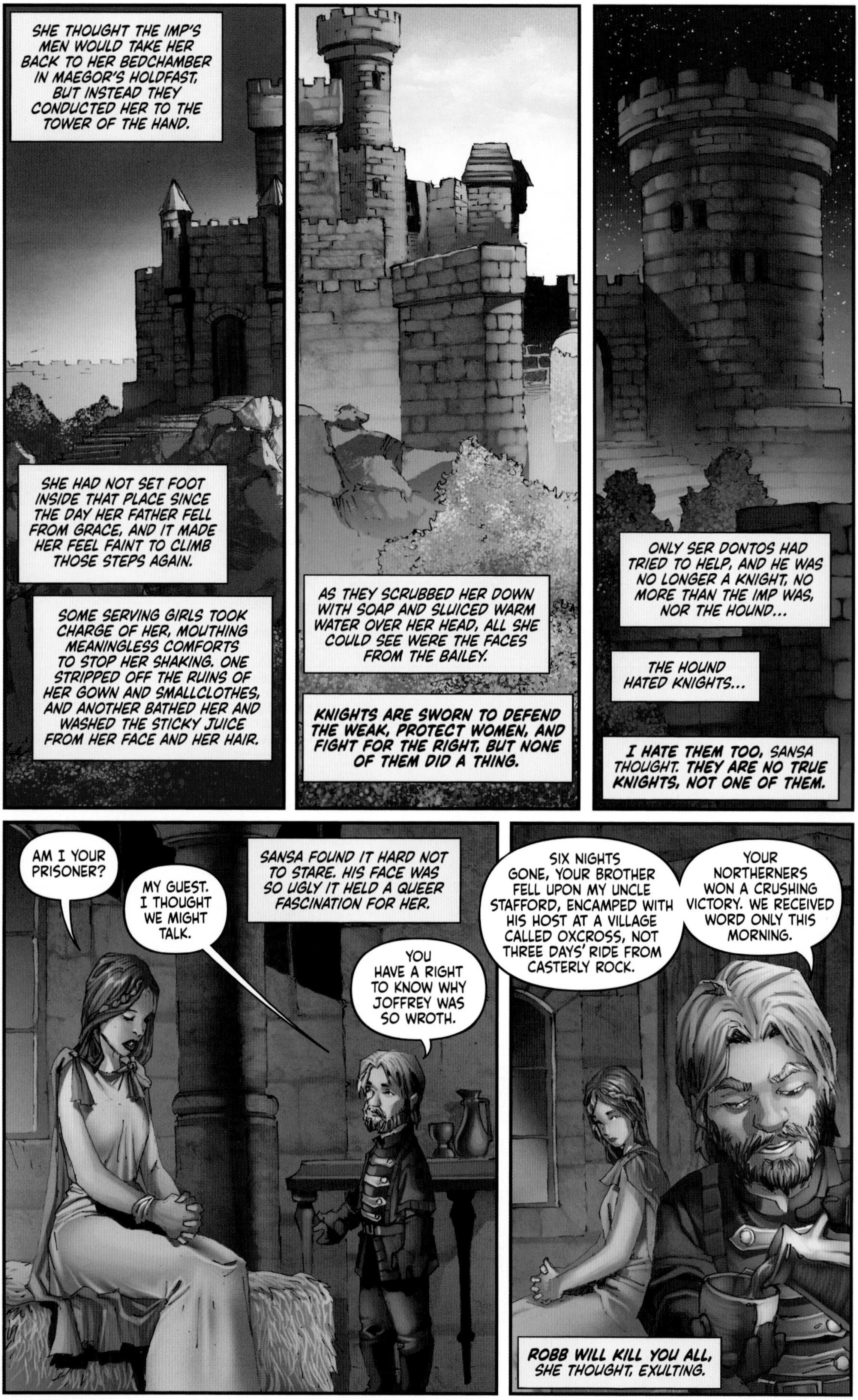
SHE THOUGHT THE IMP'S MEN WOULD TAKE HER BACK TO HER BEDCHAMBER IN MAEGOR'S HOLDFAST, BUT INSTEAD THEY CONDUCTED HER TO THE TOWER OF THE HAND.
SHE HAD NOT SET FOOT INSIDE THAT PLACE SINCE THE DAY HER FATHER FELL FROM GRACE, AND IT MADE HER FEEL FAINT TO CLIMB THOSE STEPS AGAIN.
SOME SERVING GIRLS TOOK CHARGE OF HER, MOUTHING MEANINGLESS COMFORTS TO STOP HER SHAKING. ONE STRIPPED OFF THE RUINS OF HER GOWN AND SMALLCLOTHES, AND ANOTHER BATHED HER AND WASHED THE STICKY JUICE FROM HER FACE AND HER HAIR.
AS THEY SCRUBBED HER DOWN WITH SOAP AND SLUICED WARM WATER OVER HER HEAD, ALL SHE COULD SEE WERE THE FACES FROM THE BAILEY.
KNIGHTS ARE SWORN TO DEFEND THE WEAK, PROTECT WOMEN, AND FIGHT FOR THE RIGHT, BUT NONE OF THEM DID A THING.
ONLY SER DONTOS HAD TRIED TO HELP, AND HE WAS NO LONGER A KNIGHT, NO MORE THAN THE IMP WAS, NOR THE HOUND...
THE HOUND HATED KNIGHTS...
I HATE THEM TOO, SANSA THOUGHT. THEY ARE NO TRUE KNIGHTS, NOT ONE OF THEM.
AM I YOUR PRISONER?
MY GUEST. I THOUGHT WE MIGHT TALK.
SANSA FOUND IT HARD NOT TO STARE. HIS FACE WAS SO UGLY IT HELD A QUEER FASCINATION FOR HER.
YOU HAVE A RIGHT TO KNOW WHY JOFFREY WAS SO WROTH.
SIX NIGHTS GONE, YOUR BROTHER FELL UPON MY UNCLE STAFFORD, ENCAMPED WITH HIS HOST AT A VILLAGE CALLED OXCROSS, NOT THREE DAYS' RIDE FROM CASTERLY ROCK.
YOUR NORTHERNERS WON A CRUSHING VICTORY. WE RECEIVED WORD ONLY THIS MORNING.
ROBB WILL KILL YOU ALL, SHE THOUGHT, EXULTING.

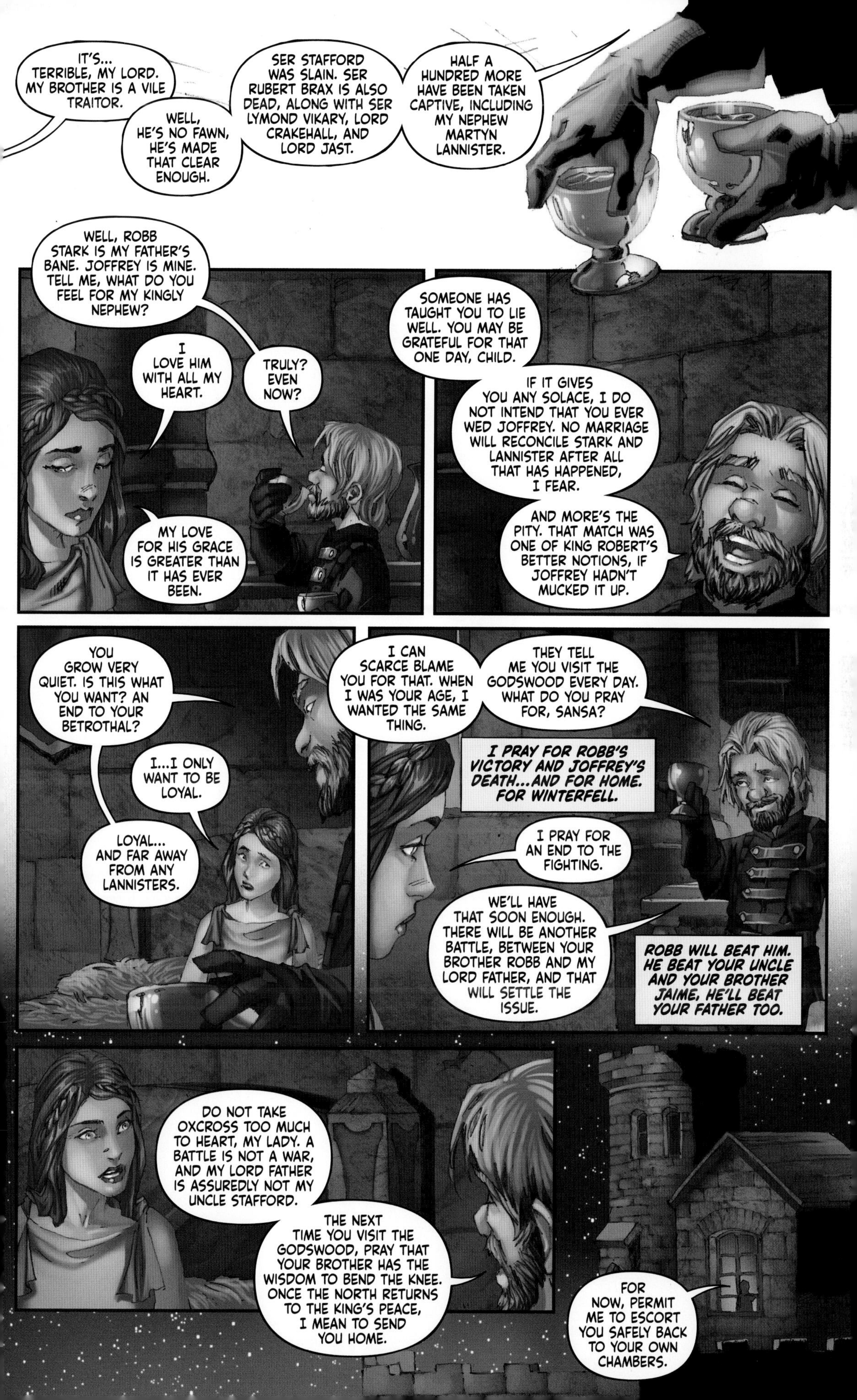
IT'S... TERRIBLE, MY LORD. MY BROTHER IS A VILE TRAITOR.
WELL, HE'S NO FAWN, HE'S MADE THAT CLEAR ENOUGH.
SER STAFFORD WAS SLAIN. SER RUBERT BRAX IS ALSO DEAD, ALONG WITH SER LYMOND VIKARY, LORD CRAKEHALL, AND LORD JAST.
HALF A HUNDRED MORE HAVE BEEN TAKEN CAPTIVE, INCLUDING MY NEPHEW MARTYN LANNISTER.
WELL, ROBB STARK IS MY FATHER'S BANE. JOFFREY IS MINE. TELL ME, WHAT DO YOU FEEL FOR MY KINGLY NEPHEW?
I LOVE HIM WITH ALL MY HEART.
TRULY? EVEN NOW?
MY LOVE FOR HIS GRACE IS GREATER THAN IT HAS EVER BEEN.
SOMEONE HAS TAUGHT YOU TO LIE WELL. YOU MAY BE GRATEFUL FOR THAT ONE DAY, CHILD.
IF IT GIVES YOU ANY SOLACE, I DO NOT INTEND THAT YOU EVER WED JOFFREY. NO MARRIAGE WILL RECONCILE STARK AND LANNISTER AFTER ALL THAT HAS HAPPENED, I FEAR.
AND MORE'S THE PITY. THAT MATCH WAS ONE OF KING ROBERT'S BETTER NOTIONS, IF JOFFREY HADN'T MUCKED IT UP.
YOU GROW VERY QUIET. IS THIS WHAT YOU WANT? AN END TO YOUR BETROTHAL?
I...I ONLY WANT TO BE LOYAL.
LOYAL... AND FAR AWAY FROM ANY LANNISTERS.
I CAN SCARCE BLAME YOU FOR THAT. WHEN I WAS YOUR AGE, I WANTED THE SAME THING.
THEY TELL ME YOU VISIT THE GODSWOOD EVERY DAY. WHAT DO YOU PRAY FOR, SANSA?
I PRAY FOR ROBB'S VICTORY AND JOFFREY'S DEATH...AND FOR HOME. FOR WINTERFELL.
I PRAY FOR AN END TO THE FIGHTING.
WE'LL HAVE THAT SOON ENOUGH. THERE WILL BE ANOTHER BATTLE, BETWEEN YOUR BROTHER ROBB AND MY LORD FATHER, AND THAT WILL SETTLE THE ISSUE.
ROBB WILL BEAT HIM. HE BEAT YOUR UNCLE AND YOUR BROTHER JAIME, HE'LL BEAT YOUR FATHER TOO.
DO NOT TAKE OXCROSS TOO MUCH TO HEART, MY LADY. A BATTLE IS NOT A WAR, AND MY LORD FATHER IS ASSUREDLY NOT MY UNCLE STAFFORD.
THE NEXT TIME YOU VISIT THE GODSWOOD, PRAY THAT YOUR BROTHER HAS THE WISDOM TO BEND THE KNEE. ONCE THE NORTH RETURNS TO THE KING'S PEACE, I MEAN TO SEND YOU HOME.
FOR NOW, PERMIT ME TO ESCORT YOU SAFELY BACK TO YOUR OWN CHAMBERS.

BRAN

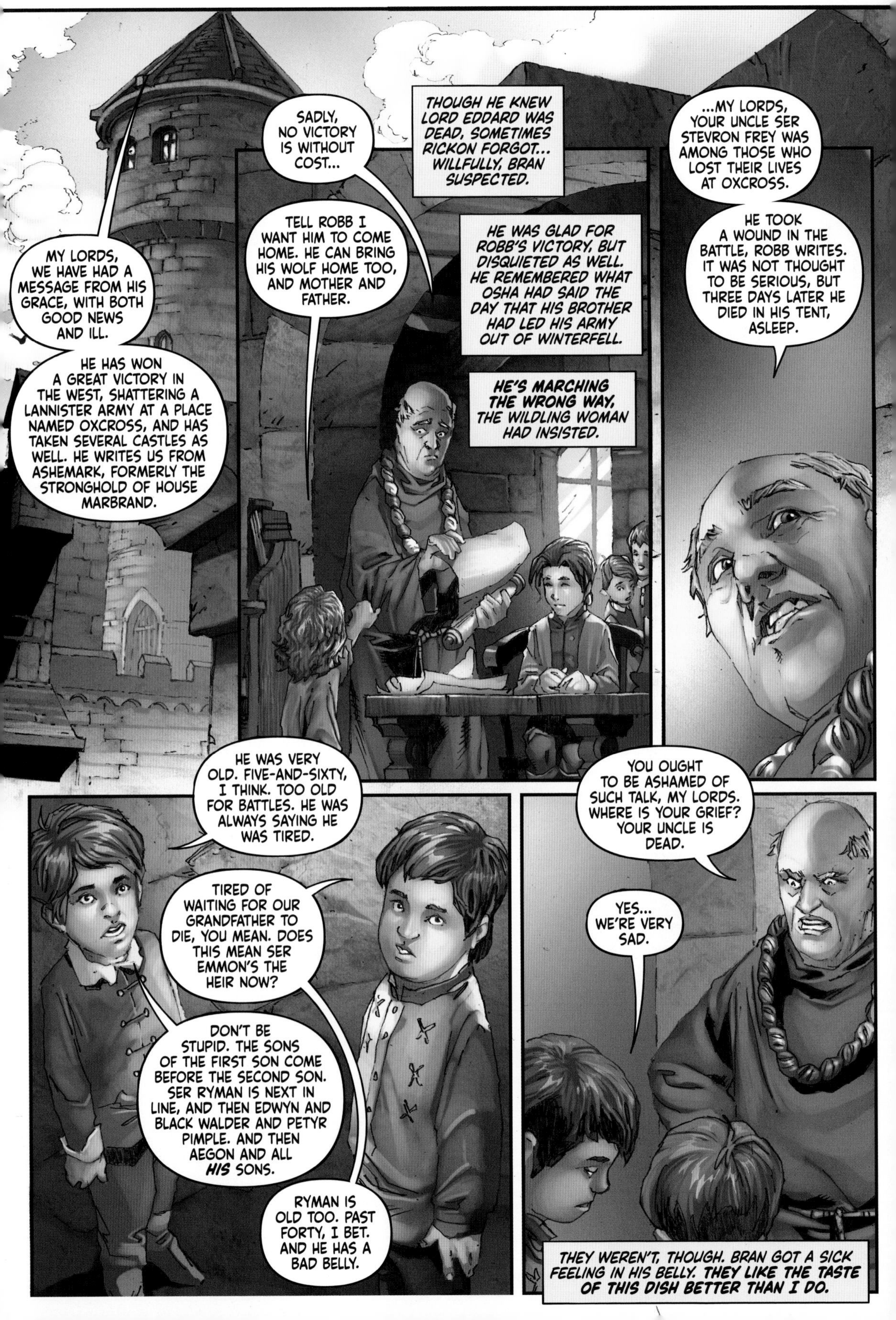
MY LORDS, WE HAVE HAD A MESSAGE FROM HIS GRACE, WITH BOTH GOOD NEWS AND ILL.
HE HAS WON A GREAT VICTORY IN THE WEST, SHATTERING A LANNISTER ARMY AT A PLACE NAMED OXCROSS, AND HAS TAKEN SEVERAL CASTLES AS WELL. HE WRITES US FROM ASHEMARK, FORMERLY THE STRONGHOLD OF HOUSE MARBRAND.
SADLY, NO VICTORY IS WITHOUT COST...
TELL ROBB I WANT HIM TO COME HOME. HE CAN BRING HIS WOLF HOME TOO, AND MOTHER AND FATHER.
THOUGH HE KNEW LORD EDDARD WAS DEAD, SOMETIMES RICKON FORGOT... WILLFULLY, BRAN SUSPECTED.
HE WAS GLAD FOR ROBB'S VICTORY, BUT DISQUIETED AS WELL. HE REMEMBERED WHAT OSHA HAD SAID THE DAY THAT HIS BROTHER HAD LED HIS ARMY OUT OF WINTERFELL.
HE'S MARCHING THE WRONG WAY, THE WILDLING WOMAN HAD INSISTED.
...MY LORDS, YOUR UNCLE SER STEVRON FREY WAS AMONG THOSE WHO LOST THEIR LIVES AT OXCROSS.
HE TOOK A WOUND IN THE BATTLE, ROBB WRITES. IT WAS NOT THOUGHT TO BE SERIOUS, BUT THREE DAYS LATER HE DIED IN HIS TENT, ASLEEP.
HE WAS VERY OLD. FIVE-AND-SIXTY, I THINK. TOO OLD FOR BATTLES. HE WAS ALWAYS SAYING HE WAS TIRED.
TIRED OF WAITING FOR OUR GRANDFATHER TO DIE, YOU MEAN. DOES THIS MEAN SER EMMON'S THE HEIR NOW?
DON'T BE STUPID. THE SONS OF THE FIRST SON COME BEFORE THE SECOND SON. SER RYMAN IS NEXT IN LINE, AND THEN EDWYN AND BLACK WALDER AND PETYR PIMPLE. AND THEN AEGON AND ALL HIS SONS.
RYMAN IS OLD TOO. PAST FORTY, I BET. AND HE HAS A BAD BELLY.
YOU OUGHT TO BE ASHAMED OF SUCH TALK, MY LORDS. WHERE IS YOUR GRIEF? YOUR UNCLE IS DEAD.
YES... WE'RE VERY SAD.
THEY WEREN'T, THOUGH. BRAN GOT A SICK FEELING IN HIS BELLY. THEY LIKE THE TASTE OF THIS DISH BETTER THAN I DO.

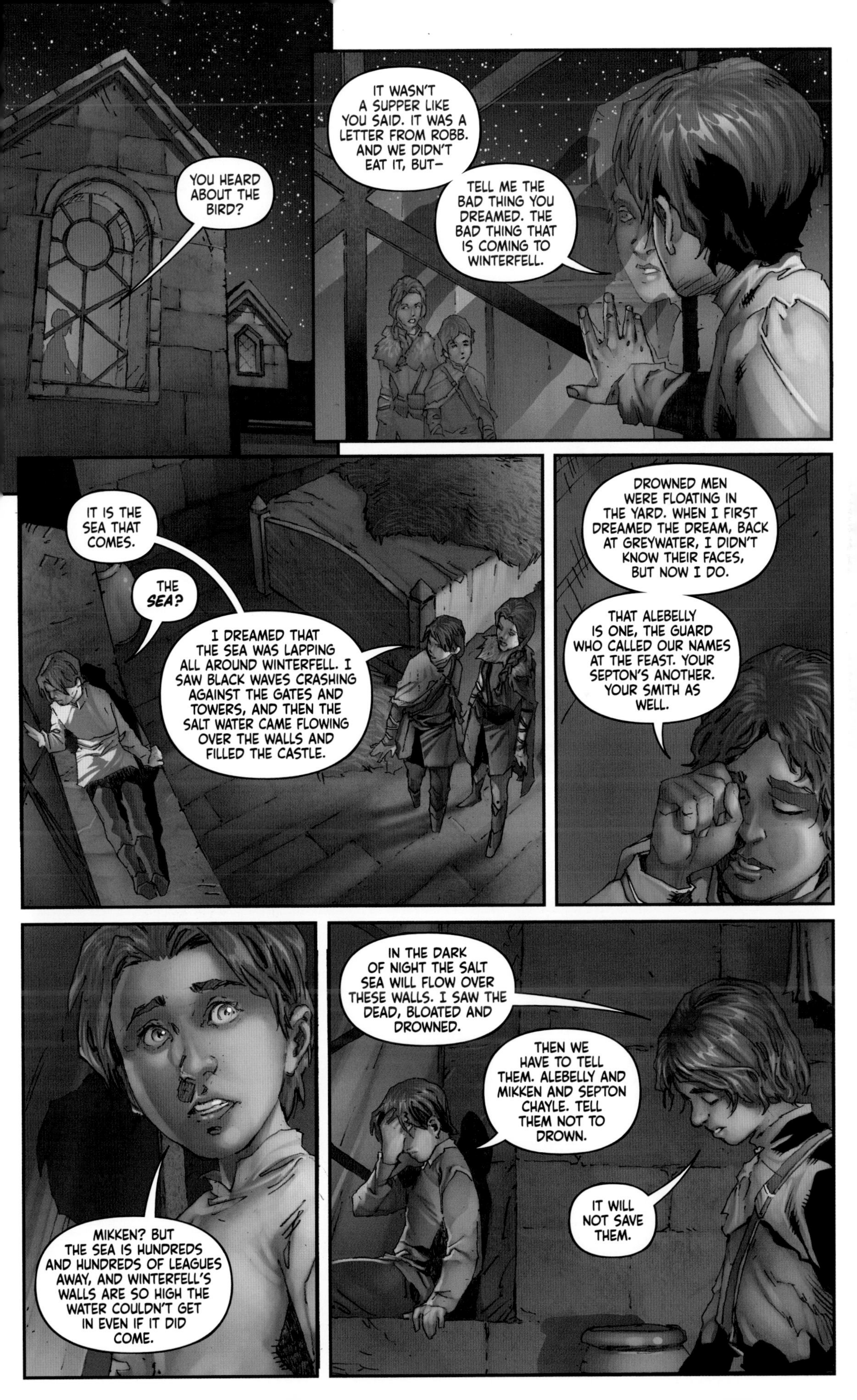
YOU HEARD ABOUT THE BIRD?
IT WASN'T A SUPPER LIKE YOU SAID. IT WAS A LETTER FROM ROBB. AND WE DIDN'T EAT IT, BUT–
TELL ME THE BAD THING YOU DREAMED. THE BAD THING THAT IS COMING TO WINTERFELL.
IT IS THE SEA THAT COMES.
THE *SEA?*
I DREAMED THAT THE SEA WAS LAPPING ALL AROUND WINTERFELL. I SAW BLACK WAVES CRASHING AGAINST THE GATES AND TOWERS, AND THEN THE SALT WATER CAME FLOWING OVER THE WALLS AND FILLED THE CASTLE.
DROWNED MEN WERE FLOATING IN THE YARD. WHEN I FIRST DREAMED THE DREAM, BACK AT GREYWATER, I DIDN'T KNOW THEIR FACES, BUT NOW I DO.
THAT ALEBELLY IS ONE, THE GUARD WHO CALLED OUR NAMES AT THE FEAST. YOUR SEPTON'S ANOTHER. YOUR SMITH AS WELL.
MIKKEN? BUT THE SEA IS HUNDREDS AND HUNDREDS OF LEAGUES AWAY, AND WINTERFELL'S WALLS ARE SO HIGH THE WATER COULDN'T GET IN EVEN IF IT DID COME.
IN THE DARK OF NIGHT THE SALT SEA WILL FLOW OVER THESE WALLS. I SAW THE DEAD, BLOATED AND DROWNED.
THEN WE HAVE TO TELL THEM. ALEBELLY AND MIKKEN AND SEPTON CHAYLE. TELL THEM NOT TO DROWN.
IT WILL NOT SAVE THEM.

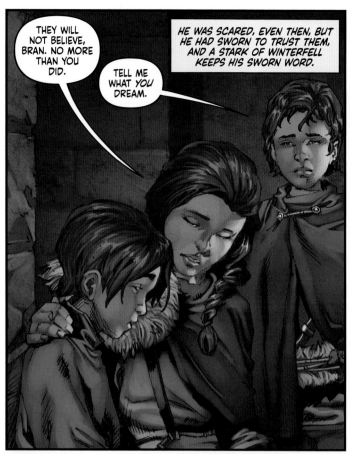

THEY WILL NOT BELIEVE, BRAN. NO MORE THAN YOU DID.

TELL ME WHAT *YOU* DREAM.

HE WAS SCARED, EVEN THEN, BUT HE HAD SWORN TO TRUST THEM, AND A STARK OF WINTERFELL KEEPS HIS SWORN WORD.

THERE'S DIFFERENT KINDS...

THERE'S THE WOLF DREAMS, THOSE AREN'T SO BAD AS THE OTHERS. I RUN AND HUNT AND KILL SQUIRRELS. AND THERE'S DREAMS WHERE THE CROW COMES AND TELLS ME TO FLY.

SOMETIMES THE TREE IS IN THOSE DREAMS TOO, CALLING MY NAME. THAT FRIGHTENS ME. BUT THE WORST DREAMS ARE WHEN I FALL.

I NEVER USED TO FALL BEFORE. WHEN I CLIMBED. I WENT EVERYPLACE, UP ON THE ROOFS AND ALONG THE WALLS. I USED TO FEED THE CROWS IN THE BURNED TOWER.

MOTHER WAS AFRAID THAT I WOULD FALL BUT I KNEW I NEVER WOULD. ONLY I DID, AND NOW WHEN I SLEEP I FALL ALL THE TIME.

IS THAT ALL?

I GUESS.

WARG.

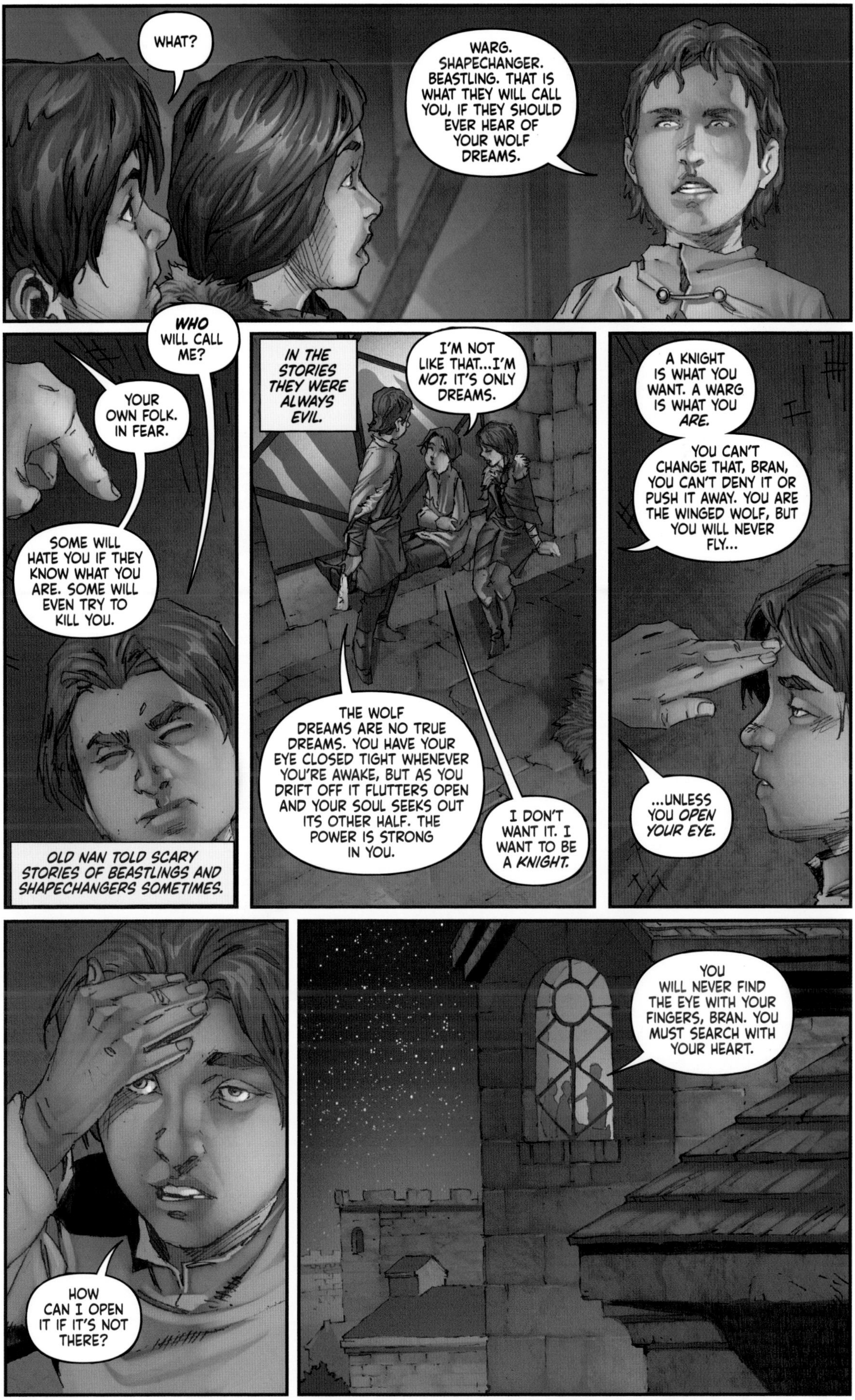
WHAT?
WARG. SHAPECHANGER. BEASTLING. THAT IS WHAT THEY WILL CALL YOU, IF THEY SHOULD EVER HEAR OF YOUR WOLF DREAMS.
WHO WILL CALL ME?
YOUR OWN FOLK. IN FEAR.
SOME WILL HATE YOU IF THEY KNOW WHAT YOU ARE. SOME WILL EVEN TRY TO KILL YOU.
OLD NAN TOLD SCARY STORIES OF BEASTLINGS AND SHAPECHANGERS SOMETIMES.
IN THE STORIES THEY WERE ALWAYS EVIL.
I'M NOT LIKE THAT...I'M NOT. IT'S ONLY DREAMS.
THE WOLF DREAMS ARE NO TRUE DREAMS. YOU HAVE YOUR EYE CLOSED TIGHT WHENEVER YOU'RE AWAKE, BUT AS YOU DRIFT OFF IT FLUTTERS OPEN AND YOUR SOUL SEEKS OUT ITS OTHER HALF. THE POWER IS STRONG IN YOU.
I DON'T WANT IT. I WANT TO BE A KNIGHT.
A KNIGHT IS WHAT YOU WANT. A WARG IS WHAT YOU ARE.
YOU CAN'T CHANGE THAT, BRAN, YOU CAN'T DENY IT OR PUSH IT AWAY. YOU ARE THE WINGED WOLF, BUT YOU WILL NEVER FLY...
...UNLESS YOU OPEN YOUR EYE.
HOW CAN I OPEN IT IF IT'S NOT THERE?
YOU WILL NEVER FIND THE EYE WITH YOUR FINGERS, BRAN. YOU MUST SEARCH WITH YOUR HEART.

THEY LEFT HIM MORE MUDDLED THAN EVER. WHEN HE WAS ALONE, BRAN TRIED TO OPEN HIS THIRD EYE, BUT HE DIDN'T KNOW HOW.

NO MATTER HOW HE WRINKLED HIS FOREHEAD AND POKED AT IT, HE COULDN'T SEE ANY DIFFERENT THAN HE'D DONE BEFORE.

IN THE DAYS THAT FOLLOWED, HE TRIED TO WARN OTHERS ABOUT WHAT JOJEN HAD SEEN, BUT IT DIDN'T GO AS HE WANTED.

ALEBELLY WAS THE ONLY ONE WHO PAID THE WARNING ANY HEED. HE WENT TO TALK TO JOJEN HIMSELF, AND AFTERWARD STOPPED BATHING AND REFUSED TO GO NEAR THE WELL.

FINALLY HE STANK SO BAD THAT SIX OF THE OTHER GUARDS THREW HIM INTO A TUB OF SCALDING WATER AND SCRUBBED HIM RAW WHILE HE SCREAMED THAT THEY WERE GOING TO DROWN HIM LIKE THE FROGBOY HAD SAID.

THEREAFTER HE SCOWLED WHENEVER HE SAW BRAN OR JOJEN ABOUT THE CASTLE, AND MUTTERED UNDER HIS BREATH.

IT WAS A FEW DAYS AFTER ALEBELLY'S BATH THAT SER RODRIK RETURNED TO WINTERFELL WITH HIS PRISONER, A FLESHY YOUNG MAN WITH FAT MOIST LIPS AND LONG HAIR WHO SMELLED LIKE A PRIVY, EVEN WORSE THAN ALEBELLY HAD.

REEK, HE WAS CALLED. NO ONE KNEW HIS TRUE NAME. THEY SAID HE SERVED THE BASTARD OF BOLTON AND HELPED HIM TO MURDER LADY HORNWOOD.

THE BASTARD HIMSELF WAS DEAD, BRAN LEARNED THAT EVENING OVER SUPPER. SER RODRIK'S MEN HAD CAUGHT HIM ON HORNWOOD LAND DOING SOMETHING HORRIBLE...

...BRAN WASN'T QUITE SURE WHAT, BUT IT SEEMED TO BE SOMETHING YOU DID WITHOUT YOUR CLOTHES.

THEY CAME TOO LATE FOR POOR LADY HORNWOOD, THOUGH. AFTER THEIR WEDDING, THE BASTARD HAD LOCKED HER IN A TOWER AND NEGLECTED TO FEED HER.

BRAN HAD HEARD MEN SAYING THAT WHEN SER RODRIK HAD SMASHED DOWN THE DOOR HE FOUND HER WITH HER MOUTH ALL BLOODY AND HER FINGERS CHEWED OFF.

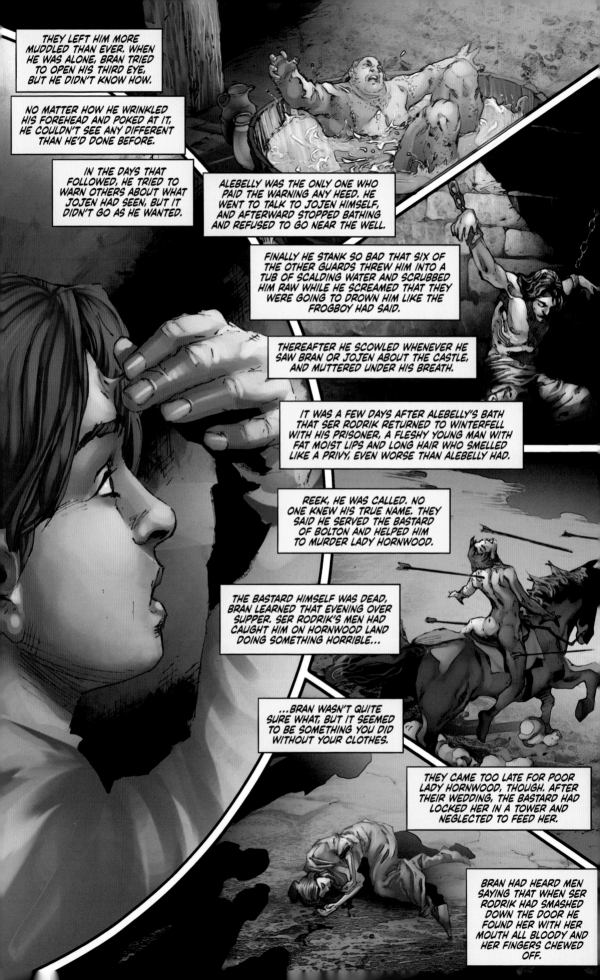

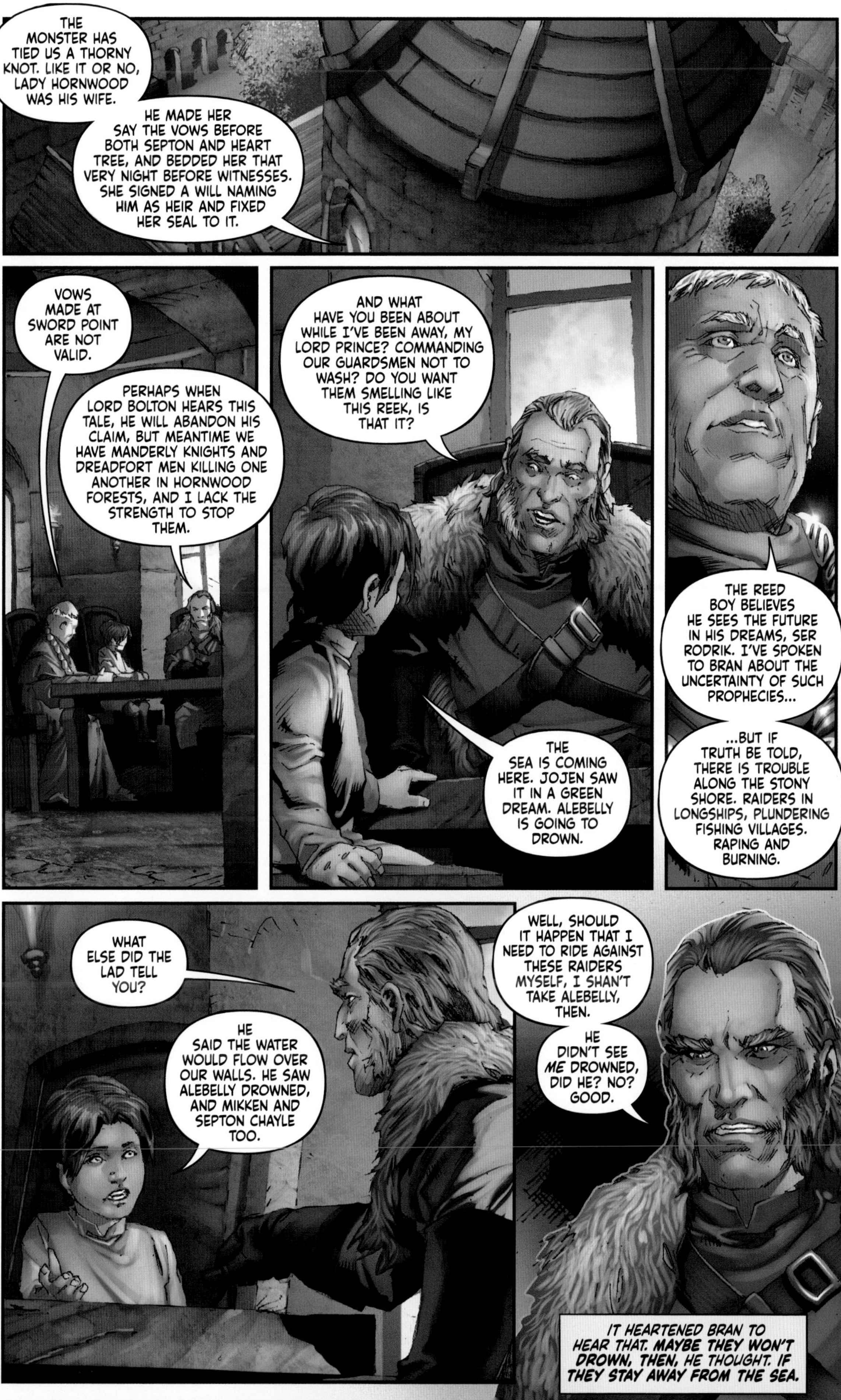
THE MONSTER HAS TIED US A THORNY KNOT. LIKE IT OR NO, LADY HORNWOOD WAS HIS WIFE.
HE MADE HER SAY THE VOWS BEFORE BOTH SEPTON AND HEART TREE, AND BEDDED HER THAT VERY NIGHT BEFORE WITNESSES. SHE SIGNED A WILL NAMING HIM AS HEIR AND FIXED HER SEAL TO IT.
VOWS MADE AT SWORD POINT ARE NOT VALID.
PERHAPS WHEN LORD BOLTON HEARS THIS TALE, HE WILL ABANDON HIS CLAIM, BUT MEANTIME WE HAVE MANDERLY KNIGHTS AND DREADFORT MEN KILLING ONE ANOTHER IN HORNWOOD FORESTS, AND I LACK THE STRENGTH TO STOP THEM.
AND WHAT HAVE YOU BEEN ABOUT WHILE I'VE BEEN AWAY, MY LORD PRINCE? COMMANDING OUR GUARDSMEN NOT TO WASH? DO YOU WANT THEM SMELLING LIKE THIS REEK, IS THAT IT?
THE SEA IS COMING HERE. JOJEN SAW IT IN A GREEN DREAM. ALEBELLY IS GOING TO DROWN.
THE REED BOY BELIEVES HE SEES THE FUTURE IN HIS DREAMS, SER RODRIK. I'VE SPOKEN TO BRAN ABOUT THE UNCERTAINTY OF SUCH PROPHECIES...
...BUT IF TRUTH BE TOLD, THERE IS TROUBLE ALONG THE STONY SHORE. RAIDERS IN LONGSHIPS, PLUNDERING FISHING VILLAGES. RAPING AND BURNING.
WHAT ELSE DID THE LAD TELL YOU?
HE SAID THE WATER WOULD FLOW OVER OUR WALLS. HE SAW ALEBELLY DROWNED, AND MIKKEN AND SEPTON CHAYLE TOO.
WELL, SHOULD IT HAPPEN THAT I NEED TO RIDE AGAINST THESE RAIDERS MYSELF, I SHAN'T TAKE ALEBELLY, THEN.
HE DIDN'T SEE *ME* DROWNED, DID HE? NO? GOOD.
IT HEARTENED BRAN TO HEAR THAT. ***MAYBE THEY WON'T DROWN, THEN, HE THOUGHT. IF THEY STAY AWAY FROM THE SEA.***

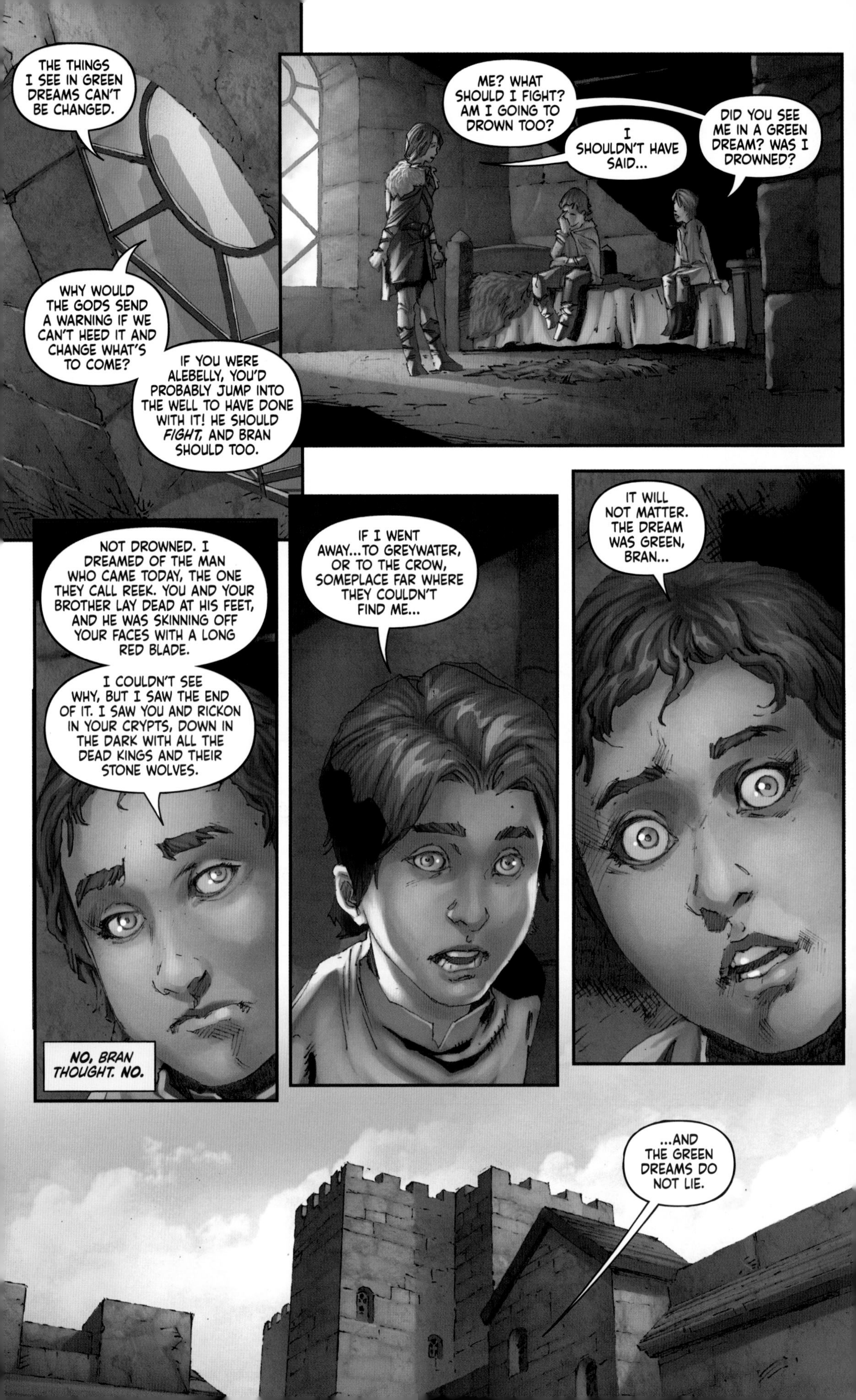
THE THINGS I SEE IN GREEN DREAMS CAN'T BE CHANGED.
ME? WHAT SHOULD I FIGHT? AM I GOING TO DROWN TOO?
DID YOU SEE ME IN A GREEN DREAM? WAS I DROWNED?
I SHOULDN'T HAVE SAID...
WHY WOULD THE GODS SEND A WARNING IF WE CAN'T HEED IT AND CHANGE WHAT'S TO COME?
IF YOU WERE ALEBELLY, YOU'D PROBABLY JUMP INTO THE WELL TO HAVE DONE WITH IT! HE SHOULD *FIGHT*, AND BRAN SHOULD TOO.
NOT DROWNED. I DREAMED OF THE MAN WHO CAME TODAY, THE ONE THEY CALL REEK. YOU AND YOUR BROTHER LAY DEAD AT HIS FEET, AND HE WAS SKINNING OFF YOUR FACES WITH A LONG RED BLADE.
I COULDN'T SEE WHY, BUT I SAW THE END OF IT. I SAW YOU AND RICKON IN YOUR CRYPTS, DOWN IN THE DARK WITH ALL THE DEAD KINGS AND THEIR STONE WOLVES.
NO, BRAN THOUGHT. NO.
IF I WENT AWAY...TO GREYWATER, OR TO THE CROW, SOMEPLACE FAR WHERE THEY COULDN'T FIND ME...
IT WILL NOT MATTER. THE DREAM WAS GREEN, BRAN...
...AND THE GREEN DREAMS DO NOT LIE.

JON

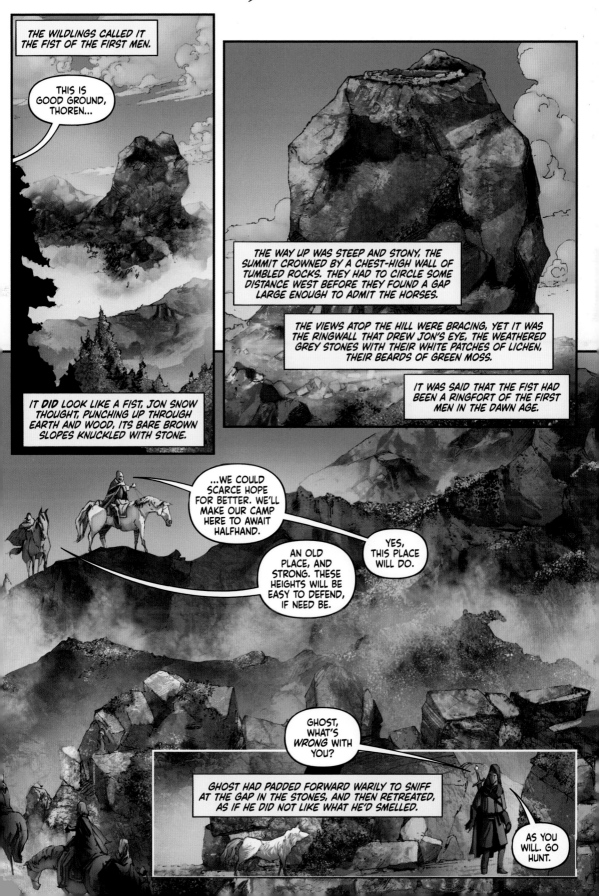

THE WILDLINGS CALLED IT THE FIST OF THE FIRST MEN.

THIS IS GOOD GROUND, THOREN...

IT *DID* LOOK LIKE A FIST, JON SNOW THOUGHT, PUNCHING UP THROUGH EARTH AND WOOD, ITS BARE BROWN SLOPES KNUCKLED WITH STONE.

THE WAY UP WAS STEEP AND STONY, THE SUMMIT CROWNED BY A CHEST-HIGH WALL OF TUMBLED ROCKS. THEY HAD TO CIRCLE SOME DISTANCE WEST BEFORE THEY FOUND A GAP LARGE ENOUGH TO ADMIT THE HORSES.

THE VIEWS ATOP THE HILL WERE BRACING, YET IT WAS THE RINGWALL THAT DREW JON'S EYE, THE WEATHERED GREY STONES WITH THEIR WHITE PATCHES OF LICHEN, THEIR BEARDS OF GREEN MOSS.

IT WAS SAID THAT THE FIST HAD BEEN A RINGFORT OF THE FIRST MEN IN THE DAWN AGE.

...WE COULD SCARCE HOPE FOR BETTER. WE'LL MAKE OUR CAMP HERE TO AWAIT HALFHAND.

YES, THIS PLACE WILL DO.

AN OLD PLACE, AND STRONG. THESE HEIGHTS WILL BE EASY TO DEFEND, IF NEED BE.

GHOST, WHAT'S *WRONG* WITH YOU?

GHOST HAD PADDED FORWARD WARILY TO SNIFF AT THE GAP IN THE STONES, AND THEN RETREATED, AS IF HE DID NOT LIKE WHAT HE'D SMELLED.

AS YOU WILL. GO HUNT.

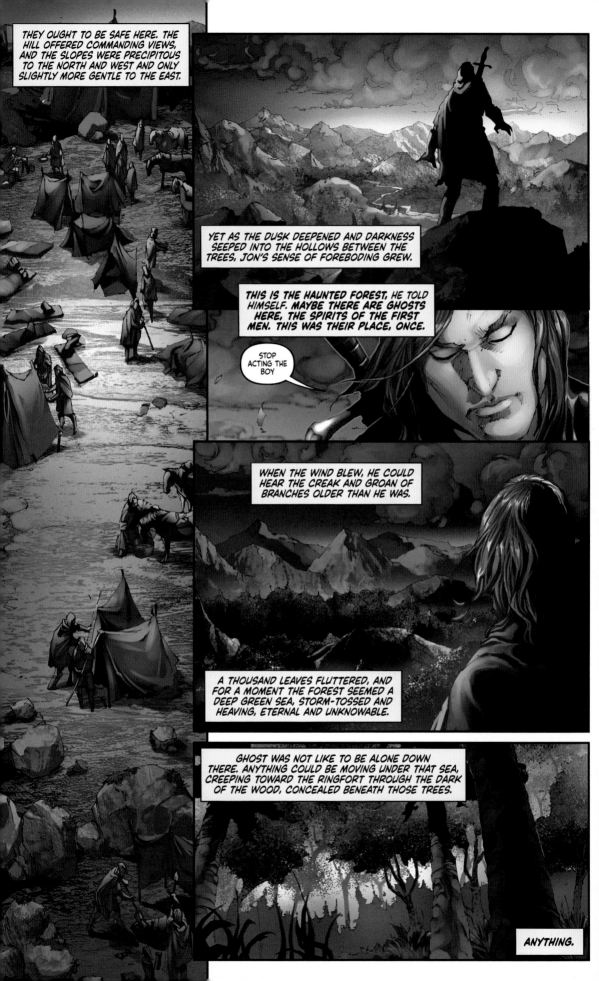

THEY OUGHT TO BE SAFE HERE. THE HILL OFFERED COMMANDING VIEWS, AND THE SLOPES WERE PRECIPITOUS TO THE NORTH AND WEST AND ONLY SLIGHTLY MORE GENTLE TO THE EAST.

YET AS THE DUSK DEEPENED AND DARKNESS SEEPED INTO THE HOLLOWS BETWEEN THE TREES, JON'S SENSE OF FOREBODING GREW.

THIS IS THE HAUNTED FOREST, HE TOLD HIMSELF. MAYBE THERE ARE GHOSTS HERE, THE SPIRITS OF THE FIRST MEN. THIS WAS THEIR PLACE, ONCE.

STOP ACTING THE BOY

WHEN THE WIND BLEW, HE COULD HEAR THE CREAK AND GROAN OF BRANCHES OLDER THAN HE WAS.

A THOUSAND LEAVES FLUTTERED, AND FOR A MOMENT THE FOREST SEEMED A DEEP GREEN SEA, STORM-TOSSED AND HEAVING, ETERNAL AND UNKNOWABLE.

GHOST WAS NOT LIKE TO BE ALONE DOWN THERE. ANYTHING COULD BE MOVING UNDER THAT SEA, CREEPING TOWARD THE RINGFORT THROUGH THE DARK OF THE WOOD, CONCEALED BENEATH THOSE TREES.

ANYTHING.

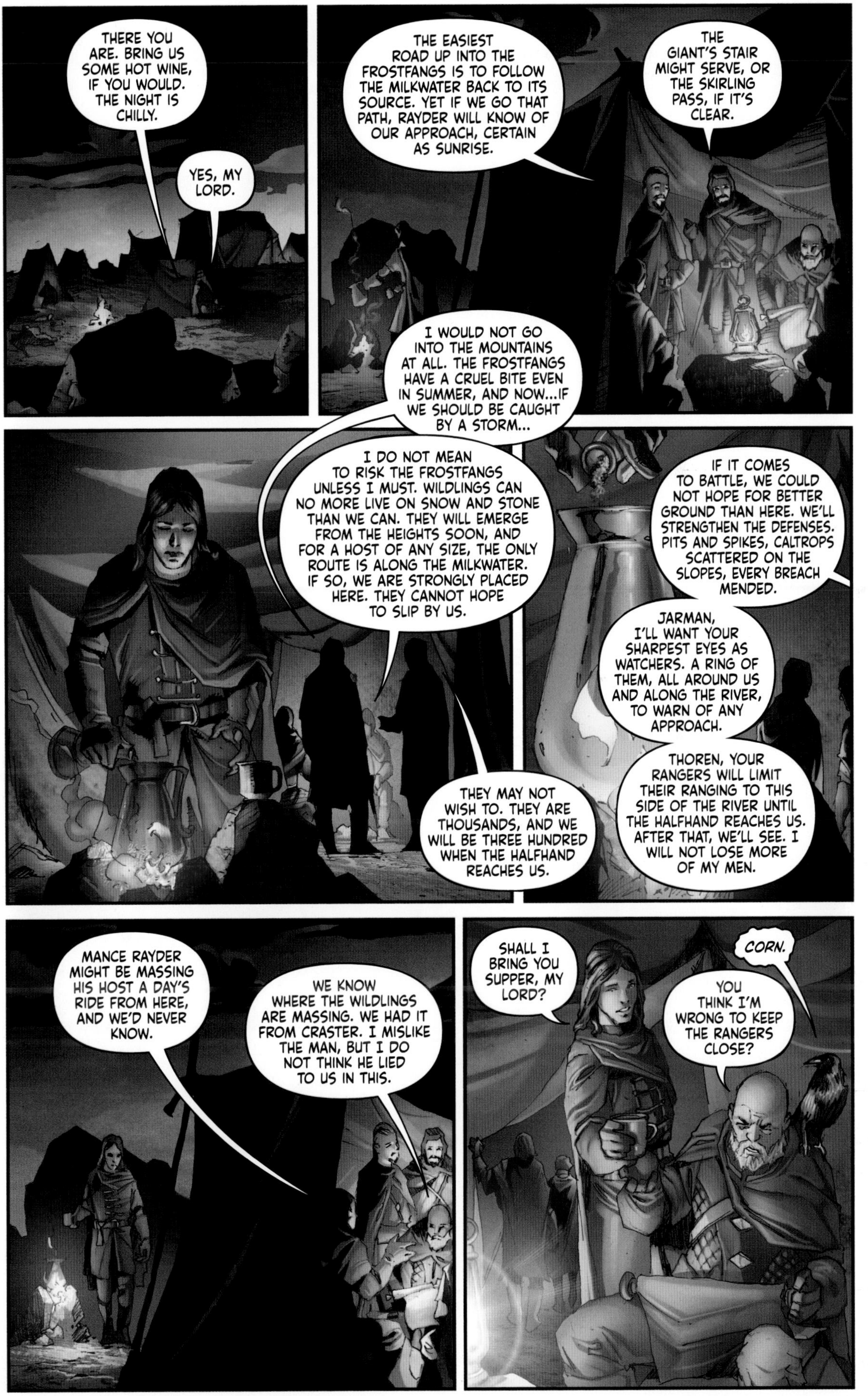

THERE YOU ARE. BRING US SOME HOT WINE, IF YOU WOULD. THE NIGHT IS CHILLY.
YES, MY LORD.
THE EASIEST ROAD UP INTO THE FROSTFANGS IS TO FOLLOW THE MILKWATER BACK TO ITS SOURCE. YET IF WE GO THAT PATH, RAYDER WILL KNOW OF OUR APPROACH, CERTAIN AS SUNRISE.
THE GIANT'S STAIR MIGHT SERVE, OR THE SKIRLING PASS, IF IT'S CLEAR.
I WOULD NOT GO INTO THE MOUNTAINS AT ALL. THE FROSTFANGS HAVE A CRUEL BITE EVEN IN SUMMER, AND NOW...IF WE SHOULD BE CAUGHT BY A STORM...
I DO NOT MEAN TO RISK THE FROSTFANGS UNLESS I MUST. WILDLINGS CAN NO MORE LIVE ON SNOW AND STONE THAN WE CAN. THEY WILL EMERGE FROM THE HEIGHTS SOON, AND FOR A HOST OF ANY SIZE, THE ONLY ROUTE IS ALONG THE MILKWATER. IF SO, WE ARE STRONGLY PLACED HERE. THEY CANNOT HOPE TO SLIP BY US.
THEY MAY NOT WISH TO. THEY ARE THOUSANDS, AND WE WILL BE THREE HUNDRED WHEN THE HALFHAND REACHES US.
IF IT COMES TO BATTLE, WE COULD NOT HOPE FOR BETTER GROUND THAN HERE. WE'LL STRENGTHEN THE DEFENSES. PITS AND SPIKES, CALTROPS SCATTERED ON THE SLOPES, EVERY BREACH MENDED.
JARMAN, I'LL WANT YOUR SHARPEST EYES AS WATCHERS. A RING OF THEM, ALL AROUND US AND ALONG THE RIVER, TO WARN OF ANY APPROACH.
THOREN, YOUR RANGERS WILL LIMIT THEIR RANGING TO THIS SIDE OF THE RIVER UNTIL THE HALFHAND REACHES US. AFTER THAT, WE'LL SEE. I WILL NOT LOSE MORE OF MY MEN.
MANCE RAYDER MIGHT BE MASSING HIS HOST A DAY'S RIDE FROM HERE, AND WE'D NEVER KNOW.
WE KNOW WHERE THE WILDLINGS ARE MASSING. WE HAD IT FROM CRASTER. I MISLIKE THE MAN, BUT I DO NOT THINK HE LIED TO US IN THIS.
SHALL I BRING YOU SUPPER, MY LORD?
CORN.
YOU THINK I'M WRONG TO KEEP THE RANGERS CLOSE?

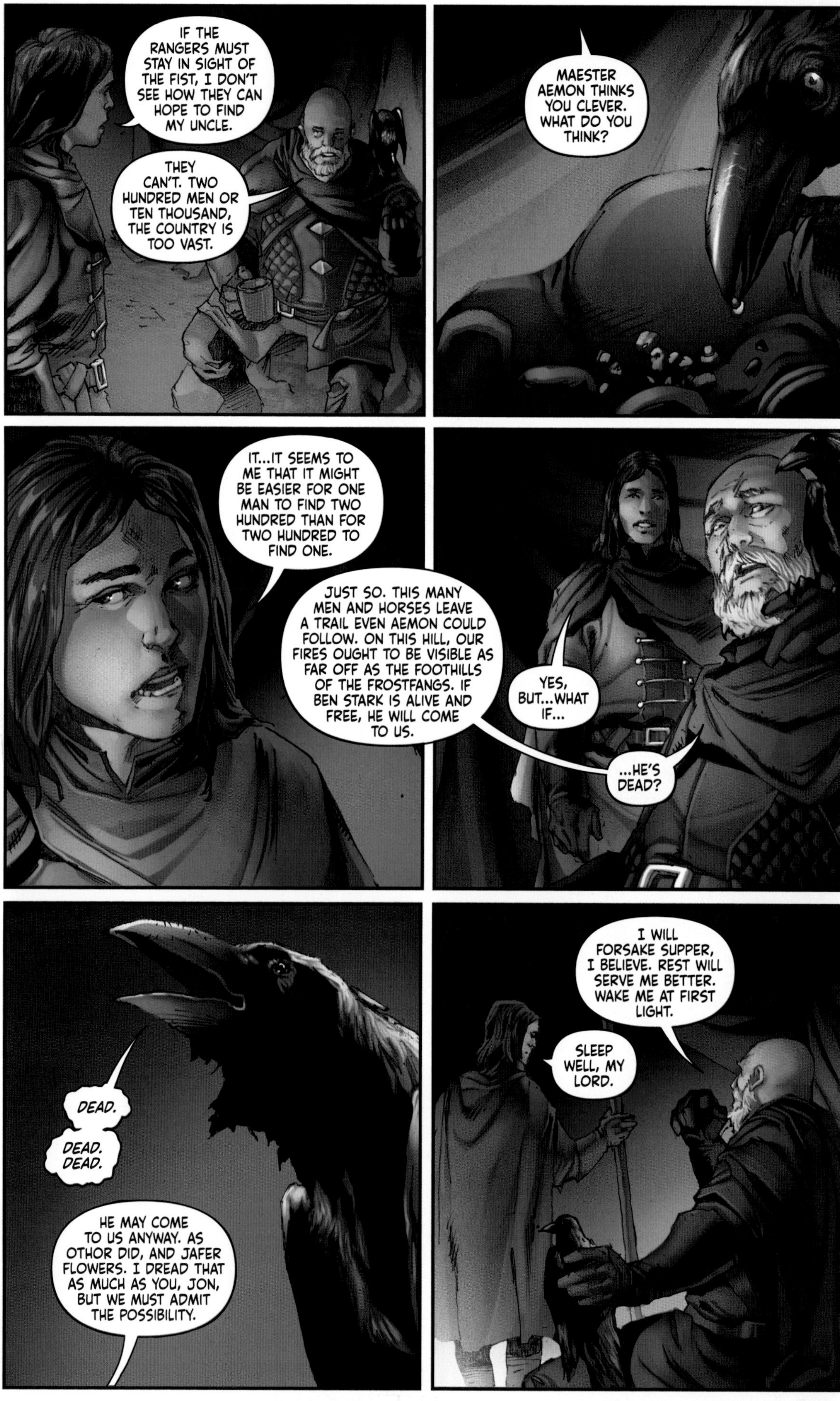
IF THE RANGERS MUST STAY IN SIGHT OF THE FIST, I DON'T SEE HOW THEY CAN HOPE TO FIND MY UNCLE.
THEY CAN'T. TWO HUNDRED MEN OR TEN THOUSAND, THE COUNTRY IS TOO VAST.
MAESTER AEMON THINKS YOU CLEVER. WHAT DO YOU THINK?
IT...IT SEEMS TO ME THAT IT MIGHT BE EASIER FOR ONE MAN TO FIND TWO HUNDRED THAN FOR TWO HUNDRED TO FIND ONE.
JUST SO. THIS MANY MEN AND HORSES LEAVE A TRAIL EVEN AEMON COULD FOLLOW. ON THIS HILL, OUR FIRES OUGHT TO BE VISIBLE AS FAR OFF AS THE FOOTHILLS OF THE FROSTFANGS. IF BEN STARK IS ALIVE AND FREE, HE WILL COME TO US.
YES, BUT...WHAT IF...
...HE'S DEAD?
DEAD.
DEAD. DEAD.
HE MAY COME TO US ANYWAY. AS OTHOR DID, AND JAFER FLOWERS. I DREAD THAT AS MUCH AS YOU, JON, BUT WE MUST ADMIT THE POSSIBILITY.
I WILL FORSAKE SUPPER, I BELIEVE. REST WILL SERVE ME BETTER. WAKE ME AT FIRST LIGHT.
SLEEP WELL, MY LORD.

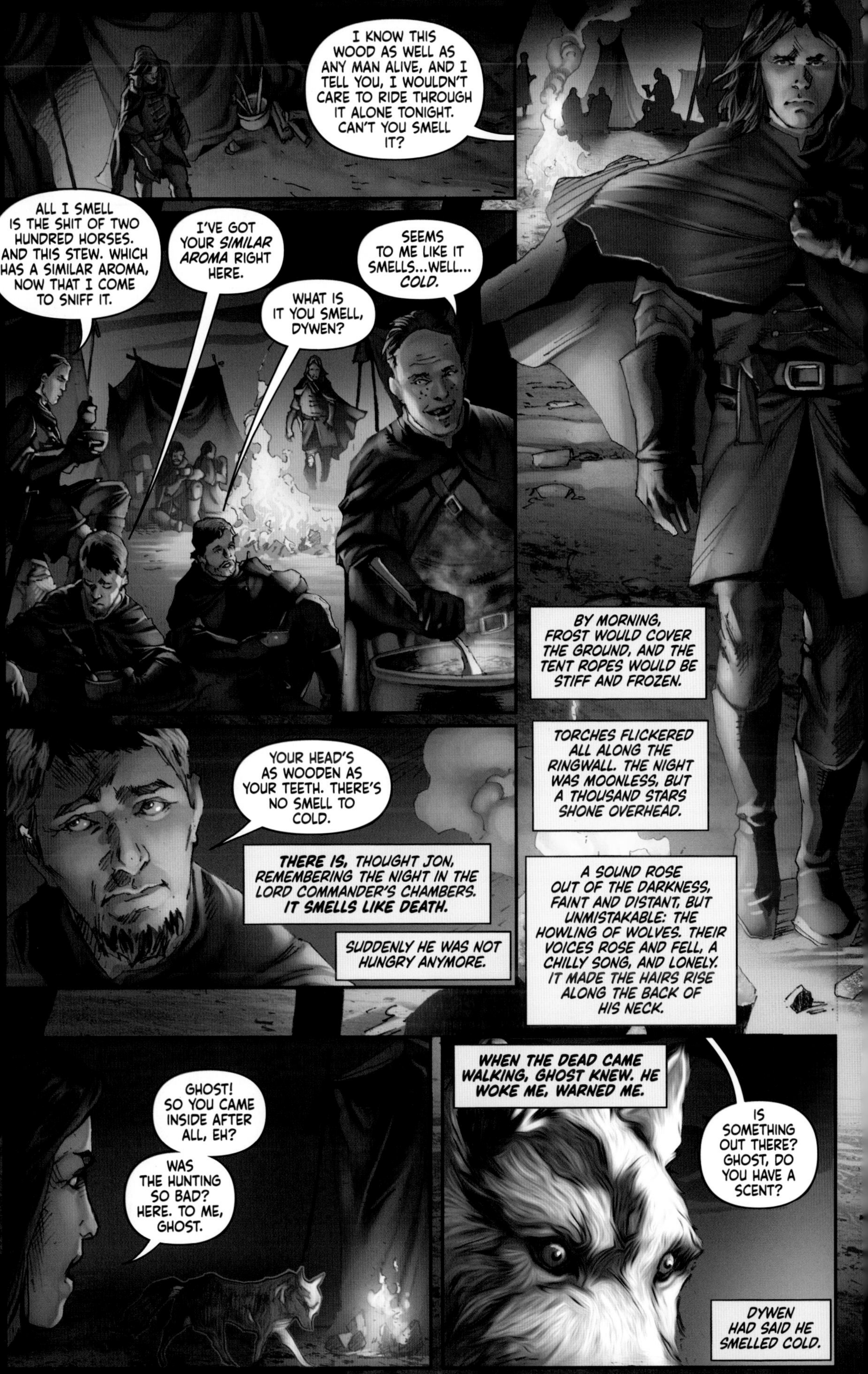
I KNOW THIS WOOD AS WELL AS ANY MAN ALIVE, AND I TELL YOU, I WOULDN'T CARE TO RIDE THROUGH IT ALONE TONIGHT. CAN'T YOU SMELL IT?
ALL I SMELL IS THE SHIT OF TWO HUNDRED HORSES. AND THIS STEW. WHICH HAS A SIMILAR AROMA, NOW THAT I COME TO SNIFF IT.
I'VE GOT YOUR *SIMILAR AROMA* RIGHT HERE.
WHAT IS IT YOU SMELL, DYWEN?
SEEMS TO ME LIKE IT SMELLS...WELL... *COLD.*
YOUR HEAD'S AS WOODEN AS YOUR TEETH. THERE'S NO SMELL TO COLD.
THERE IS, THOUGHT JON, REMEMBERING THE NIGHT IN THE LORD COMMANDER'S CHAMBERS. IT SMELLS LIKE DEATH.
SUDDENLY HE WAS NOT HUNGRY ANYMORE.
BY MORNING, FROST WOULD COVER THE GROUND, AND THE TENT ROPES WOULD BE STIFF AND FROZEN.
TORCHES FLICKERED ALL ALONG THE RINGWALL. THE NIGHT WAS MOONLESS, BUT A THOUSAND STARS SHONE OVERHEAD.
A SOUND ROSE OUT OF THE DARKNESS, FAINT AND DISTANT, BUT UNMISTAKABLE: THE HOWLING OF WOLVES. THEIR VOICES ROSE AND FELL, A CHILLY SONG, AND LONELY. IT MADE THE HAIRS RISE ALONG THE BACK OF HIS NECK.
GHOST! SO YOU CAME INSIDE AFTER ALL, EH?
WAS THE HUNTING SO BAD? HERE. TO ME, GHOST.
WHEN THE DEAD CAME WALKING, GHOST KNEW. HE WOKE ME, WARNED ME.
IS SOMETHING OUT THERE? GHOST, DO YOU HAVE A SCENT?
DYWEN HAD SAID HE SMELLED COLD.

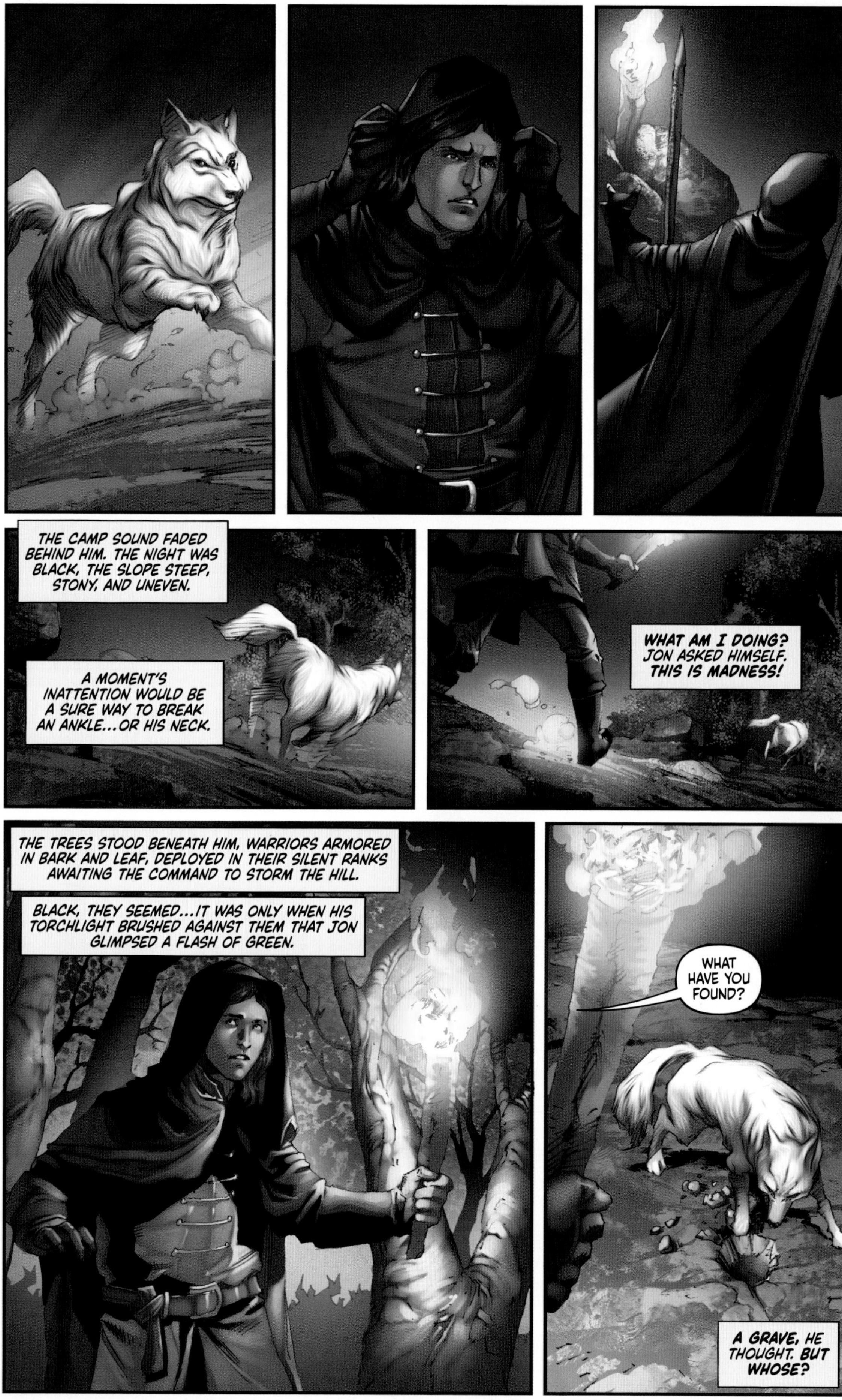

THE CAMP SOUND FADED BEHIND HIM. THE NIGHT WAS BLACK, THE SLOPE STEEP, STONY, AND UNEVEN.
A MOMENT'S INATTENTION WOULD BE A SURE WAY TO BREAK AN ANKLE...OR HIS NECK.
WHAT AM I DOING? JON ASKED HIMSELF. THIS IS MADNESS!
THE TREES STOOD BENEATH HIM, WARRIORS ARMORED IN BARK AND LEAF, DEPLOYED IN THEIR SILENT RANKS AWAITING THE COMMAND TO STORM THE HILL.
BLACK, THEY SEEMED...IT WAS ONLY WHEN HIS TORCHLIGHT BRUSHED AGAINST THEM THAT JON GLIMPSED A FLASH OF GREEN.
WHAT HAVE YOU FOUND?
A GRAVE, HE THOUGHT. BUT WHOSE?

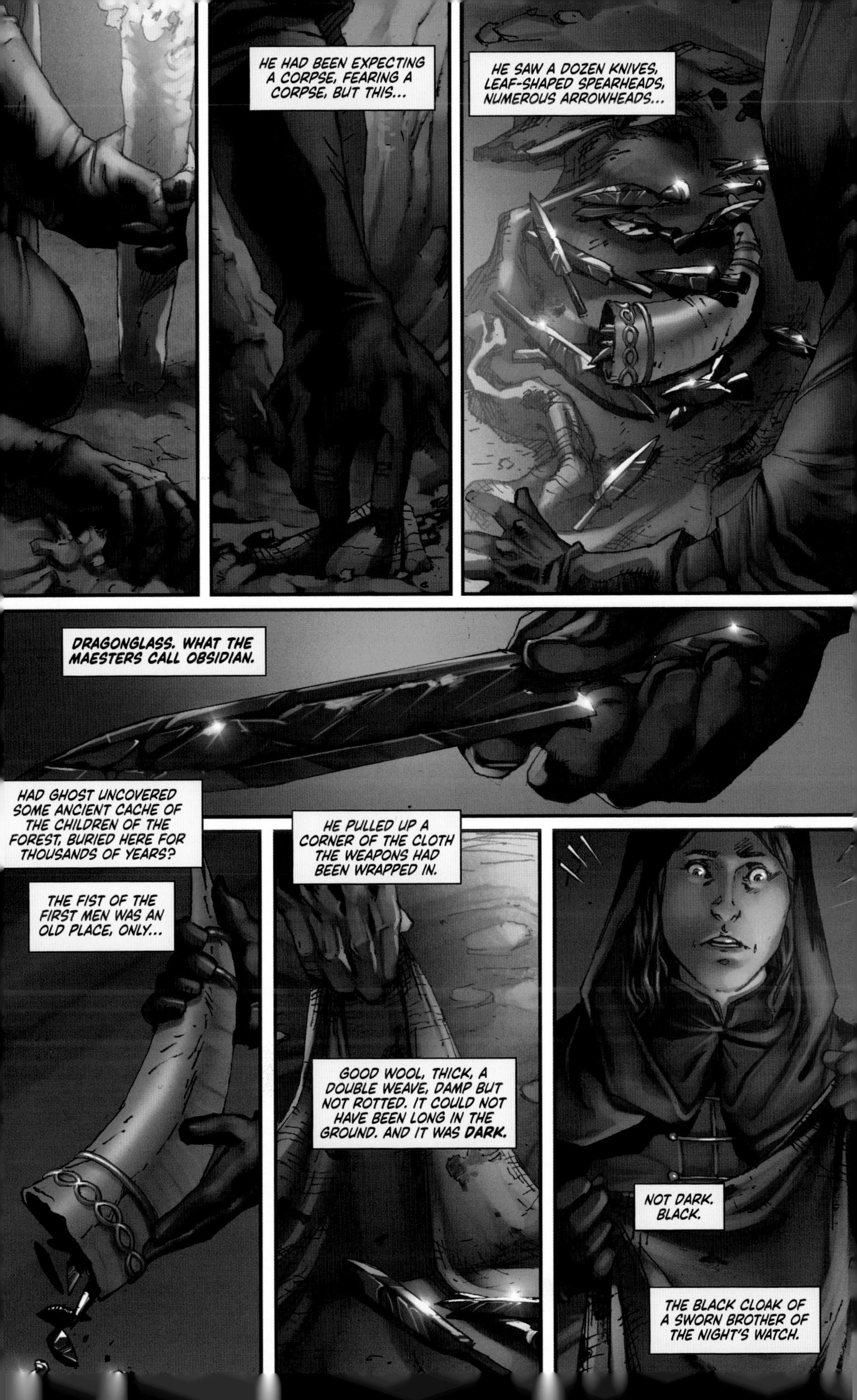
HE HAD BEEN EXPECTING A CORPSE, FEARING A CORPSE, BUT THIS...
HE SAW A DOZEN KNIVES, LEAF-SHAPED SPEARHEADS, NUMEROUS ARROWHEADS...
DRAGONGLASS. WHAT THE MAESTERS CALL OBSIDIAN.
HAD GHOST UNCOVERED SOME ANCIENT CACHE OF THE CHILDREN OF THE FOREST, BURIED HERE FOR THOUSANDS OF YEARS?
THE FIST OF THE FIRST MEN WAS AN OLD PLACE, ONLY...
HE PULLED UP A CORNER OF THE CLOTH THE WEAPONS HAD BEEN WRAPPED IN.
GOOD WOOL, THICK, A DOUBLE WEAVE, DAMP BUT NOT ROTTED. IT COULD NOT HAVE BEEN LONG IN THE GROUND. AND IT WAS DARK.
NOT DARK. BLACK.
THE BLACK CLOAK OF A SWORN BROTHER OF THE NIGHT'S WATCH.

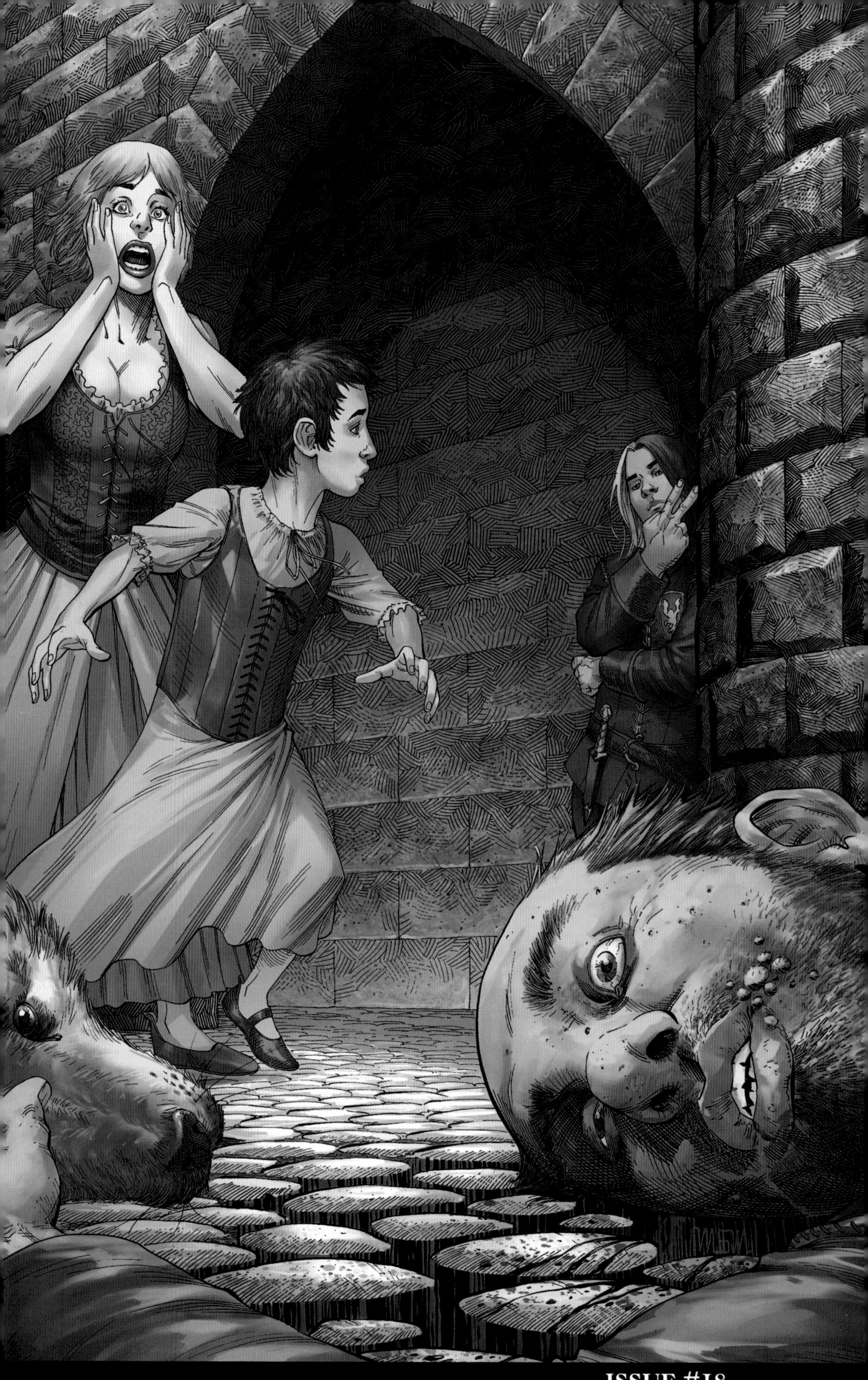

ISSUE #18

TYRION

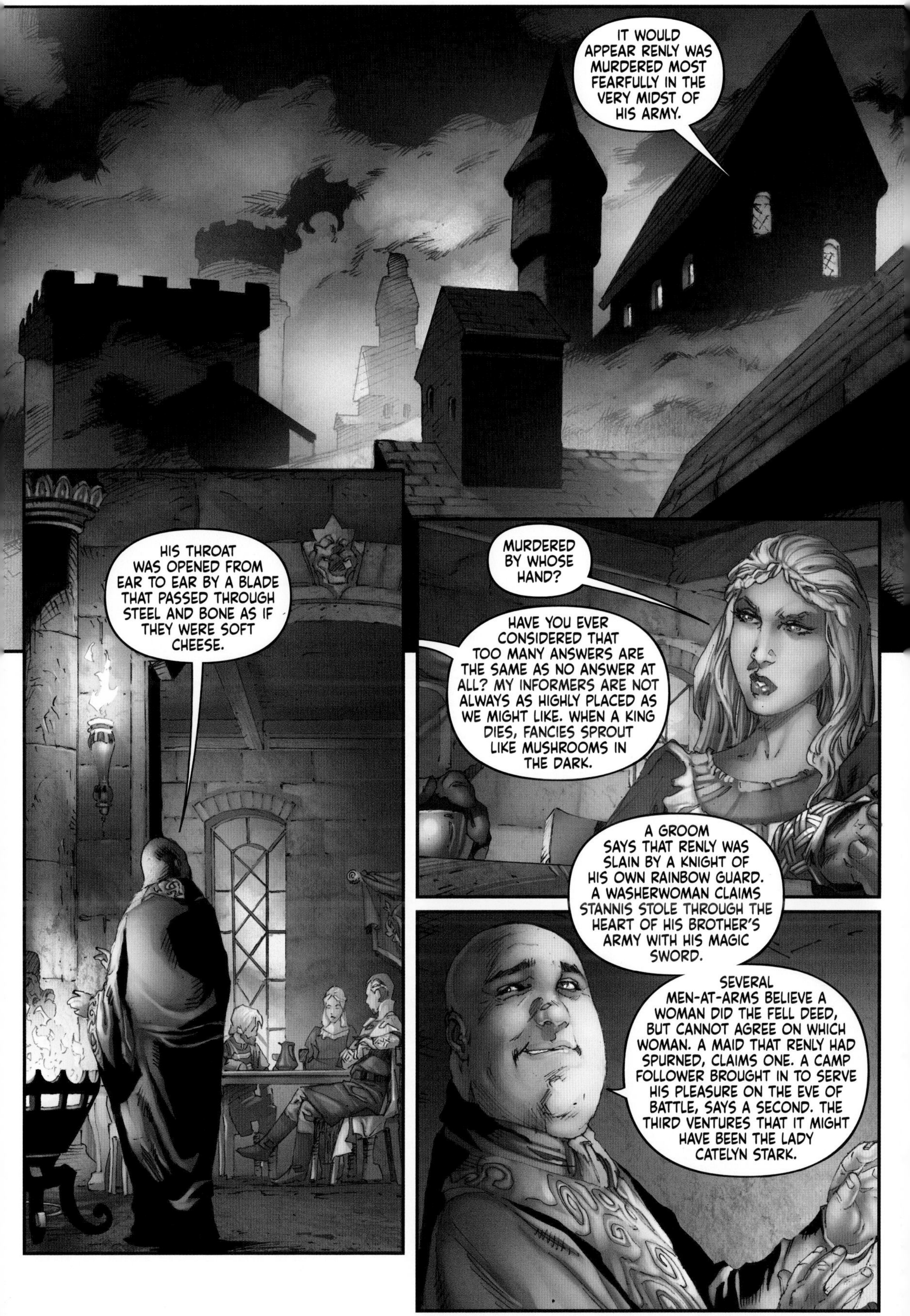
IT WOULD APPEAR RENLY WAS MURDERED MOST FEARFULLY IN THE VERY MIDST OF HIS ARMY.
HIS THROAT WAS OPENED FROM EAR TO EAR BY A BLADE THAT PASSED THROUGH STEEL AND BONE AS IF THEY WERE SOFT CHEESE.
MURDERED BY WHOSE HAND?
HAVE YOU EVER CONSIDERED THAT TOO MANY ANSWERS ARE THE SAME AS NO ANSWER AT ALL? MY INFORMERS ARE NOT ALWAYS AS HIGHLY PLACED AS WE MIGHT LIKE. WHEN A KING DIES, FANCIES SPROUT LIKE MUSHROOMS IN THE DARK.
A GROOM SAYS THAT RENLY WAS SLAIN BY A KNIGHT OF HIS OWN RAINBOW GUARD. A WASHERWOMAN CLAIMS STANNIS STOLE THROUGH THE HEART OF HIS BROTHER'S ARMY WITH HIS MAGIC SWORD.
SEVERAL MEN-AT-ARMS BELIEVE A WOMAN DID THE FELL DEED, BUT CANNOT AGREE ON WHICH WOMAN. A MAID THAT RENLY HAD SPURNED, CLAIMS ONE. A CAMP FOLLOWER BROUGHT IN TO SERVE HIS PLEASURE ON THE EVE OF BATTLE, SAYS A SECOND. THE THIRD VENTURES THAT IT MIGHT HAVE BEEN THE LADY CATELYN STARK.

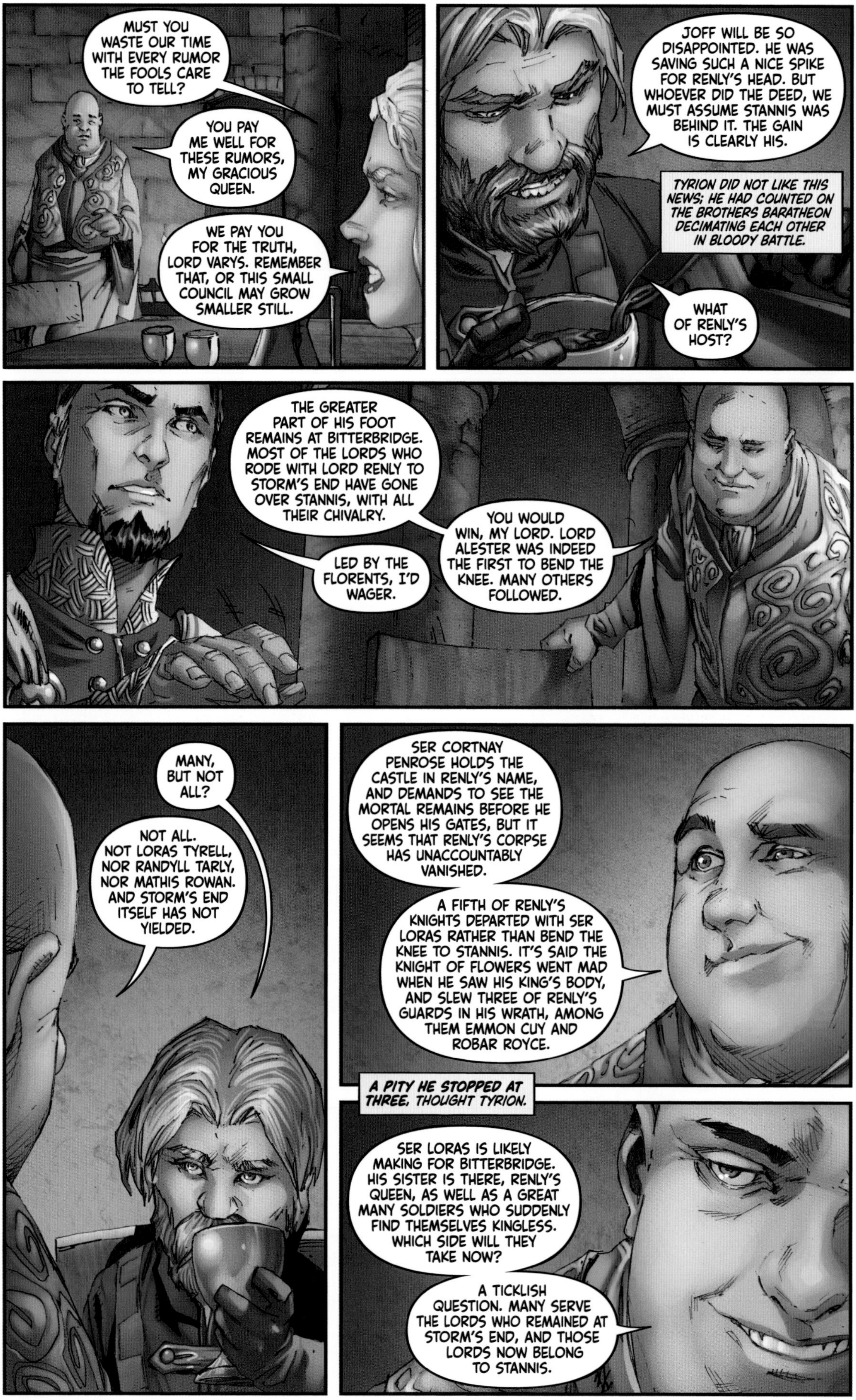
MUST YOU WASTE OUR TIME WITH EVERY RUMOR THE FOOLS CARE TO TELL?
YOU PAY ME WELL FOR THESE RUMORS, MY GRACIOUS QUEEN.
WE PAY YOU FOR THE TRUTH, LORD VARYS. REMEMBER THAT, OR THIS SMALL COUNCIL MAY GROW SMALLER STILL.
JOFF WILL BE SO DISAPPOINTED. HE WAS SAVING SUCH A NICE SPIKE FOR RENLY'S HEAD. BUT WHOEVER DID THE DEED, WE MUST ASSUME STANNIS WAS BEHIND IT. THE GAIN IS CLEARLY HIS.
TYRION DID NOT LIKE THIS NEWS; HE HAD COUNTED ON THE BROTHERS BARATHEON DECIMATING EACH OTHER IN BLOODY BATTLE.
WHAT OF RENLY'S HOST?
THE GREATER PART OF HIS FOOT REMAINS AT BITTERBRIDGE. MOST OF THE LORDS WHO RODE WITH LORD RENLY TO STORM'S END HAVE GONE OVER STANNIS, WITH ALL THEIR CHIVALRY.
LED BY THE FLORENTS, I'D WAGER.
YOU WOULD WIN, MY LORD. LORD ALESTER WAS INDEED THE FIRST TO BEND THE KNEE. MANY OTHERS FOLLOWED.
MANY, BUT NOT ALL?
NOT ALL. NOT LORAS TYRELL, NOR RANDYLL TARLY, NOR MATHIS ROWAN. AND STORM'S END ITSELF HAS NOT YIELDED.
SER CORTNAY PENROSE HOLDS THE CASTLE IN RENLY'S NAME, AND DEMANDS TO SEE THE MORTAL REMAINS BEFORE HE OPENS HIS GATES, BUT IT SEEMS THAT RENLY'S CORPSE HAS UNACCOUNTABLY VANISHED.
A FIFTH OF RENLY'S KNIGHTS DEPARTED WITH SER LORAS RATHER THAN BEND THE KNEE TO STANNIS. IT'S SAID THE KNIGHT OF FLOWERS WENT MAD WHEN HE SAW HIS KING'S BODY, AND SLEW THREE OF RENLY'S GUARDS IN HIS WRATH, AMONG THEM EMMON CUY AND ROBAR ROYCE.
A PITY HE STOPPED AT THREE, THOUGHT TYRION.
SER LORAS IS LIKELY MAKING FOR BITTERBRIDGE. HIS SISTER IS THERE, RENLY'S QUEEN, AS WELL AS A GREAT MANY SOLDIERS WHO SUDDENLY FIND THEMSELVES KINGLESS. WHICH SIDE WILL THEY TAKE NOW?
A TICKLISH QUESTION. MANY SERVE THE LORDS WHO REMAINED AT STORM'S END, AND THOSE LORDS NOW BELONG TO STANNIS.

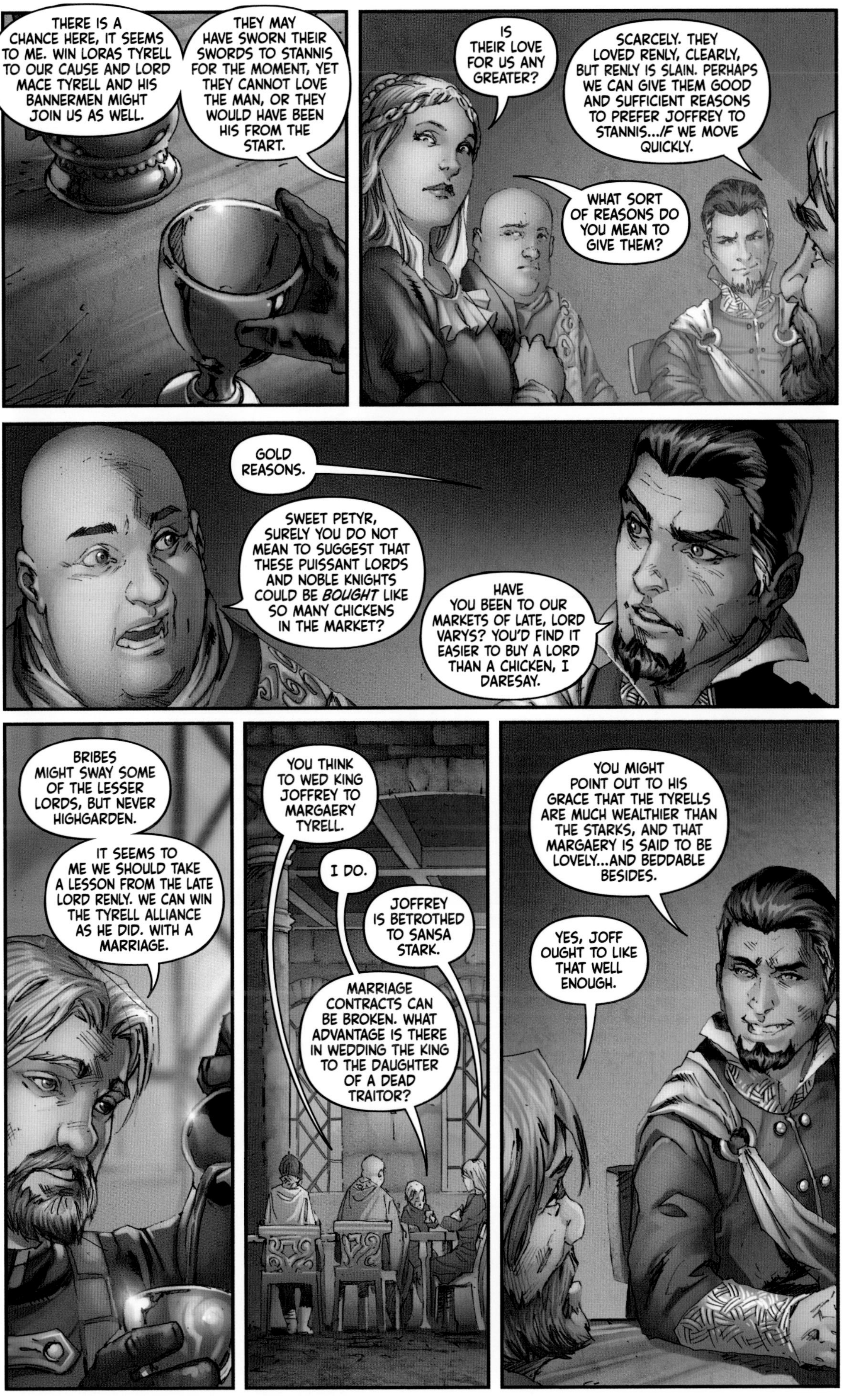
THERE IS A CHANCE HERE, IT SEEMS TO ME. WIN LORAS TYRELL TO OUR CAUSE AND LORD MACE TYRELL AND HIS BANNERMEN MIGHT JOIN US AS WELL.
THEY MAY HAVE SWORN THEIR SWORDS TO STANNIS FOR THE MOMENT, YET THEY CANNOT LOVE THE MAN, OR THEY WOULD HAVE BEEN HIS FROM THE START.
IS THEIR LOVE FOR US ANY GREATER?
SCARCELY. THEY LOVED RENLY, CLEARLY, BUT RENLY IS SLAIN. PERHAPS WE CAN GIVE THEM GOOD AND SUFFICIENT REASONS TO PREFER JOFFREY TO STANNIS...*IF* WE MOVE QUICKLY.
WHAT SORT OF REASONS DO YOU MEAN TO GIVE THEM?
GOLD REASONS.
SWEET PETYR, SURELY YOU DO NOT MEAN TO SUGGEST THAT THESE PUISSANT LORDS AND NOBLE KNIGHTS COULD BE *BOUGHT* LIKE SO MANY CHICKENS IN THE MARKET?
HAVE YOU BEEN TO OUR MARKETS OF LATE, LORD VARYS? YOU'D FIND IT EASIER TO BUY A LORD THAN A CHICKEN, I DARESAY.
BRIBES MIGHT SWAY SOME OF THE LESSER LORDS, BUT NEVER HIGHGARDEN.
IT SEEMS TO ME WE SHOULD TAKE A LESSON FROM THE LATE LORD RENLY. WE CAN WIN THE TYRELL ALLIANCE AS HE DID. WITH A MARRIAGE.
YOU THINK TO WED KING JOFFREY TO MARGAERY TYRELL.
I DO.
JOFFREY IS BETROTHED TO SANSA STARK.
MARRIAGE CONTRACTS CAN BE BROKEN. WHAT ADVANTAGE IS THERE IN WEDDING THE KING TO THE DAUGHTER OF A DEAD TRAITOR?
YOU MIGHT POINT OUT TO HIS GRACE THAT THE TYRELLS ARE MUCH WEALTHIER THAN THE STARKS, AND THAT MARGAERY IS SAID TO BE LOVELY...AND BEDDABLE BESIDES.
YES, JOFF OUGHT TO LIKE THAT WELL ENOUGH.

MY SON IS TOO YOUNG TO CARE ABOUT SUCH THINGS.

YOU THINK SO? HE'S THIRTEEN, CERSEI. THE SAME AGE AT WHICH I MARRIED.

YOU SHAMED US ALL WITH THAT SORRY EPISODE. JOFFREY IS MADE OF FINER STUFF.

SO FINE THAT HE HAD SER BOROS RIP OFF SANSA'S GOWN.

HE WAS ANGRY WITH THE GIRL.

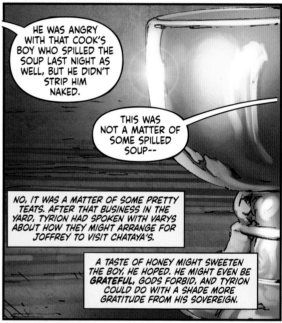

HE WAS ANGRY WITH THAT COOK'S BOY WHO SPILLED THE SOUP LAST NIGHT AS WELL, BUT HE DIDN'T STRIP HIM NAKED.

THIS WAS NOT A MATTER OF SOME SPILLED SOUP--

NO, IT WAS A MATTER OF SOME PRETTY TEATS. AFTER THAT BUSINESS IN THE YARD, TYRION HAD SPOKEN WITH VARYS ABOUT HOW THEY MIGHT ARRANGE FOR JOFFREY TO VISIT CHATAYA'S.

*A TASTE OF HONEY MIGHT SWEETEN THE BOY, HE HOPED. HE MIGHT EVEN BE **GRATEFUL**, GODS FORBID, AND TYRION COULD DO WITH A SHADE MORE GRATITUDE FROM HIS SOVEREIGN.*

DOUBTLESS YOU KNOW YOUR SON BETTER THAN I DO, BUT REGARDLESS, THERE'S STILL MUCH TO BE SAID FOR A TYRELL MARRIAGE. IT MAY BE THE ONLY WAY THAT JOFFREY LIVES LONG ENOUGH TO REACH HIS WEDDING NIGHT.

THE STARK GIRL BRINGS JOFFREY NOTHING BUT HER BODY, SWEET AS THAT MAY BE.

MARGAERY TYRELL BRINGS FIFTY THOUSAND SWORDS AND ALL THE STRENGTH OF HIGHGARDEN.

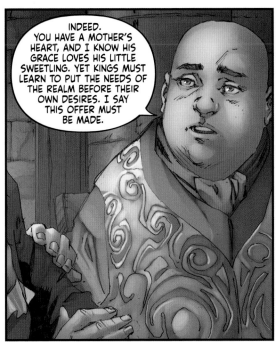

INDEED. YOU HAVE A MOTHER'S HEART, AND I KNOW HIS GRACE LOVES HIS LITTLE SWEETLING. YET KINGS MUST LEARN TO PUT THE NEEDS OF THE REALM BEFORE THEIR OWN DESIRES. I SAY THIS OFFER MUST BE MADE.

YOU WOULD NOT SPEAK SO IF YOU WERE WOMEN!

SAY WHAT YOU WILL, MY LORDS, BUT JOFFREY IS TOO PROUD TO SETTLE FOR RENLY'S LEAVINGS. HE WILL NEVER CONSENT.

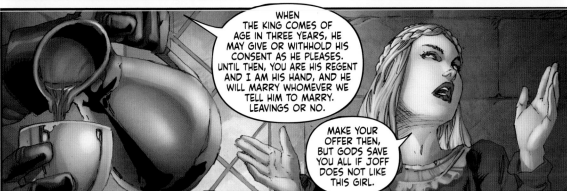

WHEN THE KING COMES OF AGE IN THREE YEARS, HE MAY GIVE OR WITHHOLD HIS CONSENT AS HE PLEASES. UNTIL THEN, YOU ARE HIS REGENT AND I AM HIS HAND, AND HE WILL MARRY WHOMEVER WE TELL HIM TO MARRY. LEAVINGS OR NO.

MAKE YOUR OFFER THEN, BUT GODS SAVE YOU ALL IF JOFF DOES NOT LIKE THIS GIRL.

I'M SO PLEASED WE CAN AGREE. NOW, WHICH OF US SHALL GO TO BITTERBRIDGE? WE MUST REACH SER LORAS WITH OUR OFFER BEFORE HIS BLOOD CAN COOL.

YOU MEAN TO SEND ONE OF THE COUNCIL?

I CAN SCARCELY EXPECT THE KNIGHT OF FLOWERS TO TREAT WITH BRONN OR SHAGGA, CAN I? THE TYRELLS ARE PROUD.

YOUR GRACE, MY LORD HAND, LET ME GO.

YOU?

WHAT GAIN DOES HE SEE IN THIS? TYRION WONDERED.

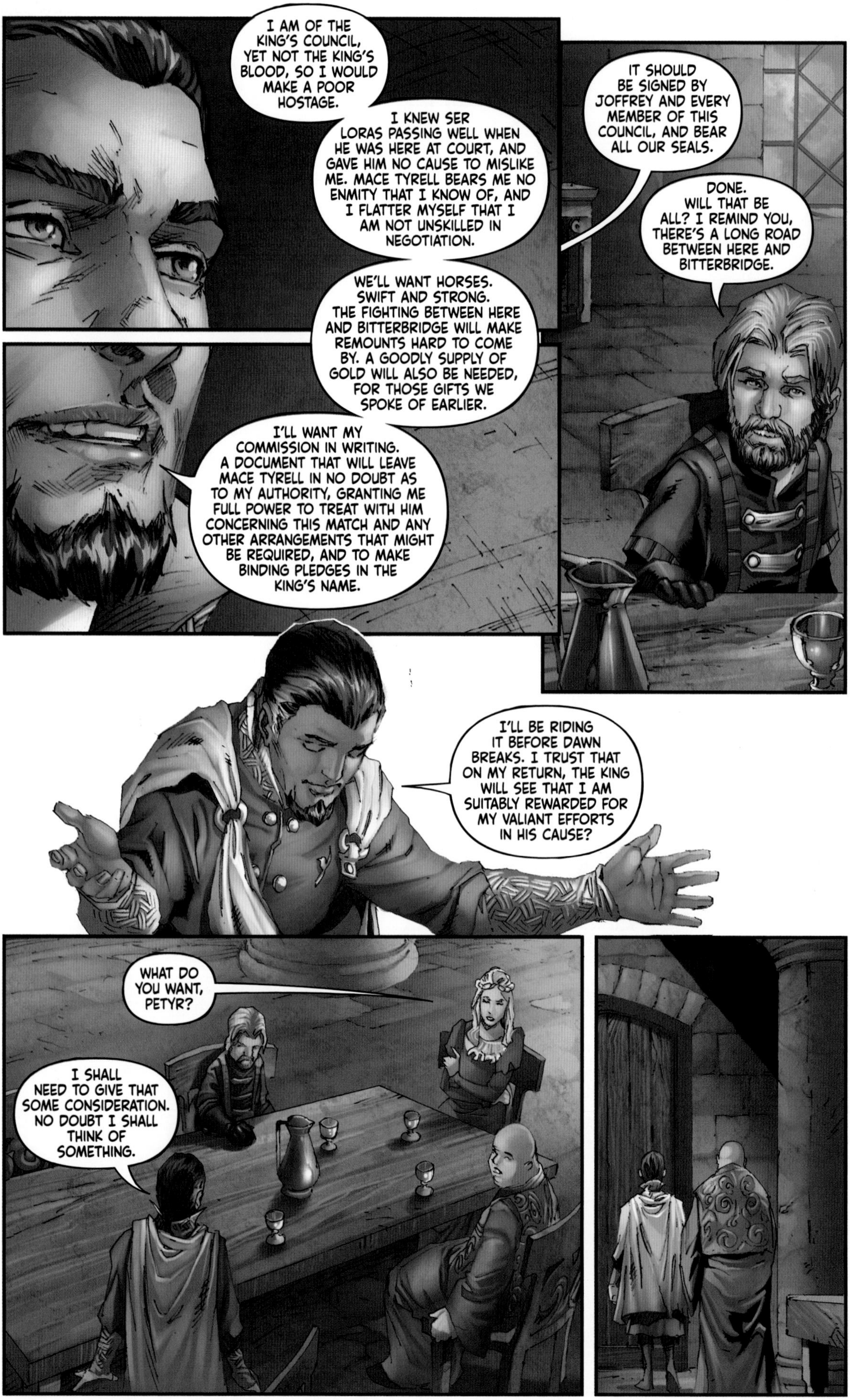
I AM OF THE KING'S COUNCIL, YET NOT THE KING'S BLOOD, SO I WOULD MAKE A POOR HOSTAGE.
I KNEW SER LORAS PASSING WELL WHEN HE WAS HERE AT COURT, AND GAVE HIM NO CAUSE TO MISLIKE ME. MACE TYRELL BEARS ME NO ENMITY THAT I KNOW OF, AND I FLATTER MYSELF THAT I AM NOT UNSKILLED IN NEGOTIATION.
WE'LL WANT HORSES. SWIFT AND STRONG. THE FIGHTING BETWEEN HERE AND BITTERBRIDGE WILL MAKE REMOUNTS HARD TO COME BY. A GOODLY SUPPLY OF GOLD WILL ALSO BE NEEDED, FOR THOSE GIFTS WE SPOKE OF EARLIER.
I'LL WANT MY COMMISSION IN WRITING. A DOCUMENT THAT WILL LEAVE MACE TYRELL IN NO DOUBT AS TO MY AUTHORITY, GRANTING ME FULL POWER TO TREAT WITH HIM CONCERNING THIS MATCH AND ANY OTHER ARRANGEMENTS THAT MIGHT BE REQUIRED, AND TO MAKE BINDING PLEDGES IN THE KING'S NAME.
IT SHOULD BE SIGNED BY JOFFREY AND EVERY MEMBER OF THIS COUNCIL, AND BEAR ALL OUR SEALS.
DONE. WILL THAT BE ALL? I REMIND YOU, THERE'S A LONG ROAD BETWEEN HERE AND BITTERBRIDGE.
I'LL BE RIDING IT BEFORE DAWN BREAKS. I TRUST THAT ON MY RETURN, THE KING WILL SEE THAT I AM SUITABLY REWARDED FOR MY VALIANT EFFORTS IN HIS CAUSE?
WHAT DO YOU WANT, PETYR?
I SHALL NEED TO GIVE THAT SOME CONSIDERATION. NO DOUBT I SHALL THINK OF SOMETHING.

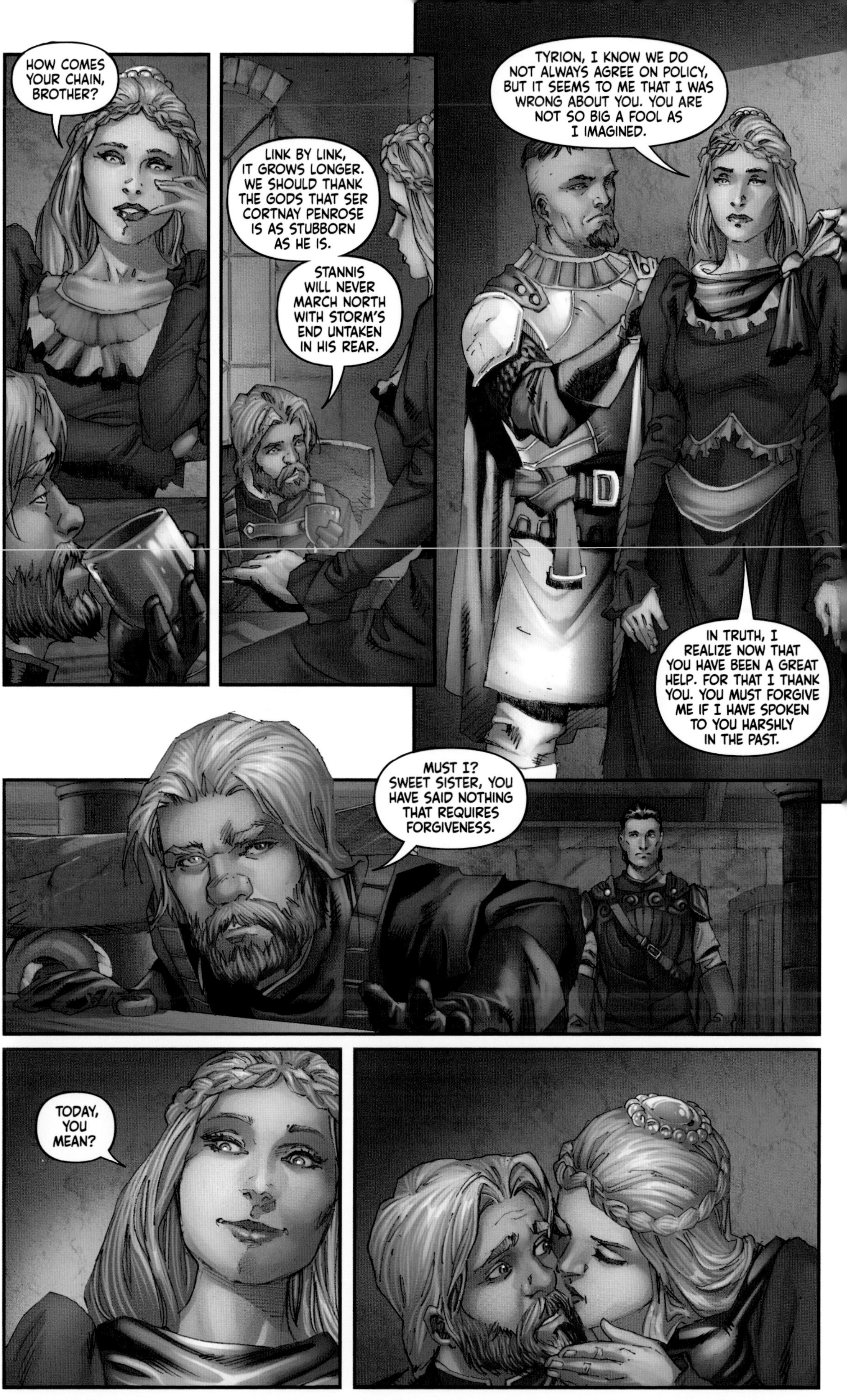
HOW COMES YOUR CHAIN, BROTHER?
LINK BY LINK, IT GROWS LONGER. WE SHOULD THANK THE GODS THAT SER CORTNAY PENROSE IS AS STUBBORN AS HE IS.
STANNIS WILL NEVER MARCH NORTH WITH STORM'S END UNTAKEN IN HIS REAR.
TYRION, I KNOW WE DO NOT ALWAYS AGREE ON POLICY, BUT IT SEEMS TO ME THAT I WAS WRONG ABOUT YOU. YOU ARE NOT SO BIG A FOOL AS I IMAGINED.
IN TRUTH, I REALIZE NOW THAT YOU HAVE BEEN A GREAT HELP. FOR THAT I THANK YOU. YOU MUST FORGIVE ME IF I HAVE SPOKEN TO YOU HARSHLY IN THE PAST.
MUST I? SWEET SISTER, YOU HAVE SAID NOTHING THAT REQUIRES FORGIVENESS.
TODAY, YOU MEAN?

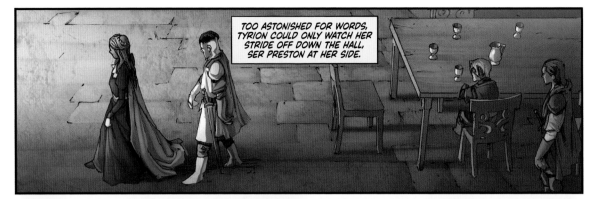

TOO ASTONISHED FOR WORDS, TYRION COULD ONLY WATCH HER STRIDE OFF DOWN THE HALL, SER PRESTON AT HER SIDE.

HAVE I LOST MY WITS, OR DID MY SISTER JUST KISS ME?

WAS IT SO SWEET?

IT WAS... UNANTICIPATED.

CERSEI HAD BEEN BEHAVING QUEERLY OF LATE. TYRION FOUND IT VERY UNSETTLING.

I AM TRYING TO RECALL THE LAST TIME SHE KISSED ME. I COULD NOT HAVE BEEN MORE THAN SIX OR SEVEN. JAIME HAD DARED HER TO DO IT.

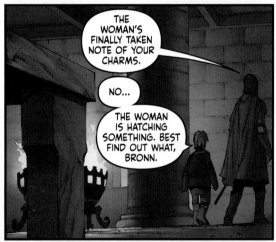

THE WOMAN'S FINALLY TAKEN NOTE OF YOUR CHARMS.

NO...

THE WOMAN IS HATCHING SOMETHING. BEST FIND OUT WHAT, BRONN.

"YOU KNOW I HATE SURPRISES."

THEON

ROBB WILL GUT YOU, GREYJOY! HE'LL FEED YOUR TURNCLOAK'S HEART TO HIS WOLF, YOU PIECE OF SHEEP DUNG!

NOW YOU MUST KILL HIM.

I HAVE QUESTIONS FOR HIM FIRST.

WHEN HE SPITS ON YOU, HE SPITS ON ALL OF US. HE SPITS ON THE DROWNED GOD. HE MUST DIE.

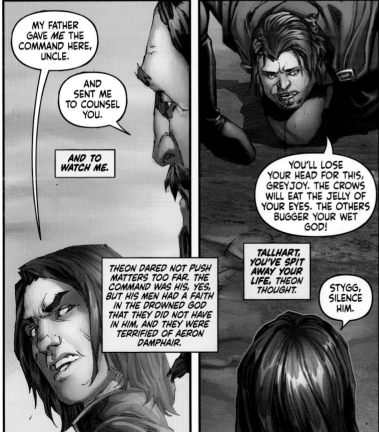

MY FATHER GAVE *ME* THE COMMAND HERE, UNCLE.

AND SENT ME TO COUNSEL YOU.

AND TO WATCH ME.

YOU'LL LOSE YOUR HEAD FOR THIS, GREYJOY. THE CROWS WILL EAT THE JELLY OF YOUR EYES. THE OTHERS BUGGER YOUR WET GOD!

TALLHART, YOU'VE SPIT AWAY YOUR LIFE, THEON THOUGHT.

STYGG, SILENCE HIM.

THEON DARED NOT PUSH MATTERS TOO FAR. THE COMMAND WAS HIS, YES, BUT HIS MEN HAD A FAITH IN THE DROWNED GOD THAT THEY DID NOT HAVE IN HIM, AND THEY WERE TERRIFIED OF AERON DAMPHAIR.

NO! HE MUST BE GIVEN TO THE GOD. THE OLD WAY.

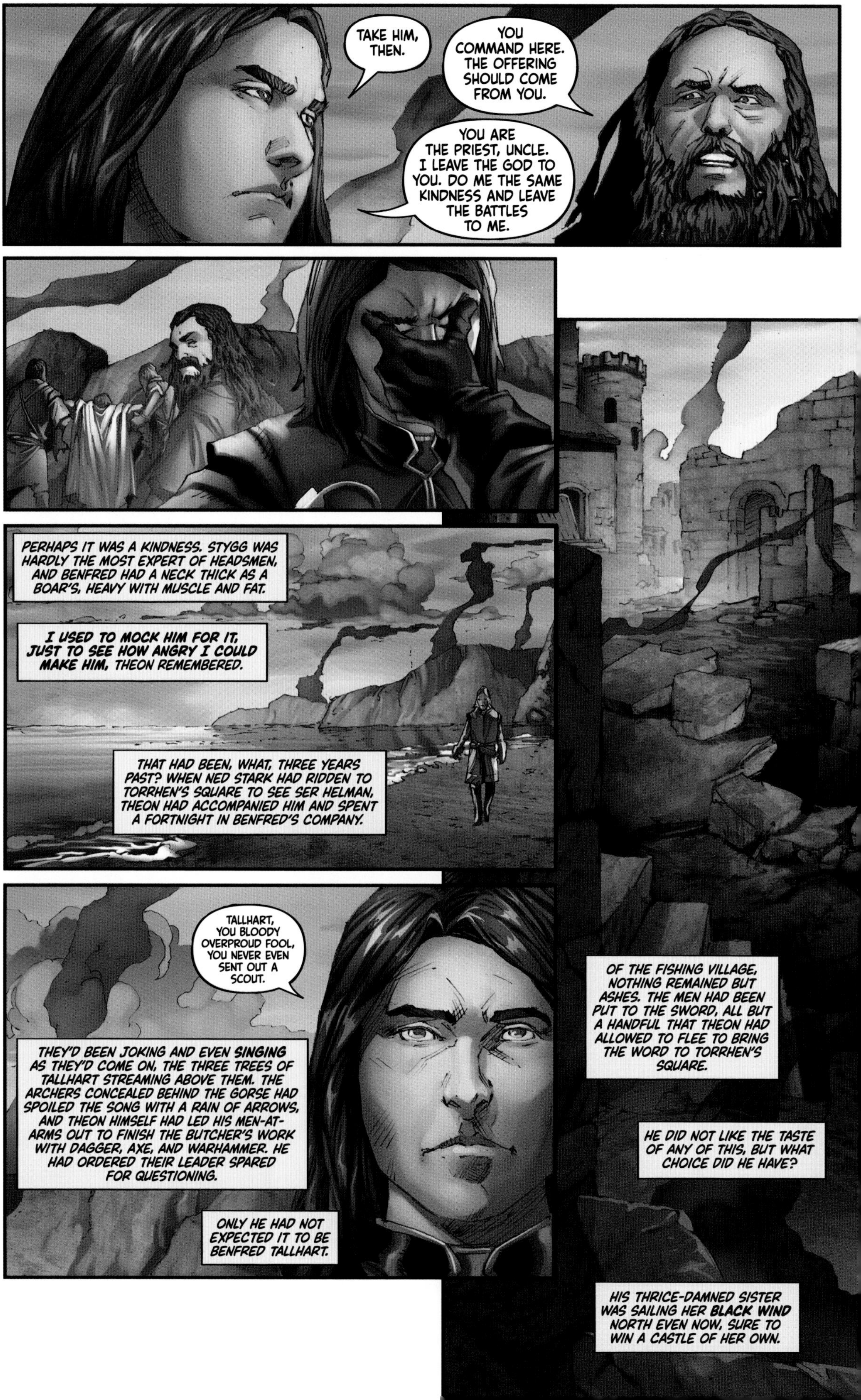

TAKE HIM, THEN.
YOU COMMAND HERE. THE OFFERING SHOULD COME FROM YOU.
YOU ARE THE PRIEST, UNCLE. I LEAVE THE GOD TO YOU. DO ME THE SAME KINDNESS AND LEAVE THE BATTLES TO ME.
PERHAPS IT WAS A KINDNESS. STYGG WAS HARDLY THE MOST EXPERT OF HEADSMEN, AND BENFRED HAD A NECK THICK AS A BOAR'S, HEAVY WITH MUSCLE AND FAT.
I USED TO MOCK HIM FOR IT, JUST TO SEE HOW ANGRY I COULD MAKE HIM, THEON REMEMBERED.
THAT HAD BEEN, WHAT, THREE YEARS PAST? WHEN NED STARK HAD RIDDEN TO TORRHEN'S SQUARE TO SEE SER HELMAN, THEON HAD ACCOMPANIED HIM AND SPENT A FORTNIGHT IN BENFRED'S COMPANY.
TALLHART, YOU BLOODY OVERPROUD FOOL, YOU NEVER EVEN SENT OUT A SCOUT.
THEY'D BEEN JOKING AND EVEN SINGING AS THEY'D COME ON, THE THREE TREES OF TALLHART STREAMING ABOVE THEM. THE ARCHERS CONCEALED BEHIND THE GORSE HAD SPOILED THE SONG WITH A RAIN OF ARROWS, AND THEON HIMSELF HAD LED HIS MEN-AT-ARMS OUT TO FINISH THE BUTCHER'S WORK WITH DAGGER, AXE, AND WARHAMMER. HE HAD ORDERED THEIR LEADER SPARED FOR QUESTIONING.
ONLY HE HAD NOT EXPECTED IT TO BE BENFRED TALLHART.
OF THE FISHING VILLAGE, NOTHING REMAINED BUT ASHES. THE MEN HAD BEEN PUT TO THE SWORD, ALL BUT A HANDFUL THAT THEON HAD ALLOWED TO FLEE TO BRING THE WORD TO TORRHEN'S SQUARE.
HE DID NOT LIKE THE TASTE OF ANY OF THIS, BUT WHAT CHOICE DID HE HAVE?
HIS THRICE-DAMNED SISTER WAS SAILING HER BLACK WIND NORTH EVEN NOW, SURE TO WIN A CASTLE OF HER OWN.

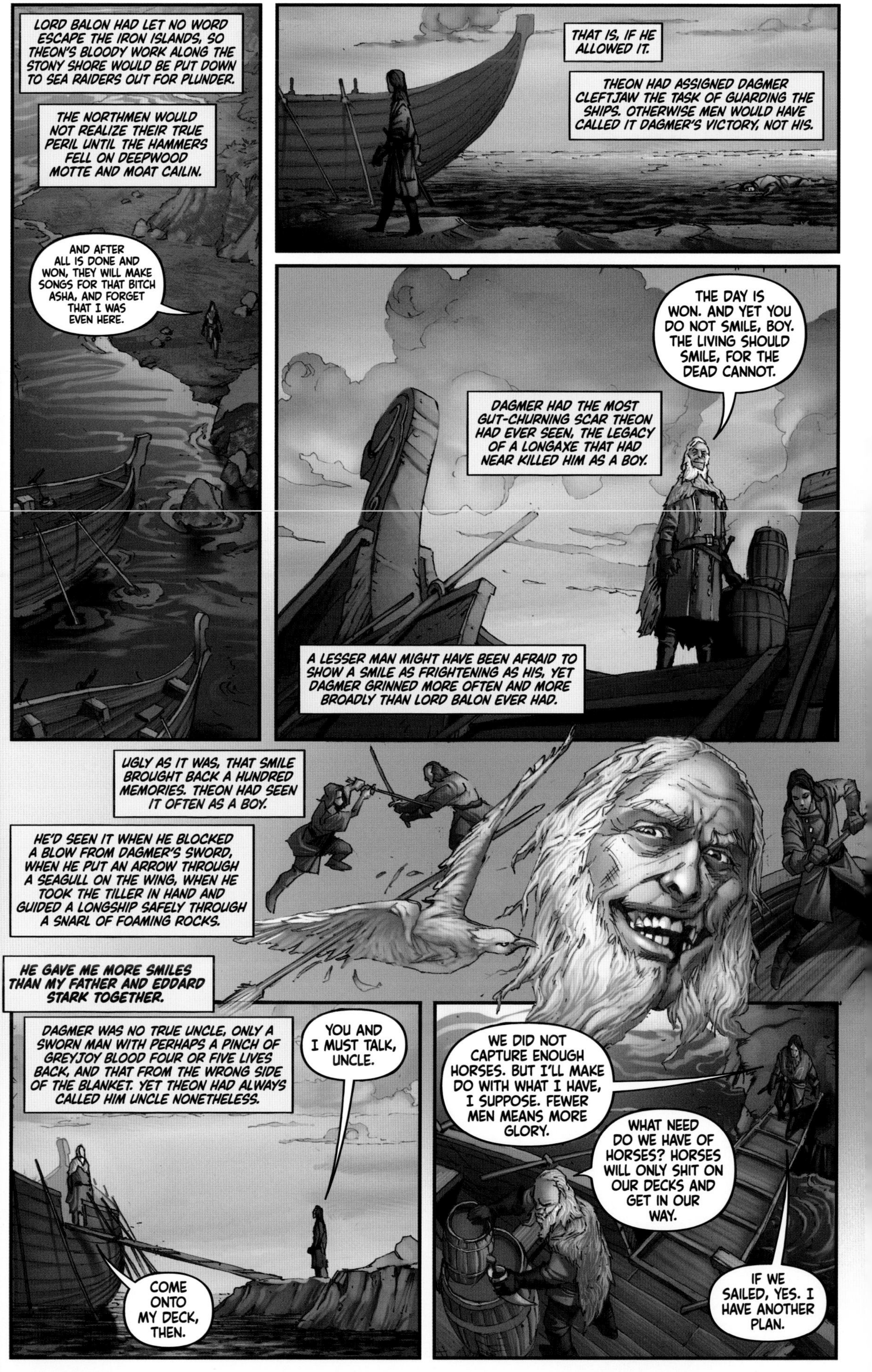
LORD BALON HAD LET NO WORD ESCAPE THE IRON ISLANDS, SO THEON'S BLOODY WORK ALONG THE STONY SHORE WOULD BE PUT DOWN TO SEA RAIDERS OUT FOR PLUNDER.
THE NORTHMEN WOULD NOT REALIZE THEIR TRUE PERIL UNTIL THE HAMMERS FELL ON DEEPWOOD MOTTE AND MOAT CAILIN.
AND AFTER ALL IS DONE AND WON, THEY WILL MAKE SONGS FOR THAT BITCH ASHA, AND FORGET THAT I WAS EVEN HERE.
THAT IS, IF HE ALLOWED IT.
THEON HAD ASSIGNED DAGMER CLEFTJAW THE TASK OF GUARDING THE SHIPS. OTHERWISE MEN WOULD HAVE CALLED IT DAGMER'S VICTORY, NOT HIS.
THE DAY IS WON. AND YET YOU DO NOT SMILE, BOY. THE LIVING SHOULD SMILE, FOR THE DEAD CANNOT.
DAGMER HAD THE MOST GUT-CHURNING SCAR THEON HAD EVER SEEN, THE LEGACY OF A LONGAXE THAT HAD NEAR KILLED HIM AS A BOY.
A LESSER MAN MIGHT HAVE BEEN AFRAID TO SHOW A SMILE AS FRIGHTENING AS HIS, YET DAGMER GRINNED MORE OFTEN AND MORE BROADLY THAN LORD BALON EVER HAD.
UGLY AS IT WAS, THAT SMILE BROUGHT BACK A HUNDRED MEMORIES. THEON HAD SEEN IT OFTEN AS A BOY.
HE'D SEEN IT WHEN HE BLOCKED A BLOW FROM DAGMER'S SWORD, WHEN HE PUT AN ARROW THROUGH A SEAGULL ON THE WING, WHEN HE TOOK THE TILLER IN HAND AND GUIDED A LONGSHIP SAFELY THROUGH A SNARL OF FOAMING ROCKS.
HE GAVE ME MORE SMILES THAN MY FATHER AND EDDARD STARK TOGETHER.
DAGMER WAS NO TRUE UNCLE, ONLY A SWORN MAN WITH PERHAPS A PINCH OF GREYJOY BLOOD FOUR OR FIVE LIVES BACK, AND THAT FROM THE WRONG SIDE OF THE BLANKET. YET THEON HAD ALWAYS CALLED HIM UNCLE NONETHELESS.
YOU AND I MUST TALK, UNCLE.
COME ONTO MY DECK, THEN.
WE DID NOT CAPTURE ENOUGH HORSES. BUT I'LL MAKE DO WITH WHAT I HAVE, I SUPPOSE. FEWER MEN MEANS MORE GLORY.
WHAT NEED DO WE HAVE OF HORSES? HORSES WILL ONLY SHIT ON OUR DECKS AND GET IN OUR WAY.
IF WE SAILED, YES. I HAVE ANOTHER PLAN.

YOUR LORD FATHER COMMANDED US TO HARRY THE COAST, NO MORE.

HIS *BEST* MAN, AND ALWAYS HAVE BEEN.

YOU ARE MY FATHER'S MAN.

PRIDE, THEON THOUGHT. HIS PRIDE WILL BE THE KEY.

IF I HAD A MAN LIKE YOU IN MY SERVICE, I SHOULD NOT WASTE HIM ON THIS CHILD'S BUSINESS OF HARRYING AND BURNING. THIS IS NO WORK FOR LORD BALON'S BEST MAN.

NOR FOR HIS TRUEBORN SON?

I KNOW YOU TOO WELL, THEON. 'TIS NOT ME WHO FEELS WASTED.

BY RIGHTS I SHOULD HAVE MY SISTER'S COMMAND.

YOU TAKE THIS BUSINESS TOO HARD, BOY. IT IS ONLY THAT YOUR LORD FATHER DOES NOT KNOW YOU.

WITH YOUR BROTHERS DEAD AND YOU TAKEN BY THE WOLVES, YOUR SISTER WAS HIS SOLACE. HE LEARNED TO RELY ON HER, AND SHE HAS NEVER FAILED HIM.

NOR HAVE I. THE STARKS KNEW MY WORTH. I CHARGED WITH THE FIRST WAVE IN THE WHISPERING WOOD.

I WAS *THAT* CLOSE TO CROSSING SWORDS WITH THE KINGSLAYER HIMSELF.

WHY DO YOU TELL ME THIS? IT WAS ME WHO PUT YOUR FIRST SWORD IN YOUR HAND. I KNOW YOU ARE NO CRAVEN.

DOES MY FATHER?

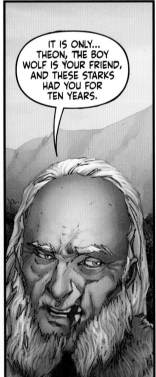

IT IS ONLY... THEON, THE BOY WOLF IS YOUR FRIEND, AND THESE STARKS HAD YOU FOR TEN YEARS.

I AM NO STARK.

LORD EDDARD SAW TO THAT.

I AM A GREYJOY, AND I MEAN TO BE MY FATHER'S HEIR. HOW CAN I DO THAT UNLESS I PROVE MYSELF WITH SOME GREAT DEED?

YOU ARE YOUNG. OTHER WARS WILL COME, AND YOU SHALL DO YOUR GREAT DEEDS. FOR NOW, WE ARE COMMANDED TO HARRY THE STONY SHORE.

LET MY UNCLE AERON SEE TO IT. I'LL GIVE HIM SIX SHIPS, AND HE CAN BURN AND DROWN TO HIS GOD'S SURFEIT.

SO LONG AS THE HARRYING IS DONE, WHAT DOES IT MATTER? I HAVE A TASK THAT ONLY DAGMER CLEFTJAW CAN ACCOMPLISH.

TELL ME.

HE IS TEMPTED, THEON THOUGHT. HE LIKES THIS REAVER'S WORK NO BETTER THAN I DO.

IF MY SISTER CAN TAKE A CASTLE, SO CAN I.

ASHA HAS FOUR OR FIVE TIMES THE MEN WE DO.

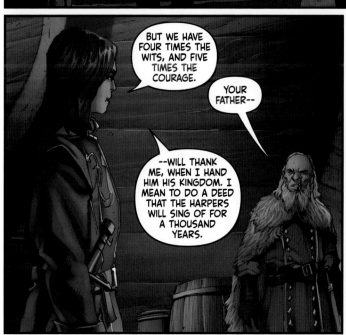

BUT WE HAVE FOUR TIMES THE WITS, AND FIVE TIMES THE COURAGE.

YOUR FATHER--

--WILL THANK ME, WHEN I HAND HIM HIS KINGDOM. I MEAN TO DO A DEED THAT THE HARPERS WILL SING OF FOR A THOUSAND YEARS.

WHAT WOULD MY PART BE IN THIS SCHEME OF YOURS, BOY?

HE KNEW THAT WOULD GIVE DAGMER PAUSE. A SINGER HAD MADE A SONG ABOUT THE AXE THAT CRACKED HIS JAW IN HALF, AND THE OLD MAN LOVED TO HEAR IT.

HIS HAIR IS WHITE AND HIS TEETH ARE ROTTEN, BUT HE STILL HAS A TASTE FOR GLORY.

TO STRIKE TERROR INTO THE HEART OF THE FOE, AS ONLY ONE OF YOUR NAME COULD DO. YOU'LL TAKE THE GREAT PART OF OUR FORCE AND MARCH ON TORRHEN'S SQUARE. HELMAN TALLHART TOOK HIS BEST MEN SOUTH, AND BENFRED DIED HERE WITH THEIR SONS. HIS UNCLE LEOBALD WILL REMAIN, WITH SOME SMALL GARRISON.

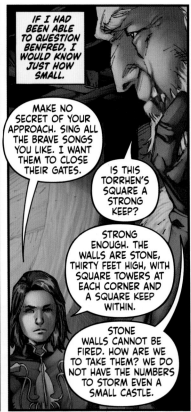

IF I HAD BEEN ABLE TO QUESTION BENFRED, I WOULD KNOW JUST HOW SMALL.

MAKE NO SECRET OF YOUR APPROACH. SING ALL THE BRAVE SONGS YOU LIKE. I WANT THEM TO CLOSE THEIR GATES.

IS THIS TORRHEN'S SQUARE A STRONG KEEP?

STRONG ENOUGH. THE WALLS ARE STONE, THIRTY FEET HIGH, WITH SQUARE TOWERS AT EACH CORNER AND A SQUARE KEEP WITHIN.

STONE WALLS CANNOT BE FIRED. HOW ARE WE TO TAKE THEM? WE DO NOT HAVE THE NUMBERS TO STORM EVEN A SMALL CASTLE.

YOU WILL MAKE CAMP OUTSIDE THEIR WALLS AND SET TO BUILDING CATAPULTS AND SIEGE ENGINES.

THAT IS NOT THE OLD WAY. HAVE YOU FORGOTTEN? IRONMEN FIGHT WITH SWORDS AND AXES, NOT BY FLINGING ROCKS. THERE IS NO GLORY IN STARVING OUT A FOEMAN.

LEOBALD WILL NOT KNOW THAT. WHEN HE SEES YOU RAISING SIEGE TOWERS, HIS OLD WOMAN'S BLOOD WILL RUN COLD, AND HE WILL BLEAT FOR HELP. STAY YOUR ARCHERS, UNCLE, AND LET THE RAVEN FLY.

THE CASTELLAN AT WINTERFELL IS A BRAVE MAN, BUT AGE HAS STIFFENED HIS WITS AS WELL AS HIS LIMBS. WHEN HE LEARNS THAT ONE OF HIS KING'S BANNERMEN IS UNDER ATTACK BY THE FEARSOME DAGMER CLEFTJAW, HE WILL SUMMON HIS STRENGTH AND RIDE TO TALLHART'S AID.

ANY FORCE HE SUMMONS WILL BE LARGER THAN MINE. YOU SET US A BATTLE WE CANNOT HOPE TO WIN, THEON. THIS TORRHEN'S SQUARE WILL NEVER FALL.

IT'S NOT TORRHEN'S SQUARE I MEAN TO TAKE.

ARYA

CONFUSION AND CLANGOR RULED THE CASTLE. MEN STOOD ON THE BEDS OF WAGONS LOADING CASKS OF WINE, SACKS OF FLOUR, AND BUNDLES OF NEW-FLETCHED ARROWS.

SMITHS STRAIGHTENED SWORDS, KNOCKED DENTS FROM BREASTPLATES, AND SHOED DESTRIERS AND PACK MULES ALIKE.

LORD TYWIN LANNISTER WAS MARCHING AT LAST.

HE WAS GOING TO FIGHT ROBB, ARYA KNEW. ROBB HAD WON SOME GREAT VICTORY IN THE WEST.

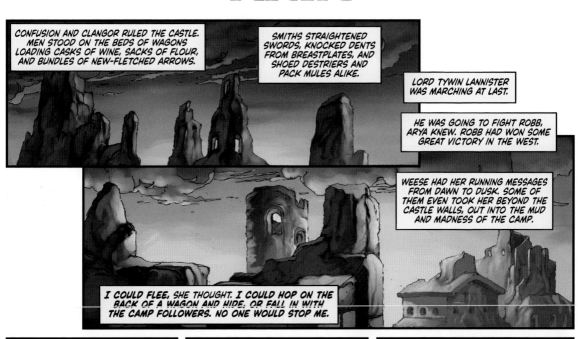

WEESE HAD HER RUNNING MESSAGES FROM DAWN TO DUSK. SOME OF THEM EVEN TOOK HER BEYOND THE CASTLE WALLS, OUT INTO THE MUD AND MADNESS OF THE CAMP.

I COULD FLEE, SHE THOUGHT. I COULD HOP ON THE BACK OF A WAGON AND HIDE, OR FALL IN WITH THE CAMP FOLLOWERS. NO ONE WOULD STOP ME.

SHE MIGHT HAVE DONE IT IF NOT FOR WEESE. HE'D TOLD THEM MORE THAN ONCE WHAT HE'D DO TO ANYONE WHO TRIED TO RUN OFF.

"IT WON'T BE A BEATING, OH, NO. I'LL JUST SAVE YOU FOR THE QOHORIK. WHEN VARGO HOAT GETS BACK HE'LL CUT OFF YOUR FEET."

MAYBE IF WEESE WERE DEAD, ARYA THOUGHT...BUT NOT WHEN SHE WAS WITH HIM. HE COULD LOOK AT YOU AND SMELL WHAT YOU WERE THINKING, HE ALWAYS SAID SO.

HE NEVER IMAGINED SHE COULD READ, THOUGH, SO HE NEVER BOTHERED TO SEAL THE MESSAGES HE GAVE HER.

ARYA PEEKED AT THEM ALL, BUT THEY WERE NEVER ANYTHING GOOD, JUST STUPID STUFF SENDING THIS CART TO THE GRANARY AND THAT ONE TO THE ARMORY.

ONE WAS A DEMAND FOR PAYMENT ON A GAMBLING DEBT, BUT THE KNIGHT SHE GAVE IT TO TRIED TO HIT HER. ARYA DUCKED UNDER THE BLOW, SNATCHED A SILVER-BANDED DRINKING HORN OFF HIS SADDLE, AND DARTED AWAY.

WHEN SHE GAVE THE HORN TO WEESE, HE TOLD HER THAT A SMART LITTLE WEASEL LIKE HER DESERVED A REWARD.

"I'VE GOT MY EYE ON A PLUMP CRISP CAPON TO SUP ON," WEESE SAID. "WE'LL SHARE IT, ME AND YOU."

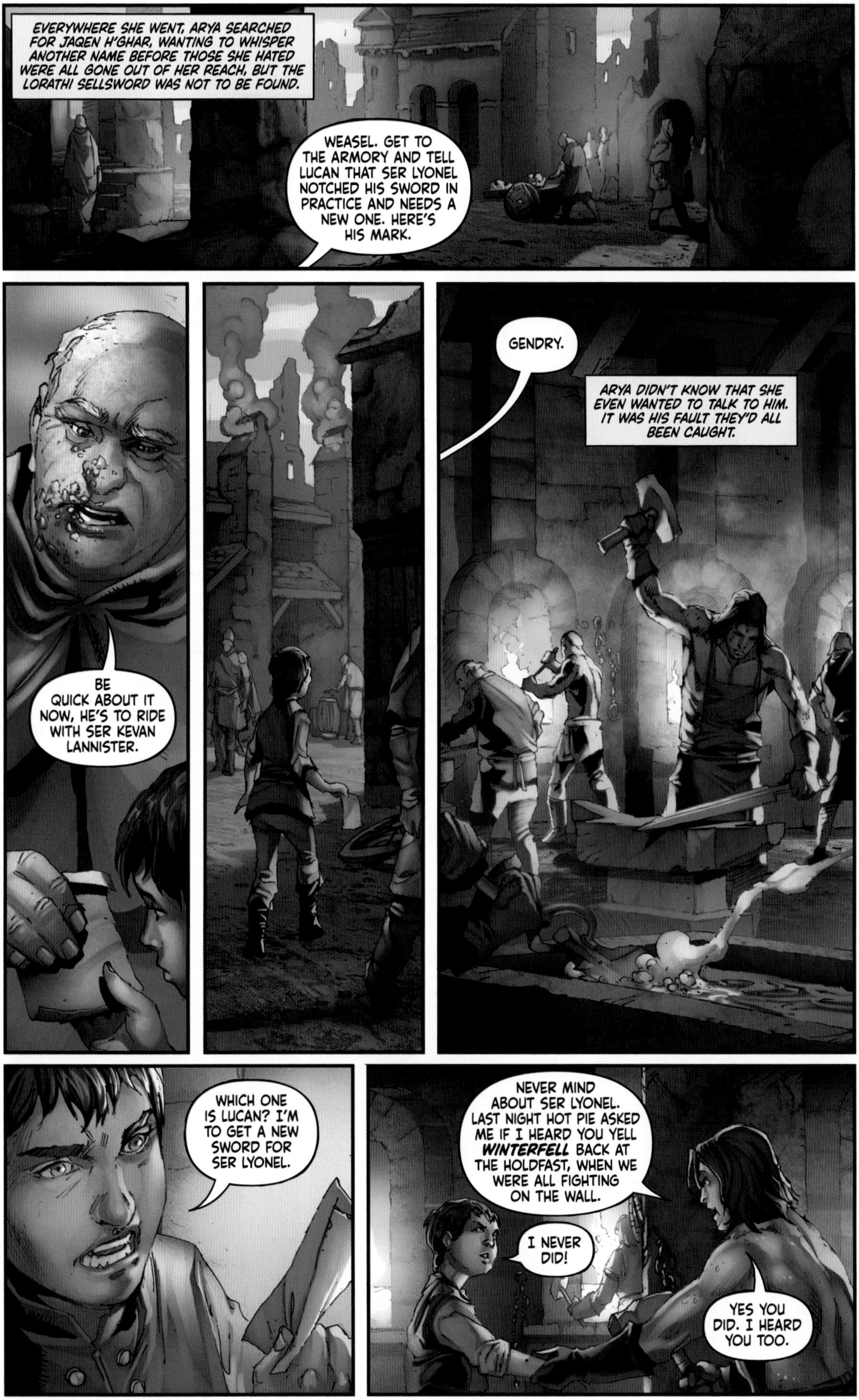
EVERYWHERE SHE WENT, ARYA SEARCHED FOR JAQEN H'GHAR, WANTING TO WHISPER ANOTHER NAME BEFORE THOSE SHE HATED WERE ALL GONE OUT OF HER REACH, BUT THE LORATHI SELLSWORD WAS NOT TO BE FOUND.
WEASEL. GET TO THE ARMORY AND TELL LUCAN THAT SER LYONEL NOTCHED HIS SWORD IN PRACTICE AND NEEDS A NEW ONE. HERE'S HIS MARK.
BE QUICK ABOUT IT NOW, HE'S TO RIDE WITH SER KEVAN LANNISTER.
GENDRY.
ARYA DIDN'T KNOW THAT SHE EVEN WANTED TO TALK TO HIM. IT WAS HIS FAULT THEY'D ALL BEEN CAUGHT.
WHICH ONE IS LUCAN? I'M TO GET A NEW SWORD FOR SER LYONEL.
NEVER MIND ABOUT SER LYONEL. LAST NIGHT HOT PIE ASKED ME IF I HEARD YOU YELL WINTERFELL BACK AT THE HOLDFAST, WHEN WE WERE ALL FIGHTING ON THE WALL.
I NEVER DID!
YES YOU DID. I HEARD YOU TOO.

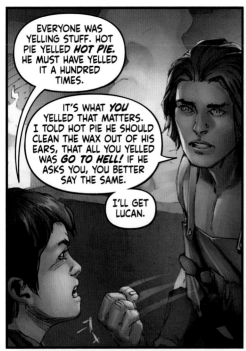

EVERYONE WAS YELLING STUFF. HOT PIE YELLED *HOT PIE*. HE MUST HAVE YELLED IT A HUNDRED TIMES.

IT'S WHAT *YOU* YELLED THAT MATTERS. I TOLD HOT PIE HE SHOULD CLEAN THE WAX OUT OF HIS EARS, THAT ALL YOU YELLED WAS *GO TO HELL!* IF HE ASKS YOU, YOU BETTER SAY THE SAME.

I'LL GET LUCAN.

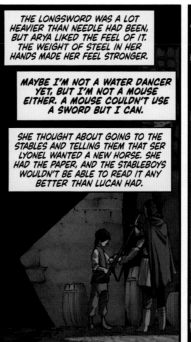

THE LONGSWORD WAS A LOT HEAVIER THAN NEEDLE HAD BEEN, BUT ARYA LIKED THE FEEL OF IT. THE WEIGHT OF STEEL IN HER HANDS MADE HER FEEL STRONGER.

MAYBE I'M NOT A WATER DANCER YET, BUT I'M NOT A MOUSE EITHER. A MOUSE COULDN'T USE A SWORD BUT I CAN.

SHE THOUGHT ABOUT GOING TO THE STABLES AND TELLING THEM THAT SER LYONEL WANTED A NEW HORSE. SHE HAD THE PAPER, AND THE STABLEBOYS WOULDN'T BE ABLE TO READ IT ANY BETTER THAN LUCAN HAD.

I COULD TAKE THE HORSE AND THE SWORD AND JUST RIDE OUT.

BUT IF THE GUARDS QUESTIONED HER, THEY'D KNOW, AND THEN WEESE... WEESE...

SHE CHEWED HER LIP, TRYING NOT TO THINK ABOUT HOW IT WOULD FEEL TO HAVE HER FEET CUT OFF.

...GIANTS I TELL YOU, HE'S GOT *GIANTS* TWENTY FOOT TALL COME DOWN FROM BEYOND THE WALL, FOLLOW HIM LIKE DOGS...

...NOT NATURAL, COMING ON THEM SO FAST, IN THE NIGHT AND ALL. HE'S MORE WOLF THAN MAN, ALL THEM STARKS ARE...

YES, ARYA THOUGHT. ALL OF YOU BETTER RUN OR MY BROTHER WILL KILL YOU. HE'S A STARK, HE'S MORE WOLF THAN MAN, AND SO AM I.

WEASEL!

GIVE ME THAT! TOOK YOU LONG ENOUGH.

NEXT TIME BE QUICKER ABOUT IT.

NOW, GET DOWN TO THE BREWHOUSE AND TELL TUFFLEBERRY THAT I HAVE TWO DOZEN BARRELS FOR HIM, BUT HE BETTER SEND HIS LADS TO FETCH THEM OR I'LL FIND SOMEONE WANTS 'EM WORSE.

YOU *RUN* IF YOU WANT TO EAT TONIGHT!

AND DON'T BE GETTING LOST AGAIN, OR I SWEAR I'LL BEAT YOU BLOODY.

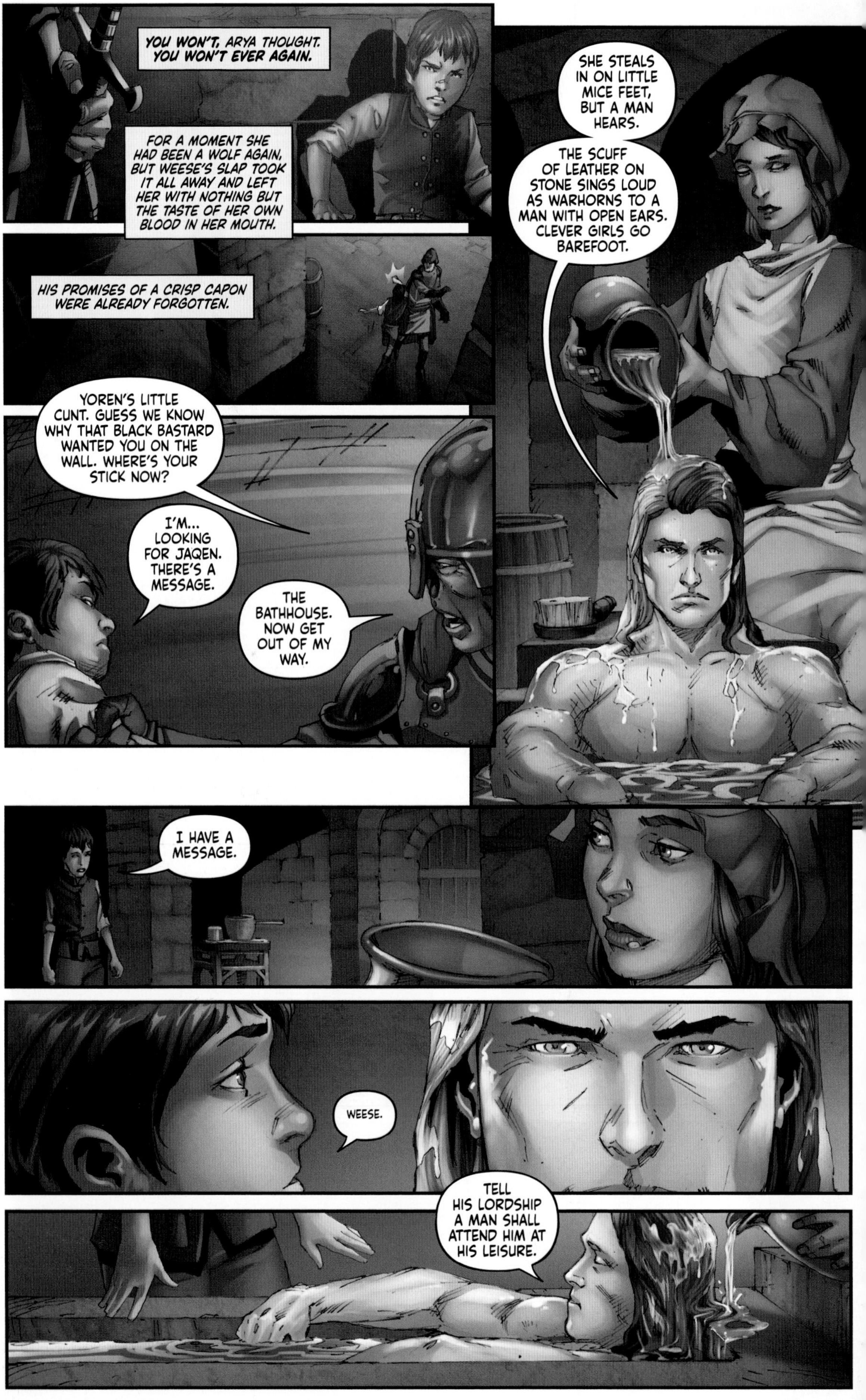

YOU WON'T, ARYA THOUGHT. YOU WON'T EVER AGAIN.
FOR A MOMENT SHE HAD BEEN A WOLF AGAIN, BUT WEESE'S SLAP TOOK IT ALL AWAY AND LEFT HER WITH NOTHING BUT THE TASTE OF HER OWN BLOOD IN HER MOUTH.
HIS PROMISES OF A CRISP CAPON WERE ALREADY FORGOTTEN.
YOREN'S LITTLE CUNT. GUESS WE KNOW WHY THAT BLACK BASTARD WANTED YOU ON THE WALL. WHERE'S YOUR STICK NOW?
I'M... LOOKING FOR JAQEN. THERE'S A MESSAGE.
THE BATHHOUSE. NOW GET OUT OF MY WAY.
SHE STEALS IN ON LITTLE MICE FEET, BUT A MAN HEARS.
THE SCUFF OF LEATHER ON STONE SINGS LOUD AS WARHORNS TO A MAN WITH OPEN EARS. CLEVER GIRLS GO BAREFOOT.
I HAVE A MESSAGE.
WEESE.
TELL HIS LORDSHIP A MAN SHALL ATTEND HIM AT HIS LEISURE.

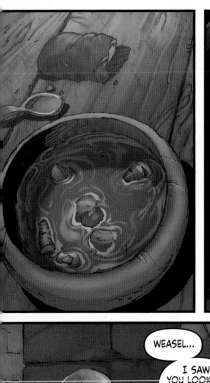

WEASEL...

I SAW YOU LOOKING AT ME. WHAT DID I TELL YOU?

KEEP THOSE EYES TO YOURSELF, OR NEXT TIME I'LL SPOON ONE OUT AND FEED IT TO MY BITCH.

SHE WONDERED HOW MUCH LONGER SHE WOULD HAVE TO INCLUDE WEESE IN HER PRAYER...

WEESE, DUNSEN, POLLIVER, RAFF THE SWEETLING...

THE TICKLER AND THE HOUND. SER GREGOR, SER AMORY, SER ILYN, SER MERYN, KING JOFFREY, QUEEN CERSEI.

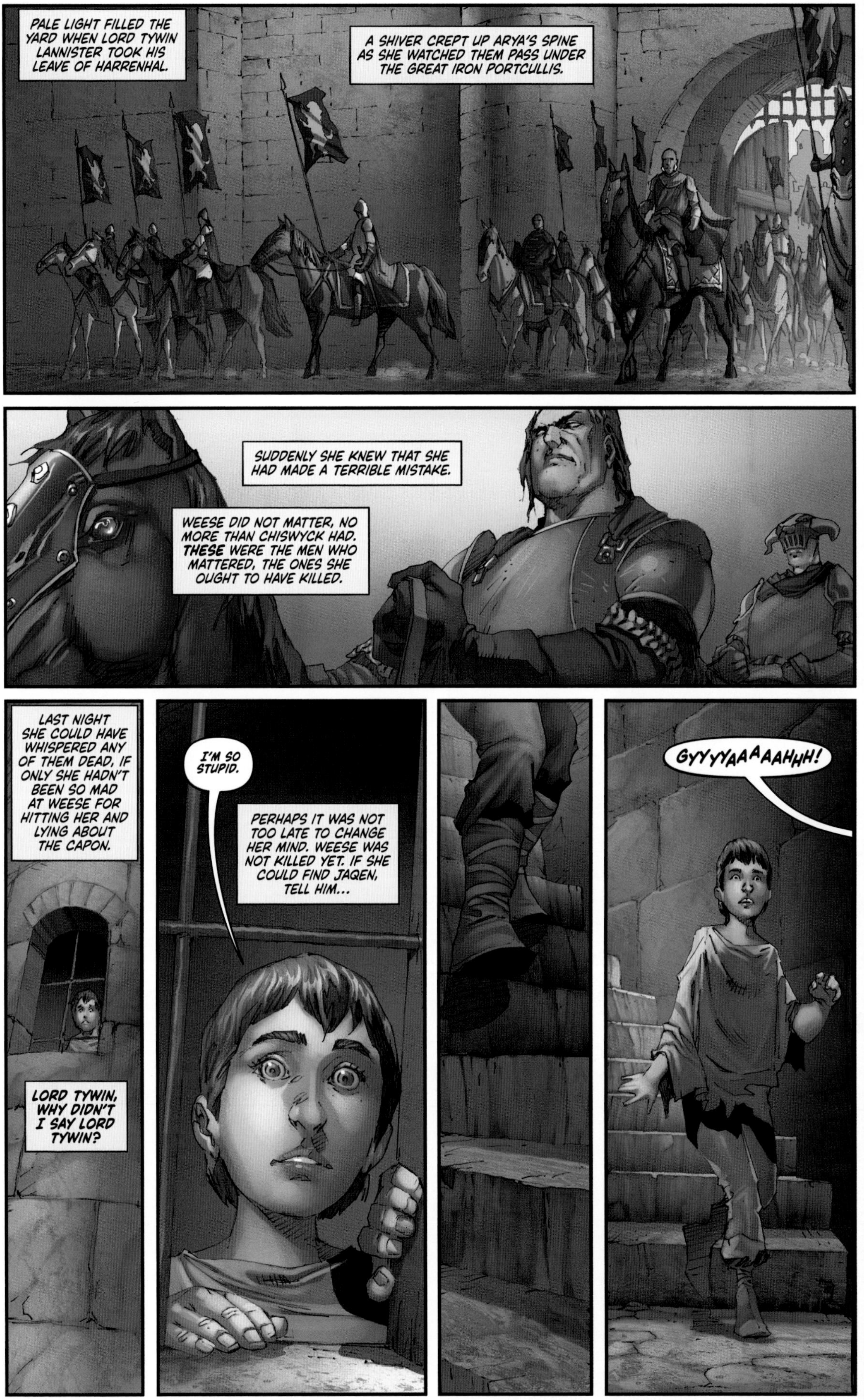
PALE LIGHT FILLED THE YARD WHEN LORD TYWIN LANNISTER TOOK HIS LEAVE OF HARRENHAL.
A SHIVER CREPT UP ARYA'S SPINE AS SHE WATCHED THEM PASS UNDER THE GREAT IRON PORTCULLIS.
SUDDENLY SHE KNEW THAT SHE HAD MADE A TERRIBLE MISTAKE.
WEESE DID NOT MATTER, NO MORE THAN CHISWYCK HAD. THESE WERE THE MEN WHO MATTERED, THE ONES SHE OUGHT TO HAVE KILLED.
LAST NIGHT SHE COULD HAVE WHISPERED ANY OF THEM DEAD, IF ONLY SHE HADN'T BEEN SO MAD AT WEESE FOR HITTING HER AND LYING ABOUT THE CAPON.
LORD TYWIN, WHY DIDN'T I SAY LORD TYWIN?
I'M SO STUPID.
PERHAPS IT WAS NOT TOO LATE TO CHANGE HER MIND. WEESE WAS NOT KILLED YET. IF SHE COULD FIND JAQEN, TELL HIM...
GYYYYAAAAAHHH!

DAMNEDEST THING. HE HAD THAT BITCH DOG SINCE SHE WAS A PUP.

THIS PLACE IS CURSED.

IT'S HARREN'S GHOST, THAT'S WHAT IT IS. I'LL NOT SLEEP HERE ANOTHER NIGHT, I SWEAR IT.

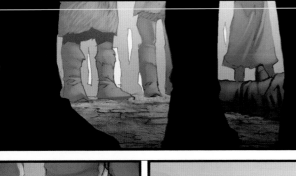

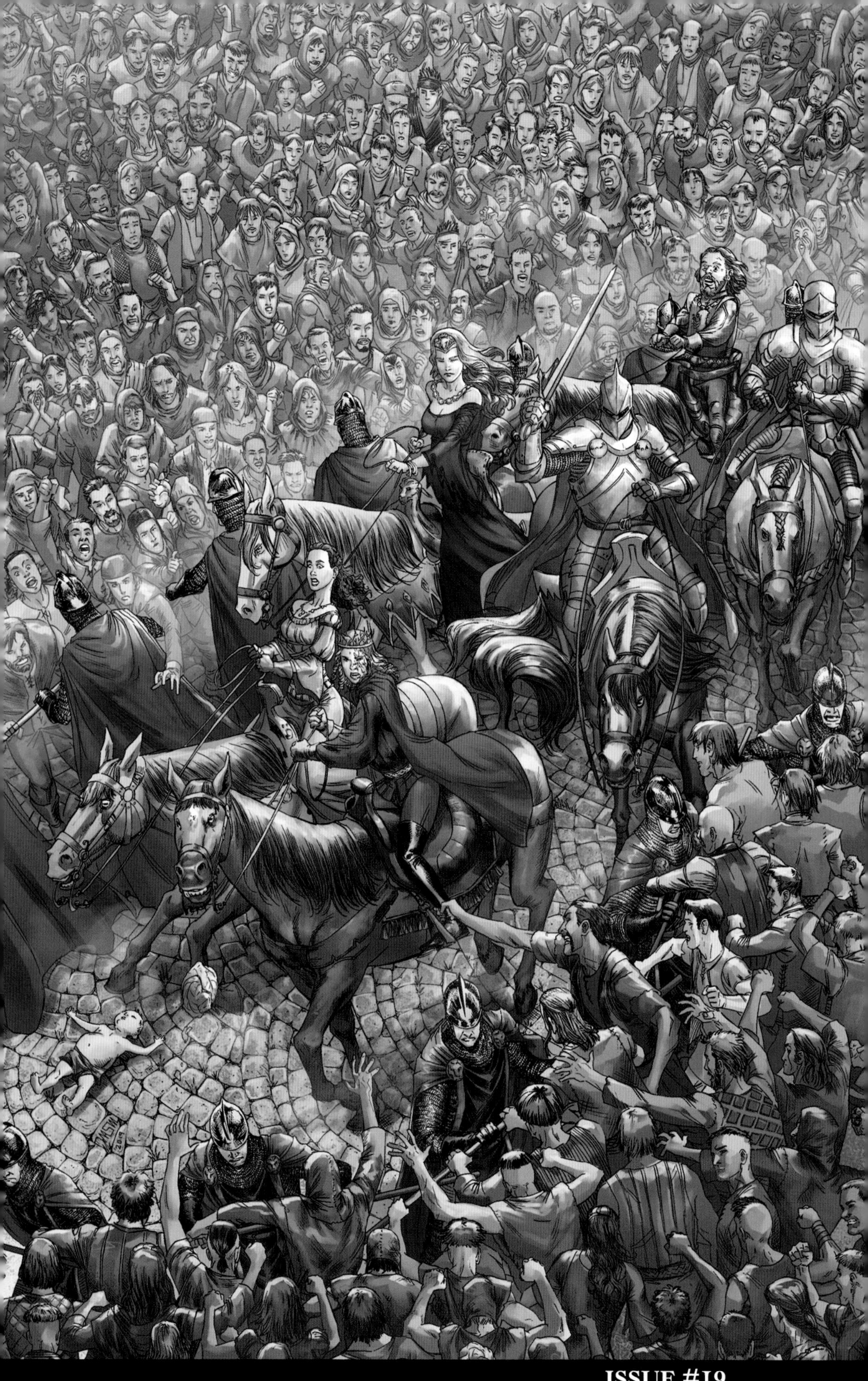

ISSUE #19

CATELYN

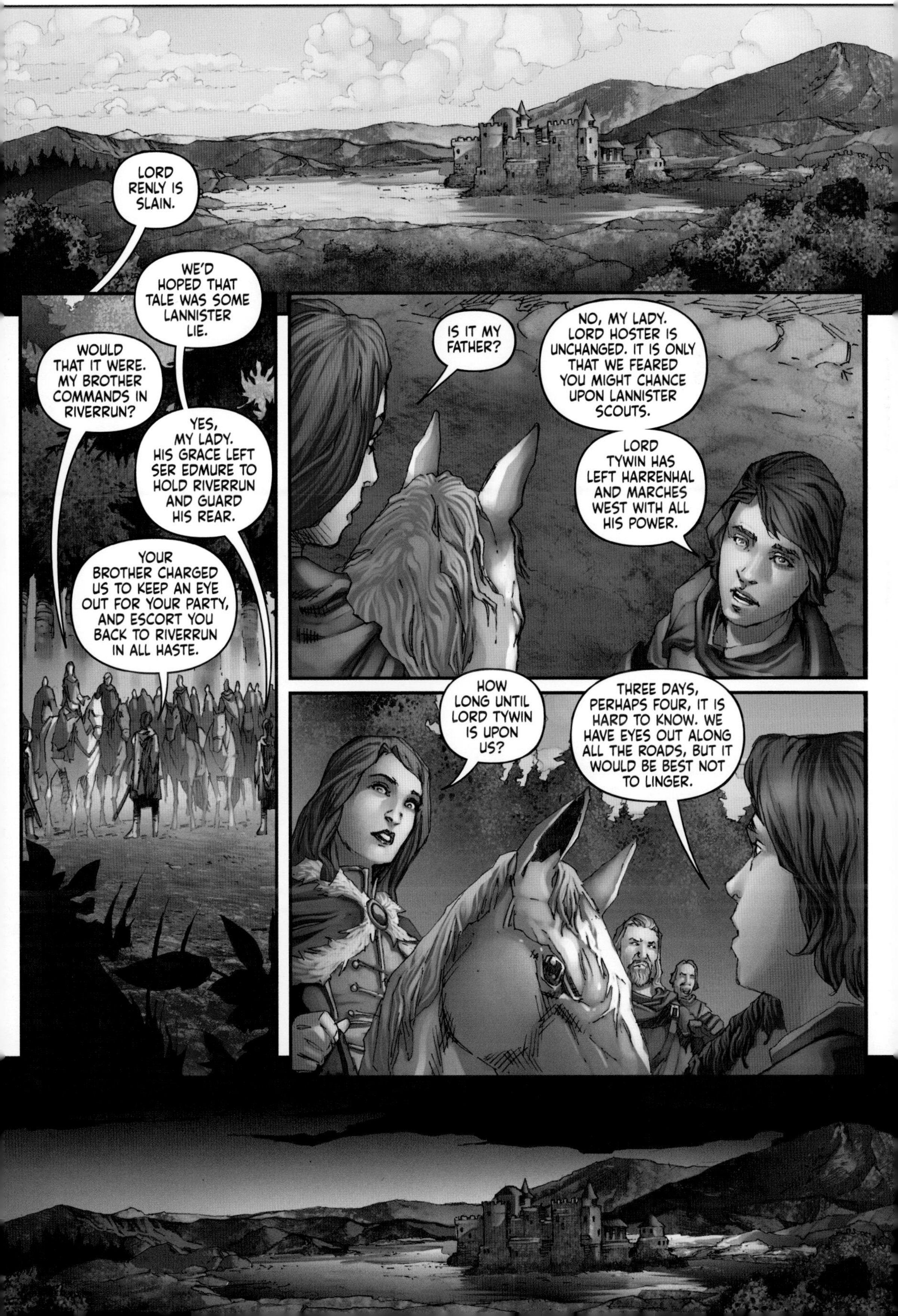
LORD RENLY IS SLAIN.
WE'D HOPED THAT TALE WAS SOME LANNISTER LIE.
WOULD THAT IT WERE. MY BROTHER COMMANDS IN RIVERRUN?
YES, MY LADY. HIS GRACE LEFT SER EDMURE TO HOLD RIVERRUN AND GUARD HIS REAR.
YOUR BROTHER CHARGED US TO KEEP AN EYE OUT FOR YOUR PARTY, AND ESCORT YOU BACK TO RIVERRUN IN ALL HASTE.
IS IT MY FATHER?
NO, MY LADY. LORD HOSTER IS UNCHANGED. IT IS ONLY THAT WE FEARED YOU MIGHT CHANCE UPON LANNISTER SCOUTS.
LORD TYWIN HAS LEFT HARRENHAL AND MARCHES WEST WITH ALL HIS POWER.
HOW LONG UNTIL LORD TYWIN IS UPON US?
THREE DAYS, PERHAPS FOUR, IT IS HARD TO KNOW. WE HAVE EYES OUT ALONG ALL THE ROADS, BUT IT WOULD BE BEST NOT TO LINGER.

MY LADY, YOU ARE SAFELY BACK AMONG YOUR OWN NOW, A DAY'S RIDE FROM YOUR BROTHER'S CASTLE. GIVE ME LEAVE TO GO.

CATELYN SHOULD NOT HAVE BEEN SURPRISED. THE HOMELY YOUNG WOMAN HAD KEPT TO HERSELF ALL THROUGH THEIR JOURNEY.

ANY TASK CATELYN ASKED OF HER, BRIENNE HAD PERFORMED DEFTLY AND WITHOUT COMPLAINT, BUT SHE NEVER CHATTERED, NOR WEPT, NOR LAUGHED. SHE HAD RIDDEN WITH THEM WITHOUT EVER TRULY BECOMING ONE OF THEM.

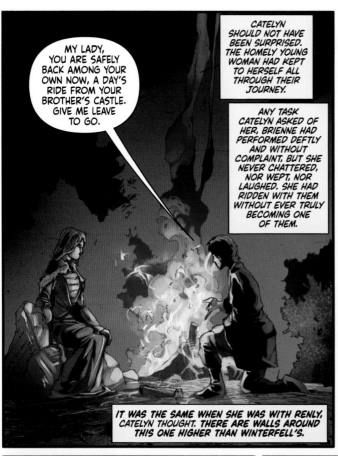

IT WAS THE SAME WHEN SHE WAS WITH RENLY, CATELYN THOUGHT. THERE ARE WALLS AROUND THIS ONE HIGHER THAN WINTERFELL'S.

IF YOU LEFT US, WHERE WOULD YOU GO?

BACK. TO STORM'S END. I SWORE A VOW. THREE TIMES I SWORE. YOU HEARD ME.

YOU MEAN TO KILL STANNIS.

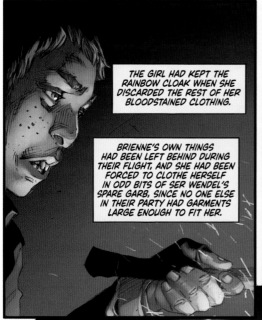

THE GIRL HAD KEPT THE RAINBOW CLOAK WHEN SHE DISCARDED THE REST OF HER BLOODSTAINED CLOTHING.

BRIENNE'S OWN THINGS HAD BEEN LEFT BEHIND DURING THEIR FLIGHT, AND SHE HAD BEEN FORCED TO CLOTHE HERSELF IN ODD BITS OF SER WENDEL'S SPARE GARB, SINCE NO ONE ELSE IN THEIR PARTY HAD GARMENTS LARGE ENOUGH TO FIT HER.

RENLY'S DEATH WAS NO FAULT OF YOURS. YOU SERVED HIM VALIANTLY, BUT WHEN YOU SEEK TO FOLLOW HIM INTO THE EARTH, YOU SERVE NO ONE.

I KNOW HOW HARD IT IS--

NO ONE KNOWS.

YOU'RE WRONG. EVERY MORNING, WHEN I WAKE, I REMEMBER THAT NED IS GONE.

I HAVE NO SKILL WITH SWORDS, BUT THAT DOES NOT MEAN THAT I DO NOT DREAM OF RIDING TO KING'S LANDING AND WRAPPING MY HANDS AROUND CERSEI LANNISTER'S WHITE THROAT AND SQUEEZING UNTIL HER FACE TURNS BLACK.

IF YOU DREAM THAT, WHY WOULD YOU SEEK TO HOLD ME BACK?

I WAS TAUGHT THAT GOOD MEN MUST FIGHT EVIL IN THIS WORLD, AND RENLY'S DEATH WAS EVIL BEYOND ALL DOUBT. YET I WAS ALSO TAUGHT THAT THE GODS MAKE KINGS, NOT THE SWORDS OF MEN. IF STANNIS IS OUR RIGHTFUL KING--

HE'S NOT. ROBERT WAS NEVER THE RIGHTFUL KING EITHER. JAIME LANNISTER *MURDERED* THE RIGHTFUL KING, AFTER ROBERT KILLED HIS LAWFUL HEIR ON THE TRIDENT.

WHERE WERE THE GODS THEN? THE GODS DON'T CARE ABOUT MEN, NO MORE THAN KINGS CARE ABOUT PEASANTS.

A GOOD KING DOES CARE.

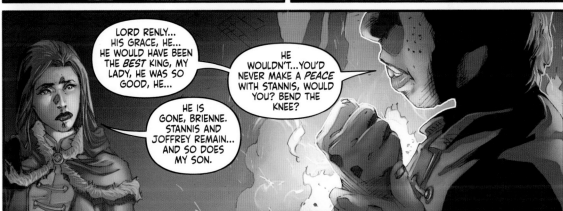

LORD RENLY... HIS GRACE, HE... HE WOULD HAVE BEEN THE *BEST* KING, MY LADY, HE WAS SO GOOD, HE...

HE WOULDN'T...YOU'D NEVER MAKE A *PEACE* WITH STANNIS, WOULD YOU? BEND THE KNEE?

HE IS GONE, BRIENNE. STANNIS AND JOFFREY REMAIN... AND SO DOES MY SON.

I WILL TELL YOU TRUE, BRIENNE. I DO NOT KNOW.

MY SON MAY BE A KING, BUT I AM NO QUEEN... ONLY A MOTHER WHO WOULD KEEP HER CHILDREN SAFE, HOWEVER SHE COULD.

I AM NOT MADE TO BE A MOTHER. I NEED TO FIGHT.

THEN FIGHT... BUT FOR THE LIVING, NOT THE DEAD. RENLY'S ENEMIES ARE ROBB'S ENEMIES AS WELL.

I DO NOT KNOW YOUR SON, MY LADY. BUT I COULD SERVE YOU. IF YOU WOULD HAVE ME.

YOU HELPED ME. IN THE PAVILION...WHEN THEY THOUGHT THAT I HAD...THAT I HAD...

YOU COULD HAVE LET THEM KILL ME. I WAS NOTHING TO YOU.

PERHAPS I DID NOT WANT TO BE THE ONLY ONE WHO KNEW THE DARK TRUTH OF WHAT HAD HAPPENED THERE, CATELYN THOUGHT.

BRIENNE, I HAVE TAKEN MANY WELLBORN LADIES INTO MY SERVICE OVER THE YEARS, BUT NEVER ONE LIKE YOU. I AM NO BATTLE COMMANDER.

NO, BUT YOU HAVE COURAGE. NOT BATTLE COURAGE PERHAPS BUT...A KIND OF *WOMAN'S* COURAGE.

AND I THINK, WHEN THE TIME COMES, YOU WILL NOT TRY AND HOLD ME BACK. PROMISE ME THAT. THAT YOU WILL NOT HOLD ME BACK FROM STANNIS.

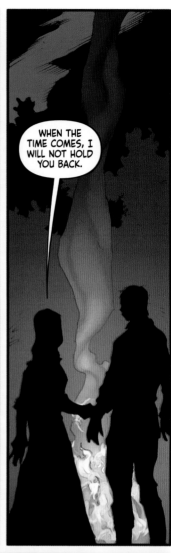

WHEN THE TIME COMES, I WILL NOT HOLD YOU BACK.

THEN I AM YOURS, MY LADY. YOUR LIEGE MAN, OR...WHATEVER YOU WOULD HAVE ME BE. I WILL SHIELD YOUR BACK AND KEEP YOUR COUNSEL AND GIVE MY LIFE FOR YOURS, IF NEED BE. I SWEAR IT BY THE OLD GODS AND THE NEW.

AND I VOW THAT YOU SHALL ALWAYS HAVE A PLACE BY MY HEARTH AND MEAT AND MEAD AT MY TABLE, AND PLEDGE TO ASK NO SERVICE OF YOU THAT MIGHT BRING YOU INTO DISHONOR. I SWEAR IT BY THE OLD GODS AND THE NEW.

ARISE.

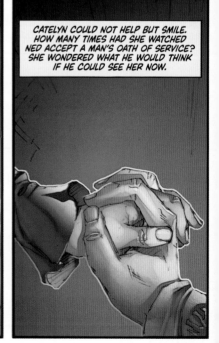

CATELYN COULD NOT HELP BUT SMILE. HOW MANY TIMES HAD SHE WATCHED NED ACCEPT A MAN'S OATH OF SERVICE? SHE WONDERED WHAT HE WOULD THINK IF HE COULD SEE HER NOW.

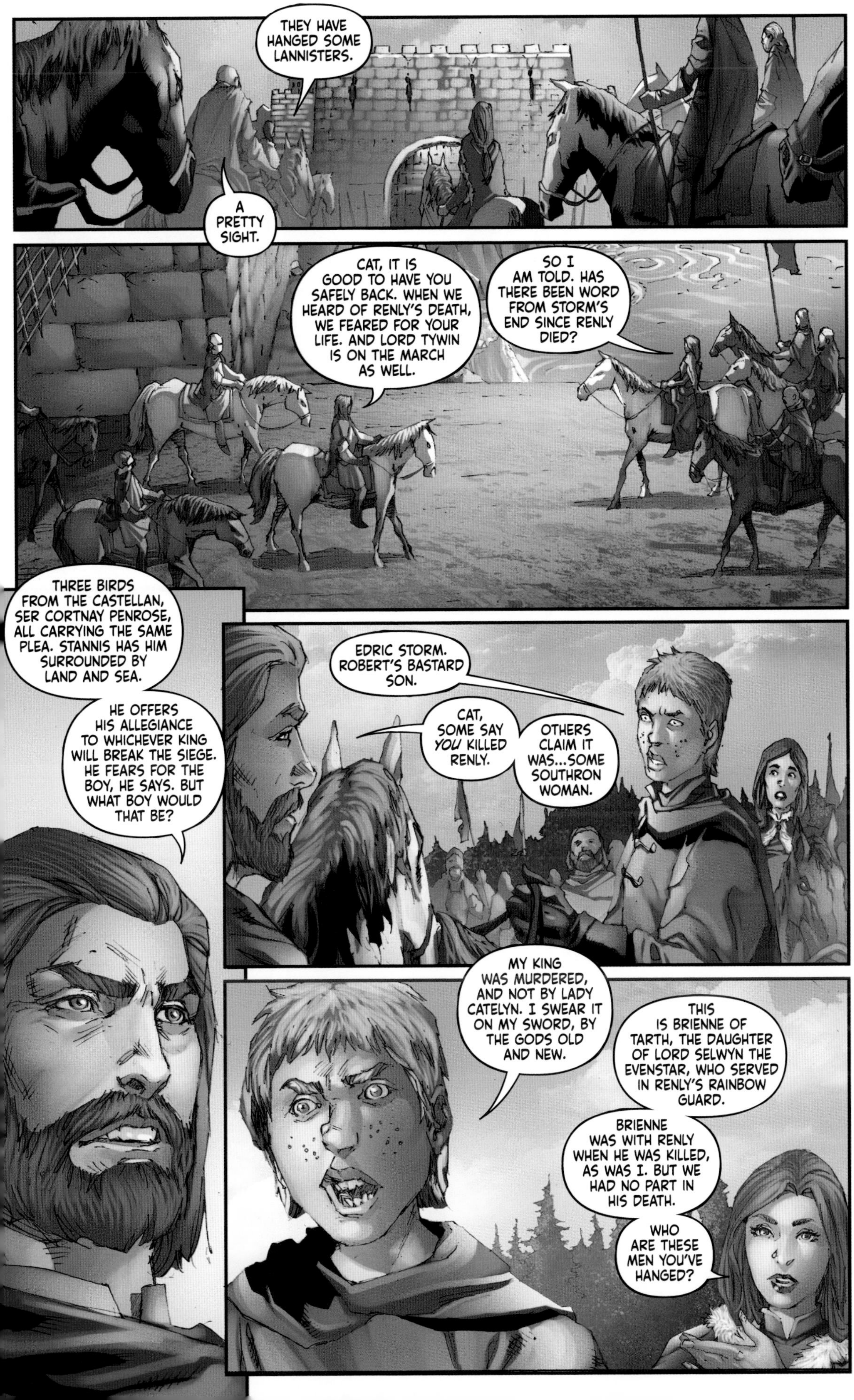
THEY HAVE HANGED SOME LANNISTERS.
A PRETTY SIGHT.
CAT, IT IS GOOD TO HAVE YOU SAFELY BACK. WHEN WE HEARD OF RENLY'S DEATH, WE FEARED FOR YOUR LIFE. AND LORD TYWIN IS ON THE MARCH AS WELL.
SO I AM TOLD. HAS THERE BEEN WORD FROM STORM'S END SINCE RENLY DIED?
THREE BIRDS FROM THE CASTELLAN, SER CORTNAY PENROSE, ALL CARRYING THE SAME PLEA. STANNIS HAS HIM SURROUNDED BY LAND AND SEA.
HE OFFERS HIS ALLEGIANCE TO WHICHEVER KING WILL BREAK THE SIEGE. HE FEARS FOR THE BOY, HE SAYS. BUT WHAT BOY WOULD THAT BE?
EDRIC STORM. ROBERT'S BASTARD SON.
CAT, SOME SAY *YOU* KILLED RENLY.
OTHERS CLAIM IT WAS...SOME SOUTHRON WOMAN.
MY KING WAS MURDERED, AND NOT BY LADY CATELYN. I SWEAR IT ON MY SWORD, BY THE GODS OLD AND NEW.
THIS IS BRIENNE OF TARTH, THE DAUGHTER OF LORD SELWYN THE EVENSTAR, WHO SERVED IN RENLY'S RAINBOW GUARD.
BRIENNE WAS WITH RENLY WHEN HE WAS KILLED, AS WAS I. BUT WE HAD NO PART IN HIS DEATH.
WHO ARE THESE MEN YOU'VE HANGED?

THEY CAME WITH SER CLEOS WHEN HE BROUGHT THE QUEEN'S ANSWER TO OUR PEACE OFFER.

THEY PLEDGED ME THEIR PEACE AND SURRENDERED THEIR WEAPONS, SO I ALLOWED THEM FREEDOM OF THE CASTLE. ON THE FOURTH NIGHT, THEY TRIED TO FREE THE KINGSLAYER.

THIS WAS THE IMP'S WORK, CATELYN SUSPECTED. ONCE, SHE WOULD HAVE NAMED TYRION THE LEAST DANGEROUS OF THE LANNISTERS. NOW SHE WAS NOT SO CERTAIN.

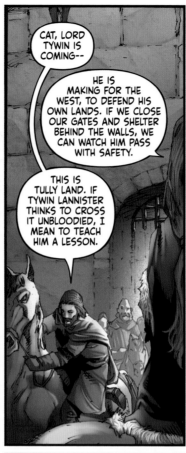

CAT, LORD TYWIN IS COMING--

HE IS MAKING FOR THE WEST, TO DEFEND HIS OWN LANDS. IF WE CLOSE OUR GATES AND SHELTER BEHIND THE WALLS, WE CAN WATCH HIM PASS WITH SAFETY.

THIS IS TULLY LAND. IF TYWIN LANNISTER THINKS TO CROSS IT UNBLOODIED, I MEAN TO TEACH HIM A LESSON.

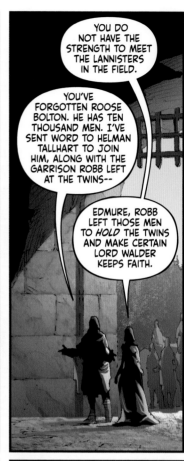

YOU DO NOT HAVE THE STRENGTH TO MEET THE LANNISTERS IN THE FIELD.

YOU'VE FORGOTTEN ROOSE BOLTON. HE HAS TEN THOUSAND MEN. I'VE SENT WORD TO HELMAN TALLHART TO JOIN HIM, ALONG WITH THE GARRISON ROBB LEFT AT THE TWINS--

EDMURE, ROBB LEFT THOSE MEN TO *HOLD* THE TWINS AND MAKE CERTAIN LORD WALDER KEEPS FAITH.

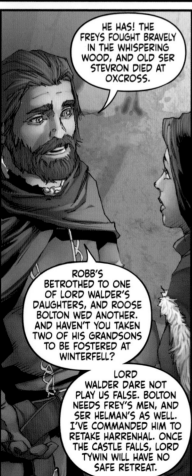

HE HAS! THE FREYS FOUGHT BRAVELY IN THE WHISPERING WOOD, AND OLD SER STEVRON DIED AT OXCROSS.

ROBB'S BETROTHED TO ONE OF LORD WALDER'S DAUGHTERS, AND ROOSE BOLTON WED ANOTHER. AND HAVEN'T YOU TAKEN TWO OF HIS GRANDSONS TO BE FOSTERED AT WINTERFELL?

LORD WALDER DARE NOT PLAY US FALSE. BOLTON NEEDS FREY'S MEN, AND SER HELMAN'S AS WELL. I'VE COMMANDED HIM TO RETAKE HARRENHAL. ONCE THE CASTLE FALLS, LORD TYWIN WILL HAVE NO SAFE RETREAT.

CATELYN WAS SUDDENLY WEARY. PERHAPS IT WAS A SPLENDID PLAN, AND HER MISGIVINGS ONLY A WOMAN'S FEARS. SHE WISHED NED WERE HERE, OR HER UNCLE BRYNDEN, OR...

HAVE YOU ASKED FATHER ABOUT THIS?

FATHER IS IN NO STATE TO WEIGH STRATEGIES. TWO DAYS AGO HE WAS MAKING PLANS FOR YOUR MARRIAGE TO BRANDON STARK! THIS PLAN WILL WORK, CAT, YOU'LL SEE.

I HOPE SO, EDMURE. I TRULY DO.

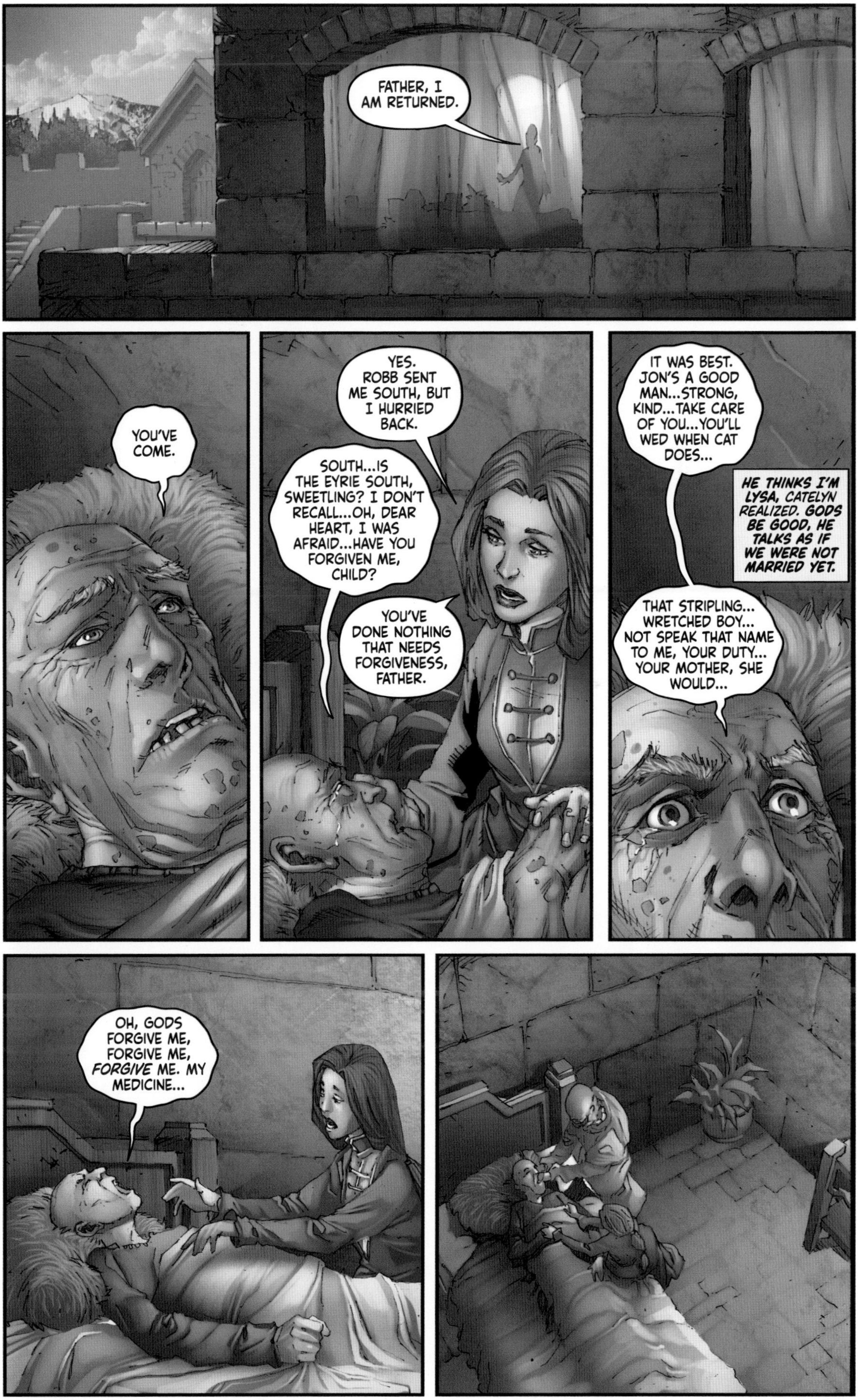
FATHER, I AM RETURNED.
YOU'VE COME.
YES. ROBB SENT ME SOUTH, BUT I HURRIED BACK.
SOUTH...IS THE EYRIE SOUTH, SWEETLING? I DON'T RECALL...OH, DEAR HEART, I WAS AFRAID...HAVE YOU FORGIVEN ME, CHILD?
YOU'VE DONE NOTHING THAT NEEDS FORGIVENESS, FATHER.
IT WAS BEST. JON'S A GOOD MAN...STRONG, KIND...TAKE CARE OF YOU...YOU'LL WED WHEN CAT DOES...
HE THINKS I'M LYSA, CATELYN REALIZED. GODS BE GOOD, HE TALKS AS IF WE WERE NOT MARRIED YET.
THAT STRIPLING... WRETCHED BOY... NOT SPEAK THAT NAME TO ME, YOUR DUTY... YOUR MOTHER, SHE WOULD...
OH, GODS FORGIVE ME, FORGIVE ME, FORGIVE ME. MY MEDICINE...

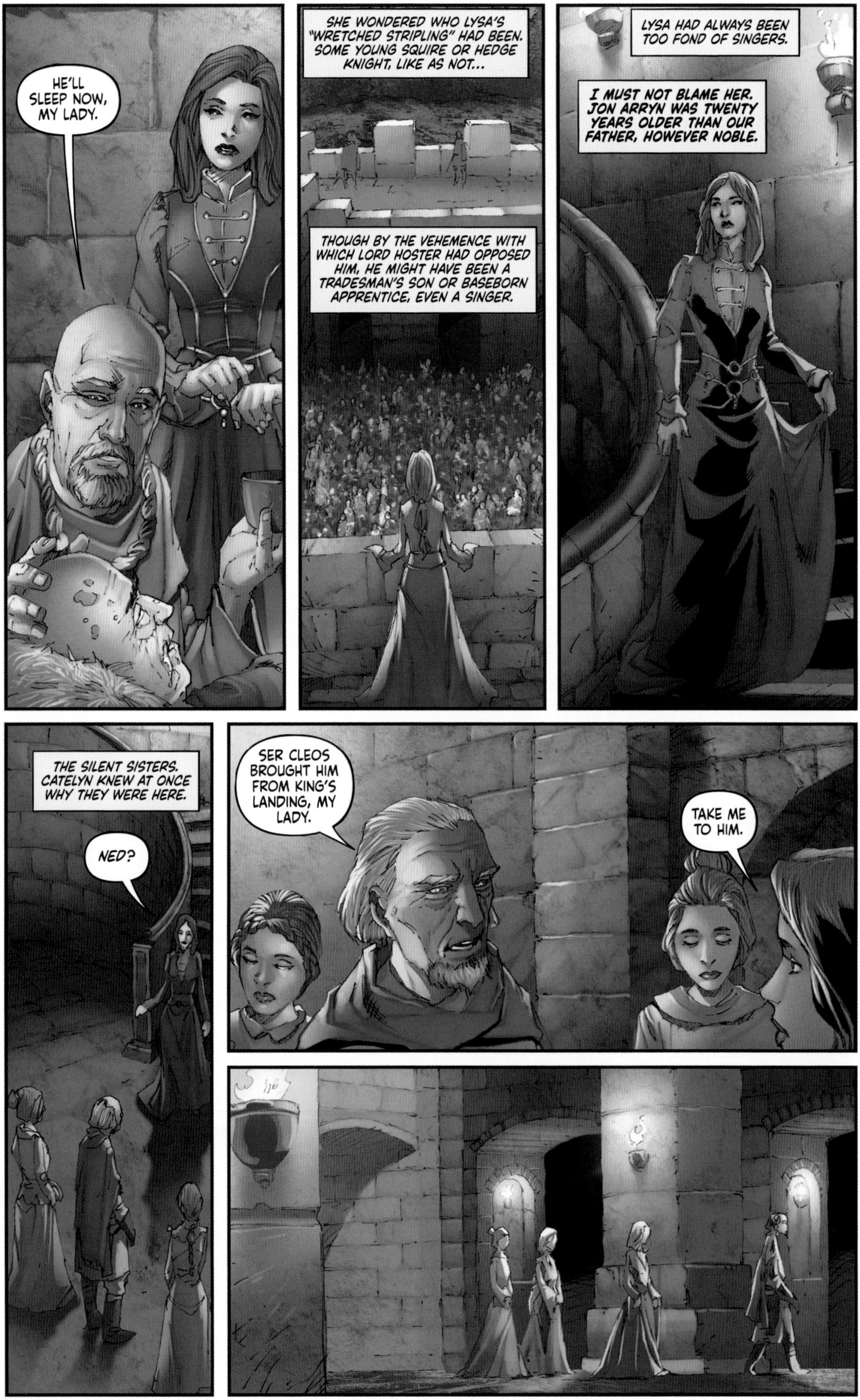
HE'LL SLEEP NOW, MY LADY.
SHE WONDERED WHO LYSA'S "WRETCHED STRIPLING" HAD BEEN. SOME YOUNG SQUIRE OR HEDGE KNIGHT, LIKE AS NOT...
THOUGH BY THE VEHEMENCE WITH WHICH LORD HOSTER HAD OPPOSED HIM, HE MIGHT HAVE BEEN A TRADESMAN'S SON OR BASEBORN APPRENTICE, EVEN A SINGER.
LYSA HAD ALWAYS BEEN TOO FOND OF SINGERS.
I MUST NOT BLAME HER. JON ARRYN WAS TWENTY YEARS OLDER THAN OUR FATHER, HOWEVER NOBLE.
THE SILENT SISTERS. CATELYN KNEW AT ONCE WHY THEY WERE HERE.
NED?
SER CLEOS BROUGHT HIM FROM KING'S LANDING, MY LADY.
TAKE ME TO HIM.

NOTHING REMAINED OF THE WARM FLESH THAT HAD PILLOWED HER HEAD SO MANY NIGHTS, THE ARMS THAT HAD HELD HER.

THIS IS NOT NED, THIS IS NOT THE MAN I LOVED, THE FATHER OF MY CHILDREN.

I WOULD LOOK ON HIM.

ONLY THE BONES REMAIN, MY LADY.

I AM GRATEFUL FOR YOUR SERVICE, SISTERS, BUT I MUST LAY ANOTHER TASK UPON YOU. LORD EDDARD WAS A STARK, AND HIS BONES MUST BE LAID TO REST BENEATH WINTERFELL.

THEY WILL MAKE A STATUE OF HIM, A STONE LIKENESS THAT WILL SIT IN THE DARK WITH A DIREWOLF AT HIS FEET AND A SWORD ACROSS HIS KNEES.

MAKE CERTAIN THE SISTERS HAVE FRESH HORSES, AND AUGHT ELSE THEY NEED FOR THE JOURNEY. HAL MOLLEN WILL ESCORT THEM BACK TO WINTERFELL, AS CAPTAIN OF GUARDS.

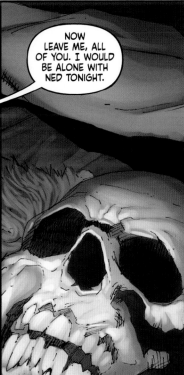

NOW LEAVE ME, ALL OF YOU. I WOULD BE ALONE WITH NED TONIGHT.

THE SILENT SISTERS DO NOT SPEAK TO THE LIVING, CATELYN REMEMBERED DULLY, BUT SOME SAY THEY CAN TALK TO THE DEAD.

AND HOW SHE ENVIED THAT...

TYRION

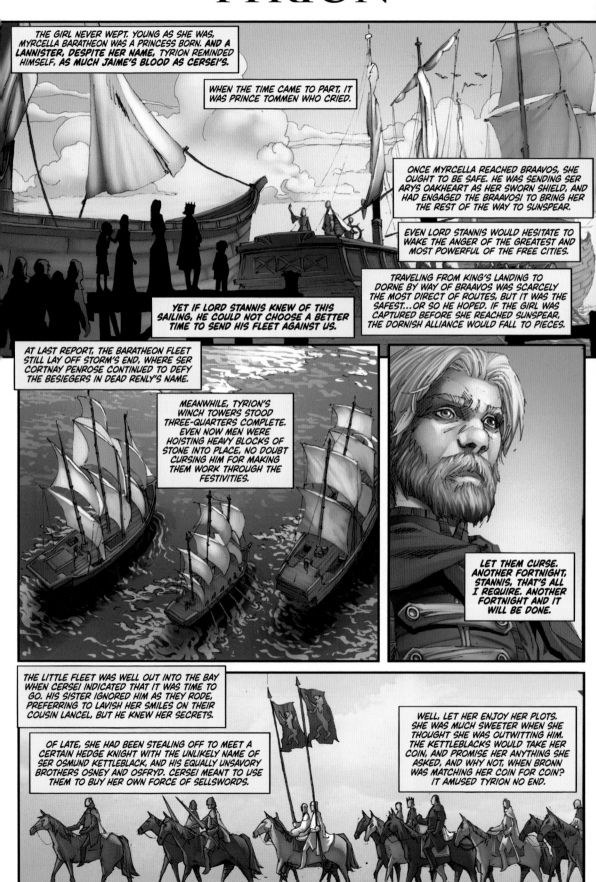

THE GIRL NEVER WEPT. YOUNG AS SHE WAS, MYRCELLA BARATHEON WAS A PRINCESS BORN. AND A LANNISTER, DESPITE HER NAME, TYRION REMINDED HIMSELF, AS MUCH JAIME'S BLOOD AS CERSEI'S.

WHEN THE TIME CAME TO PART, IT WAS PRINCE TOMMEN WHO CRIED.

ONCE MYRCELLA REACHED BRAAVOS, SHE OUGHT TO BE SAFE. HE WAS SENDING SER ARYS OAKHEART AS HER SWORN SHIELD, AND HAD ENGAGED THE BRAAVOSI TO BRING HER THE REST OF THE WAY TO SUNSPEAR.

EVEN LORD STANNIS WOULD HESITATE TO WAKE THE ANGER OF THE GREATEST AND MOST POWERFUL OF THE FREE CITIES.

YET IF LORD STANNIS KNEW OF THIS SAILING, HE COULD NOT CHOOSE A BETTER TIME TO SEND HIS FLEET AGAINST US.

TRAVELING FROM KING'S LANDING TO DORNE BY WAY OF BRAAVOS WAS SCARCELY THE MOST DIRECT OF ROUTES, BUT IT WAS THE SAFEST...OR SO HE HOPED. IF THE GIRL WAS CAPTURED BEFORE SHE REACHED SUNSPEAR, THE DORNISH ALLIANCE WOULD FALL TO PIECES.

AT LAST REPORT, THE BARATHEON FLEET STILL LAY OFF STORM'S END, WHERE SER CORTNAY PENROSE CONTINUED TO DEFY THE BESIEGERS IN DEAD RENLY'S NAME.

MEANWHILE, TYRION'S WINCH TOWERS STOOD THREE-QUARTERS COMPLETE. EVEN NOW MEN WERE HOISTING HEAVY BLOCKS OF STONE INTO PLACE, NO DOUBT CURSING HIM FOR MAKING THEM WORK THROUGH THE FESTIVITIES.

LET THEM CURSE. ANOTHER FORTNIGHT, STANNIS, THAT'S ALL I REQUIRE. ANOTHER FORTNIGHT AND IT WILL BE DONE.

THE LITTLE FLEET WAS WELL OUT INTO THE BAY WHEN CERSEI INDICATED THAT IT WAS TIME TO GO. HIS SISTER IGNORED HIM AS THEY RODE, PREFERRING TO LAVISH HER SMILES ON THEIR COUSIN LANCEL, BUT HE KNEW HER SECRETS.

OF LATE, SHE HAD BEEN STEALING OFF TO MEET A CERTAIN HEDGE KNIGHT WITH THE UNLIKELY NAME OF SER OSMUND KETTLEBLACK, AND HIS EQUALLY UNSAVORY BROTHERS OSNEY AND OSFRYD. CERSEI MEANT TO USE THEM TO BUY HER OWN FORCE OF SELLSWORDS.

WELL, LET HER ENJOY HER PLOTS. SHE WAS MUCH SWEETER WHEN SHE THOUGHT SHE WAS OUTWITTING HIM. THE KETTLEBLACKS WOULD TAKE HER COIN, AND PROMISE HER ANYTHING SHE ASKED, AND WHY NOT, WHEN BRONN WAS MATCHING HER COIN FOR COIN? IT AMUSED TYRION NO END.

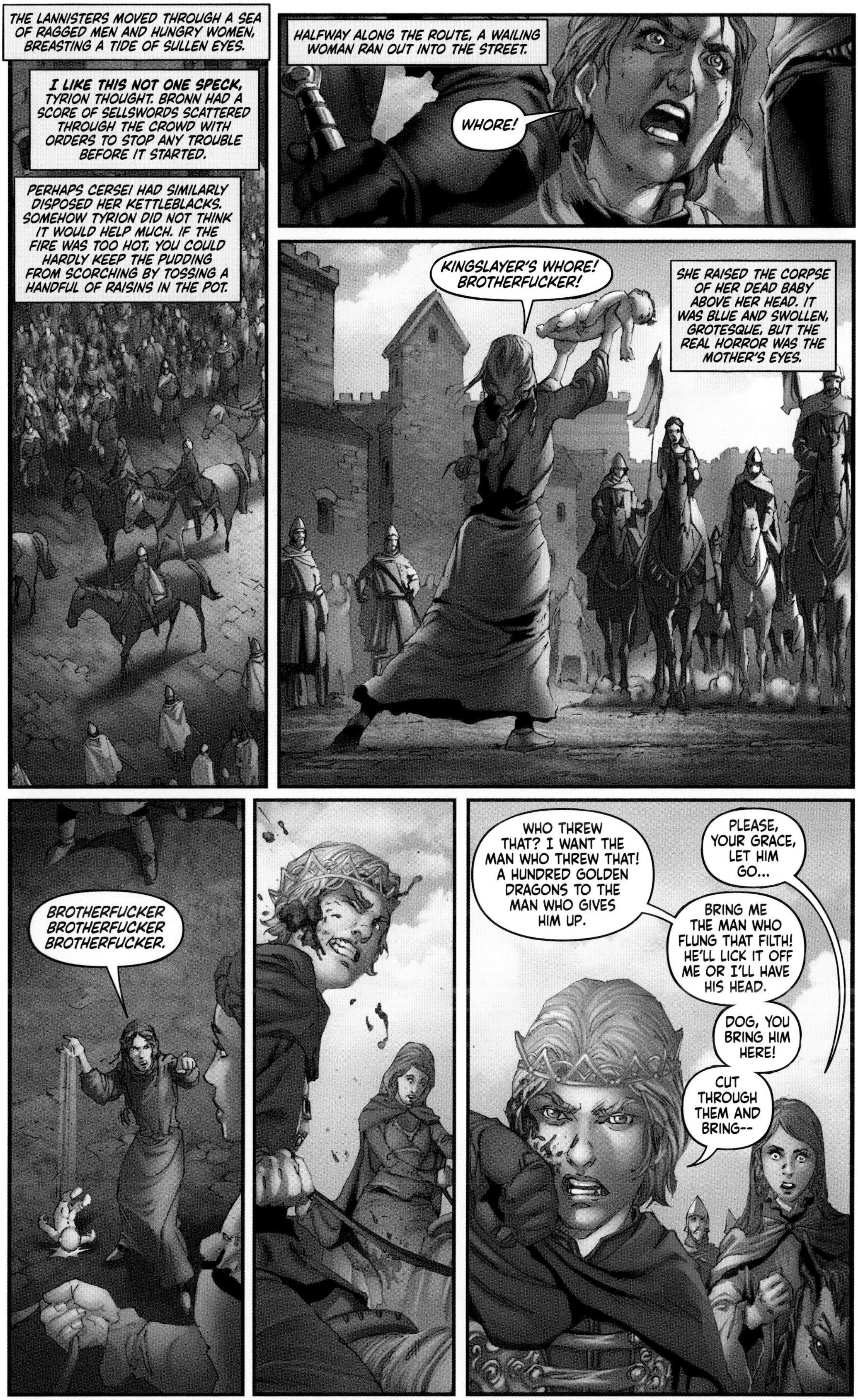
THE LANNISTERS MOVED THROUGH A SEA OF RAGGED MEN AND HUNGRY WOMEN, BREASTING A TIDE OF SULLEN EYES.
I LIKE THIS NOT ONE SPECK, TYRION THOUGHT. BRONN HAD A SCORE OF SELLSWORDS SCATTERED THROUGH THE CROWD WITH ORDERS TO STOP ANY TROUBLE BEFORE IT STARTED.
PERHAPS CERSEI HAD SIMILARLY DISPOSED HER KETTLEBLACKS. SOMEHOW TYRION DID NOT THINK IT WOULD HELP MUCH. IF THE FIRE WAS TOO HOT, YOU COULD HARDLY KEEP THE PUDDING FROM SCORCHING BY TOSSING A HANDFUL OF RAISINS IN THE POT.
HALFWAY ALONG THE ROUTE, A WAILING WOMAN RAN OUT INTO THE STREET.
WHORE!
KINGSLAYER'S WHORE! BROTHERFUCKER!
SHE RAISED THE CORPSE OF HER DEAD BABY ABOVE HER HEAD. IT WAS BLUE AND SWOLLEN, GROTESQUE, BUT THE REAL HORROR WAS THE MOTHER'S EYES.
BROTHERFUCKER BROTHERFUCKER BROTHERFUCKER.
WHO THREW THAT? I WANT THE MAN WHO THREW THAT! A HUNDRED GOLDEN DRAGONS TO THE MAN WHO GIVES HIM UP.
PLEASE, YOUR GRACE, LET HIM GO...
BRING ME THE MAN WHO FLUNG THAT FILTH! HE'LL LICK IT OFF ME OR I'LL HAVE HIS HEAD.
DOG, YOU BRING HIM HERE!
CUT THROUGH THEM AND BRING--

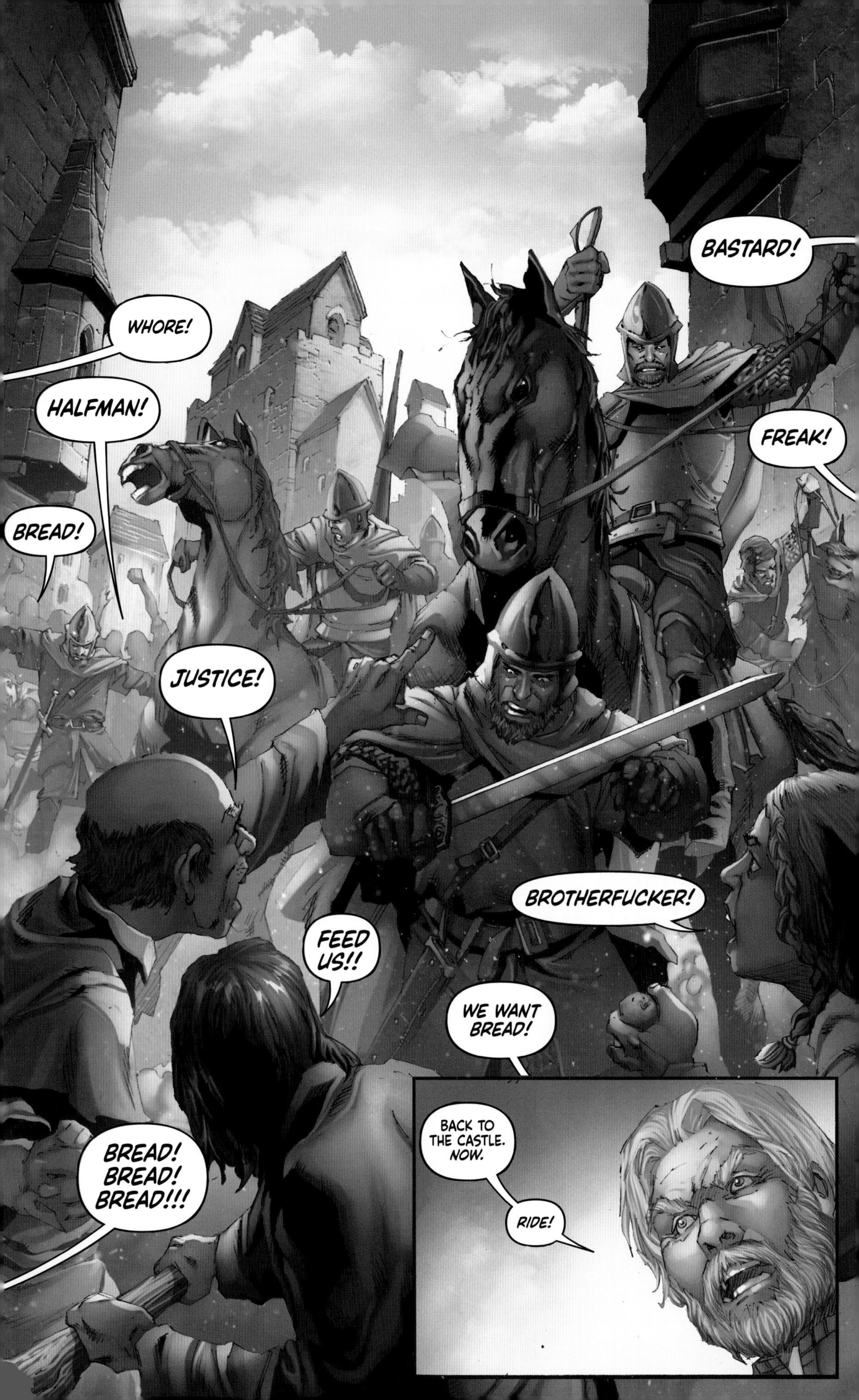
BASTARD!
WHORE!
HALFMAN!
FREAK!
BREAD!
JUSTICE!
BROTHERFUCKER!
FEED US!!
WE WANT BREAD!
BREAD! BREAD! BREAD!!!
BACK TO THE CASTLE. NOW.
RIDE!

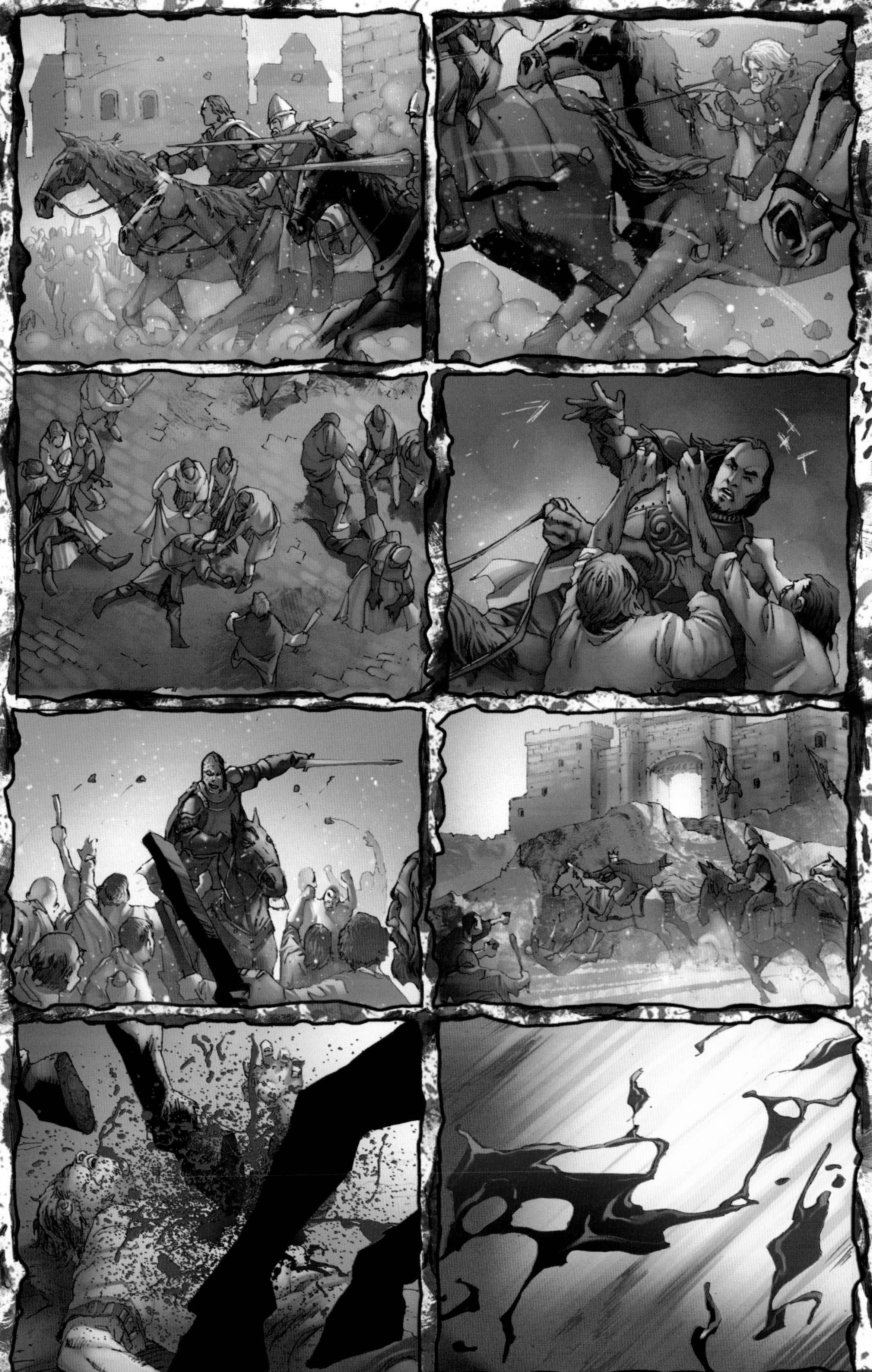

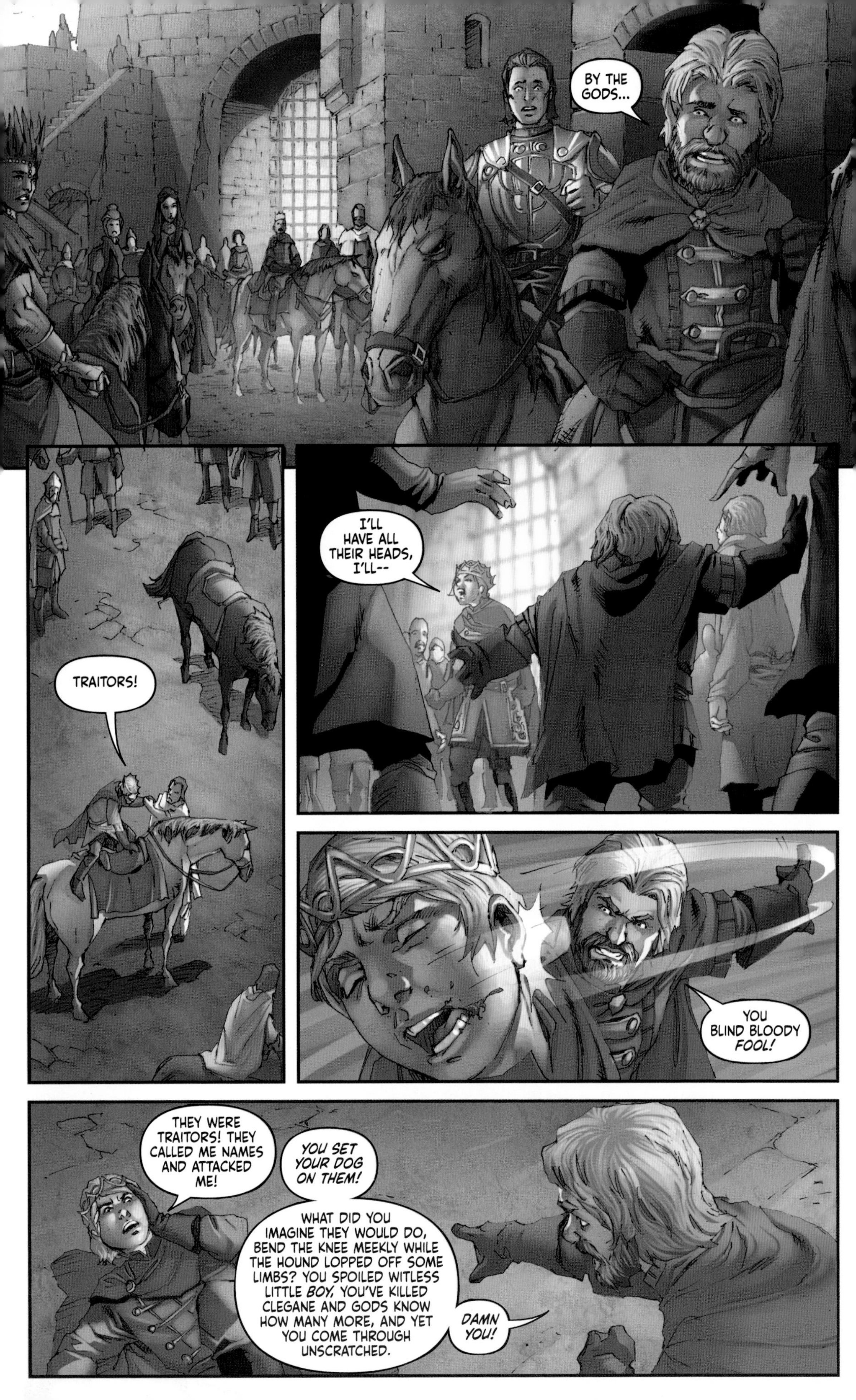
BY THE GODS...
TRAITORS!
I'LL HAVE ALL THEIR HEADS, I'LL--
YOU BLIND BLOODY *FOOL!*
THEY WERE TRAITORS! THEY CALLED ME NAMES AND ATTACKED ME!
YOU SET YOUR DOG ON THEM!
WHAT DID YOU IMAGINE THEY WOULD DO, BEND THE KNEE MEEKLY WHILE THE HOUND LOPPED OFF SOME LIMBS? YOU SPOILED WITLESS LITTLE *BOY*, YOU'VE KILLED CLEGANE AND GODS KNOW HOW MANY MORE, AND YET YOU COME THROUGH UNSCRATCHED.
DAMN YOU!

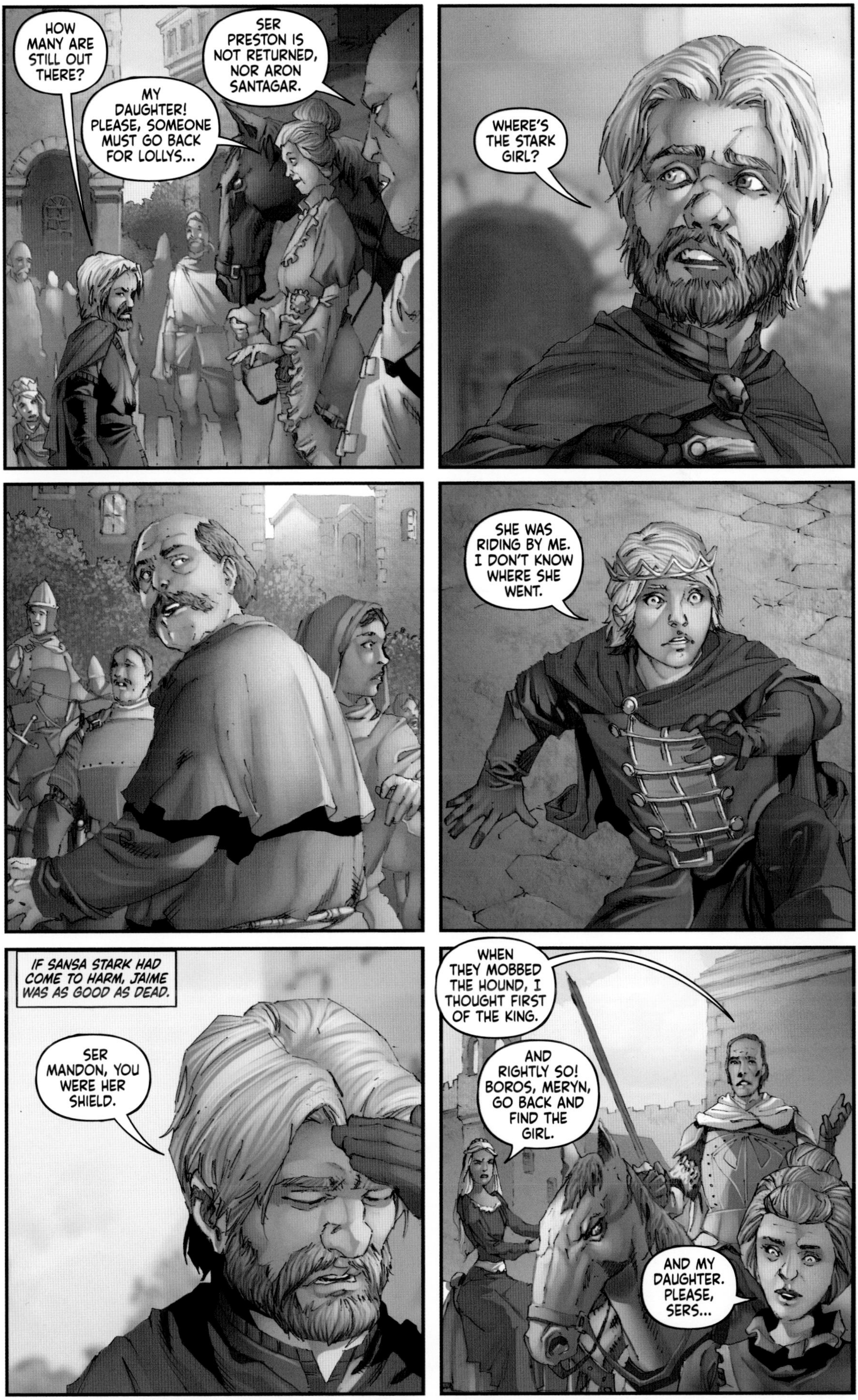
HOW MANY ARE STILL OUT THERE?
SER PRESTON IS NOT RETURNED, NOR ARON SANTAGAR.
MY DAUGHTER! PLEASE, SOMEONE MUST GO BACK FOR LOLLYS...
WHERE'S THE STARK GIRL?
SHE WAS RIDING BY ME. I DON'T KNOW WHERE SHE WENT.
IF SANSA STARK HAD COME TO HARM, JAIME WAS AS GOOD AS DEAD.
SER MANDON, YOU WERE HER SHIELD.
WHEN THEY MOBBED THE HOUND, I THOUGHT FIRST OF THE KING.
AND RIGHTLY SO! BOROS, MERYN, GO BACK AND FIND THE GIRL.
AND MY DAUGHTER. PLEASE, SERS...

YOUR GRACE, THE SIGHT OF OUR WHITE CLOAKS MIGHT ENRAGE THE MOB.

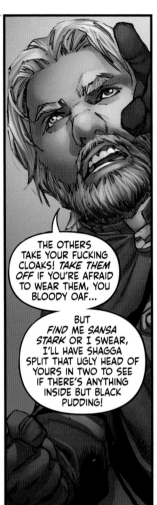

THE OTHERS TAKE YOUR FUCKING CLOAKS! *TAKE THEM OFF* IF YOU'RE AFRAID TO WEAR THEM, YOU BLOODY OAF...

BUT *FIND ME SANSA STARK* OR I SWEAR, I'LL HAVE SHAGGA SPLIT THAT UGLY HEAD OF YOURS IN TWO TO SEE IF THERE'S ANYTHING INSIDE BUT BLACK PUDDING!

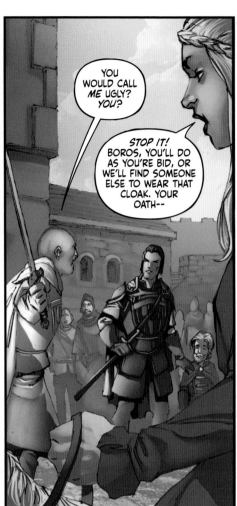

YOU WOULD CALL *ME* UGLY? *YOU?*

STOP IT! BOROS, YOU'LL DO AS YOU'RE BID, OR WE'LL FIND SOMEONE ELSE TO WEAR THAT CLOAK. YOUR OATH--

THERE SHE IS!

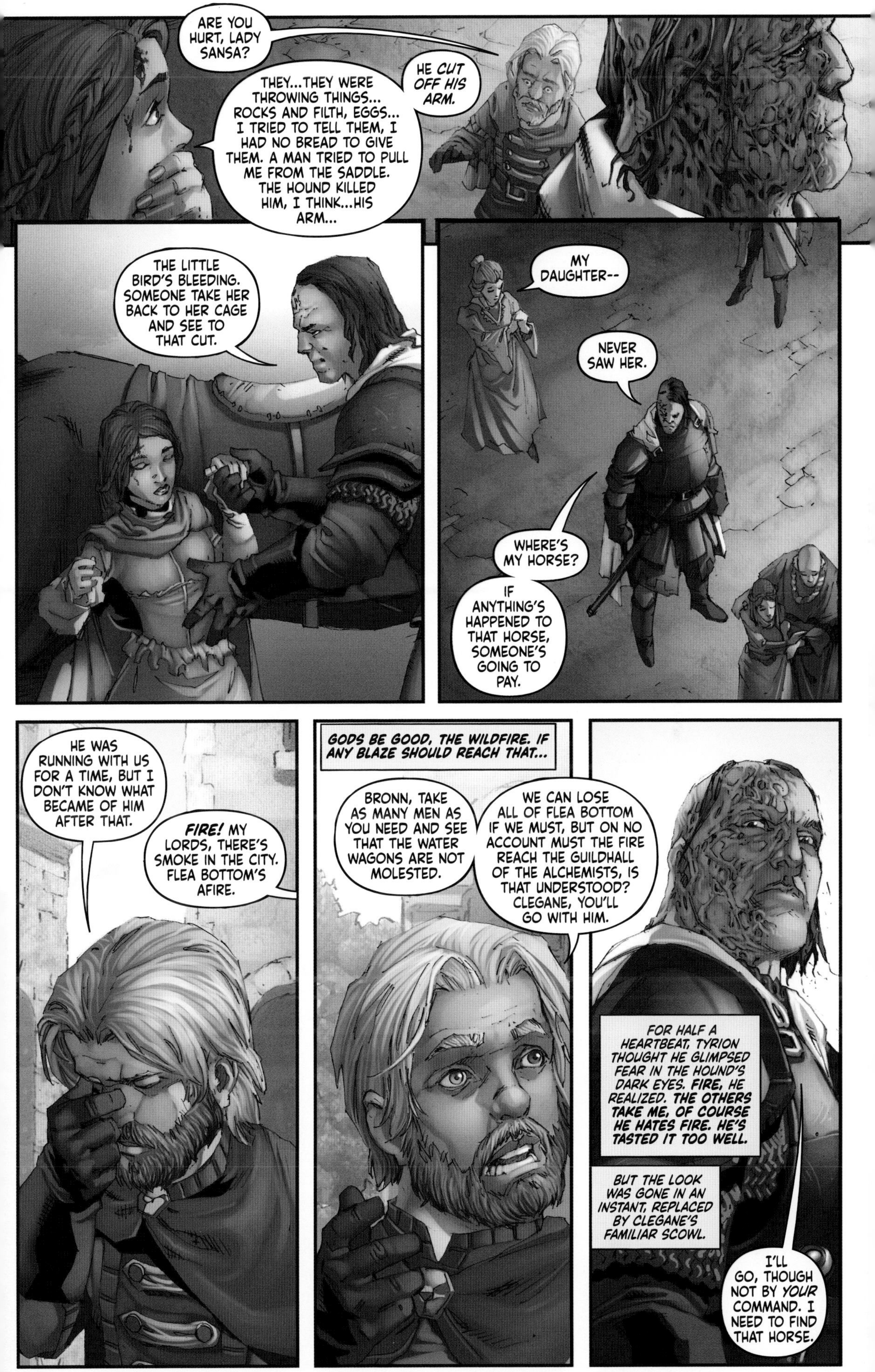
ARE YOU HURT, LADY SANSA?
THEY...THEY WERE THROWING THINGS... ROCKS AND FILTH, EGGS... I TRIED TO TELL THEM, I HAD NO BREAD TO GIVE THEM. A MAN TRIED TO PULL ME FROM THE SADDLE. THE HOUND KILLED HIM, I THINK...HIS ARM...
HE CUT OFF HIS ARM.
THE LITTLE BIRD'S BLEEDING. SOMEONE TAKE HER BACK TO HER CAGE AND SEE TO THAT CUT.
MY DAUGHTER--
NEVER SAW HER.
WHERE'S MY HORSE?
IF ANYTHING'S HAPPENED TO THAT HORSE, SOMEONE'S GOING TO PAY.
HE WAS RUNNING WITH US FOR A TIME, BUT I DON'T KNOW WHAT BECAME OF HIM AFTER THAT.
FIRE! MY LORDS, THERE'S SMOKE IN THE CITY. FLEA BOTTOM'S AFIRE.
GODS BE GOOD, THE WILDFIRE. IF ANY BLAZE SHOULD REACH THAT...
BRONN, TAKE AS MANY MEN AS YOU NEED AND SEE THAT THE WATER WAGONS ARE NOT MOLESTED.
WE CAN LOSE ALL OF FLEA BOTTOM IF WE MUST, BUT ON NO ACCOUNT MUST THE FIRE REACH THE GUILDHALL OF THE ALCHEMISTS, IS THAT UNDERSTOOD? CLEGANE, YOU'LL GO WITH HIM.
FOR HALF A HEARTBEAT, TYRION THOUGHT HE GLIMPSED FEAR IN THE HOUND'S DARK EYES. FIRE, HE REALIZED. THE OTHERS TAKE ME, OF COURSE HE HATES FIRE. HE'S TASTED IT TOO WELL.
BUT THE LOOK WAS GONE IN AN INSTANT, REPLACED BY CLEGANE'S FAMILIAR SCOWL.
I'LL GO, THOUGH NOT BY YOUR COMMAND. I NEED TO FIND THAT HORSE.

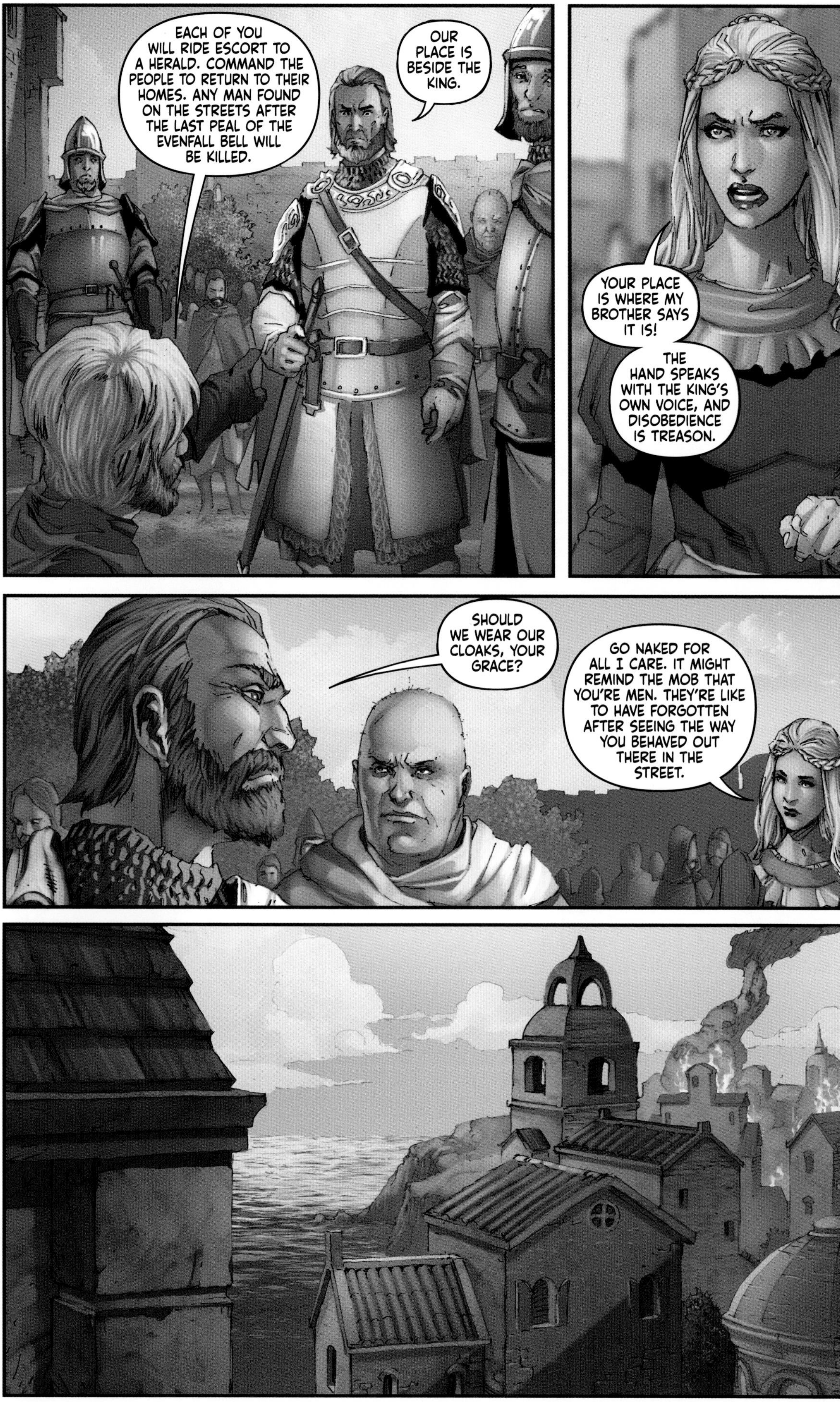
EACH OF YOU WILL RIDE ESCORT TO A HERALD. COMMAND THE PEOPLE TO RETURN TO THEIR HOMES. ANY MAN FOUND ON THE STREETS AFTER THE LAST PEAL OF THE EVENFALL BELL WILL BE KILLED.
OUR PLACE IS BESIDE THE KING.
YOUR PLACE IS WHERE MY BROTHER SAYS IT IS!
THE HAND SPEAKS WITH THE KING'S OWN VOICE, AND DISOBEDIENCE IS TREASON.
SHOULD WE WEAR OUR CLOAKS, YOUR GRACE?
GO NAKED FOR ALL I CARE. IT MIGHT REMIND THE MOB THAT YOU'RE MEN. THEY'RE LIKE TO HAVE FORGOTTEN AFTER SEEING THE WAY YOU BEHAVED OUT THERE IN THE STREET.

BY EVENFALL THE CITY WAS STILL IN TURMOIL, THOUGH BRONN REPORTED THAT THE FIRES WERE QUENCHED AND MOST OF THE ROVING MOBS DISPERSED. MUCH AS TYRION YEARNED FOR THE COMFORT OF SHAE'S ARMS, HE REALIZED HE WOULD GO NOWHERE THAT NIGHT.

SER JACELYN BYWATER DELIVERED THE BUTCHER'S BILL AS HE WAS SUPPING ON A COLD CAPON AND BROWN BREAD IN THE GLOOM OF HIS SOLAR.

THE LIST OF THE SLAIN WAS TOPPED BY THE HIGH SEPTON, RIPPED APART AS HE SQUEALED TO HIS GODS FOR MERCY. *STARVING MEN TAKE A HARD VIEW OF PRIESTS TOO FAT TO WALK,* TYRION REFLECTED.

SER PRESTON'S CORPSE HAD BEEN OVERLOOKED AT FIRST; THE GOLD CLOAKS HAD BEEN SEARCHING FOR A KNIGHT IN WHITE ARMOR, AND HE HAD BEEN STABBED AND HACKED SO CRUELLY THAT HE WAS RED-BROWN FROM HEAD TO HEEL.

SER ARON SANTAGAR HAD BEEN FOUND IN A GUTTER, HIS HEAD A RED PULP INSIDE A CRUSHED HELM.

LADY TANDA'S DAUGHTER HAD SURRENDERED HER MAIDENHOOD TO HALF A HUNDRED SHOUTING MEN BEHIND A TANNER'S SHOP. THE GOLD CLOAKS FOUND HER WANDERING NAKED ON SOWBELLY ROW.

TYREK LANNISTER WAS STILL MISSING, AS WAS THE HIGH SEPTON'S CRYSTAL CROWN.

NINE GOLD CLOAKS HAD BEEN SLAIN, TWO SCORE WOUNDED. NO ONE HAD TROUBLED TO COUNT HOW MANY OF THE MOB HAD DIED.

WE HELD THE CITY TODAY, MY LORD, BUT I MAKE NO PROMISES FOR THE MORROW. THE KETTLE IS CLOSE TO BOILING.

SO MANY THIEVES AND MURDERERS ARE ABROAD THAT NO MAN'S HOUSE IS SAFE, THE BLOODY FLUX IS SPREADING IN THE STEWS ALONG PISSWATER BEND, AND THERE'S NO FOOD TO BE HAD FOR COPPER NOR SILVER.

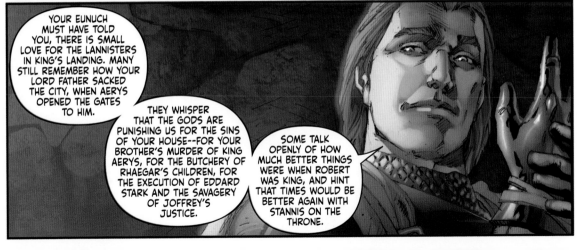

YOUR EUNUCH MUST HAVE TOLD YOU, THERE IS SMALL LOVE FOR THE LANNISTERS IN KING'S LANDING. MANY STILL REMEMBER HOW YOUR LORD FATHER SACKED THE CITY, WHEN AERYS OPENED THE GATES TO HIM.

THEY WHISPER THAT THE GODS ARE PUNISHING US FOR THE SINS OF YOUR HOUSE--FOR YOUR BROTHER'S MURDER OF KING AERYS, FOR THE BUTCHERY OF RHAEGAR'S CHILDREN, FOR THE EXECUTION OF EDDARD STARK AND THE SAVAGERY OF JOFFREY'S JUSTICE.

SOME TALK OPENLY OF HOW MUCH BETTER THINGS WERE WHEN ROBERT WAS KING, AND HINT THAT TIMES WOULD BE BETTER AGAIN WITH STANNIS ON THE THRONE.

THEY HATE MY FAMILY, IS THAT WHAT YOU ARE TELLING ME?

AYE...AND WILL TURN ON THEM, IF THE CHANCE COMES.

ME AS WELL?

ASK YOUR EUNUCH.

I'M ASKING YOU.

YOU MOST OF ALL, MY LORD.

MOST OF ALL? IT WAS JOFFREY WHO TOLD THEM TO EAT THEIR DEAD, JOFFREY WHO SET HIS DOG ON THEM. HOW COULD THEY BLAME ME?

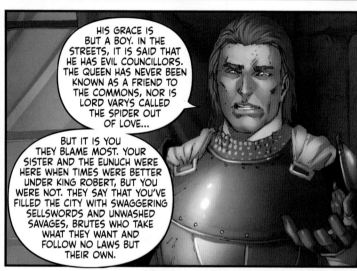

HIS GRACE IS BUT A BOY. IN THE STREETS, IT IS SAID THAT HE HAS EVIL COUNCILLORS. THE QUEEN HAS NEVER BEEN KNOWN AS A FRIEND TO THE COMMONS, NOR IS LORD VARYS CALLED THE SPIDER OUT OF LOVE...

BUT IT IS YOU THEY BLAME MOST. YOUR SISTER AND THE EUNUCH WERE HERE WHEN TIMES WERE BETTER UNDER KING ROBERT, BUT YOU WERE NOT. THEY SAY THAT YOU'VE FILLED THE CITY WITH SWAGGERING SELLSWORDS AND UNWASHED SAVAGES, BRUTES WHO TAKE WHAT THEY WANT AND FOLLOW NO LAWS BUT THEIR OWN.

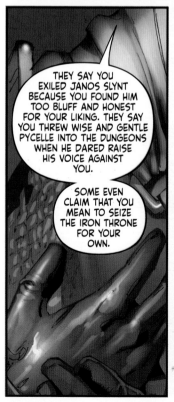

THEY SAY YOU EXILED JANOS SLYNT BECAUSE YOU FOUND HIM TOO BLUFF AND HONEST FOR YOUR LIKING. THEY SAY YOU THREW WISE AND GENTLE PYCELLE INTO THE DUNGEONS WHEN HE DARED RAISE HIS VOICE AGAINST YOU.

SOME EVEN CLAIM THAT YOU MEAN TO SEIZE THE IRON THRONE FOR YOUR OWN.

YES, AND I AM A MONSTER BESIDES, HIDEOUS AND MISSHAPEN, NEVER FORGET THAT.

I'VE HEARD ENOUGH. WE BOTH HAVE WORK TO ATTEND TO. LEAVE ME.

PERHAPS MY LORD FATHER WAS RIGHT TO DESPISE ME ALL THESE YEARS, IF THIS IS THE BEST I CAN ACHIEVE.

MY MOST TRUSTED ADVISERS ARE A EUNUCH AND A SELLSWORD, AND MY LADY'S A WHORE. WHAT DOES THAT SAY OF ME?

HE SHOUTED FOR POD, AND SENT THE BOY RUNNING TO SUMMON VARYS AND BRONN.

WHERE HAVE YOU BEEN?

ABOUT THE KING'S BUSINESS, MY SWEET LORD.

AH, YES, THE *KING*. MY NEPHEW IS NOT FIT TO SIT A PRIVY, LET ALONE THE IRON THRONE.

AN APPRENTICE MUST BE TAUGHT HIS TRADE.

HALF THE 'PRENTICES ON REEKING LANE COULD RULE BETTER THAN THIS KING OF YOURS.

I DON'T RECALL GIVING YOU LEAVE TO FINISH MY SUPPER.

YOU DIDN'T LOOK TO BE EATING IT. CITY'S STARVING; IT'S A CRIME TO WASTE FOOD. YOU HAVE ANY WINE?

YOU GO TOO FAR.

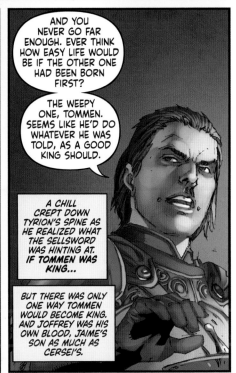

AND YOU NEVER GO FAR ENOUGH. EVER THINK HOW EASY LIFE WOULD BE IF THE OTHER ONE HAD BEEN BORN FIRST?

THE WEEPY ONE, TOMMEN. SEEMS LIKE HE'D DO WHATEVER HE WAS TOLD, AS A GOOD KING SHOULD.

A CHILL CREPT DOWN TYRION'S SPINE AS HE REALIZED WHAT THE SELLSWORD WAS HINTING AT. *IF TOMMEN WAS KING...*

BUT THERE WAS ONLY ONE WAY TOMMEN WOULD BECOME KING. AND JOFFREY WAS HIS OWN BLOOD, JAIME'S SON AS MUCH AS CERSEI'S.

I COULD HAVE YOUR HEAD OFF FOR SAYING THAT.

FRIENDS, QUARRELING WILL NOT SERVE US. I BEG YOU BOTH, TAKE HEART.

WHOSE?

HE COULD THINK OF SEVERAL TEMPTING CHOICES.

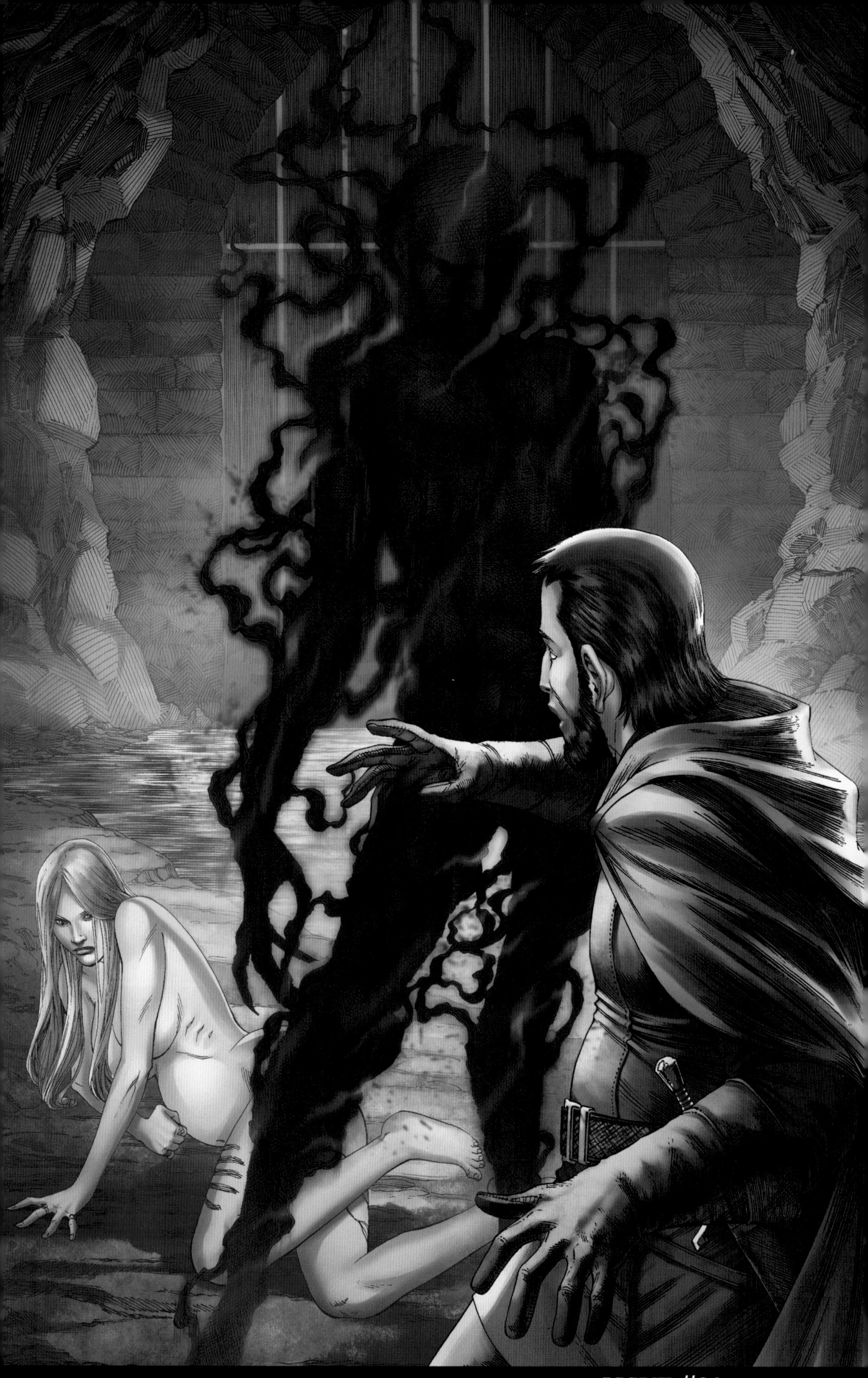

ISSUE #20

DAENERYS

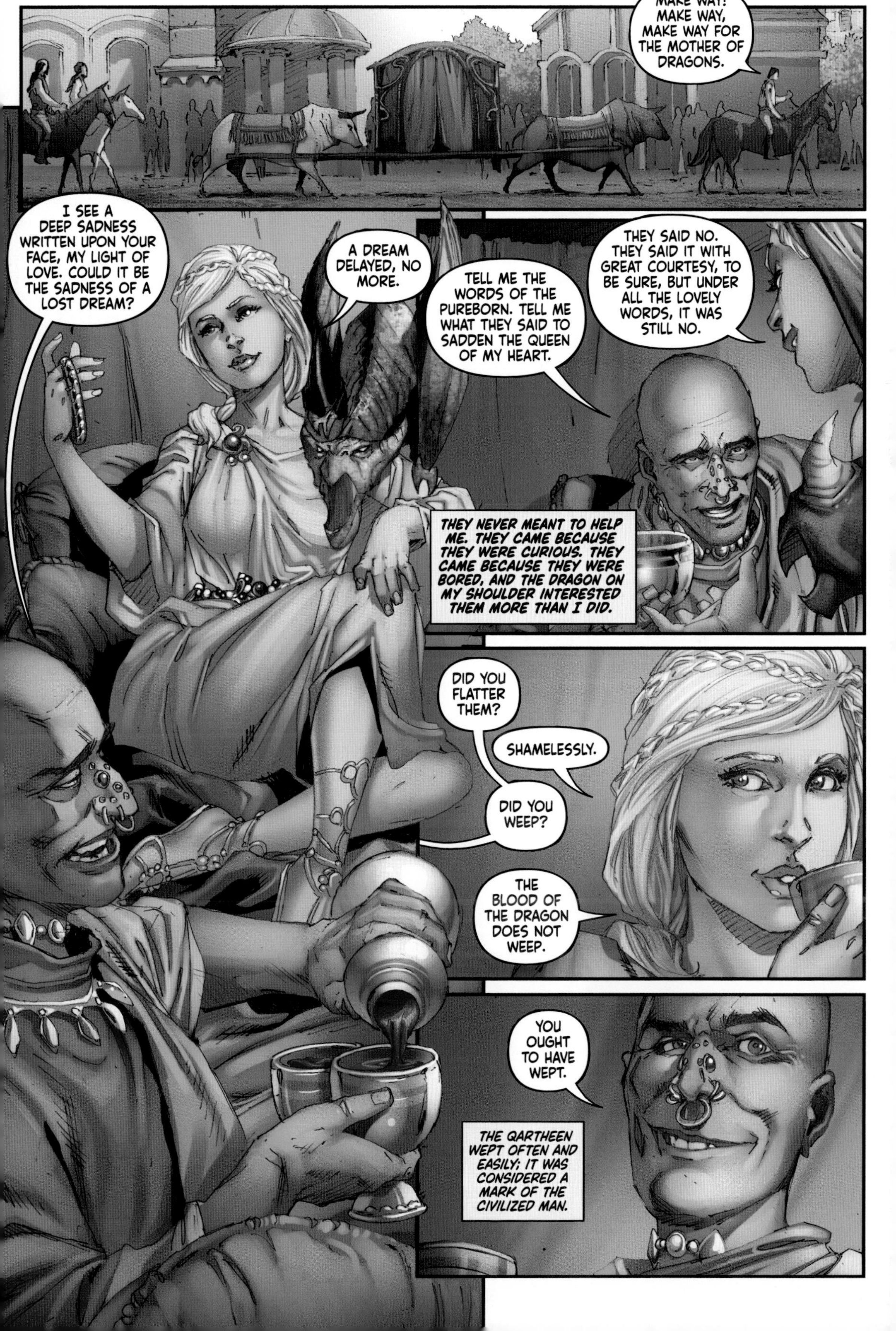

MAKE WAY! MAKE WAY, MAKE WAY FOR THE MOTHER OF DRAGONS.
I SEE A DEEP SADNESS WRITTEN UPON YOUR FACE, MY LIGHT OF LOVE. COULD IT BE THE SADNESS OF A LOST DREAM?
A DREAM DELAYED, NO MORE.
TELL ME THE WORDS OF THE PUREBORN. TELL ME WHAT THEY SAID TO SADDEN THE QUEEN OF MY HEART.
THEY SAID NO. THEY SAID IT WITH GREAT COURTESY, TO BE SURE, BUT UNDER ALL THE LOVELY WORDS, IT WAS STILL NO.
THEY NEVER MEANT TO HELP ME. THEY CAME BECAUSE THEY WERE CURIOUS. THEY CAME BECAUSE THEY WERE BORED, AND THE DRAGON ON MY SHOULDER INTERESTED THEM MORE THAN I DID.
DID YOU FLATTER THEM?
SHAMELESSLY.
DID YOU WEEP?
THE BLOOD OF THE DRAGON DOES NOT WEEP.
YOU OUGHT TO HAVE WEPT.
THE QARTHEEN WEPT OFTEN AND EASILY; IT WAS CONSIDERED A MARK OF THE CIVILIZED MAN.

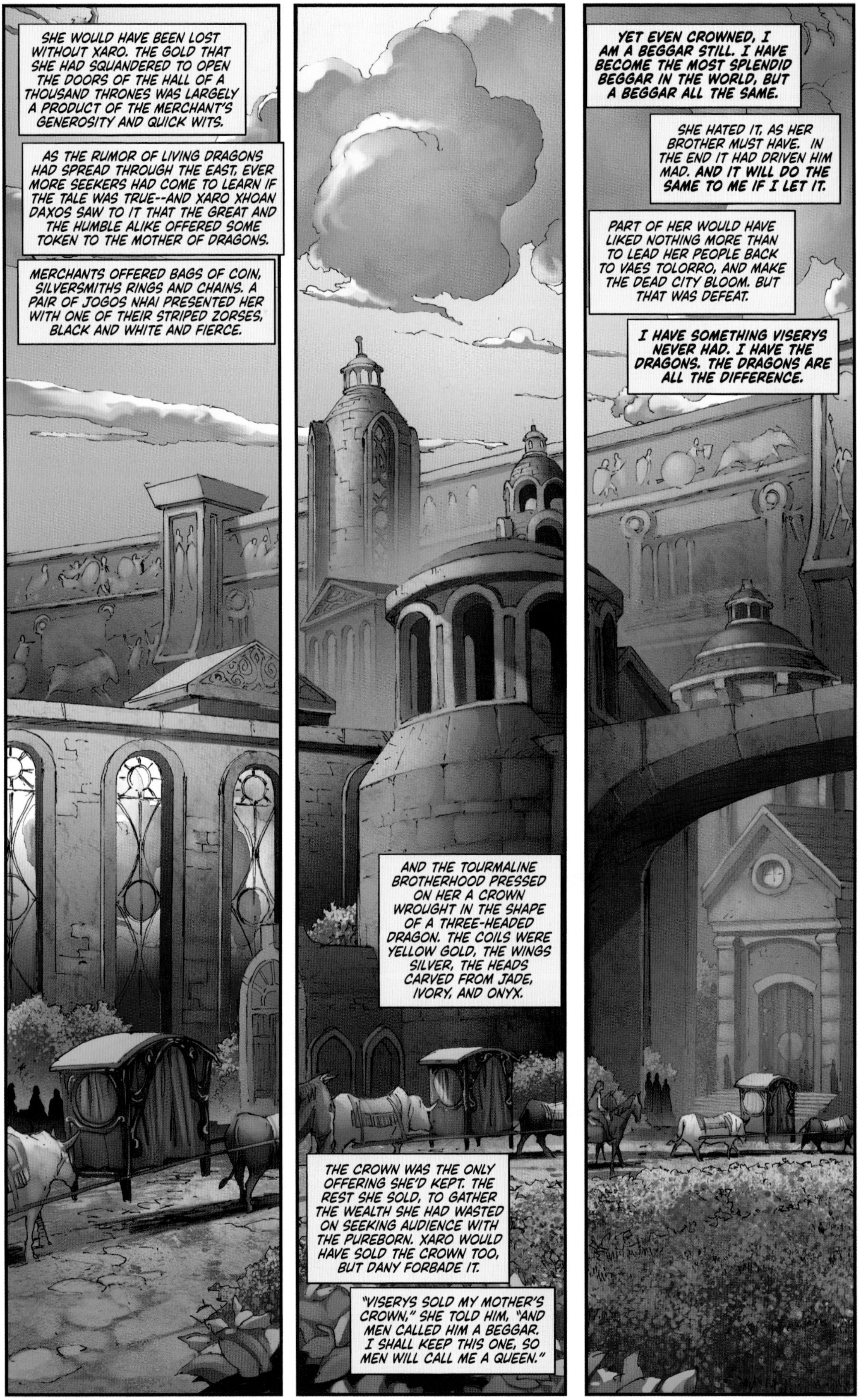
SHE WOULD HAVE BEEN LOST WITHOUT XARO. THE GOLD THAT SHE HAD SQUANDERED TO OPEN THE DOORS OF THE HALL OF A THOUSAND THRONES WAS LARGELY A PRODUCT OF THE MERCHANT'S GENEROSITY AND QUICK WITS.
AS THE RUMOR OF LIVING DRAGONS HAD SPREAD THROUGH THE EAST, EVER MORE SEEKERS HAD COME TO LEARN IF THE TALE WAS TRUE--AND XARO XHOAN DAXOS SAW TO IT THAT THE GREAT AND THE HUMBLE ALIKE OFFERED SOME TOKEN TO THE MOTHER OF DRAGONS.
MERCHANTS OFFERED BAGS OF COIN, SILVERSMITHS RINGS AND CHAINS. A PAIR OF JOGOS NHAI PRESENTED HER WITH ONE OF THEIR STRIPED ZORSES, BLACK AND WHITE AND FIERCE.
AND THE TOURMALINE BROTHERHOOD PRESSED ON HER A CROWN WROUGHT IN THE SHAPE OF A THREE-HEADED DRAGON. THE COILS WERE YELLOW GOLD, THE WINGS SILVER, THE HEADS CARVED FROM JADE, IVORY, AND ONYX.
THE CROWN WAS THE ONLY OFFERING SHE'D KEPT. THE REST SHE SOLD, TO GATHER THE WEALTH SHE HAD WASTED ON SEEKING AUDIENCE WITH THE PUREBORN. XARO WOULD HAVE SOLD THE CROWN TOO, BUT DANY FORBADE IT.
"VISERYS SOLD MY MOTHER'S CROWN," SHE TOLD HIM, "AND MEN CALLED HIM A BEGGAR. I SHALL KEEP THIS ONE, SO MEN WILL CALL ME A QUEEN."
YET EVEN CROWNED, I AM A BEGGAR STILL. I HAVE BECOME THE MOST SPLENDID BEGGAR IN THE WORLD, BUT A BEGGAR ALL THE SAME.
SHE HATED IT, AS HER BROTHER MUST HAVE. IN THE END IT HAD DRIVEN HIM MAD. AND IT WILL DO THE SAME TO ME IF I LET IT.
PART OF HER WOULD HAVE LIKED NOTHING MORE THAN TO LEAD HER PEOPLE BACK TO VAES TOLORRO, AND MAKE THE DEAD CITY BLOOM. BUT THAT WAS DEFEAT.
I HAVE SOMETHING VISERYS NEVER HAD. I HAVE THE DRAGONS. THE DRAGONS ARE ALL THE DIFFERENCE.

YOUR DRAGON HAS A GOOD NOSE. THE WINE IS ORDINARY. IT IS SAID THAT ACROSS THE JADE SEA THEY MAKE A GOLDEN VINTAGE SO FINE THAT ONE SIP MAKES ALL OTHER WINES TASTE LIKE VINEGAR.

LET US TAKE MY PLEASURE BARGE AND GO IN SEARCH OF IT, YOU AND I. LET THIS BE YOUR KINGDOM, MOST EXQUISITE OF QUEENS, AND LET ME BE YOUR KING.

MARRY ME, BRIGHT LIGHT. I CANNOT SLEEP AT NIGHT FOR THINKING OF YOUR BEAUTY.

I WILL GIVE YOU A THRONE OF GOLD, IF YOU LIKE. WHEN QARTH BEGINS TO PALL, WE CAN JOURNEY ROUND YI TI AND SEARCH FOR THE DREAMING CITY OF THE POETS, TO SIP THE WINE OF WISDOM FROM A DEAD MAN'S SKULL.

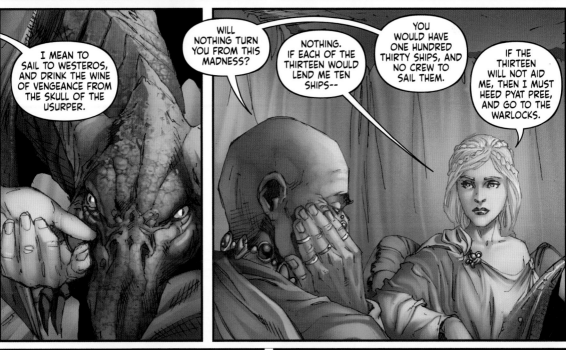

I MEAN TO SAIL TO WESTEROS, AND DRINK THE WINE OF VENGEANCE FROM THE SKULL OF THE USURPER.

WILL NOTHING TURN YOU FROM THIS MADNESS?

NOTHING. IF EACH OF THE THIRTEEN WOULD LEND ME TEN SHIPS--

YOU WOULD HAVE ONE HUNDRED THIRTY SHIPS, AND NO CREW TO SAIL THEM.

IF THE THIRTEEN WILL NOT AID ME, THEN I MUST HEED PYAT PREE, AND GO TO THE WARLOCKS.

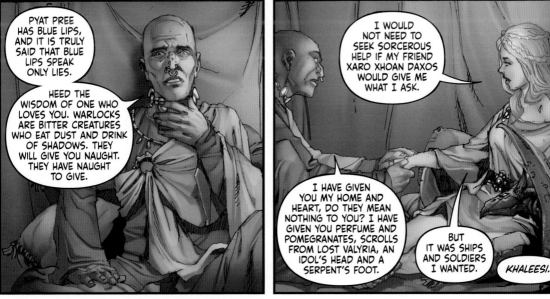

PYAT PREE HAS BLUE LIPS, AND IT IS TRULY SAID THAT BLUE LIPS SPEAK ONLY LIES.

HEED THE WISDOM OF ONE WHO LOVES YOU. WARLOCKS ARE BITTER CREATURES WHO EAT DUST AND DRINK OF SHADOWS. THEY WILL GIVE YOU NAUGHT. THEY HAVE NAUGHT TO GIVE.

I WOULD NOT NEED TO SEEK SORCEROUS HELP IF MY FRIEND XARO XHOAN DAXOS WOULD GIVE ME WHAT I ASK.

I HAVE GIVEN YOU MY HOME AND HEART, DO THEY MEAN NOTHING TO YOU? I HAVE GIVEN YOU PERFUME AND POMEGRANATES, SCROLLS FROM LOST VALYRIA, AN IDOL'S HEAD AND A SERPENT'S FOOT.

BUT IT WAS SHIPS AND SOLDIERS I WANTED.

KHALEESI.

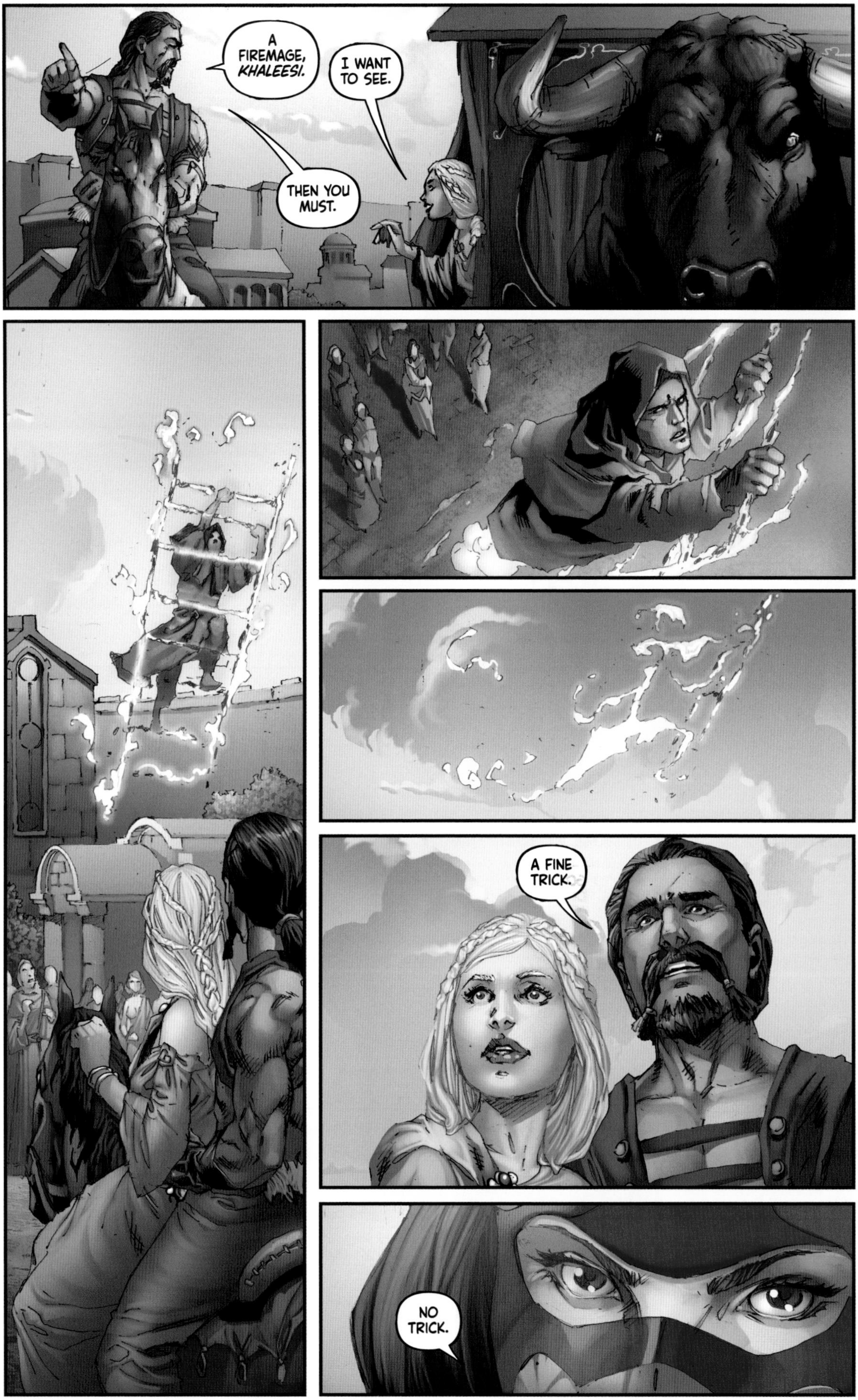
A FIREMAGE, KHALEESI.
I WANT TO SEE.
THEN YOU MUST.
A FINE TRICK.
NO TRICK.

DANY HAD NOT NOTICED QUAITHE IN THE CROWD, YET THERE SHE STOOD, EYES WET AND SHINY BEHIND THE IMPLACABLE RED LACQUER MASK.

WHAT MEAN YOU, MY LADY?

HALF A YEAR GONE, THAT MAN COULD SCARCELY WAKE FIRE FROM DRAGONGLASS. HE COULD WALK ACROSS HOT COALS AND MAKE BURNING ROSES BLOOM IN THE AIR, BUT HE COULD NO MORE ASPIRE TO CLIMB THE FIERY LADDER THAN A COMMON FISHERMAN COULD HOPE TO CATCH A KRAKEN IN HIS NETS.

AND NOW?

HIS POWERS GROW, *KHALEESI*. AND YOU ARE THE CAUSE OF IT.

ME? HOW COULD THAT BE?

YOU ARE THE MOTHER OF DRAGONS, ARE YOU NOT?

YOU MUST LEAVE THIS CITY SOON, DAENERYS TARGARYEN, OR YOU WILL NEVER BE PERMITTED TO LEAVE IT AT ALL.

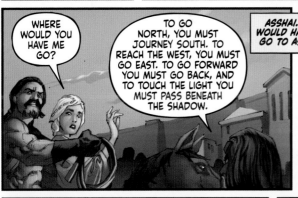

WHERE WOULD YOU HAVE ME GO?

TO GO NORTH, YOU MUST JOURNEY SOUTH. TO REACH THE WEST, YOU MUST GO EAST. TO GO FORWARD YOU MUST GO BACK, AND TO TOUCH THE LIGHT YOU MUST PASS BENEATH THE SHADOW.

ASSHAI. SHE WOULD HAVE ME GO TO ASSHAI.

WILL THE ASSHAI'I GIVE ME AN ARMY? WILL THERE BE GOLD FOR ME IN ASSHAI? WILL THERE BE SHIPS?

WHAT IS THERE IN ASSHAI THAT I WILL NOT FIND IN QARTH?

TRUTH.

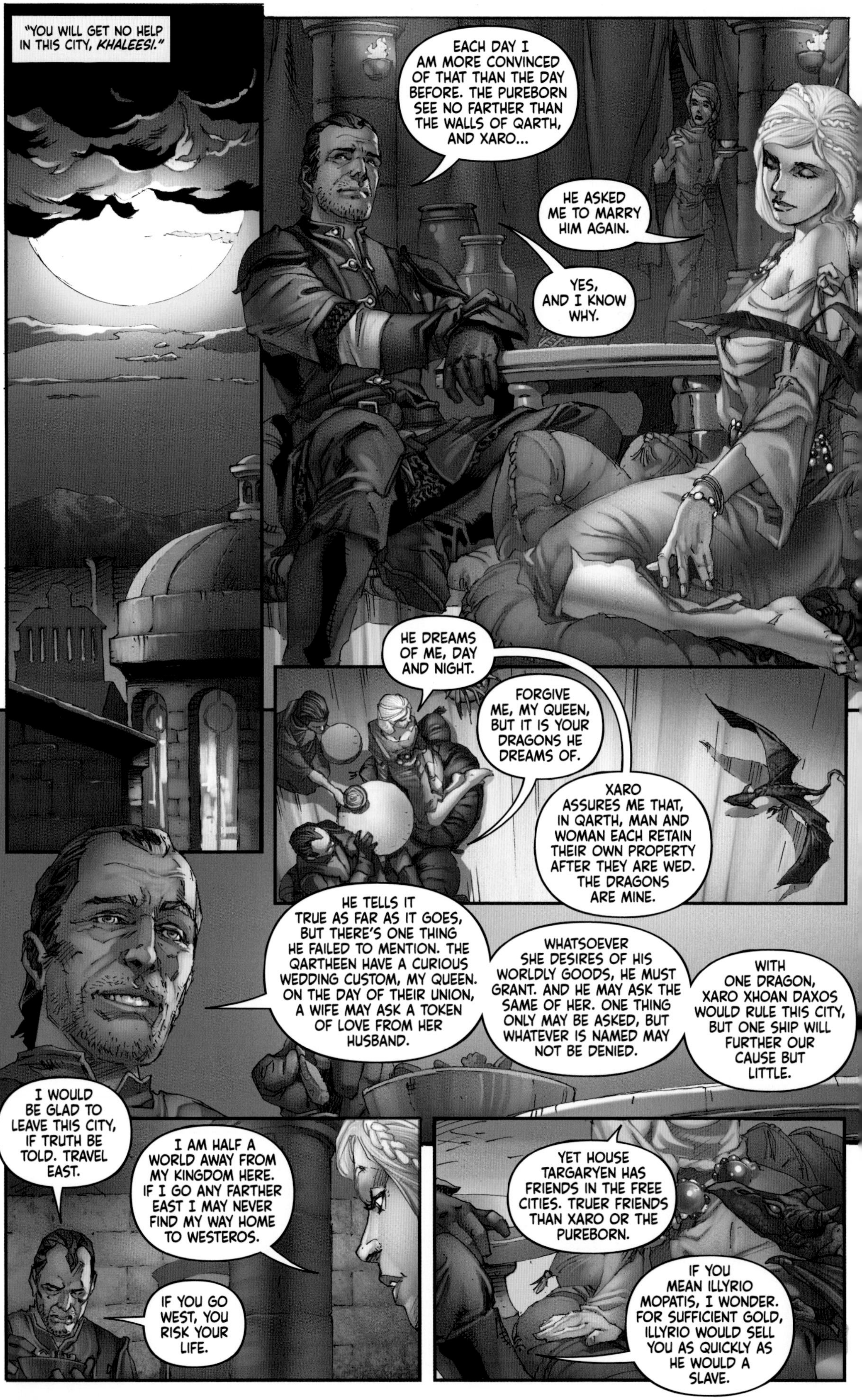
"YOU WILL GET NO HELP IN THIS CITY, *KHALEESI.*"
EACH DAY I AM MORE CONVINCED OF THAT THAN THE DAY BEFORE. THE PUREBORN SEE NO FARTHER THAN THE WALLS OF QARTH, AND XARO...
HE ASKED ME TO MARRY HIM AGAIN.
YES, AND I KNOW WHY.
HE DREAMS OF ME, DAY AND NIGHT.
FORGIVE ME, MY QUEEN, BUT IT IS YOUR DRAGONS HE DREAMS OF.
XARO ASSURES ME THAT, IN QARTH, MAN AND WOMAN EACH RETAIN THEIR OWN PROPERTY AFTER THEY ARE WED. THE DRAGONS ARE MINE.
HE TELLS IT TRUE AS FAR AS IT GOES, BUT THERE'S ONE THING HE FAILED TO MENTION. THE QARTHEEN HAVE A CURIOUS WEDDING CUSTOM, MY QUEEN. ON THE DAY OF THEIR UNION, A WIFE MAY ASK A TOKEN OF LOVE FROM HER HUSBAND.
WHATSOEVER SHE DESIRES OF HIS WORLDLY GOODS, HE MUST GRANT. AND HE MAY ASK THE SAME OF HER. ONE THING ONLY MAY BE ASKED, BUT WHATEVER IS NAMED MAY NOT BE DENIED.
WITH ONE DRAGON, XARO XHOAN DAXOS WOULD RULE THIS CITY, BUT ONE SHIP WILL FURTHER OUR CAUSE BUT LITTLE.
I WOULD BE GLAD TO LEAVE THIS CITY, IF TRUTH BE TOLD. TRAVEL EAST.
I AM HALF A WORLD AWAY FROM MY KINGDOM HERE. IF I GO ANY FARTHER EAST I MAY NEVER FIND MY WAY HOME TO WESTEROS.
IF YOU GO WEST, YOU RISK YOUR LIFE.
YET HOUSE TARGARYEN HAS FRIENDS IN THE FREE CITIES. TRUER FRIENDS THAN XARO OR THE PUREBORN.
IF YOU MEAN ILLYRIO MOPATIS, I WONDER. FOR SUFFICIENT GOLD, ILLYRIO WOULD SELL YOU AS QUICKLY AS HE WOULD A SLAVE.

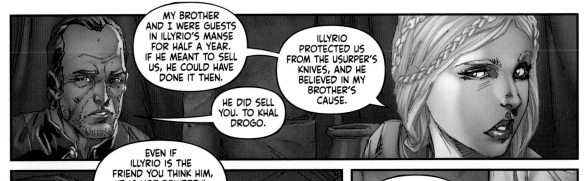

MY BROTHER AND I WERE GUESTS IN ILLYRIO'S MANSE FOR HALF A YEAR. IF HE MEANT TO SELL US, HE COULD HAVE DONE IT THEN.

ILLYRIO PROTECTED US FROM THE USURPER'S KNIVES, AND HE BELIEVED IN MY BROTHER'S CAUSE.

HE DID SELL YOU. TO KHAL DROGO.

EVEN IF ILLYRIO IS THE FRIEND YOU THINK HIM, HE IS NOT POWERFUL ENOUGH TO ENTHRONE YOU BY HIMSELF, NO MORE THAN HE COULD YOUR BROTHER.

HE IS RICH. NOT SO RICH AS XARO, PERHAPS, BUT RICH ENOUGH TO HIRE SHIPS FOR ME, AND MEN AS WELL.

SELLSWORDS HAVE THEIR USES, BUT YOU WILL NOT WIN YOUR FATHER'S THRONE WITH SWEEPINGS FROM THE FREE CITIES. NOTHING KNITS A BROKEN REALM TOGETHER SO QUICK AS AN INVADING ARMY ON ITS SOIL.

BUT I AM THEIR RIGHTFUL QUEEN!

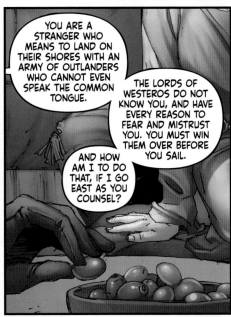

YOU ARE A STRANGER WHO MEANS TO LAND ON THEIR SHORES WITH AN ARMY OF OUTLANDERS WHO CANNOT EVEN SPEAK THE COMMON TONGUE.

THE LORDS OF WESTEROS DO NOT KNOW YOU, AND HAVE EVERY REASON TO FEAR AND MISTRUST YOU. YOU MUST WIN THEM OVER BEFORE YOU SAIL.

AND HOW AM I TO DO THAT, IF I GO EAST AS YOU COUNSEL?

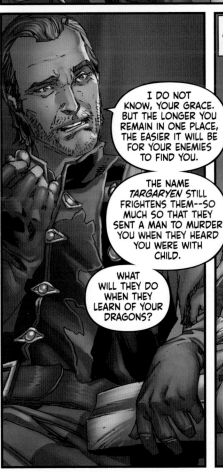

I DO NOT KNOW, YOUR GRACE. BUT THE LONGER YOU REMAIN IN ONE PLACE, THE EASIER IT WILL BE FOR YOUR ENEMIES TO FIND YOU.

THE NAME *TARGARYEN* STILL FRIGHTENS THEM--SO MUCH SO THAT THEY SENT A MAN TO MURDER YOU WHEN THEY HEARD YOU WERE WITH CHILD.

WHAT WILL THEY DO WHEN THEY LEARN OF YOUR DRAGONS?

MY FURIOUS CHILDREN...THEY MUST NOT COME TO HARM.

THE COMET LED ME TO QARTH FOR A REASON. I HAD HOPED TO FIND MY ARMY HERE, BUT IT SEEMS THAT WILL NOT BE. WHAT ELSE REMAINS?

I AM AFRAID, SHE REALIZED, BUT I MUST BE BRAVE.

COME THE MORROW, YOU MUST GO TO PYAT PREE.

DAVOS

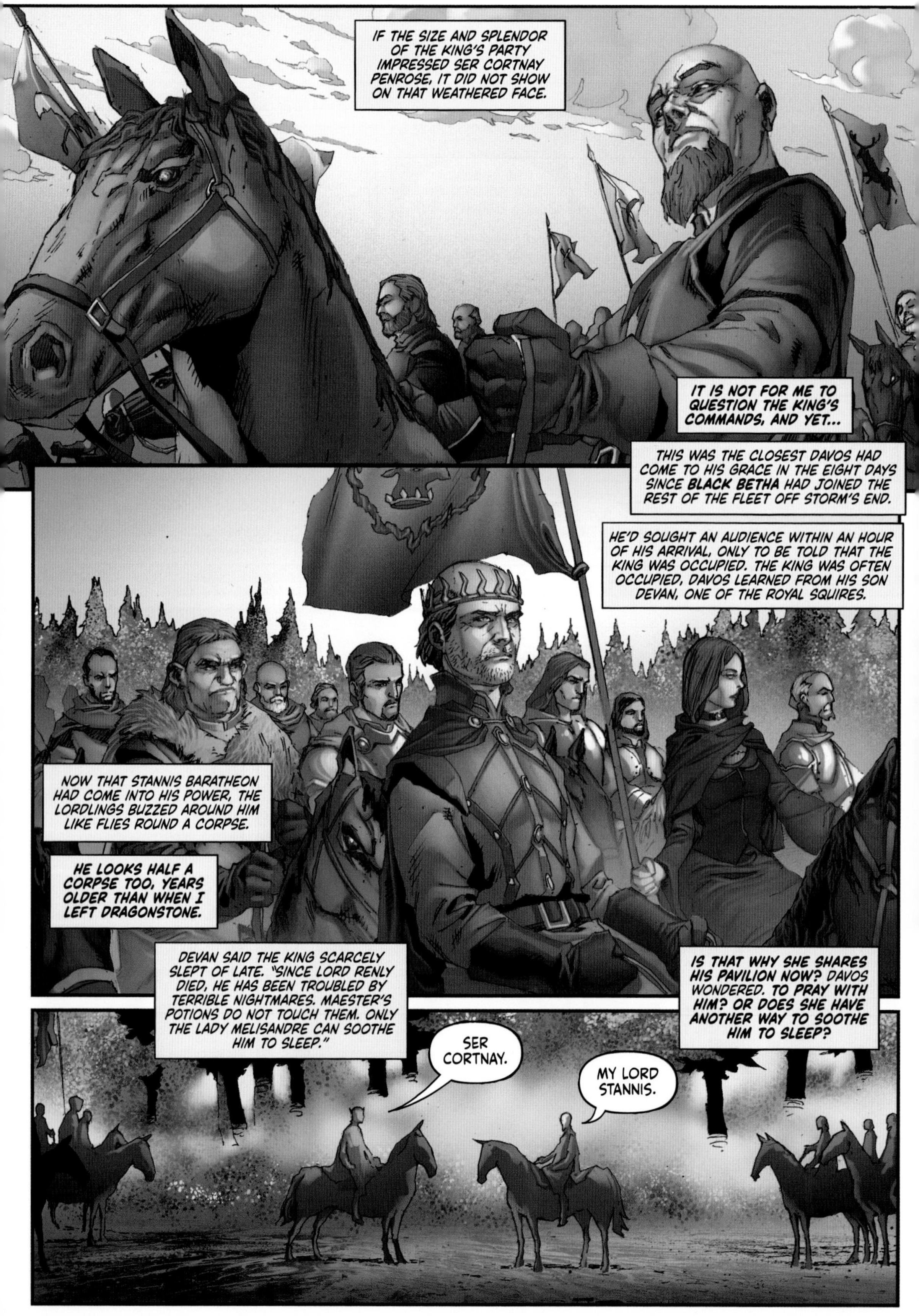

IF THE SIZE AND SPLENDOR OF THE KING'S PARTY IMPRESSED SER CORTNAY PENROSE, IT DID NOT SHOW ON THAT WEATHERED FACE.
IT IS NOT FOR ME TO QUESTION THE KING'S COMMANDS, AND YET...
THIS WAS THE CLOSEST DAVOS HAD COME TO HIS GRACE IN THE EIGHT DAYS SINCE BLACK BETHA HAD JOINED THE REST OF THE FLEET OFF STORM'S END.
HE'D SOUGHT AN AUDIENCE WITHIN AN HOUR OF HIS ARRIVAL, ONLY TO BE TOLD THAT THE KING WAS OCCUPIED. THE KING WAS OFTEN OCCUPIED, DAVOS LEARNED FROM HIS SON DEVAN, ONE OF THE ROYAL SQUIRES.
NOW THAT STANNIS BARATHEON HAD COME INTO HIS POWER, THE LORDLINGS BUZZED AROUND HIM LIKE FLIES ROUND A CORPSE.
HE LOOKS HALF A CORPSE TOO, YEARS OLDER THAN WHEN I LEFT DRAGONSTONE.
DEVAN SAID THE KING SCARCELY SLEPT OF LATE. "SINCE LORD RENLY DIED, HE HAS BEEN TROUBLED BY TERRIBLE NIGHTMARES. MAESTER'S POTIONS DO NOT TOUCH THEM. ONLY THE LADY MELISANDRE CAN SOOTHE HIM TO SLEEP."
IS THAT WHY SHE SHARES HIS PAVILION NOW? DAVOS WONDERED. TO PRAY WITH HIM? OR DOES SHE HAVE ANOTHER WAY TO SOOTHE HIM TO SLEEP?
SER CORTNAY.
MY LORD STANNIS.

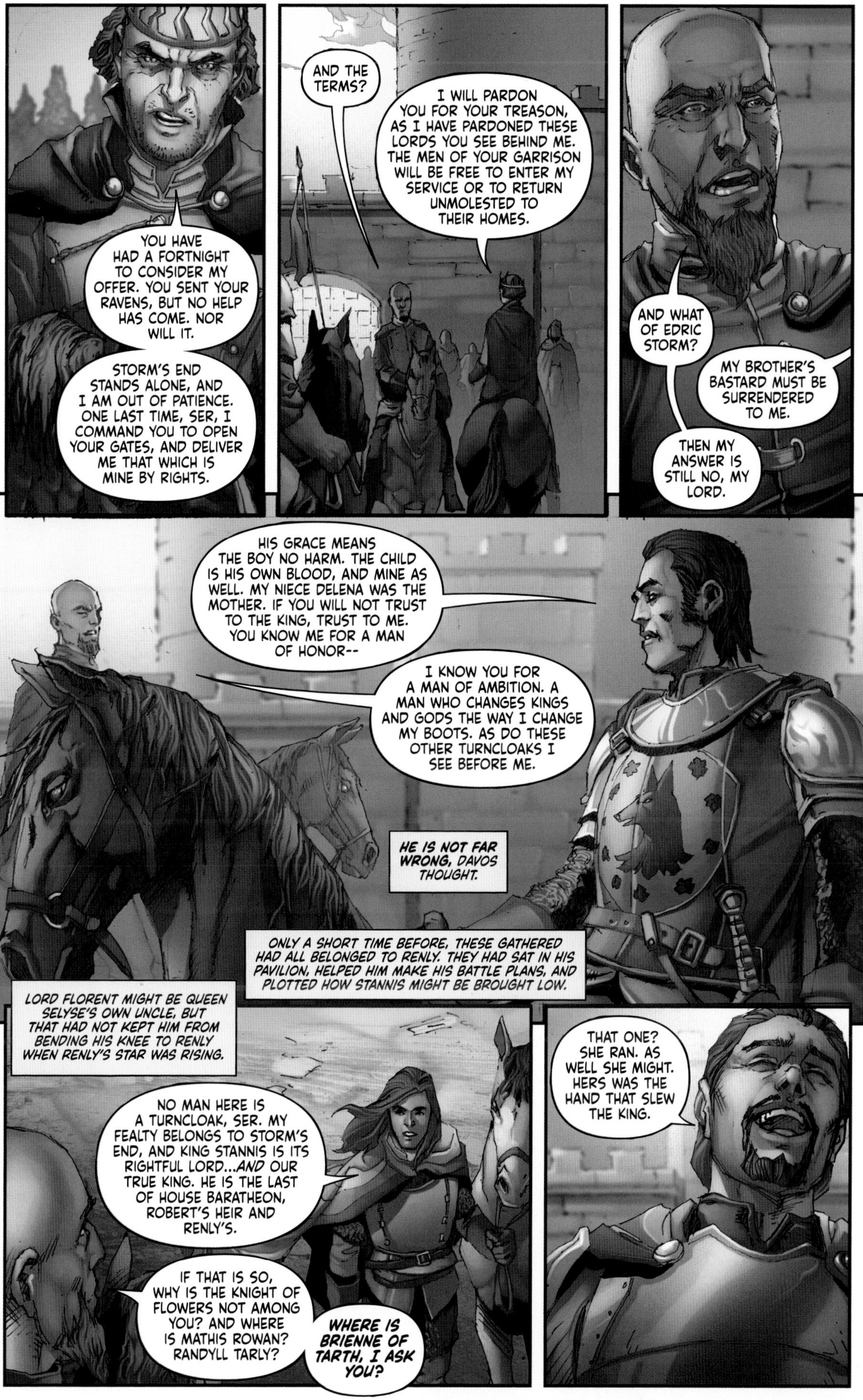
YOU HAVE HAD A FORTNIGHT TO CONSIDER MY OFFER. YOU SENT YOUR RAVENS, BUT NO HELP HAS COME. NOR WILL IT.
STORM'S END STANDS ALONE, AND I AM OUT OF PATIENCE. ONE LAST TIME, SER, I COMMAND YOU TO OPEN YOUR GATES, AND DELIVER ME THAT WHICH IS MINE BY RIGHTS.
AND THE TERMS?
I WILL PARDON YOU FOR YOUR TREASON, AS I HAVE PARDONED THESE LORDS YOU SEE BEHIND ME. THE MEN OF YOUR GARRISON WILL BE FREE TO ENTER MY SERVICE OR TO RETURN UNMOLESTED TO THEIR HOMES.
AND WHAT OF EDRIC STORM?
MY BROTHER'S BASTARD MUST BE SURRENDERED TO ME.
THEN MY ANSWER IS STILL NO, MY LORD.
HIS GRACE MEANS THE BOY NO HARM. THE CHILD IS HIS OWN BLOOD, AND MINE AS WELL. MY NIECE DELENA WAS THE MOTHER. IF YOU WILL NOT TRUST TO THE KING, TRUST TO ME. YOU KNOW ME FOR A MAN OF HONOR--
I KNOW YOU FOR A MAN OF AMBITION. A MAN WHO CHANGES KINGS AND GODS THE WAY I CHANGE MY BOOTS. AS DO THESE OTHER TURNCLOAKS I SEE BEFORE ME.
HE IS NOT FAR WRONG, DAVOS THOUGHT.
ONLY A SHORT TIME BEFORE, THESE GATHERED HAD ALL BELONGED TO RENLY. THEY HAD SAT IN HIS PAVILION, HELPED HIM MAKE HIS BATTLE PLANS, AND PLOTTED HOW STANNIS MIGHT BE BROUGHT LOW.
LORD FLORENT MIGHT BE QUEEN SELYSE'S OWN UNCLE, BUT THAT HAD NOT KEPT HIM FROM BENDING HIS KNEE TO RENLY WHEN RENLY'S STAR WAS RISING.
NO MAN HERE IS A TURNCLOAK, SER. MY FEALTY BELONGS TO STORM'S END, AND KING STANNIS IS ITS RIGHTFUL LORD...AND OUR TRUE KING. HE IS THE LAST OF HOUSE BARATHEON, ROBERT'S HEIR AND RENLY'S.
IF THAT IS SO, WHY IS THE KNIGHT OF FLOWERS NOT AMONG YOU? AND WHERE IS MATHIS ROWAN? RANDYLL TARLY?
WHERE IS BRIENNE OF TARTH, I ASK YOU?
THAT ONE? SHE RAN. AS WELL SHE MIGHT. HERS WAS THE HAND THAT SLEW THE KING.

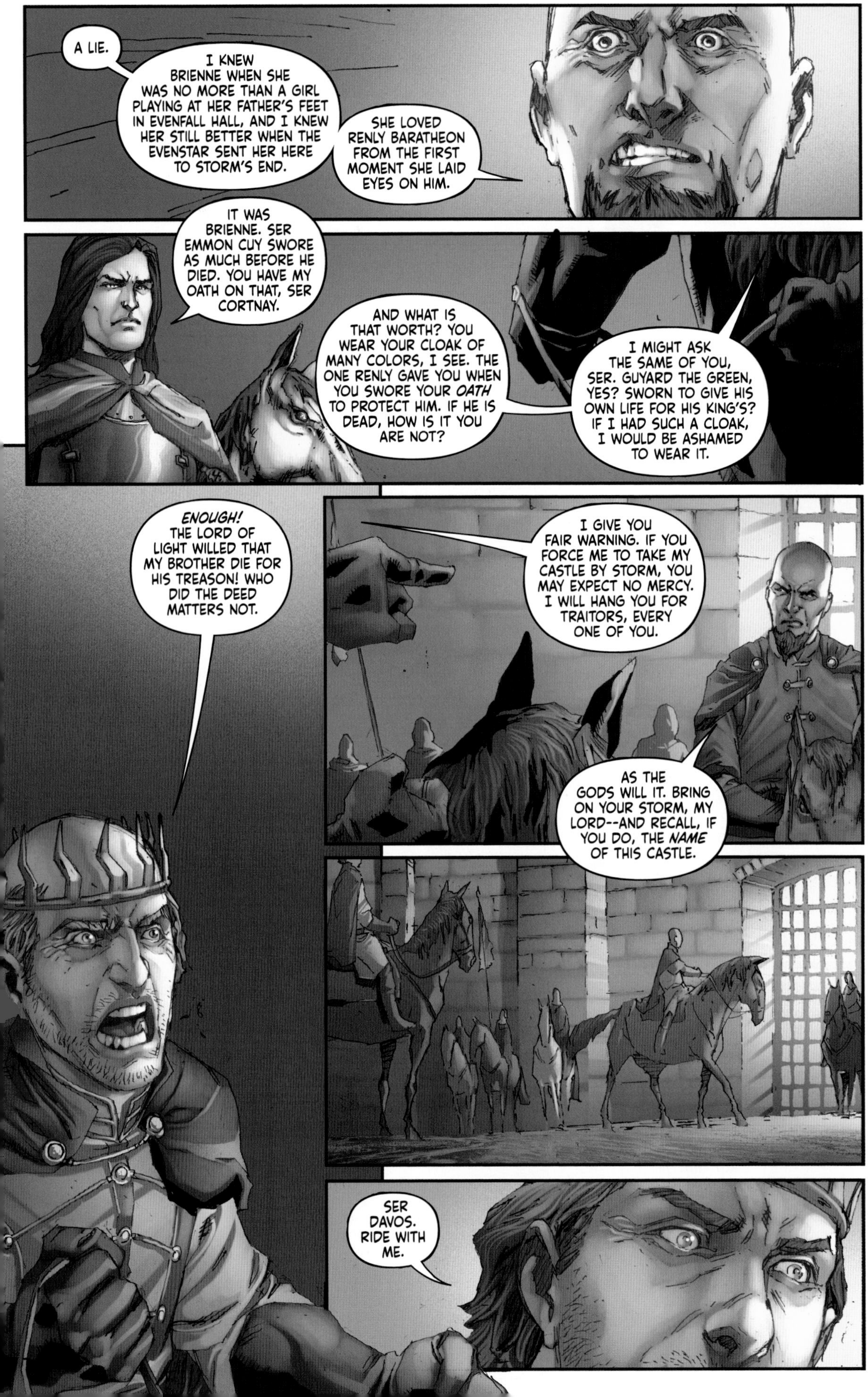

A LIE.
I KNEW BRIENNE WHEN SHE WAS NO MORE THAN A GIRL PLAYING AT HER FATHER'S FEET IN EVENFALL HALL, AND I KNEW HER STILL BETTER WHEN THE EVENSTAR SENT HER HERE TO STORM'S END.
SHE LOVED RENLY BARATHEON FROM THE FIRST MOMENT SHE LAID EYES ON HIM.
IT WAS BRIENNE. SER EMMON CUY SWORE AS MUCH BEFORE HE DIED. YOU HAVE MY OATH ON THAT, SER CORTNAY.
AND WHAT IS THAT WORTH? YOU WEAR YOUR CLOAK OF MANY COLORS, I SEE. THE ONE RENLY GAVE YOU WHEN YOU SWORE YOUR *OATH* TO PROTECT HIM. IF HE IS DEAD, HOW IS IT YOU ARE NOT?
I MIGHT ASK THE SAME OF YOU, SER. GUYARD THE GREEN, YES? SWORN TO GIVE HIS OWN LIFE FOR HIS KING'S? IF I HAD SUCH A CLOAK, I WOULD BE ASHAMED TO WEAR IT.
ENOUGH! THE LORD OF LIGHT WILLED THAT MY BROTHER DIE FOR HIS TREASON! WHO DID THE DEED MATTERS NOT.
I GIVE YOU FAIR WARNING. IF YOU FORCE ME TO TAKE MY CASTLE BY STORM, YOU MAY EXPECT NO MERCY. I WILL HANG YOU FOR TRAITORS, EVERY ONE OF YOU.
AS THE GODS WILL IT. BRING ON YOUR STORM, MY LORD--AND RECALL, IF YOU DO, THE *NAME* OF THIS CASTLE.
SER DAVOS. RIDE WITH ME.

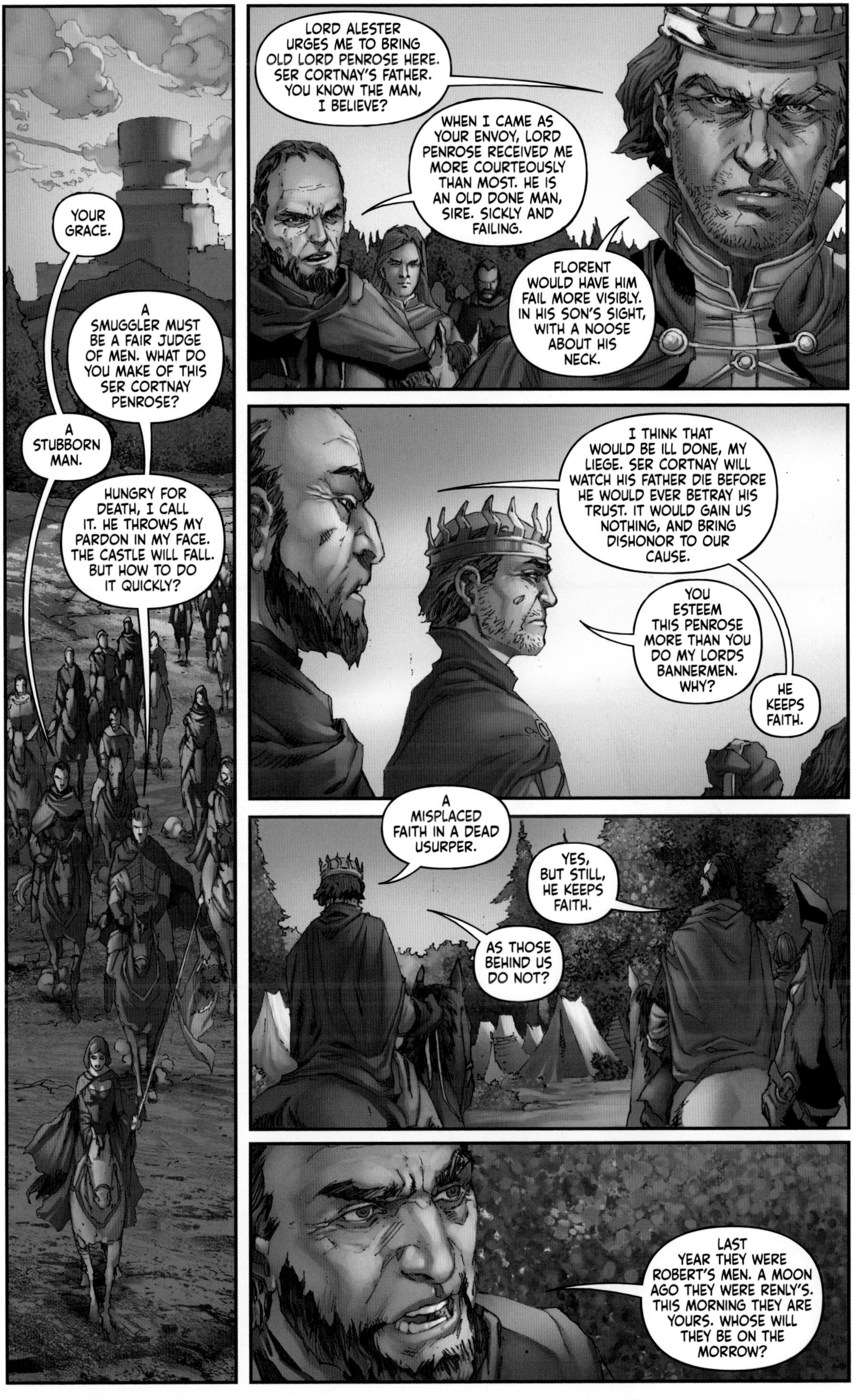
YOUR GRACE.
A SMUGGLER MUST BE A FAIR JUDGE OF MEN. WHAT DO YOU MAKE OF THIS SER CORTNAY PENROSE?
A STUBBORN MAN.
HUNGRY FOR DEATH, I CALL IT. HE THROWS MY PARDON IN MY FACE. THE CASTLE WILL FALL. BUT HOW TO DO IT QUICKLY?
LORD ALESTER URGES ME TO BRING OLD LORD PENROSE HERE. SER CORTNAY'S FATHER. YOU KNOW THE MAN, I BELIEVE?
WHEN I CAME AS YOUR ENVOY, LORD PENROSE RECEIVED ME MORE COURTEOUSLY THAN MOST. HE IS AN OLD DONE MAN, SIRE. SICKLY AND FAILING.
FLORENT WOULD HAVE HIM FAIL MORE VISIBLY. IN HIS SON'S SIGHT, WITH A NOOSE ABOUT HIS NECK.
I THINK THAT WOULD BE ILL DONE, MY LIEGE. SER CORTNAY WILL WATCH HIS FATHER DIE BEFORE HE WOULD EVER BETRAY HIS TRUST. IT WOULD GAIN US NOTHING, AND BRING DISHONOR TO OUR CAUSE.
YOU ESTEEM THIS PENROSE MORE THAN YOU DO MY LORDS BANNERMEN. WHY?
HE KEEPS FAITH.
A MISPLACED FAITH IN A DEAD USURPER.
YES, BUT STILL, HE KEEPS FAITH.
AS THOSE BEHIND US DO NOT?
LAST YEAR THEY WERE ROBERT'S MEN. A MOON AGO THEY WERE RENLY'S. THIS MORNING THEY ARE YOURS. WHOSE WILL THEY BE ON THE MORROW?

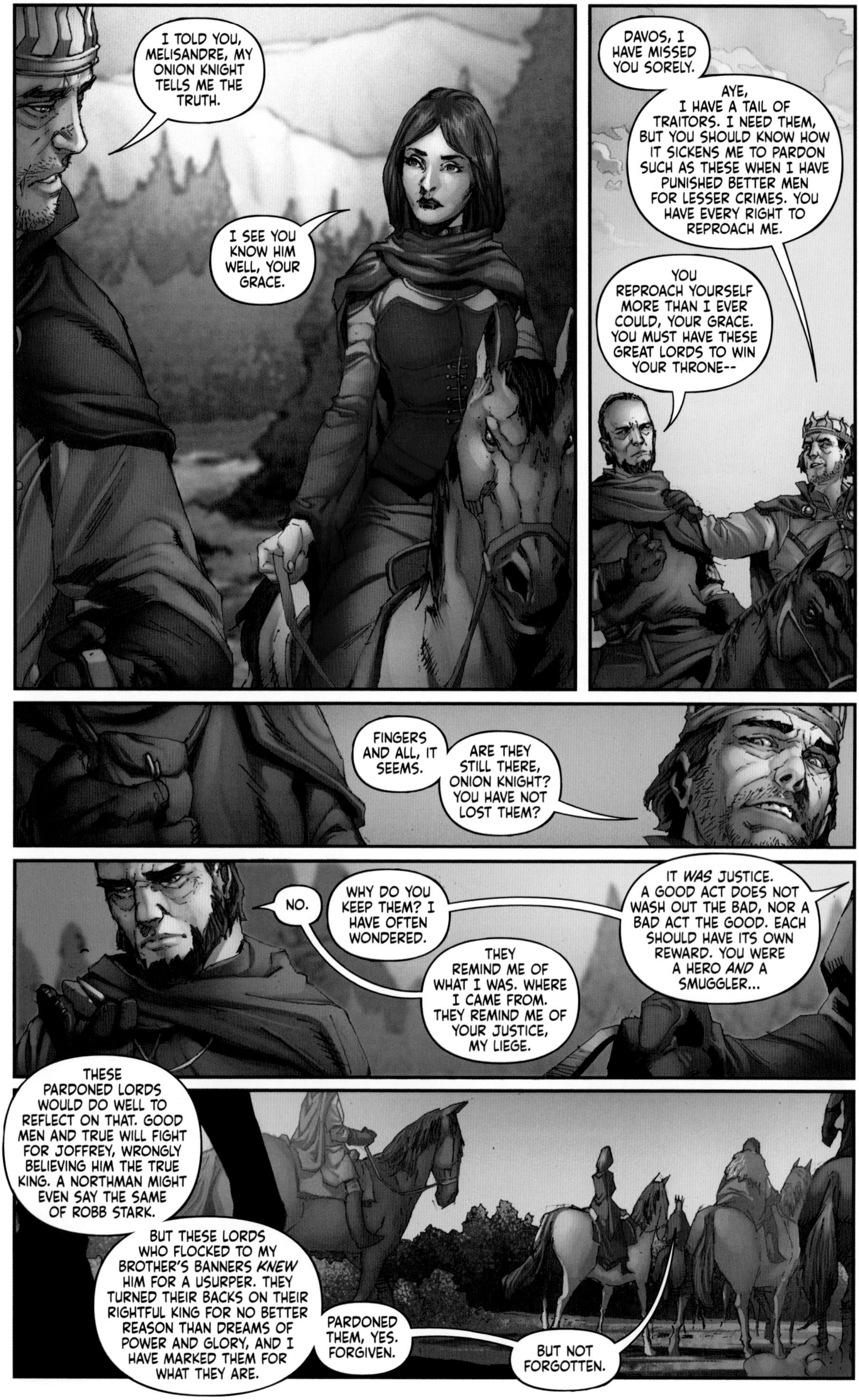
I TOLD YOU, MELISANDRE, MY ONION KNIGHT TELLS ME THE TRUTH.
I SEE YOU KNOW HIM WELL, YOUR GRACE.
DAVOS, I HAVE MISSED YOU SORELY.
AYE, I HAVE A TAIL OF TRAITORS. I NEED THEM, BUT YOU SHOULD KNOW HOW IT SICKENS ME TO PARDON SUCH AS THESE WHEN I HAVE PUNISHED BETTER MEN FOR LESSER CRIMES. YOU HAVE EVERY RIGHT TO REPROACH ME.
YOU REPROACH YOURSELF MORE THAN I EVER COULD, YOUR GRACE. YOU MUST HAVE THESE GREAT LORDS TO WIN YOUR THRONE--
ARE THEY STILL THERE, ONION KNIGHT? YOU HAVE NOT LOST THEM?
FINGERS AND ALL, IT SEEMS.
WHY DO YOU KEEP THEM? I HAVE OFTEN WONDERED.
NO.
THEY REMIND ME OF WHAT I WAS. WHERE I CAME FROM. THEY REMIND ME OF YOUR JUSTICE, MY LIEGE.
IT *WAS* JUSTICE. A GOOD ACT DOES NOT WASH OUT THE BAD, NOR A BAD ACT THE GOOD. EACH SHOULD HAVE ITS OWN REWARD. YOU WERE A HERO *AND* A SMUGGLER...
THESE PARDONED LORDS WOULD DO WELL TO REFLECT ON THAT. GOOD MEN AND TRUE WILL FIGHT FOR JOFFREY, WRONGLY BELIEVING HIM THE TRUE KING. A NORTHMAN MIGHT EVEN SAY THE SAME OF ROBB STARK.
BUT THESE LORDS WHO FLOCKED TO MY BROTHER'S BANNERS *KNEW* HIM FOR A USURPER. THEY TURNED THEIR BACKS ON THEIR RIGHTFUL KING FOR NO BETTER REASON THAN DREAMS OF POWER AND GLORY, AND I HAVE MARKED THEM FOR WHAT THEY ARE.
PARDONED THEM, YES. FORGIVEN.
BUT NOT FORGOTTEN.

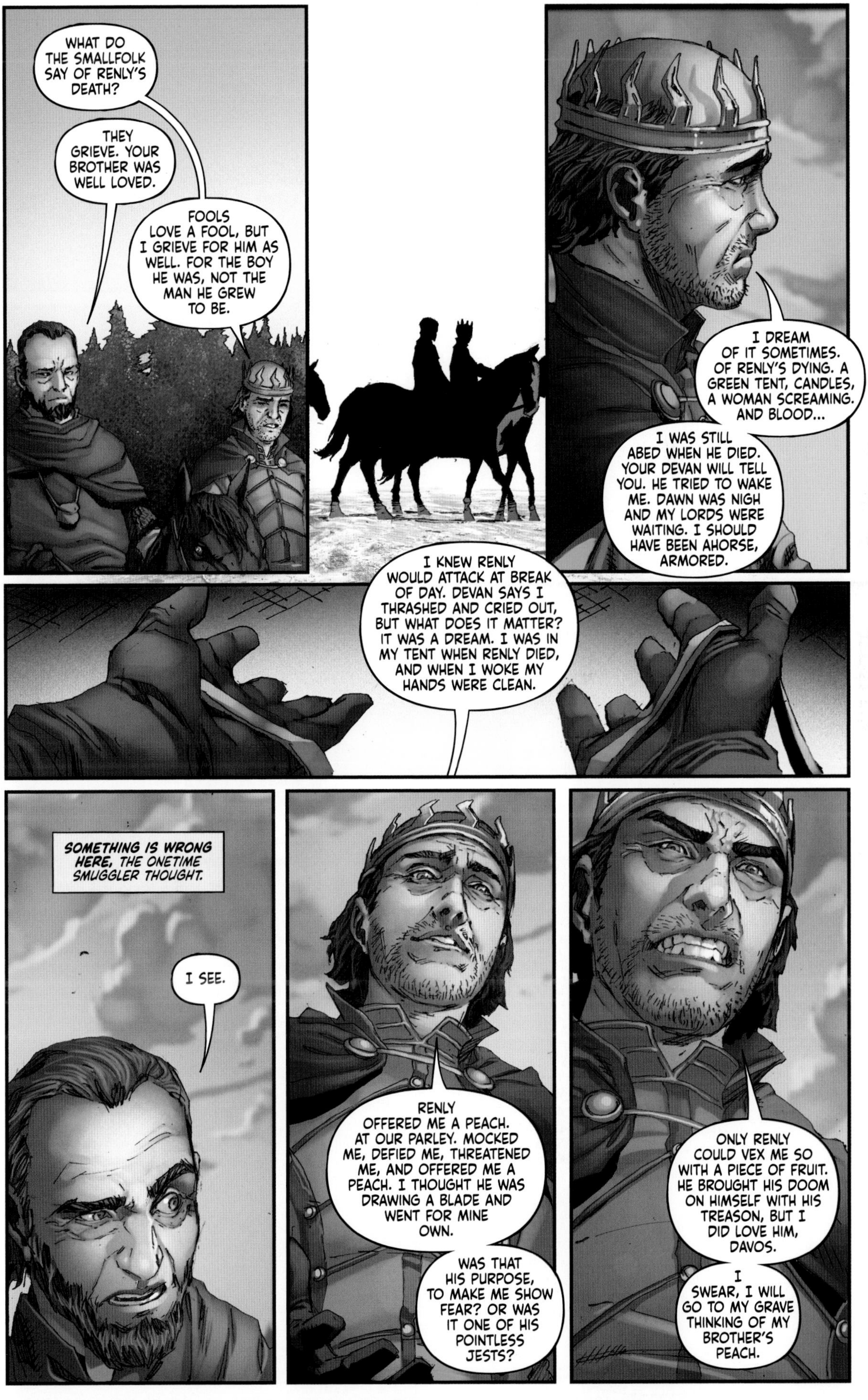
WHAT DO THE SMALLFOLK SAY OF RENLY'S DEATH?
THEY GRIEVE. YOUR BROTHER WAS WELL LOVED.
FOOLS LOVE A FOOL, BUT I GRIEVE FOR HIM AS WELL. FOR THE BOY HE WAS, NOT THE MAN HE GREW TO BE.
I DREAM OF IT SOMETIMES. OF RENLY'S DYING. A GREEN TENT, CANDLES, A WOMAN SCREAMING. AND BLOOD...
I WAS STILL ABED WHEN HE DIED. YOUR DEVAN WILL TELL YOU. HE TRIED TO WAKE ME. DAWN WAS NIGH AND MY LORDS WERE WAITING. I SHOULD HAVE BEEN AHORSE, ARMORED.
I KNEW RENLY WOULD ATTACK AT BREAK OF DAY. DEVAN SAYS I THRASHED AND CRIED OUT, BUT WHAT DOES IT MATTER? IT WAS A DREAM. I WAS IN MY TENT WHEN RENLY DIED, AND WHEN I WOKE MY HANDS WERE CLEAN.
SOMETHING IS WRONG HERE, THE ONETIME SMUGGLER THOUGHT.
I SEE.
RENLY OFFERED ME A PEACH. AT OUR PARLEY. MOCKED ME, DEFIED ME, THREATENED ME, AND OFFERED ME A PEACH. I THOUGHT HE WAS DRAWING A BLADE AND WENT FOR MINE OWN.
WAS THAT HIS PURPOSE, TO MAKE ME SHOW FEAR? OR WAS IT ONE OF HIS POINTLESS JESTS?
ONLY RENLY COULD VEX ME SO WITH A PIECE OF FRUIT. HE BROUGHT HIS DOOM ON HIMSELF WITH HIS TREASON, BUT I DID LOVE HIM, DAVOS.
I SWEAR, I WILL GO TO MY GRAVE THINKING OF MY BROTHER'S PEACH.

LET ME TELL YOU HOW IT WILL GO...

LORD VELARYON WILL URGE ME TO STORM THE CASTLE WALLS AT FIRST LIGHT, GRAPNELS AND SCALING LADDERS AGAINST ARROWS AND BOILING OIL.

ESTERMONT WILL FAVOR SETTLING DOWN TO STARVE THEM OUT, AS TYRELL AND REDWYNE ONCE TRIED WITH ME. THAT MIGHT TAKE A YEAR.

WHAT WOULD *YOU* HAVE ME DO, SMUGGLER?

STRIKE FOR KING'S LANDING AT ONCE.

SER CORTNAY DOES NOT HAVE THE POWER TO HARM YOU. THE LANNISTERS DO. A SIEGE WOULD TAKE TOO LONG, AND AN ASSAULT WOULD COST THOUSANDS OF LIVES WITH NO CERTAINTY OF SUCCESS.

AND THERE IS NO NEED. ONCE YOU DETHRONE JOFFREY, THIS CASTLE MUST COME TO YOU WITH ALL THE REST.

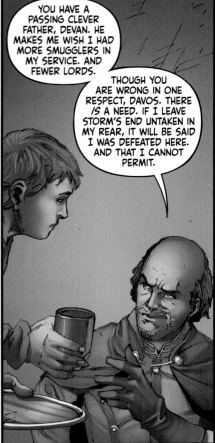

YOU HAVE A PASSING CLEVER FATHER, DEVAN. HE MAKES ME WISH I HAD MORE SMUGGLERS IN MY SERVICE. AND FEWER LORDS.

THOUGH YOU ARE WRONG IN ONE RESPECT, DAVOS. THERE *IS* A NEED. IF I LEAVE STORM'S END UNTAKEN IN MY REAR, IT WILL BE SAID I WAS DEFEATED HERE. AND THAT I CANNOT PERMIT.

MEN DO NOT LOVE ME AS THEY LOVED MY BROTHERS. THEY FOLLOW ME BECAUSE THEY FEAR ME...AND DEFEAT IS DEATH TO FEAR. THE CASTLE MUST FALL.

AYE, AND *QUICKLY*.

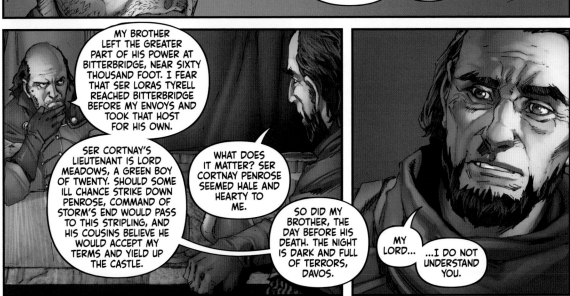

MY BROTHER LEFT THE GREATER PART OF HIS POWER AT BITTERBRIDGE, NEAR SIXTY THOUSAND FOOT. I FEAR THAT SER LORAS TYRELL REACHED BITTERBRIDGE BEFORE MY ENVOYS AND TOOK THAT HOST FOR HIS OWN.

SER CORTNAY'S LIEUTENANT IS LORD MEADOWS, A GREEN BOY OF TWENTY. SHOULD SOME ILL CHANCE STRIKE DOWN PENROSE, COMMAND OF STORM'S END WOULD PASS TO THIS STRIPLING, AND HIS COUSINS BELIEVE HE WOULD ACCEPT MY TERMS AND YIELD UP THE CASTLE.

WHAT DOES IT MATTER? SER CORTNAY PENROSE SEEMED HALE AND HEARTY TO ME.

SO DID MY BROTHER, THE DAY BEFORE HIS DEATH. THE NIGHT IS DARK AND FULL OF TERRORS, DAVOS.

MY LORD... ...I DO NOT UNDERSTAND YOU.

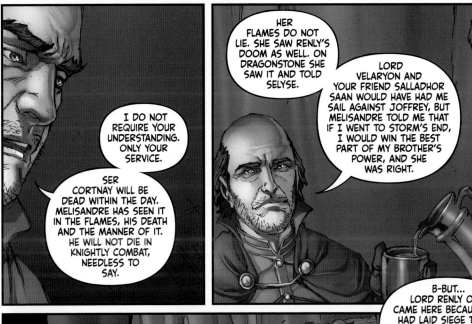

I DO NOT REQUIRE YOUR UNDERSTANDING. ONLY YOUR SERVICE.

SER CORTNAY WILL BE DEAD WITHIN THE DAY. MELISANDRE HAS SEEN IT IN THE FLAMES, HIS DEATH AND THE MANNER OF IT. HE WILL NOT DIE IN KNIGHTLY COMBAT, NEEDLESS TO SAY.

HER FLAMES DO NOT LIE. SHE SAW RENLY'S DOOM AS WELL. ON DRAGONSTONE SHE SAW IT AND TOLD SELYSE.

LORD VELARYON AND YOUR FRIEND SALLADHOR SAAN WOULD HAVE HAD ME SAIL AGAINST JOFFREY, BUT MELISANDRE TOLD ME THAT IF I WENT TO STORM'S END, I WOULD WIN THE BEST PART OF MY BROTHER'S POWER, AND SHE WAS RIGHT.

B-BUT... LORD RENLY ONLY CAME HERE BECAUSE YOU HAD LAID SIEGE TO THE CASTLE. HE WAS MARCHING TOWARD KING'S LANDING, AGAINST THE LANNISTERS. HE WOULD HAVE--

WAS, WOULD HAVE, WHAT IS THAT? HE CAME HERE WITH HIS BANNERS AND HIS PEACHES, TO HIS DOOM... AND IT WAS WELL FOR ME HE DID.

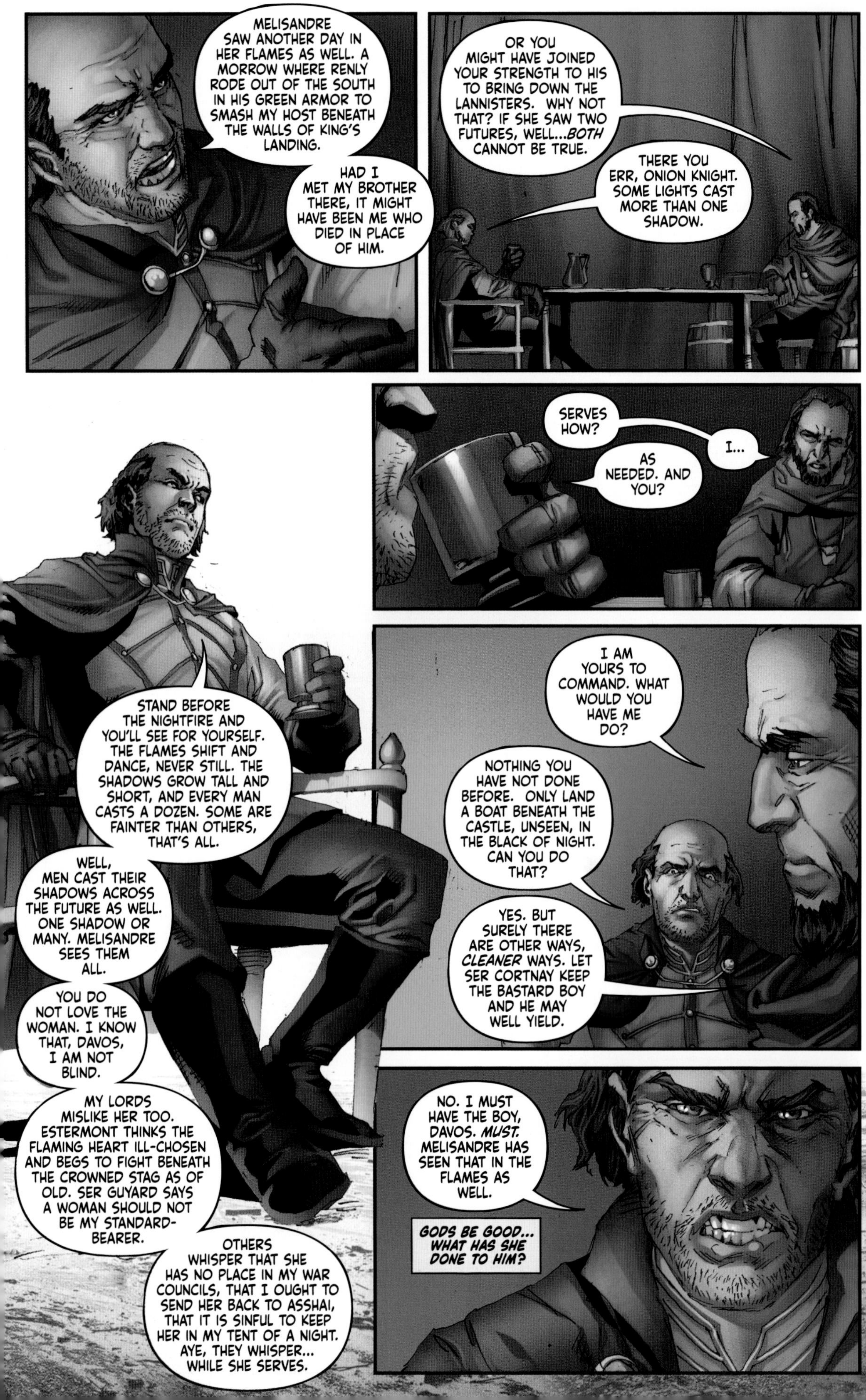
MELISANDRE SAW ANOTHER DAY IN HER FLAMES AS WELL. A MORROW WHERE RENLY RODE OUT OF THE SOUTH IN HIS GREEN ARMOR TO SMASH MY HOST BENEATH THE WALLS OF KING'S LANDING.
HAD I MET MY BROTHER THERE, IT MIGHT HAVE BEEN ME WHO DIED IN PLACE OF HIM.
OR YOU MIGHT HAVE JOINED YOUR STRENGTH TO HIS TO BRING DOWN THE LANNISTERS. WHY NOT THAT? IF SHE SAW TWO FUTURES, WELL...*BOTH* CANNOT BE TRUE.
THERE YOU ERR, ONION KNIGHT. SOME LIGHTS CAST MORE THAN ONE SHADOW.
STAND BEFORE THE NIGHTFIRE AND YOU'LL SEE FOR YOURSELF. THE FLAMES SHIFT AND DANCE, NEVER STILL. THE SHADOWS GROW TALL AND SHORT, AND EVERY MAN CASTS A DOZEN. SOME ARE FAINTER THAN OTHERS, THAT'S ALL.
WELL, MEN CAST THEIR SHADOWS ACROSS THE FUTURE AS WELL. ONE SHADOW OR MANY. MELISANDRE SEES THEM ALL.
YOU DO NOT LOVE THE WOMAN. I KNOW THAT, DAVOS, I AM NOT BLIND.
MY LORDS MISLIKE HER TOO. ESTERMONT THINKS THE FLAMING HEART ILL-CHOSEN AND BEGS TO FIGHT BENEATH THE CROWNED STAG AS OF OLD. SER GUYARD SAYS A WOMAN SHOULD NOT BE MY STANDARD-BEARER.
OTHERS WHISPER THAT SHE HAS NO PLACE IN MY WAR COUNCILS, THAT I OUGHT TO SEND HER BACK TO ASSHAI, THAT IT IS SINFUL TO KEEP HER IN MY TENT OF A NIGHT. AYE, THEY WHISPER... WHILE SHE SERVES.
SERVES HOW?
AS NEEDED. AND YOU?
I...
I AM YOURS TO COMMAND. WHAT WOULD YOU HAVE ME DO?
NOTHING YOU HAVE NOT DONE BEFORE. ONLY LAND A BOAT BENEATH THE CASTLE, UNSEEN, IN THE BLACK OF NIGHT. CAN YOU DO THAT?
YES. BUT SURELY THERE ARE OTHER WAYS, *CLEANER* WAYS. LET SER CORTNAY KEEP THE BASTARD BOY AND HE MAY WELL YIELD.
NO. I MUST HAVE THE BOY, DAVOS. *MUST.* MELISANDRE HAS SEEN THAT IN THE FLAMES AS WELL.
GODS BE GOOD... WHAT HAS SHE DONE TO HIM?

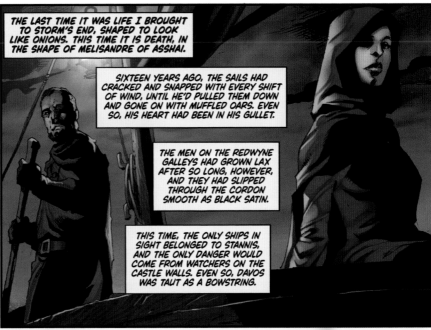

THE LAST TIME IT WAS LIFE I BROUGHT TO STORM'S END, SHAPED TO LOOK LIKE ONIONS. THIS TIME IT IS DEATH, IN THE SHAPE OF MELISANDRE OF ASSHAI.

SIXTEEN YEARS AGO, THE SAILS HAD CRACKED AND SNAPPED WITH EVERY SHIFT OF WIND, UNTIL HE'D PULLED THEM DOWN AND GONE ON WITH MUFFLED OARS. EVEN SO, HIS HEART HAD BEEN IN HIS GULLET.

THE MEN ON THE REDWYNE GALLEYS HAD GROWN LAX AFTER SO LONG, HOWEVER, AND THEY HAD SLIPPED THROUGH THE CORDON SMOOTH AS BLACK SATIN.

THIS TIME, THE ONLY SHIPS IN SIGHT BELONGED TO STANNIS, AND THE ONLY DANGER WOULD COME FROM WATCHERS ON THE CASTLE WALLS. EVEN SO, DAVOS WAS TAUT AS A BOWSTRING.

I CAN SMELL THE FEAR ON YOU, SER KNIGHT.

SOMEONE ONCE TOLD ME THE NIGHT IS DARK AND FULL OF TERRORS. AND TONIGHT I AM NO KNIGHT. TONIGHT I AM DAVOS THE SMUGGLER AGAIN.

WOULD THAT YOU WERE AN ONION.

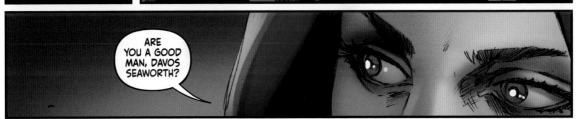

ARE YOU A GOOD MAN, DAVOS SEAWORTH?

WOULD A GOOD MAN BE DOING THIS?

I AM A MAN. I AM KIND TO MY WIFE, BUT I HAVE KNOWN OTHER WOMEN. I HAVE TRIED TO BE A FATHER TO MY SONS, TO HELP MAKE THEM A PLACE IN THIS WORLD...

AYE, I'VE BROKEN LAWS, BUT I NEVER FELT EVIL UNTIL TONIGHT. I WOULD SAY MY PARTS ARE MIXED, M'LADY. GOOD AND BAD.

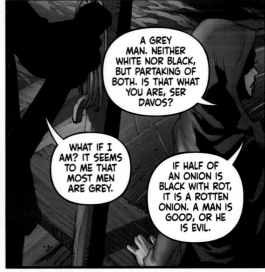

A GREY MAN. NEITHER WHITE NOR BLACK, BUT PARTAKING OF BOTH. IS THAT WHAT YOU ARE, SER DAVOS?

WHAT IF I AM? IT SEEMS TO ME THAT MOST MEN ARE GREY.

IF HALF OF AN ONION IS BLACK WITH ROT, IT IS A ROTTEN ONION. A MAN IS GOOD, OR HE IS EVIL.

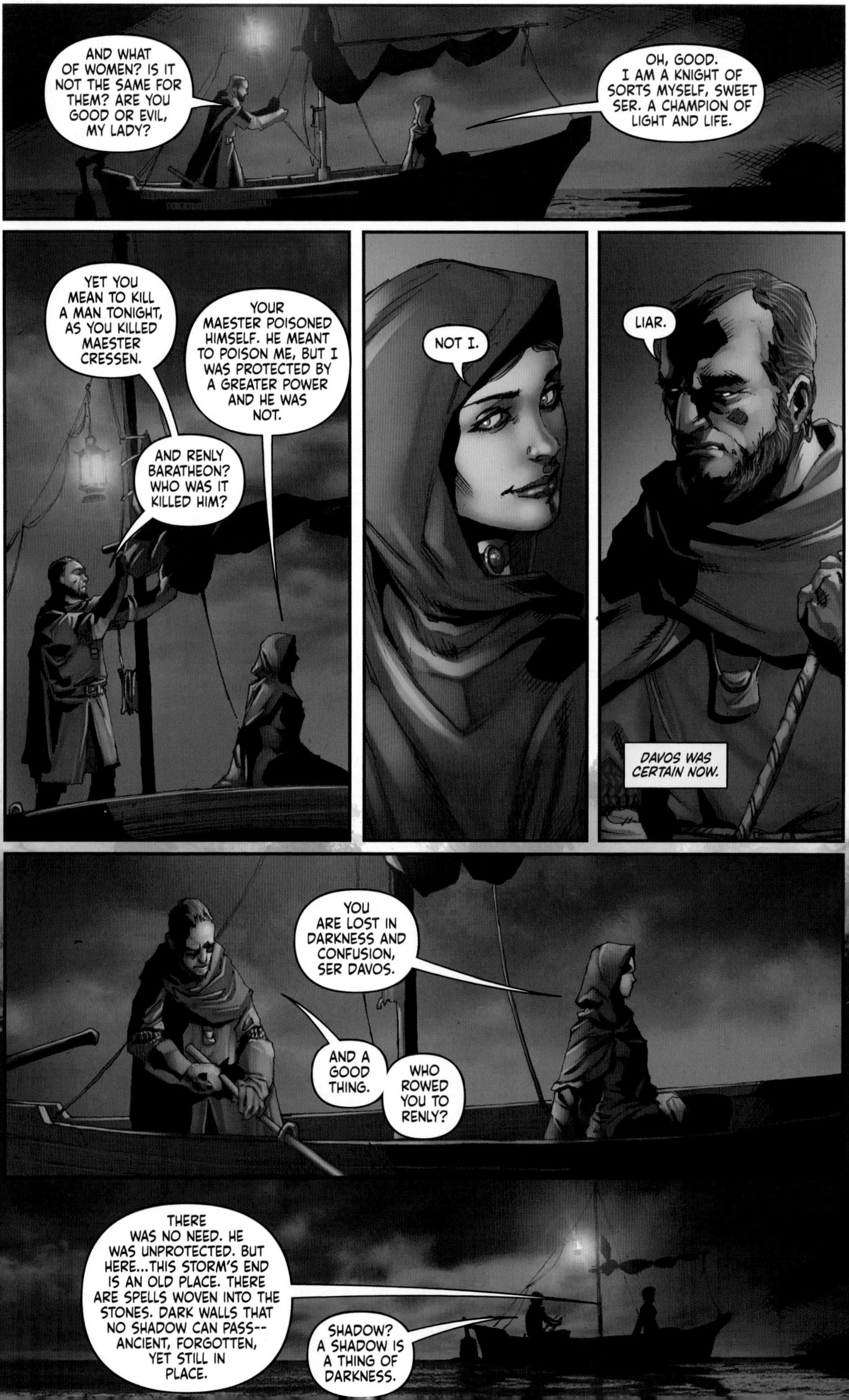
AND WHAT OF WOMEN? IS IT NOT THE SAME FOR THEM? ARE YOU GOOD OR EVIL, MY LADY?
OH, GOOD. I AM A KNIGHT OF SORTS MYSELF, SWEET SER. A CHAMPION OF LIGHT AND LIFE.
YET YOU MEAN TO KILL A MAN TONIGHT, AS YOU KILLED MAESTER CRESSEN.
YOUR MAESTER POISONED HIMSELF. HE MEANT TO POISON ME, BUT I WAS PROTECTED BY A GREATER POWER AND HE WAS NOT.
AND RENLY BARATHEON? WHO WAS IT KILLED HIM?
NOT I.
LIAR.
DAVOS WAS CERTAIN NOW.
YOU ARE LOST IN DARKNESS AND CONFUSION, SER DAVOS.
AND A GOOD THING.
WHO ROWED YOU TO RENLY?
THERE WAS NO NEED. HE WAS UNPROTECTED. BUT HERE...THIS STORM'S END IS AN OLD PLACE. THERE ARE SPELLS WOVEN INTO THE STONES. DARK WALLS THAT NO SHADOW CAN PASS--ANCIENT, FORGOTTEN, YET STILL IN PLACE.
SHADOW? A SHADOW IS A THING OF DARKNESS.

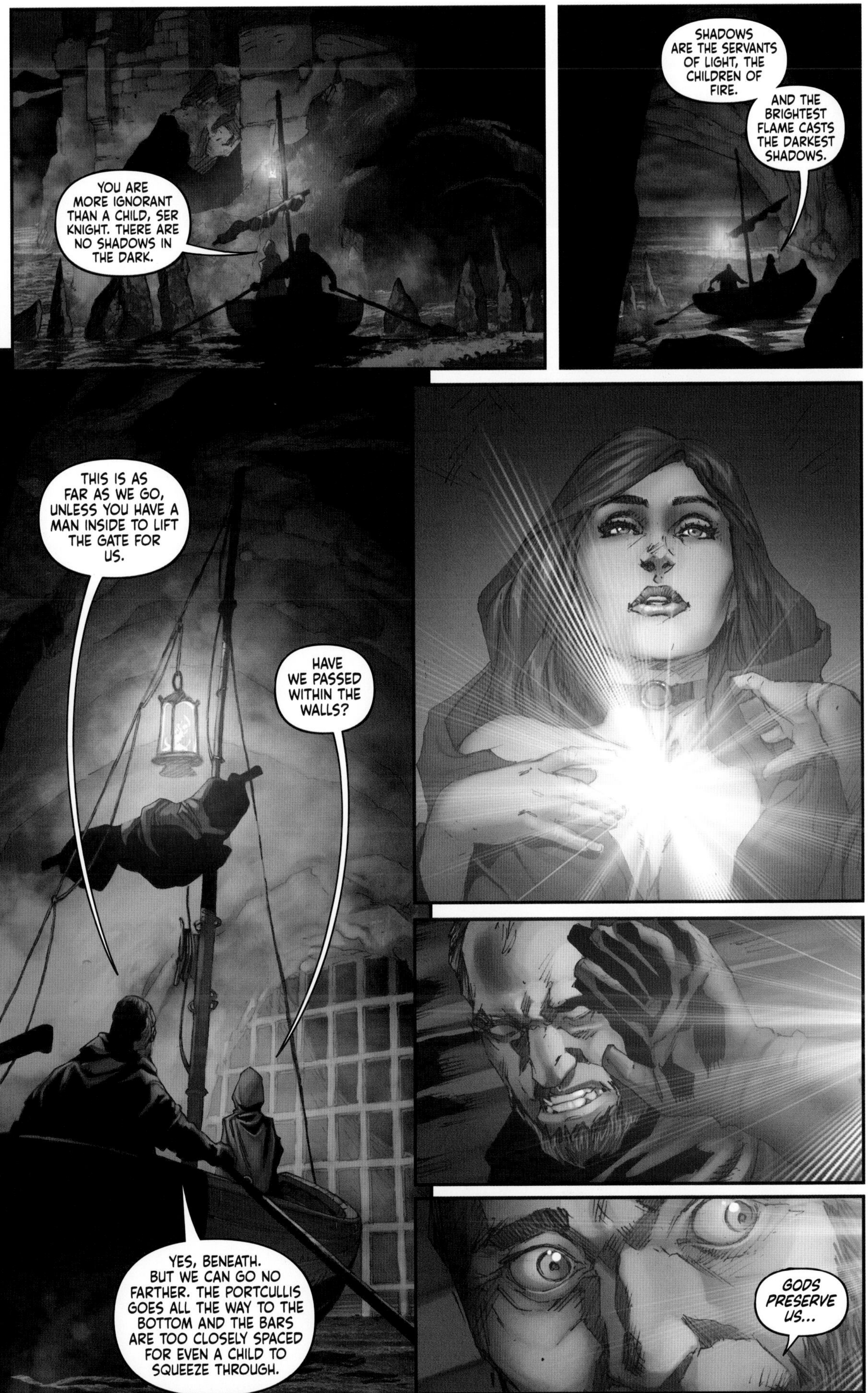
YOU ARE MORE IGNORANT THAN A CHILD, SER KNIGHT. THERE ARE NO SHADOWS IN THE DARK.
SHADOWS ARE THE SERVANTS OF LIGHT, THE CHILDREN OF FIRE.
AND THE BRIGHTEST FLAME CASTS THE DARKEST SHADOWS.
THIS IS AS FAR AS WE GO, UNLESS YOU HAVE A MAN INSIDE TO LIFT THE GATE FOR US.
HAVE WE PASSED WITHIN THE WALLS?
YES, BENEATH. BUT WE CAN GO NO FARTHER. THE PORTCULLIS GOES ALL THE WAY TO THE BOTTOM AND THE BARS ARE TOO CLOSELY SPACED FOR EVEN A CHILD TO SQUEEZE THROUGH.
GODS PRESERVE US...

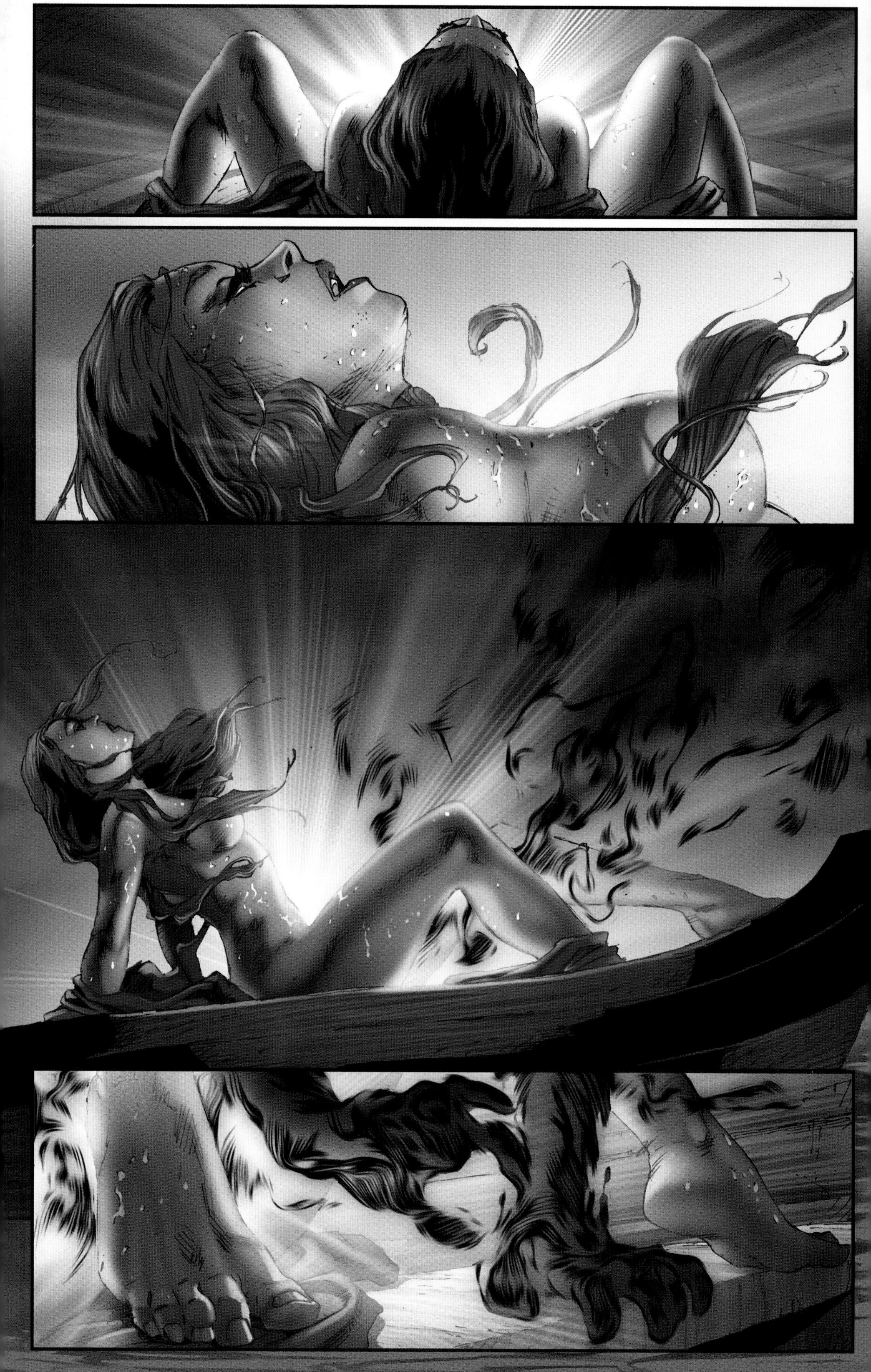

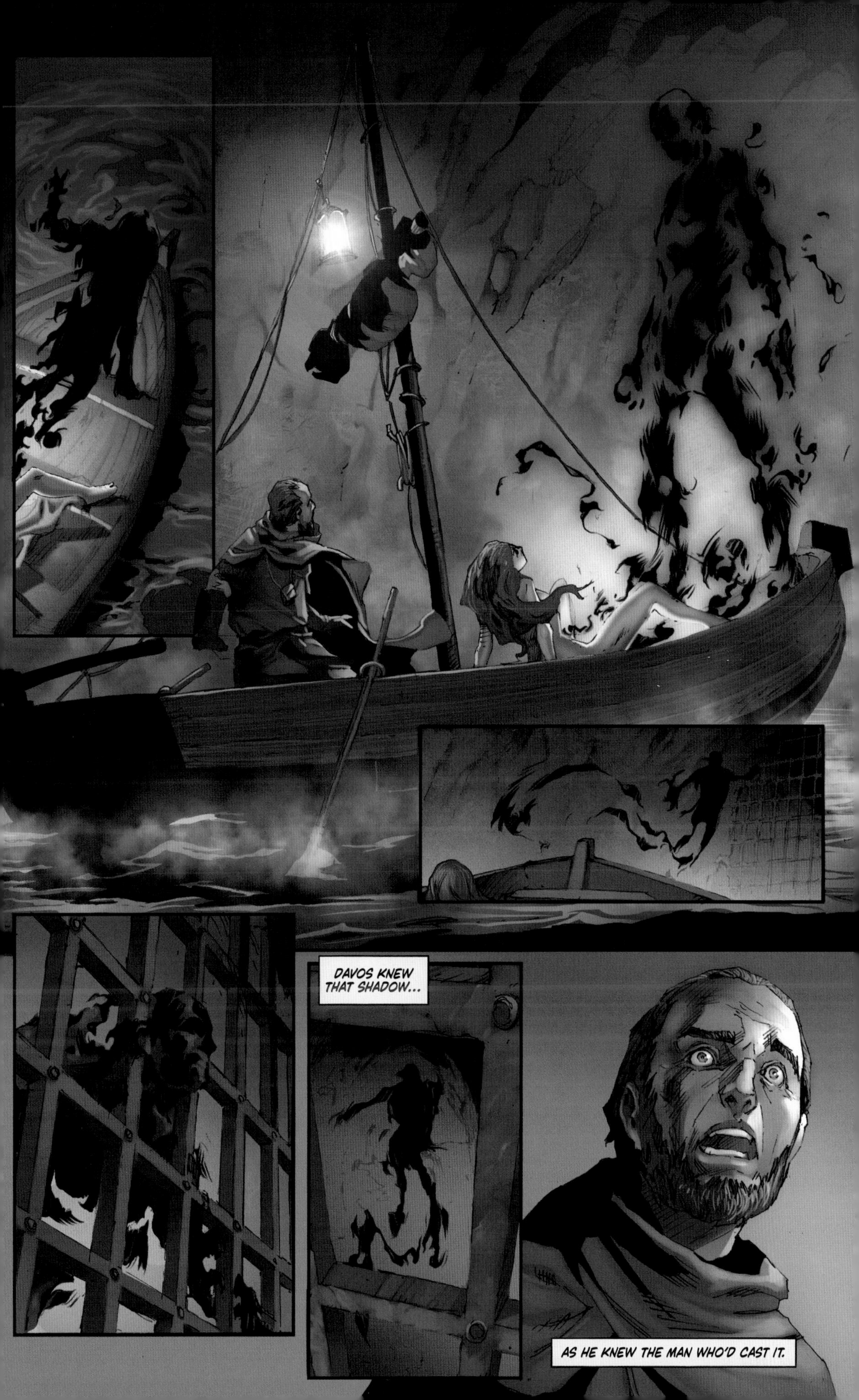
DAVOS KNEW THAT SHADOW...
AS HE KNEW THE MAN WHO'D CAST IT.

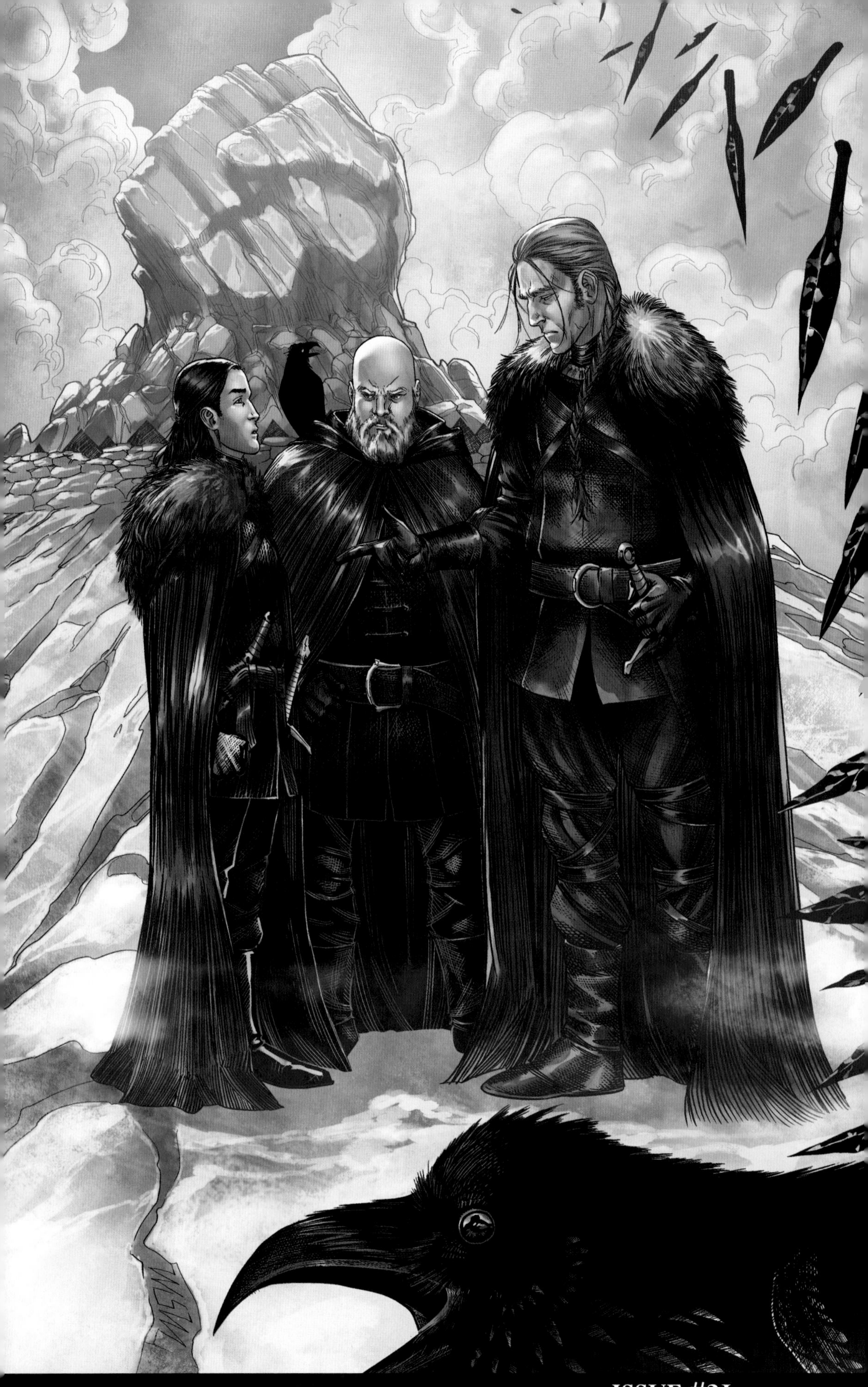

ISSUE #21

TYRION

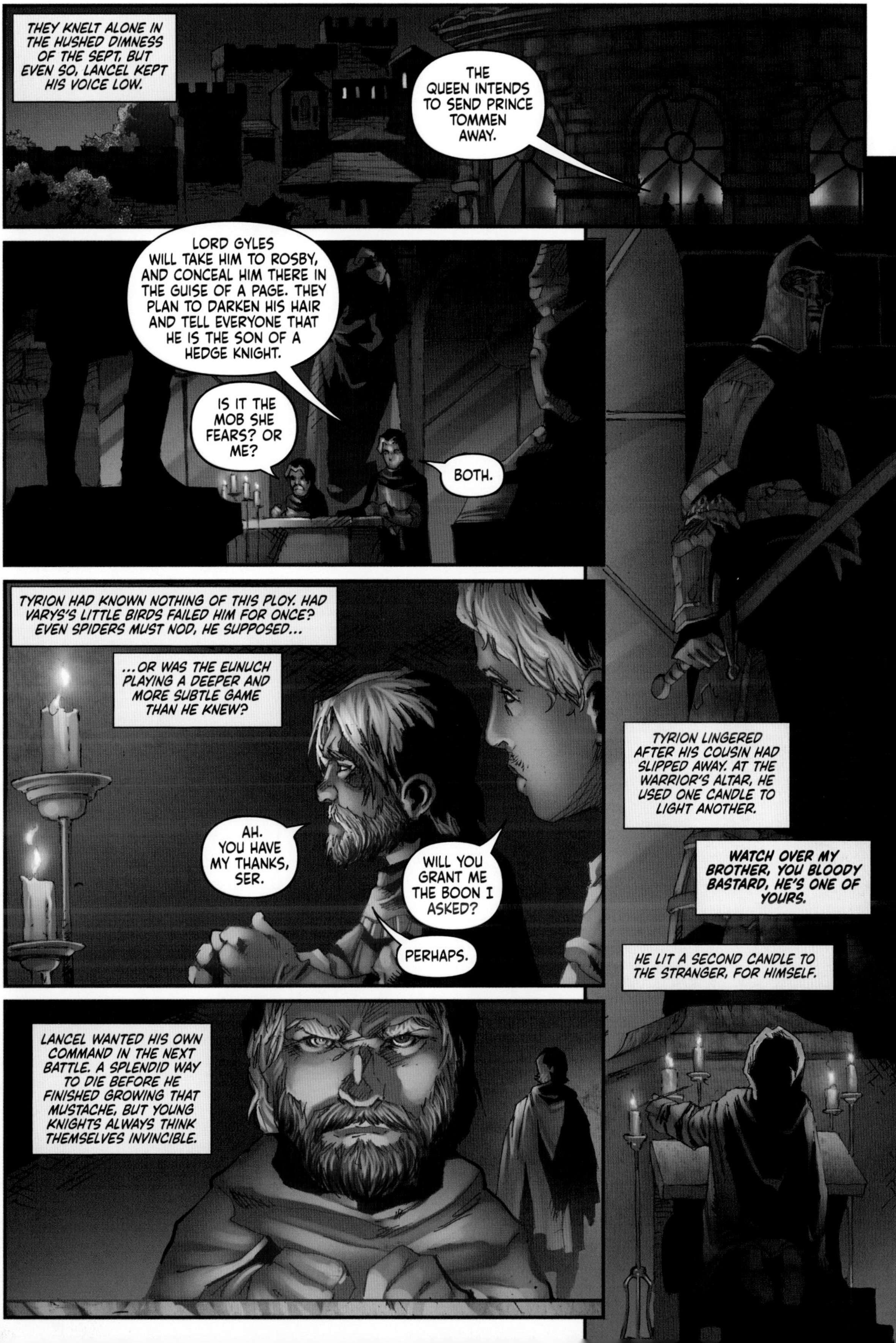

THEY KNELT ALONE IN THE HUSHED DIMNESS OF THE SEPT, BUT EVEN SO, LANCEL KEPT HIS VOICE LOW.
THE QUEEN INTENDS TO SEND PRINCE TOMMEN AWAY.
LORD GYLES WILL TAKE HIM TO ROSBY, AND CONCEAL HIM THERE IN THE GUISE OF A PAGE. THEY PLAN TO DARKEN HIS HAIR AND TELL EVERYONE THAT HE IS THE SON OF A HEDGE KNIGHT.
IS IT THE MOB SHE FEARS? OR ME?
BOTH.
TYRION HAD KNOWN NOTHING OF THIS PLOY. HAD VARYS'S LITTLE BIRDS FAILED HIM FOR ONCE? EVEN SPIDERS MUST NOD, HE SUPPOSED...
...OR WAS THE EUNUCH PLAYING A DEEPER AND MORE SUBTLE GAME THAN HE KNEW?
AH. YOU HAVE MY THANKS, SER.
WILL YOU GRANT ME THE BOON I ASKED?
PERHAPS.
LANCEL WANTED HIS OWN COMMAND IN THE NEXT BATTLE. A SPLENDID WAY TO DIE BEFORE HE FINISHED GROWING THAT MUSTACHE, BUT YOUNG KNIGHTS ALWAYS THINK THEMSELVES INVINCIBLE.
TYRION LINGERED AFTER HIS COUSIN HAD SLIPPED AWAY. AT THE WARRIOR'S ALTAR, HE USED ONE CANDLE TO LIGHT ANOTHER.
WATCH OVER MY BROTHER, YOU BLOODY BASTARD, HE'S ONE OF YOURS.
HE LIT A SECOND CANDLE TO THE STRANGER, FOR HIMSELF.

TAKE THIS TO SER JACELYN BYWATER.

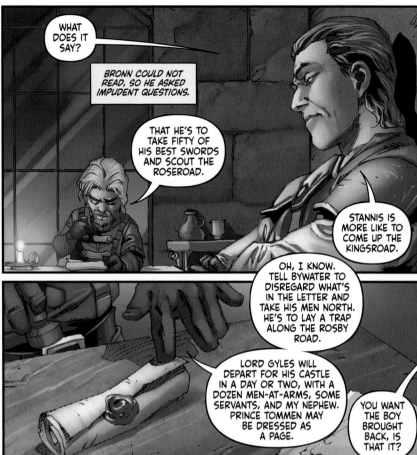

WHAT DOES IT SAY?

BRONN COULD NOT READ, SO HE ASKED IMPUDENT QUESTIONS.

THAT HE'S TO TAKE FIFTY OF HIS BEST SWORDS AND SCOUT THE ROSEROAD.

STANNIS IS MORE LIKE TO COME UP THE KINGSROAD.

OH, I KNOW. TELL BYWATER TO DISREGARD WHAT'S IN THE LETTER AND TAKE HIS MEN NORTH. HE'S TO LAY A TRAP ALONG THE ROSBY ROAD.

LORD GYLES WILL DEPART FOR HIS CASTLE IN A DAY OR TWO, WITH A DOZEN MEN-AT-ARMS, SOME SERVANTS, AND MY NEPHEW. PRINCE TOMMEN MAY BE DRESSED AS A PAGE.

YOU WANT THE BOY BROUGHT BACK, IS THAT IT?

NO, I WANT HIM TAKEN ON TO THE CASTLE.

REMOVING THE BOY FROM THE CITY WAS ONE OF HIS SISTER'S BETTER NOTIONS.

LORD GYLES IS TOO SICKLY TO RUN AND TOO CRAVEN TO FIGHT. HE'LL COMMAND HIS CASTELLAN TO OPEN THE GATES.

ONCE INSIDE THE WALLS, BYWATER IS TO EXPEL THE GARRISON AND HOLD TOMMEN THERE SAFE. ASK HIM HOW HE LIKES THE SOUND OF *LORD* BYWATER.

LORD BRONN WOULD SOUND BETTER. I COULD GRAB THE BOY FOR YOU JUST AS WELL. I'LL DANDLE HIM ON MY KNEE AND SING HIM NURSERY SONGS IF THERE'S A LORDSHIP IN IT.

I NEED YOU HERE.

AND I DON'T TRUST YOU WITH MY NEPHEW.

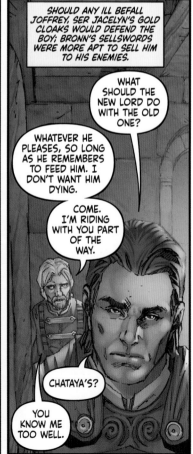

SHOULD ANY ILL BEFALL JOFFREY, SER JACELYN'S GOLD CLOAKS WOULD DEFEND THE BOY; BRONN'S SELLSWORDS WERE MORE APT TO SELL HIM TO HIS ENEMIES.

WHAT SHOULD THE NEW LORD DO WITH THE OLD ONE?

WHATEVER HE PLEASES, SO LONG AS HE REMEMBERS TO FEED HIM. I DON'T WANT HIM DYING.

COME. I'M RIDING WITH YOU PART OF THE WAY.

CHATAYA'S?

YOU KNOW ME TOO WELL.

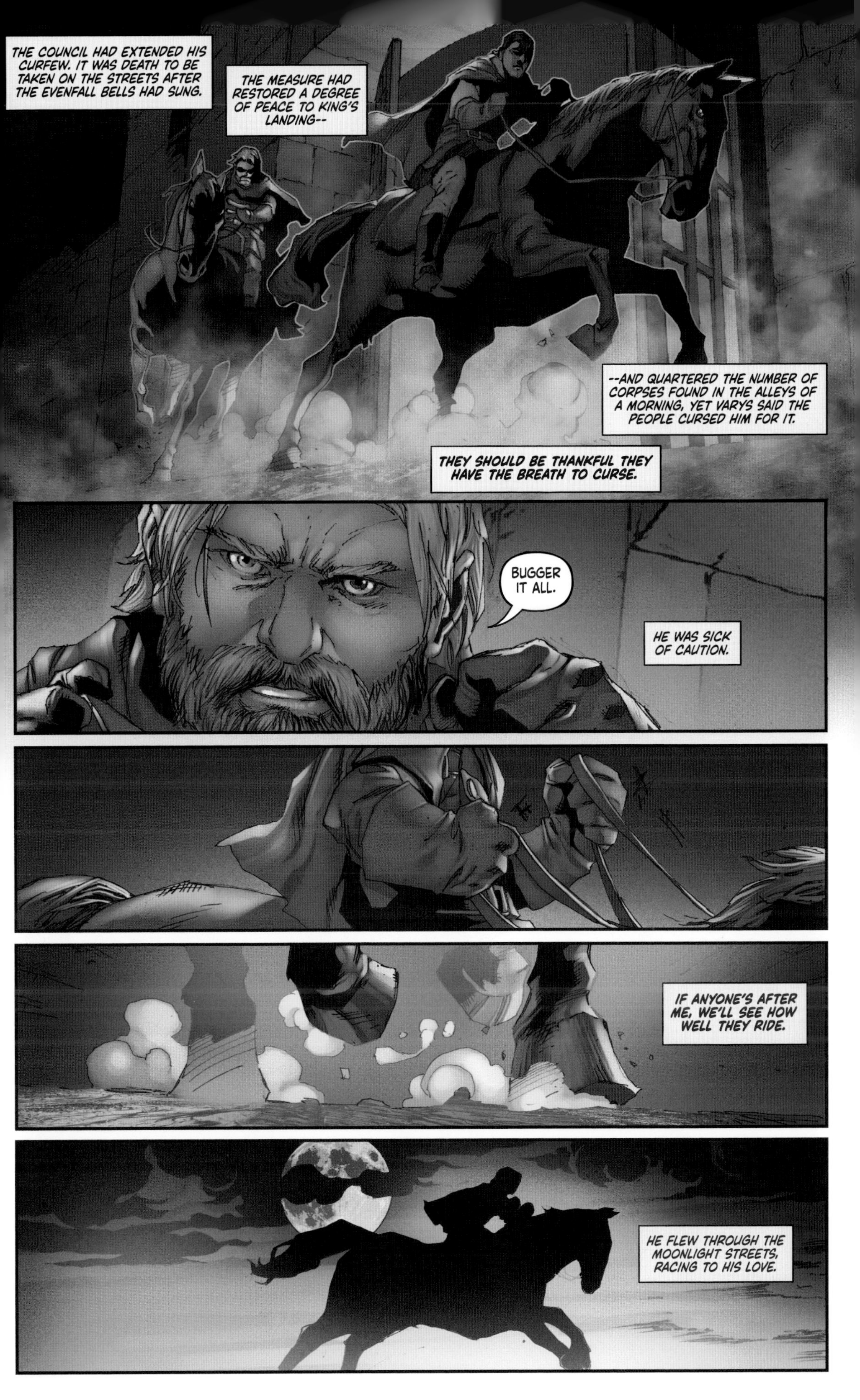
THE COUNCIL HAD EXTENDED HIS CURFEW. IT WAS DEATH TO BE TAKEN ON THE STREETS AFTER THE EVENFALL BELLS HAD SUNG.
THE MEASURE HAD RESTORED A DEGREE OF PEACE TO KING'S LANDING--
--AND QUARTERED THE NUMBER OF CORPSES FOUND IN THE ALLEYS OF A MORNING, YET VARYS SAID THE PEOPLE CURSED HIM FOR IT.
THEY SHOULD BE THANKFUL THEY HAVE THE BREATH TO CURSE.
BUGGER IT ALL.
HE WAS SICK OF CAUTION.
IF ANYONE'S AFTER ME, WE'LL SEE HOW WELL THEY RIDE.
HE FLEW THROUGH THE MOONLIGHT STREETS, RACING TO HIS LOVE.

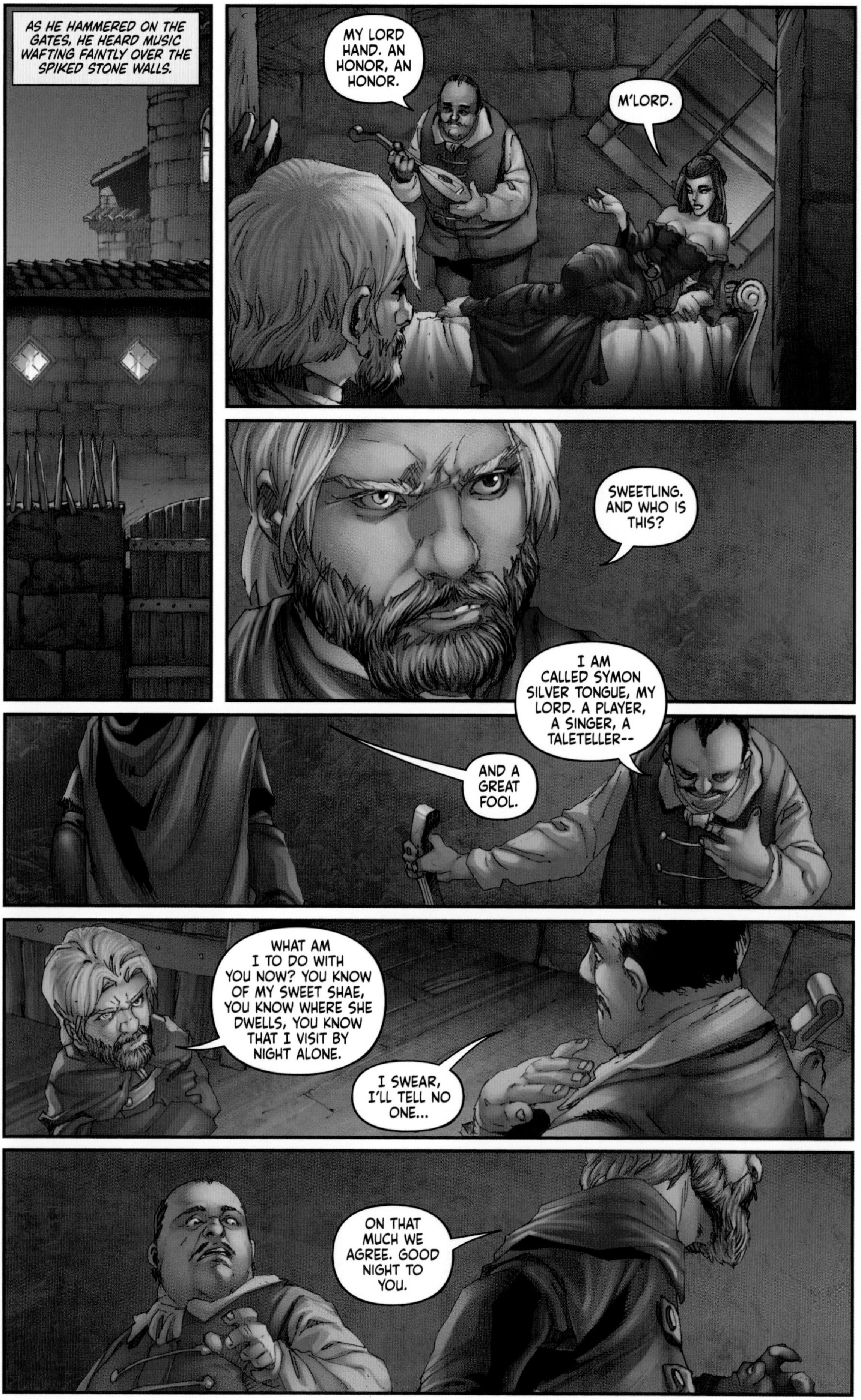
AS HE HAMMERED ON THE GATES, HE HEARD MUSIC WAFTING FAINTLY OVER THE SPIKED STONE WALLS.
MY LORD HAND. AN HONOR, AN HONOR.
M'LORD.
SWEETLING. AND WHO IS THIS?
I AM CALLED SYMON SILVER TONGUE, MY LORD. A PLAYER, A SINGER, A TALETELLER--
AND A GREAT FOOL.
WHAT AM I TO DO WITH YOU NOW? YOU KNOW OF MY SWEET SHAE, YOU KNOW WHERE SHE DWELLS, YOU KNOW THAT I VISIT BY NIGHT ALONE.
I SWEAR, I'LL TELL NO ONE...
ON THAT MUCH WE AGREE. GOOD NIGHT TO YOU.

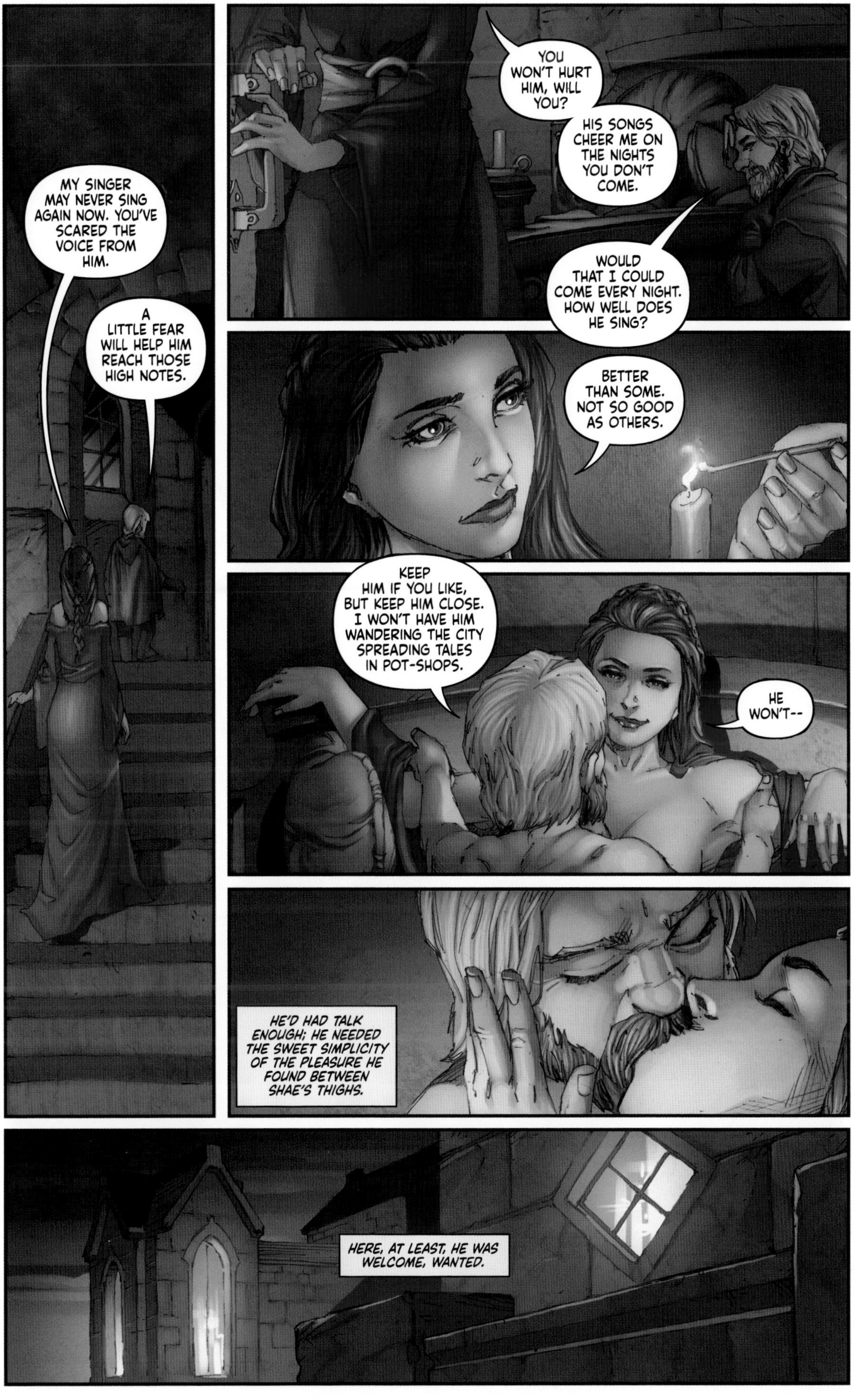
MY SINGER MAY NEVER SING AGAIN NOW. YOU'VE SCARED THE VOICE FROM HIM.
A LITTLE FEAR WILL HELP HIM REACH THOSE HIGH NOTES.
YOU WON'T HURT HIM, WILL YOU?
HIS SONGS CHEER ME ON THE NIGHTS YOU DON'T COME.
WOULD THAT I COULD COME EVERY NIGHT. HOW WELL DOES HE SING?
BETTER THAN SOME. NOT SO GOOD AS OTHERS.
KEEP HIM IF YOU LIKE, BUT KEEP HIM CLOSE. I WON'T HAVE HIM WANDERING THE CITY SPREADING TALES IN POT-SHOPS.
HE WON'T--
HE'D HAD TALK ENOUGH; HE NEEDED THE SWEET SIMPLICITY OF THE PLEASURE HE FOUND BETWEEN SHAE'S THIGHS.
HERE, AT LEAST, HE WAS WELCOME, WANTED.

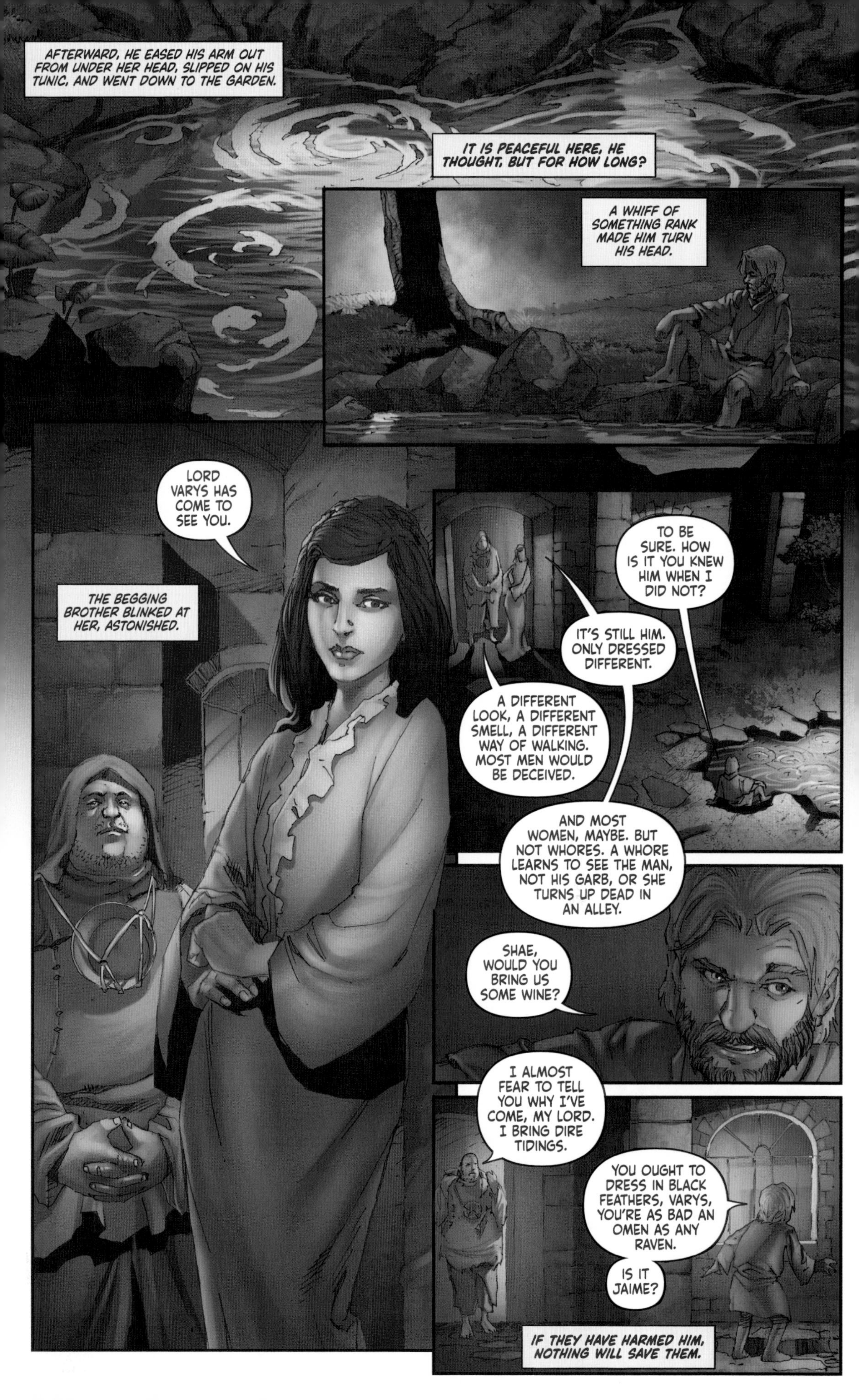
AFTERWARD, HE EASED HIS ARM OUT FROM UNDER HER HEAD, SLIPPED ON HIS TUNIC, AND WENT DOWN TO THE GARDEN.
IT IS PEACEFUL HERE, HE THOUGHT, BUT FOR HOW LONG?
A WHIFF OF SOMETHING RANK MADE HIM TURN HIS HEAD.
LORD VARYS HAS COME TO SEE YOU.
THE BEGGING BROTHER BLINKED AT HER, ASTONISHED.
TO BE SURE. HOW IS IT YOU KNEW HIM WHEN I DID NOT?
IT'S STILL HIM. ONLY DRESSED DIFFERENT.
A DIFFERENT LOOK, A DIFFERENT SMELL, A DIFFERENT WAY OF WALKING. MOST MEN WOULD BE DECEIVED.
AND MOST WOMEN, MAYBE. BUT NOT WHORES. A WHORE LEARNS TO SEE THE MAN, NOT HIS GARB, OR SHE TURNS UP DEAD IN AN ALLEY.
SHAE, WOULD YOU BRING US SOME WINE?
I ALMOST FEAR TO TELL YOU WHY I'VE COME, MY LORD. I BRING DIRE TIDINGS.
YOU OUGHT TO DRESS IN BLACK FEATHERS, VARYS, YOU'RE AS BAD AN OMEN AS ANY RAVEN.
IS IT JAIME?
IF THEY HAVE HARMED HIM, NOTHING WILL SAVE THEM.

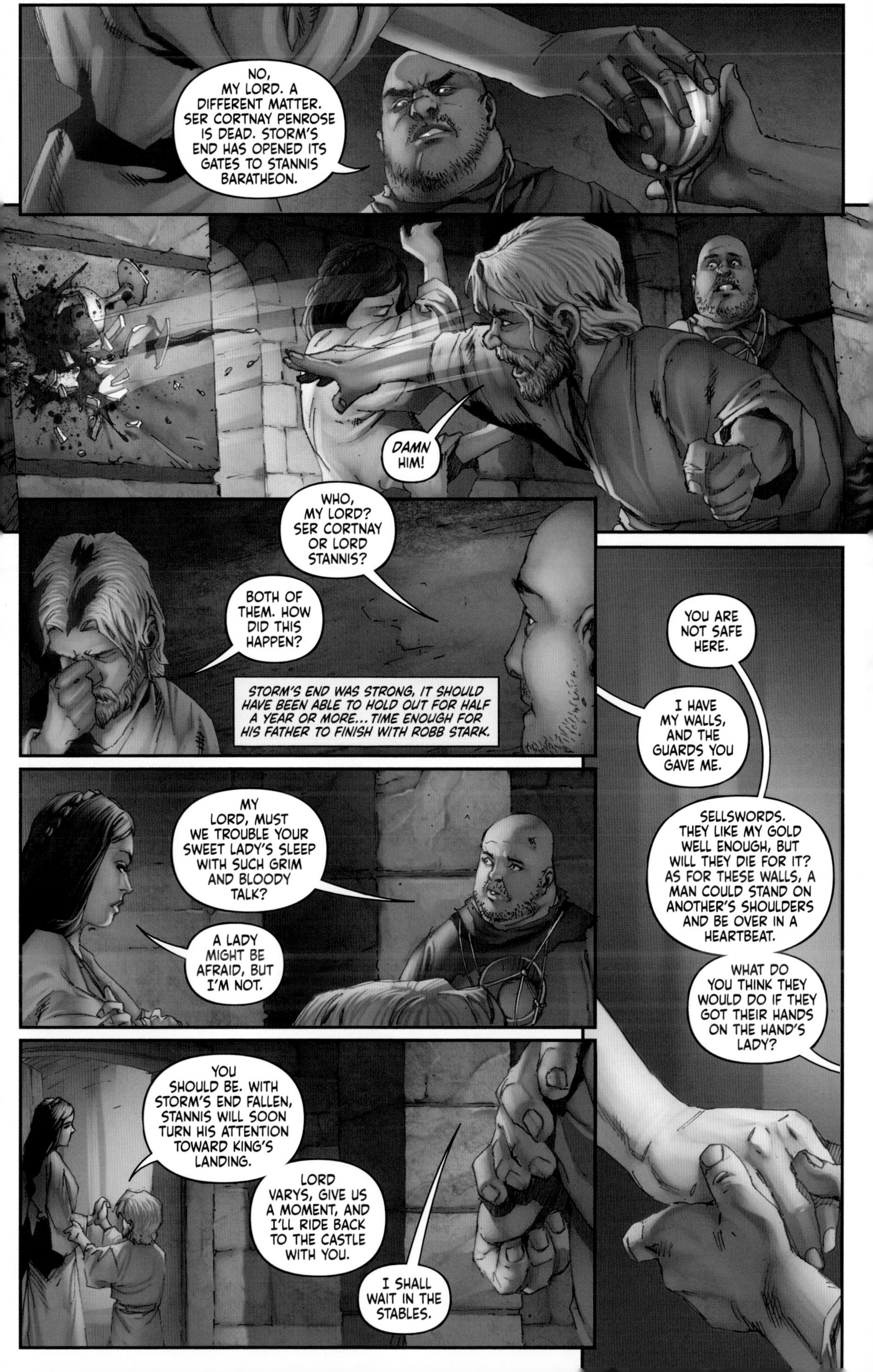
NO, MY LORD. A DIFFERENT MATTER. SER CORTNAY PENROSE IS DEAD. STORM'S END HAS OPENED ITS GATES TO STANNIS BARATHEON.
DAMN HIM!
WHO, MY LORD? SER CORTNAY OR LORD STANNIS?
BOTH OF THEM. HOW DID THIS HAPPEN?
STORM'S END WAS STRONG, IT SHOULD HAVE BEEN ABLE TO HOLD OUT FOR HALF A YEAR OR MORE...TIME ENOUGH FOR HIS FATHER TO FINISH WITH ROBB STARK.
MY LORD, MUST WE TROUBLE YOUR SWEET LADY'S SLEEP WITH SUCH GRIM AND BLOODY TALK?
A LADY MIGHT BE AFRAID, BUT I'M NOT.
YOU SHOULD BE. WITH STORM'S END FALLEN, STANNIS WILL SOON TURN HIS ATTENTION TOWARD KING'S LANDING.
LORD VARYS, GIVE US A MOMENT, AND I'LL RIDE BACK TO THE CASTLE WITH YOU.
I SHALL WAIT IN THE STABLES.
YOU ARE NOT SAFE HERE.
I HAVE MY WALLS, AND THE GUARDS YOU GAVE ME.
SELLSWORDS. THEY LIKE MY GOLD WELL ENOUGH, BUT WILL THEY DIE FOR IT? AS FOR THESE WALLS, A MAN COULD STAND ON ANOTHER'S SHOULDERS AND BE OVER IN A HEARTBEAT.
WHAT DO YOU THINK THEY WOULD DO IF THEY GOT THEIR HANDS ON THE HAND'S LADY?

THE HAND'S WHORE, YOU MEAN?

THOUGH I WOULD BE YOUR LADY, M'LORD. I'D WEAR YOUR JEWELS AND HOLD YOUR HAND AND SIT BY YOU AT FEASTS. I COULD GIVE YOU SONS, I KNOW I COULD...AND I VOW I'D NEVER SHAME YOU.

MY LOVE FOR YOU SHAMES ME ENOUGH.

A SWEET DREAM, SHAE. NOW PUT IT ASIDE, I BEG YOU. IT CAN NEVER BE.

BECAUSE OF THE QUEEN? I'M NOT AFRAID OF HER EITHER.

I AM.

THEN KILL HER AND BE DONE WITH IT. IT'S NOT AS IF THERE WAS ANY LOVE BETWEEN YOU.

SHE'S MY SISTER. THE MAN WHO KILLS HIS OWN BLOOD IS CURSED FOREVER IN THE SIGHT OF GODS AND MEN. MOREOVER, MY FATHER AND BROTHER HOLD HER DEAR.

I CAN SCHEME WITH ANY MAN IN THE SEVEN KINGDOMS, BUT THE GODS HAVE NOT EQUIPPED ME TO FACE JAIME WITH SWORDS IN HAND.

I HAVE...WELL, CALL IT THE SEED OF A PLAN. I THINK I MIGHT BE ABLE TO BRING YOU INTO THE CASTLE KITCHENS.

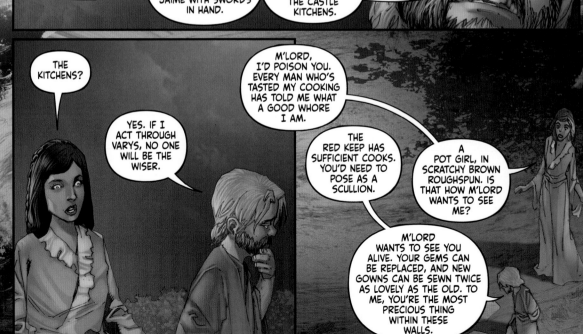

THE KITCHENS?

YES. IF I ACT THROUGH VARYS, NO ONE WILL BE THE WISER.

M'LORD, I'D POISON YOU. EVERY MAN WHO'S TASTED MY COOKING HAS TOLD ME WHAT A GOOD WHORE I AM.

THE RED KEEP HAS SUFFICIENT COOKS. YOU'D NEED TO POSE AS A SCULLION.

A POT GIRL, IN SCRATCHY BROWN ROUGHSPUN. IS THAT HOW M'LORD WANTS TO SEE ME?

M'LORD WANTS TO SEE YOU ALIVE. YOUR GEMS CAN BE REPLACED, AND NEW GOWNS CAN BE SEWN TWICE AS LOVELY AS THE OLD. TO ME, YOU'RE THE MOST PRECIOUS THING WITHIN THESE WALLS.

THE RED KEEP IS NOT SAFE EITHER, BUT IT'S A DEAL SAFER THAN HERE. I WANT YOU THERE.

IN THE KITCHENS. SCOURING POTS.

MY FATHER MADE ME HIS KITCHEN WENCH. THAT WAS WHY I RAN OFF.

YOU TOLD ME YOU RAN OFF BECAUSE YOUR FATHER MADE YOU HIS WHORE.

THAT TOO. I DIDN'T LIKE SCOURING HIS POTS NO MORE THAN I LIKED HIS COCK IN ME.

WHY CAN'T YOU KEEP ME IN YOUR TOWER? HALF THE LORDS AT COURT KEEP BEDWARMERS.

I WAS EXPRESSLY FORBIDDEN TO TAKE YOU TO COURT.

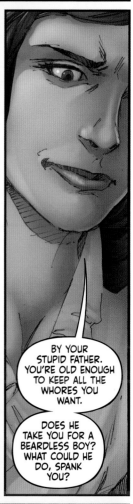

BY YOUR STUPID FATHER. YOU'RE OLD ENOUGH TO KEEP ALL THE WHORES YOU WANT.

DOES HE TAKE YOU FOR A BEARDLESS BOY? WHAT COULD HE DO, SPANK YOU?

DAMN YOU. *DAMN YOU. NEVER MOCK* ME. NOT *YOU.*

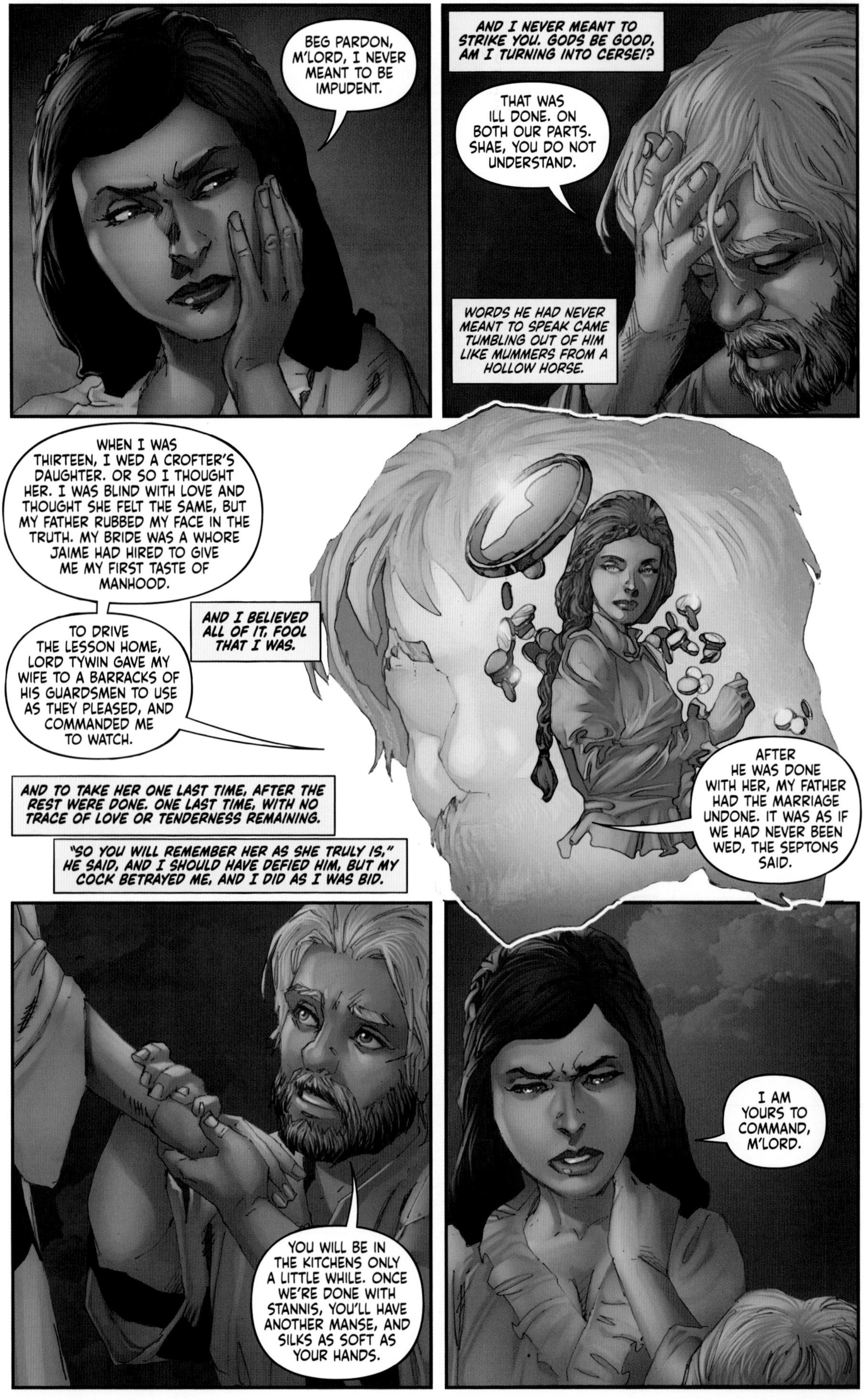
BEG PARDON, M'LORD, I NEVER MEANT TO BE IMPUDENT.
AND I NEVER MEANT TO STRIKE YOU. GODS BE GOOD, AM I TURNING INTO CERSEI?
THAT WAS ILL DONE. ON BOTH OUR PARTS. SHAE, YOU DO NOT UNDERSTAND.
WORDS HE HAD NEVER MEANT TO SPEAK CAME TUMBLING OUT OF HIM LIKE MUMMERS FROM A HOLLOW HORSE.
WHEN I WAS THIRTEEN, I WED A CROFTER'S DAUGHTER. OR SO I THOUGHT HER. I WAS BLIND WITH LOVE AND THOUGHT SHE FELT THE SAME, BUT MY FATHER RUBBED MY FACE IN THE TRUTH. MY BRIDE WAS A WHORE JAIME HAD HIRED TO GIVE ME MY FIRST TASTE OF MANHOOD.
AND I BELIEVED ALL OF IT, FOOL THAT I WAS.
TO DRIVE THE LESSON HOME, LORD TYWIN GAVE MY WIFE TO A BARRACKS OF HIS GUARDSMEN TO USE AS THEY PLEASED, AND COMMANDED ME TO WATCH.
AND TO TAKE HER ONE LAST TIME, AFTER THE REST WERE DONE. ONE LAST TIME, WITH NO TRACE OF LOVE OR TENDERNESS REMAINING.
"SO YOU WILL REMEMBER HER AS SHE TRULY IS," HE SAID, AND I SHOULD HAVE DEFIED HIM, BUT MY COCK BETRAYED ME, AND I DID AS I WAS BID.
AFTER HE WAS DONE WITH HER, MY FATHER HAD THE MARRIAGE UNDONE. IT WAS AS IF WE HAD NEVER BEEN WED, THE SEPTONS SAID.
YOU WILL BE IN THE KITCHENS ONLY A LITTLE WHILE. ONCE WE'RE DONE WITH STANNIS, YOU'LL HAVE ANOTHER MANSE, AND SILKS AS SOFT AS YOUR HANDS.
I AM YOURS TO COMMAND, M'LORD.

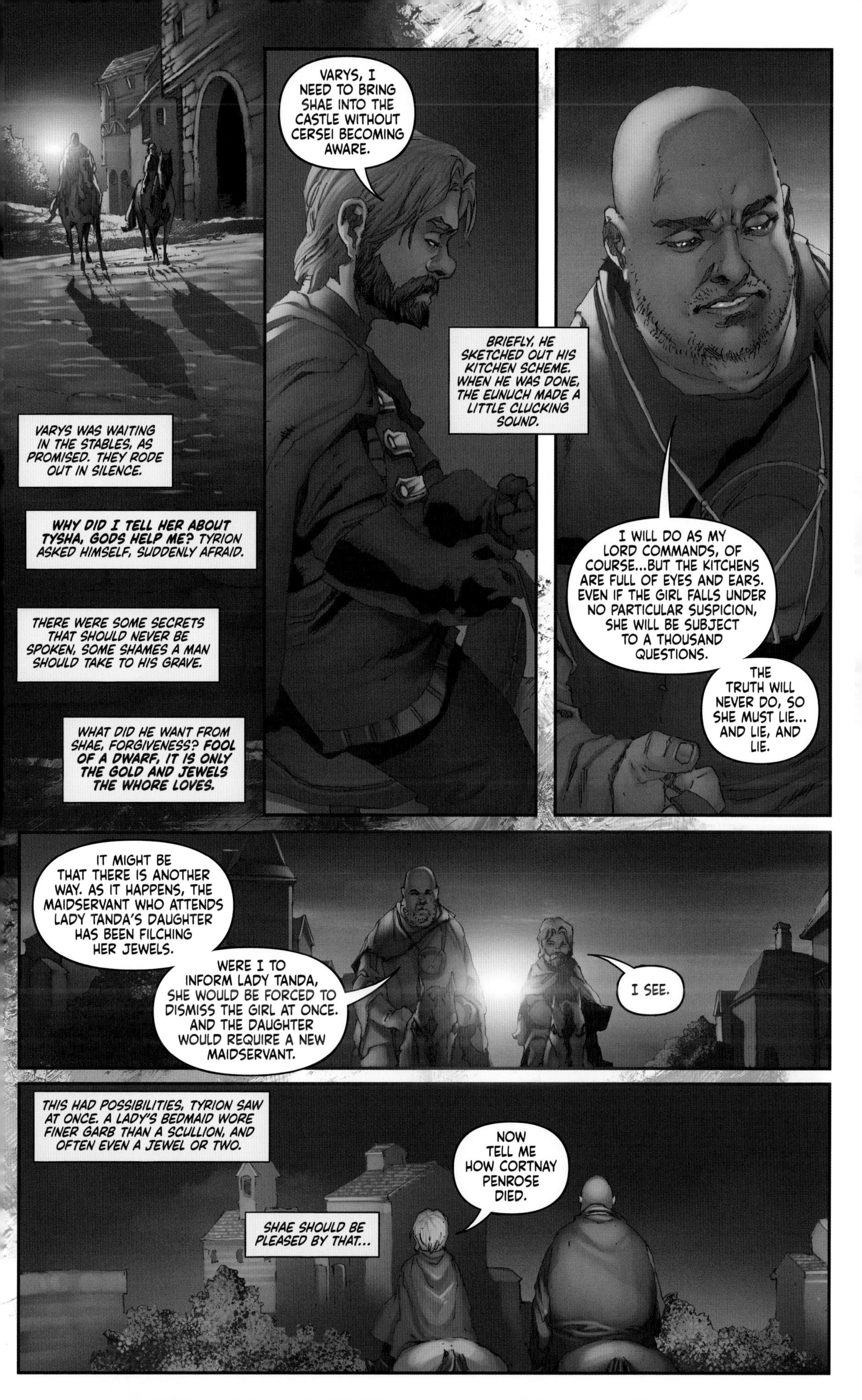
VARYS, I NEED TO BRING SHAE INTO THE CASTLE WITHOUT CERSEI BECOMING AWARE.
VARYS WAS WAITING IN THE STABLES, AS PROMISED. THEY RODE OUT IN SILENCE.
WHY DID I TELL HER ABOUT TYSHA, GODS HELP ME? TYRION ASKED HIMSELF, SUDDENLY AFRAID.
THERE WERE SOME SECRETS THAT SHOULD NEVER BE SPOKEN, SOME SHAMES A MAN SHOULD TAKE TO HIS GRAVE.
WHAT DID HE WANT FROM SHAE, FORGIVENESS? FOOL OF A DWARF, IT IS ONLY THE GOLD AND JEWELS THE WHORE LOVES.
BRIEFLY, HE SKETCHED OUT HIS KITCHEN SCHEME. WHEN HE WAS DONE, THE EUNUCH MADE A LITTLE CLUCKING SOUND.
I WILL DO AS MY LORD COMMANDS, OF COURSE...BUT THE KITCHENS ARE FULL OF EYES AND EARS. EVEN IF THE GIRL FALLS UNDER NO PARTICULAR SUSPICION, SHE WILL BE SUBJECT TO A THOUSAND QUESTIONS.
THE TRUTH WILL NEVER DO, SO SHE MUST LIE... AND LIE, AND LIE.
IT MIGHT BE THAT THERE IS ANOTHER WAY. AS IT HAPPENS, THE MAIDSERVANT WHO ATTENDS LADY TANDA'S DAUGHTER HAS BEEN FILCHING HER JEWELS.
WERE I TO INFORM LADY TANDA, SHE WOULD BE FORCED TO DISMISS THE GIRL AT ONCE. AND THE DAUGHTER WOULD REQUIRE A NEW MAIDSERVANT.
I SEE.
THIS HAD POSSIBILITIES, TYRION SAW AT ONCE. A LADY'S BEDMAID WORE FINER GARB THAN A SCULLION, AND OFTEN EVEN A JEWEL OR TWO.
SHAE SHOULD BE PLEASED BY THAT...
NOW TELL ME HOW CORTNAY PENROSE DIED.

IT IS SAID THAT HE THREW HIMSELF FROM A TOWER.

THREW *HIMSELF*? NO, I WILL NOT BELIEVE THAT!

HIS GUARDS SAW NO MAN ENTER HIS CHAMBERS, NOR DID THEY FIND ANY WITHIN AFTERWARD.

THEN THE KILLER ENTERED EARLIER AND HID UNDER THE BED. OR HE CLIMBED DOWN FROM THE ROOF ON A ROPE.

PERHAPS THE GUARDS ARE LYING. WHO'S TO SAY THEY DID NOT DO THE THING THEMSELVES?

DOUBTLESS YOU ARE RIGHT, MY LORD.

BUT YOU DO NOT THINK SO? HOW WAS IT DONE, THEN?

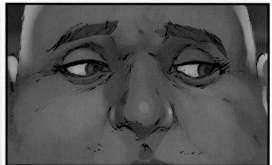

MY LORD, DO YOU BELIEVE IN THE OLD POWERS?

MAGIC, YOU MEAN? BLOODSPELLS, CURSES, SHAPESHIFTING, THOSE SORTS OF THINGS? DO YOU MEAN TO SUGGEST THAT SER CORTNAY WAS MAGICKED TO HIS DEATH?

SER CORTNAY HAD CHALLENGED LORD STANNIS TO SINGLE COMBAT ON THE MORNING HE DIED. I ASK YOU, IS THIS THE ACT OF A MAN LOST TO DESPAIR?

THEN THERE IS THE MATTER OF LORD RENLY'S MYSTERIOUS AND MOST FORTUITOUS MURDER, EVEN AS HIS BATTLE LINES WERE FORMING UP TO SWEEP HIS BROTHER FROM THE FIELD.

MY LORD, YOU ONCE ASKED ME HOW IT WAS THAT I WAS CUT.

I RECALL. YOU DID NOT WANT TO TALK OF IT.

NOR DO I, BUT...

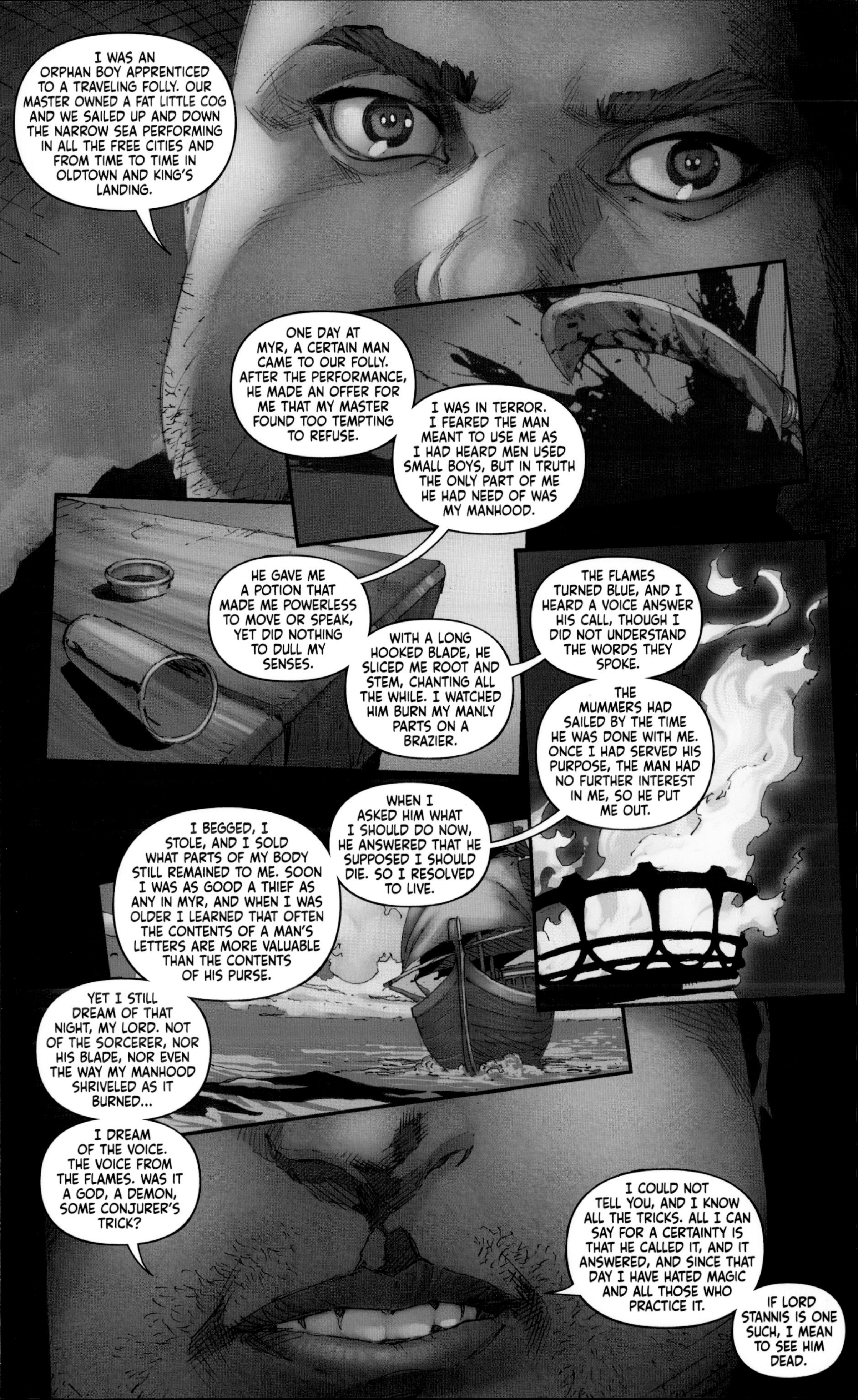
I WAS AN ORPHAN BOY APPRENTICED TO A TRAVELING FOLLY. OUR MASTER OWNED A FAT LITTLE COG AND WE SAILED UP AND DOWN THE NARROW SEA PERFORMING IN ALL THE FREE CITIES AND FROM TIME TO TIME IN OLDTOWN AND KING'S LANDING.
ONE DAY AT MYR, A CERTAIN MAN CAME TO OUR FOLLY. AFTER THE PERFORMANCE, HE MADE AN OFFER FOR ME THAT MY MASTER FOUND TOO TEMPTING TO REFUSE.
I WAS IN TERROR. I FEARED THE MAN MEANT TO USE ME AS I HAD HEARD MEN USED SMALL BOYS, BUT IN TRUTH THE ONLY PART OF ME HE HAD NEED OF WAS MY MANHOOD.
HE GAVE ME A POTION THAT MADE ME POWERLESS TO MOVE OR SPEAK, YET DID NOTHING TO DULL MY SENSES.
WITH A LONG HOOKED BLADE, HE SLICED ME ROOT AND STEM, CHANTING ALL THE WHILE. I WATCHED HIM BURN MY MANLY PARTS ON A BRAZIER.
THE FLAMES TURNED BLUE, AND I HEARD A VOICE ANSWER HIS CALL, THOUGH I DID NOT UNDERSTAND THE WORDS THEY SPOKE.
THE MUMMERS HAD SAILED BY THE TIME HE WAS DONE WITH ME. ONCE I HAD SERVED HIS PURPOSE, THE MAN HAD NO FURTHER INTEREST IN ME, SO HE PUT ME OUT.
WHEN I ASKED HIM WHAT I SHOULD DO NOW, HE ANSWERED THAT HE SUPPOSED I SHOULD DIE. SO I RESOLVED TO LIVE.
I BEGGED, I STOLE, AND I SOLD WHAT PARTS OF MY BODY STILL REMAINED TO ME. SOON I WAS AS GOOD A THIEF AS ANY IN MYR, AND WHEN I WAS OLDER I LEARNED THAT OFTEN THE CONTENTS OF A MAN'S LETTERS ARE MORE VALUABLE THAN THE CONTENTS OF HIS PURSE.
YET I STILL DREAM OF THAT NIGHT, MY LORD. NOT OF THE SORCERER, NOR HIS BLADE, NOR EVEN THE WAY MY MANHOOD SHRIVELED AS IT BURNED...
I DREAM OF THE VOICE. THE VOICE FROM THE FLAMES. WAS IT A GOD, A DEMON, SOME CONJURER'S TRICK?
I COULD NOT TELL YOU, AND I KNOW ALL THE TRICKS. ALL I CAN SAY FOR A CERTAINTY IS THAT HE CALLED IT, AND IT ANSWERED, AND SINCE THAT DAY I HAVE HATED MAGIC AND ALL THOSE WHO PRACTICE IT.
IF LORD STANNIS IS ONE SUCH, I MEAN TO SEE HIM DEAD.

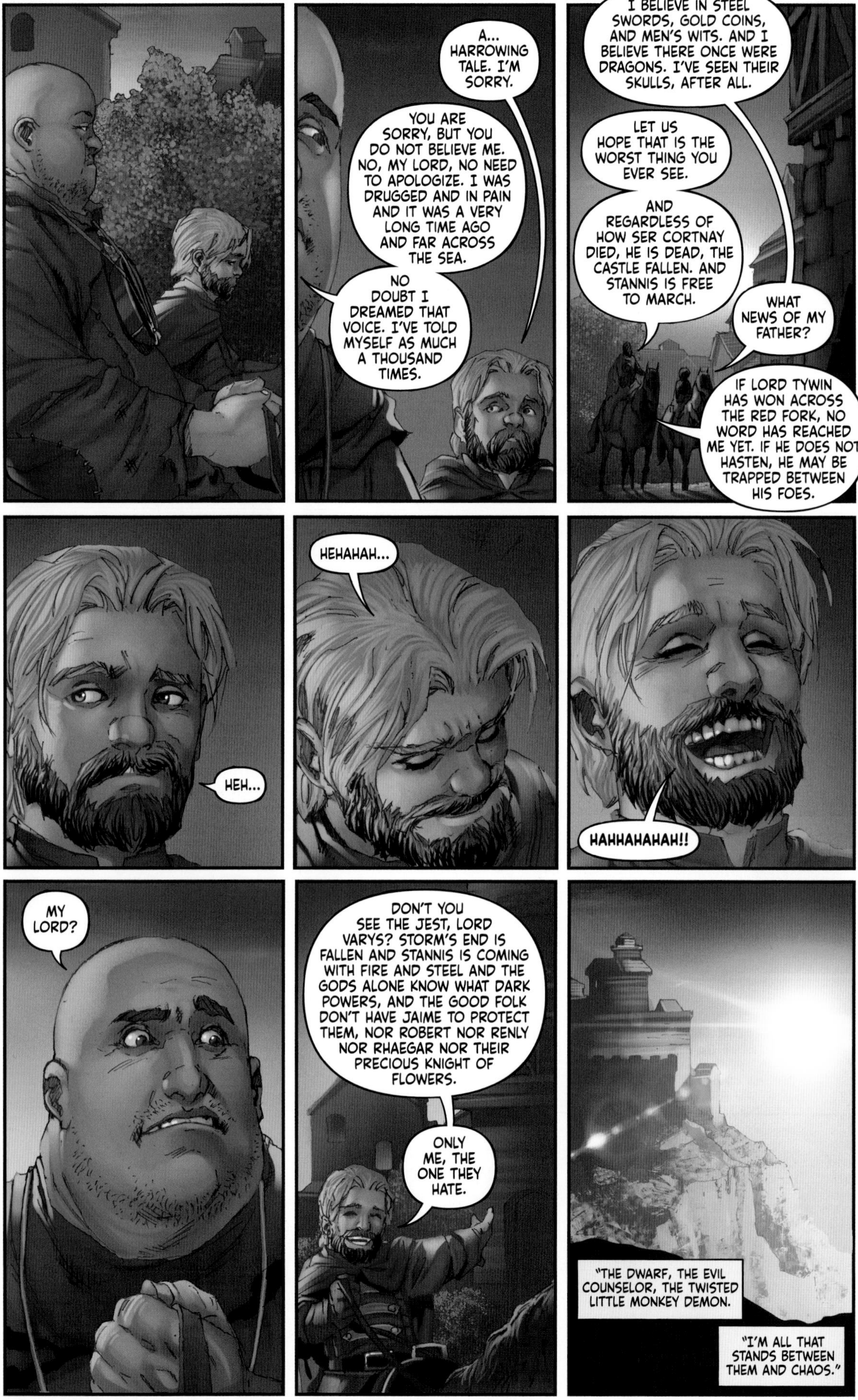
A... HARROWING TALE. I'M SORRY.
YOU ARE SORRY, BUT YOU DO NOT BELIEVE ME. NO, MY LORD, NO NEED TO APOLOGIZE. I WAS DRUGGED AND IN PAIN AND IT WAS A VERY LONG TIME AGO AND FAR ACROSS THE SEA.
NO DOUBT I DREAMED THAT VOICE. I'VE TOLD MYSELF AS MUCH A THOUSAND TIMES.
I BELIEVE IN STEEL SWORDS, GOLD COINS, AND MEN'S WITS. AND I BELIEVE THERE ONCE WERE DRAGONS. I'VE SEEN THEIR SKULLS, AFTER ALL.
LET US HOPE THAT IS THE WORST THING YOU EVER SEE.
AND REGARDLESS OF HOW SER CORTNAY DIED, HE IS DEAD, THE CASTLE FALLEN. AND STANNIS IS FREE TO MARCH.
WHAT NEWS OF MY FATHER?
IF LORD TYWIN HAS WON ACROSS THE RED FORK, NO WORD HAS REACHED ME YET. IF HE DOES NOT HASTEN, HE MAY BE TRAPPED BETWEEN HIS FOES.
HEH...
HEHAHAH...
HAHHAHAHAH!!
MY LORD?
DON'T YOU SEE THE JEST, LORD VARYS? STORM'S END IS FALLEN AND STANNIS IS COMING WITH FIRE AND STEEL AND THE GODS ALONE KNOW WHAT DARK POWERS, AND THE GOOD FOLK DON'T HAVE JAIME TO PROTECT THEM, NOR ROBERT NOR RENLY NOR RHAEGAR NOR THEIR PRECIOUS KNIGHT OF FLOWERS.
ONLY ME, THE ONE THEY HATE.
"THE DWARF, THE EVIL COUNSELOR, THE TWISTED LITTLE MONKEY DEMON.
"I'M ALL THAT STANDS BETWEEN THEM AND CHAOS."

JON

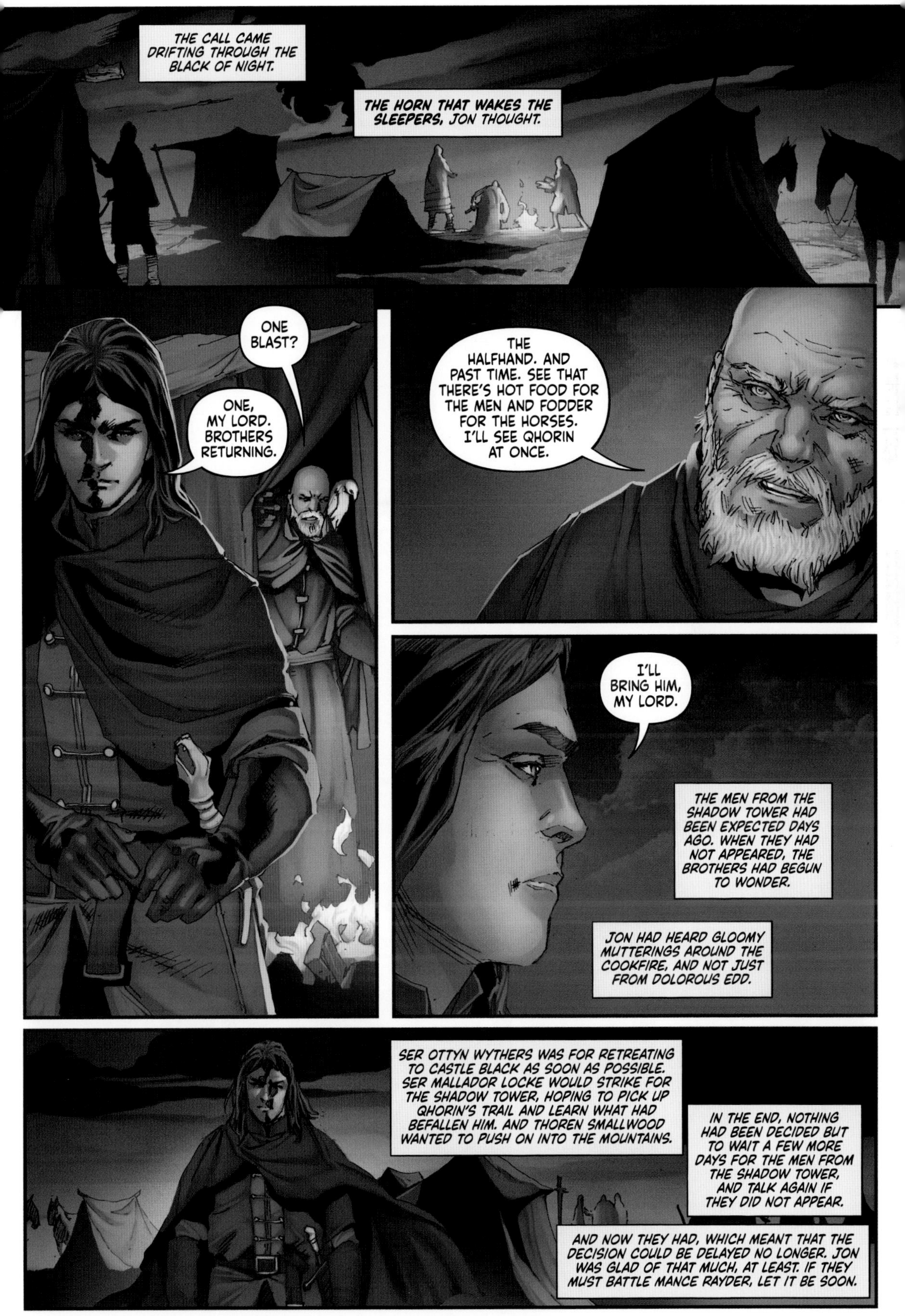
THE CALL CAME DRIFTING THROUGH THE BLACK OF NIGHT.
THE HORN THAT WAKES THE SLEEPERS, JON THOUGHT.
ONE BLAST?
ONE, MY LORD. BROTHERS RETURNING.
THE HALFHAND. AND PAST TIME. SEE THAT THERE'S HOT FOOD FOR THE MEN AND FODDER FOR THE HORSES. I'LL SEE QHORIN AT ONCE.
I'LL BRING HIM, MY LORD.
THE MEN FROM THE SHADOW TOWER HAD BEEN EXPECTED DAYS AGO. WHEN THEY HAD NOT APPEARED, THE BROTHERS HAD BEGUN TO WONDER.
JON HAD HEARD GLOOMY MUTTERINGS AROUND THE COOKFIRE, AND NOT JUST FROM DOLOROUS EDD.
SER OTTYN WYTHERS WAS FOR RETREATING TO CASTLE BLACK AS SOON AS POSSIBLE. SER MALLADOR LOCKE WOULD STRIKE FOR THE SHADOW TOWER, HOPING TO PICK UP QHORIN'S TRAIL AND LEARN WHAT HAD BEFALLEN HIM. AND THOREN SMALLWOOD WANTED TO PUSH ON INTO THE MOUNTAINS.
IN THE END, NOTHING HAD BEEN DECIDED BUT TO WAIT A FEW MORE DAYS FOR THE MEN FROM THE SHADOW TOWER, AND TALK AGAIN IF THEY DID NOT APPEAR.
AND NOW THEY HAD, WHICH MEANT THAT THE DECISION COULD BE DELAYED NO LONGER. JON WAS GLAD OF THAT MUCH, AT LEAST. IF THEY MUST BATTLE MANCE RAYDER, LET IT BE SOON.

IT WAS NOT LONG UNTIL THE FIRST OF THE BROTHERS FROM THE SHADOW TOWER BEGAN WENDING THEIR WAY UP THE SLOPE.

HEAVY BEARDS COVERED LEAN HARD FACES, AND MADE THEM LOOK AS SHAGGY AS THEIR GARRONS.

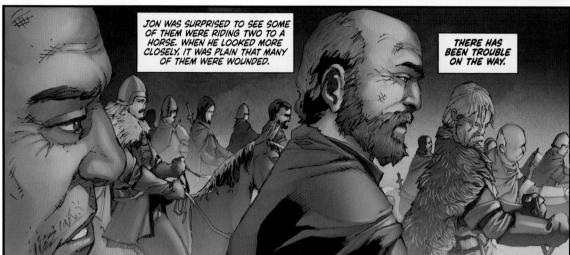

JON WAS SURPRISED TO SEE SOME OF THEM WERE RIDING TWO TO A HORSE. WHEN HE LOOKED MORE CLOSELY, IT WAS PLAIN THAT MANY OF THEM WERE WOUNDED.

THERE HAS BEEN TROUBLE ON THE WAY.

JON KNEW QHORIN HALFHAND THE INSTANT HE SAW HIM, THOUGH THEY HAD NEVER MET. THE BIG RANGER WAS HALF A LEGEND IN THE WATCH; A MAN OF SLOW WORDS AND SWIFT ACTION.

ONLY THUMB AND FOREFINGER REMAINED ON THE HAND THAT HELD THE REINS; THE OTHER FINGERS HAD BEEN SHEARED OFF CATCHING A WILDLING'S AXE THAT WOULD OTHERWISE HAVE SPLIT HIS SKULL.

IT WAS TOLD THAT HE HAD THRUST HIS MAIMED FIST INTO THE FACE OF THE AXEMAN SO THE BLOOD SPURTED INTO HIS EYES, AND SLEW HIM WHILE HE WAS BLIND. SINCE THAT DAY, THE WILDLINGS BEYOND THE WALL HAD KNOWN NO FOE MORE IMPLACABLE.

LORD COMMANDER MORMONT WOULD SEE YOU AT ONCE. I'LL SHOW YOU TO HIS TENT.

DID YOU KNOW HIM, MY LORD?

YOU ARE JON SNOW. YOU HAVE YOUR FATHER'S LOOK.

I AM NO LORDLING. ONLY A BROTHER OF THE NIGHT'S WATCH. I KNEW LORD EDDARD, YES. AND HIS FATHER BEFORE HIM.

LORD RICKARD DIED BEFORE I WAS BORN.

HE WAS A FRIEND TO THE WATCH. IT IS SAID THAT A DIREWOLF RUNS WITH YOU.

GHOST SHOULD BE BACK BY DAWN. HE HUNTS AT NIGHT.

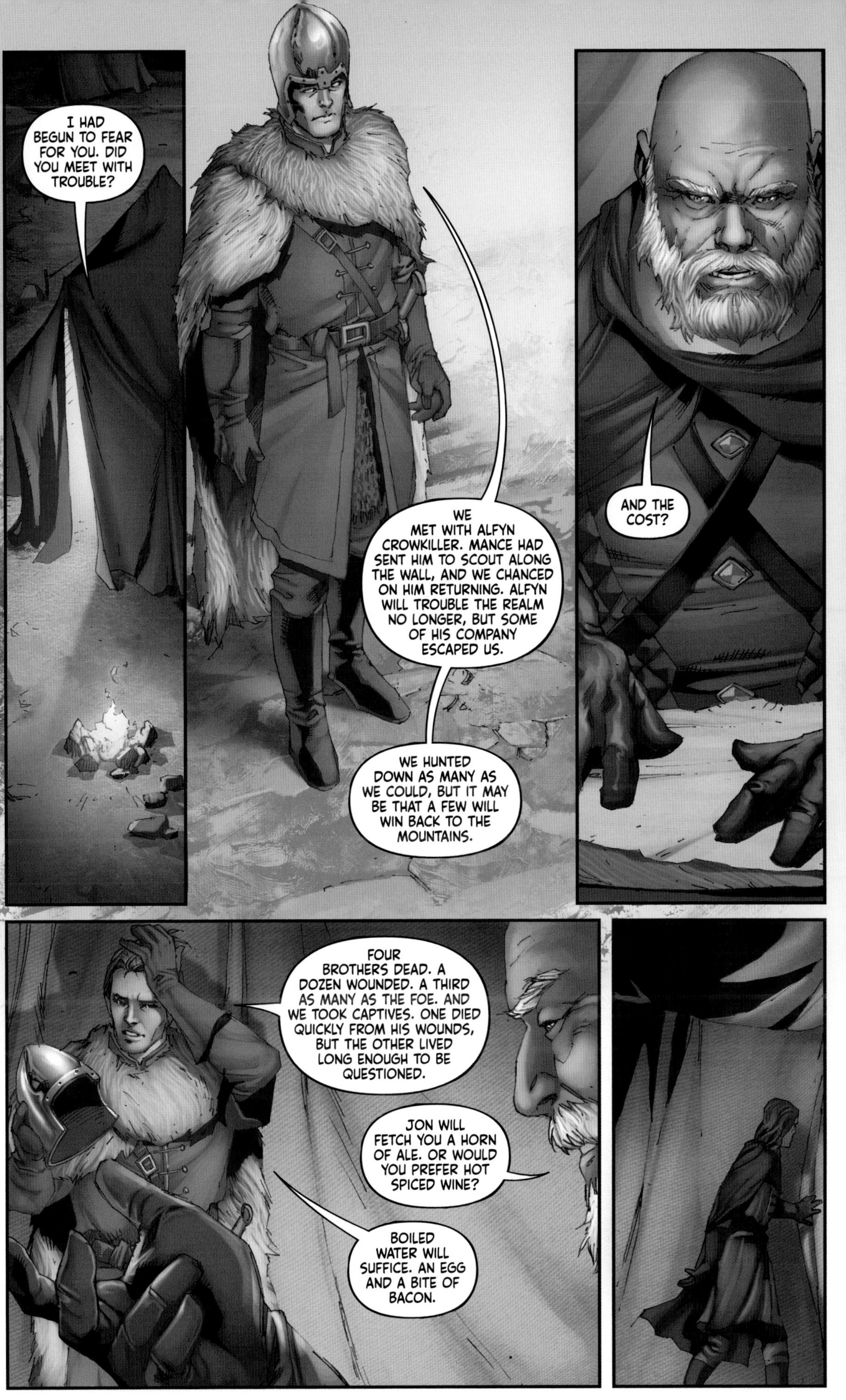
I HAD BEGUN TO FEAR FOR YOU. DID YOU MEET WITH TROUBLE?
WE MET WITH ALFYN CROWKILLER. MANCE HAD SENT HIM TO SCOUT ALONG THE WALL, AND WE CHANCED ON HIM RETURNING. ALFYN WILL TROUBLE THE REALM NO LONGER, BUT SOME OF HIS COMPANY ESCAPED US.
WE HUNTED DOWN AS MANY AS WE COULD, BUT IT MAY BE THAT A FEW WILL WIN BACK TO THE MOUNTAINS.
AND THE COST?
FOUR BROTHERS DEAD. A DOZEN WOUNDED. A THIRD AS MANY AS THE FOE. AND WE TOOK CAPTIVES. ONE DIED QUICKLY FROM HIS WOUNDS, BUT THE OTHER LIVED LONG ENOUGH TO BE QUESTIONED.
JON WILL FETCH YOU A HORN OF ALE. OR WOULD YOU PREFER HOT SPICED WINE?
BOILED WATER WILL SUFFICE. AN EGG AND A BITE OF BACON.

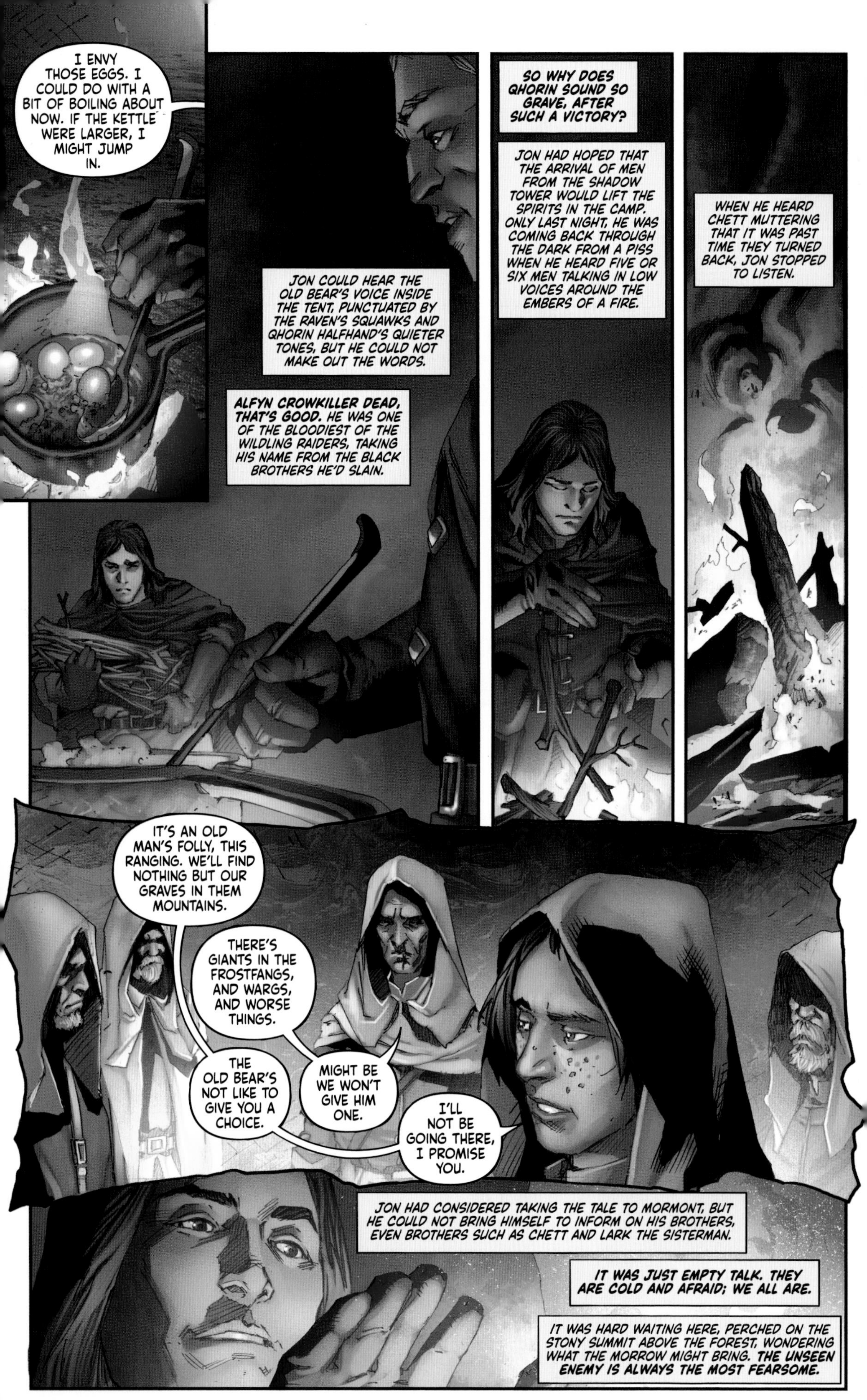
I ENVY THOSE EGGS. I COULD DO WITH A BIT OF BOILING ABOUT NOW. IF THE KETTLE WERE LARGER, I MIGHT JUMP IN.
JON COULD HEAR THE OLD BEAR'S VOICE INSIDE THE TENT, PUNCTUATED BY THE RAVEN'S SQUAWKS AND QHORIN HALFHAND'S QUIETER TONES, BUT HE COULD NOT MAKE OUT THE WORDS.
ALFYN CROWKILLER DEAD, THAT'S GOOD. HE WAS ONE OF THE BLOODIEST OF THE WILDLING RAIDERS, TAKING HIS NAME FROM THE BLACK BROTHERS HE'D SLAIN.
SO WHY DOES QHORIN SOUND SO GRAVE, AFTER SUCH A VICTORY?
JON HAD HOPED THAT THE ARRIVAL OF MEN FROM THE SHADOW TOWER WOULD LIFT THE SPIRITS IN THE CAMP. ONLY LAST NIGHT, HE WAS COMING BACK THROUGH THE DARK FROM A PISS WHEN HE HEARD FIVE OR SIX MEN TALKING IN LOW VOICES AROUND THE EMBERS OF A FIRE.
WHEN HE HEARD CHETT MUTTERING THAT IT WAS PAST TIME THEY TURNED BACK, JON STOPPED TO LISTEN.
IT'S AN OLD MAN'S FOLLY, THIS RANGING. WE'LL FIND NOTHING BUT OUR GRAVES IN THEM MOUNTAINS.
THERE'S GIANTS IN THE FROSTFANGS, AND WARGS, AND WORSE THINGS.
THE OLD BEAR'S NOT LIKE TO GIVE YOU A CHOICE.
MIGHT BE WE WON'T GIVE HIM ONE.
I'LL NOT BE GOING THERE, I PROMISE YOU.
JON HAD CONSIDERED TAKING THE TALE TO MORMONT, BUT HE COULD NOT BRING HIMSELF TO INFORM ON HIS BROTHERS, EVEN BROTHERS SUCH AS CHETT AND LARK THE SISTERMAN.
IT WAS JUST EMPTY TALK. THEY ARE COLD AND AFRAID; WE ALL ARE.
IT WAS HARD WAITING HERE, PERCHED ON THE STONY SUMMIT ABOVE THE FOREST, WONDERING WHAT THE MORROW MIGHT BRING. THE UNSEEN ENEMY IS ALWAYS THE MOST FEARSOME.

JON SLID HIS NEW DAGGER FROM ITS SHEATH. HE HAD FASHIONED THE WOODEN HILT HIMSELF, AND WOUND HEMPEN TWINE AROUND IT TO MAKE A GRIP.

DOLOROUS EDD OPINED THAT GLASS KNIVES WERE ABOUT AS USEFUL AS NIPPLES ON A KNIGHT'S BREASTPLATE, BUT JON WAS NOT SO CERTAIN. THE DRAGONGLASS BLADE WAS SHARPER THAN STEEL, ALBEIT FAR MORE BRITTLE.

IT MUST HAVE BEEN BURIED FOR A REASON.

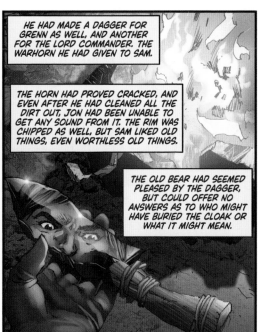

HE HAD MADE A DAGGER FOR GRENN AS WELL, AND ANOTHER FOR THE LORD COMMANDER. THE WARHORN HE HAD GIVEN TO SAM.

THE HORN HAD PROVED CRACKED, AND EVEN AFTER HE HAD CLEANED ALL THE DIRT OUT, JON HAD BEEN UNABLE TO GET ANY SOUND FROM IT. THE RIM WAS CHIPPED AS WELL, BUT SAM LIKED OLD THINGS, EVEN WORTHLESS OLD THINGS.

THE OLD BEAR HAD SEEMED PLEASED BY THE DAGGER, BUT COULD OFFER NO ANSWERS AS TO WHO MIGHT HAVE BURIED THE CLOAK OR WHAT IT MIGHT MEAN.

PERHAPS QHORIN WILL KNOW. THE HALFHAND HAD VENTURED DEEPER INTO THE WILD THAN ANY OTHER LIVING MAN.

YOU WANT TO SERVE, OR SHALL I?

I'LL DO IT.

...RATTLESHIRT, THE WEEPING MAN, AND EVERY OTHER CHIEF GREAT AND SMALL.

THEY HAVE WARGS AS WELL, AND MAMMOTHS, AND MORE STRENGTH THAN WE WOULD HAVE DREAMED.

OR SO HE CLAIMED. I WILL NOT SWEAR AS TO THE TRUTH OF IT. EBBEN BELIEVES THE MAN WAS TELLING US TALES TO MAKE HIS LIFE LAST A LITTLE LONGER.

TRUE OR FALSE, THE WALL MUST BE WARNED. AND THE KING.

WHICH KING?

ALL OF THEM. THE TRUE AND THE FALSE ALIKE. IF THEY WOULD CLAIM THE REALM, LET THEM DEFEND IT.

THESE KINGS WILL DO WHAT THEY WILL. LIKELY IT WILL BE LITTLE ENOUGH. THE BEST HOPE IS WINTERFELL. THE STARKS MUST RALLY THE NORTH.

YES. TO BE SURE.

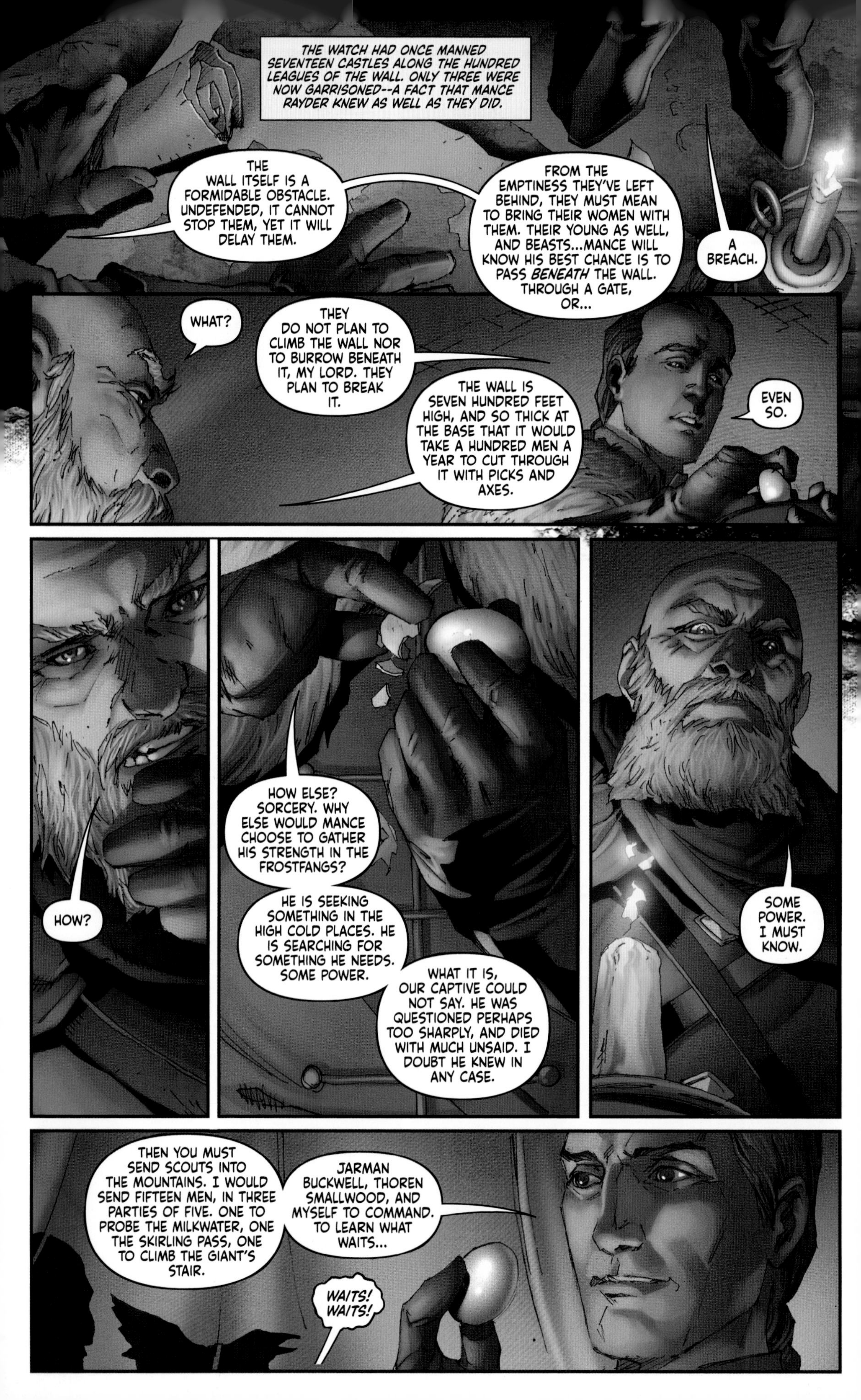
THE WATCH HAD ONCE MANNED SEVENTEEN CASTLES ALONG THE HUNDRED LEAGUES OF THE WALL. ONLY THREE WERE NOW GARRISONED--A FACT THAT MANCE RAYDER KNEW AS WELL AS THEY DID.
THE WALL ITSELF IS A FORMIDABLE OBSTACLE. UNDEFENDED, IT CANNOT STOP THEM, YET IT WILL DELAY THEM.
FROM THE EMPTINESS THEY'VE LEFT BEHIND, THEY MUST MEAN TO BRING THEIR WOMEN WITH THEM. THEIR YOUNG AS WELL, AND BEASTS...MANCE WILL KNOW HIS BEST CHANCE IS TO PASS *BENEATH* THE WALL. THROUGH A GATE, OR...
A BREACH.
WHAT?
THEY DO NOT PLAN TO CLIMB THE WALL NOR TO BURROW BENEATH IT, MY LORD. THEY PLAN TO BREAK IT.
THE WALL IS SEVEN HUNDRED FEET HIGH, AND SO THICK AT THE BASE THAT IT WOULD TAKE A HUNDRED MEN A YEAR TO CUT THROUGH IT WITH PICKS AND AXES.
EVEN SO.
HOW?
HOW ELSE? SORCERY. WHY ELSE WOULD MANCE CHOOSE TO GATHER HIS STRENGTH IN THE FROSTFANGS?
HE IS SEEKING SOMETHING IN THE HIGH COLD PLACES. HE IS SEARCHING FOR SOMETHING HE NEEDS. SOME POWER.
WHAT IT IS, OUR CAPTIVE COULD NOT SAY. HE WAS QUESTIONED PERHAPS TOO SHARPLY, AND DIED WITH MUCH UNSAID. I DOUBT HE KNEW IN ANY CASE.
SOME POWER. I MUST KNOW.
THEN YOU MUST SEND SCOUTS INTO THE MOUNTAINS. I WOULD SEND FIFTEEN MEN, IN THREE PARTIES OF FIVE. ONE TO PROBE THE MILKWATER, ONE THE SKIRLING PASS, ONE TO CLIMB THE GIANT'S STAIR.
JARMAN BUCKWELL, THOREN SMALLWOOD, AND MYSELF TO COMMAND. TO LEARN WHAT WAITS...
WAITS! WAITS!

I SEE NO OTHER CHOICE. BUT IF YOU DO NOT RETURN...

MAY THE GODS FORGIVE ME. CHOOSE YOUR MEN.

VERY WELL. I CHOOSE JON SNOW.

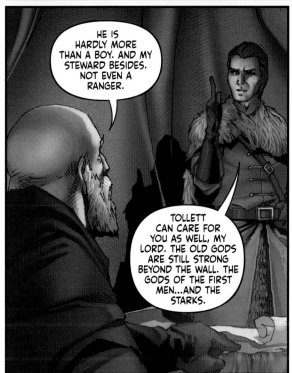

HE IS HARDLY MORE THAN A BOY. AND MY STEWARD BESIDES. NOT EVEN A RANGER.

TOLLETT CAN CARE FOR YOU AS WELL, MY LORD. THE OLD GODS ARE STILL STRONG BEYOND THE WALL. THE GODS OF THE FIRST MEN...AND THE STARKS.

WHAT IS YOUR WILL IN THIS?

TO GO.

I THOUGHT IT MIGHT BE.

WE RIDE AT NOON...

...BEST FIND THAT WOLF OF YOURS.

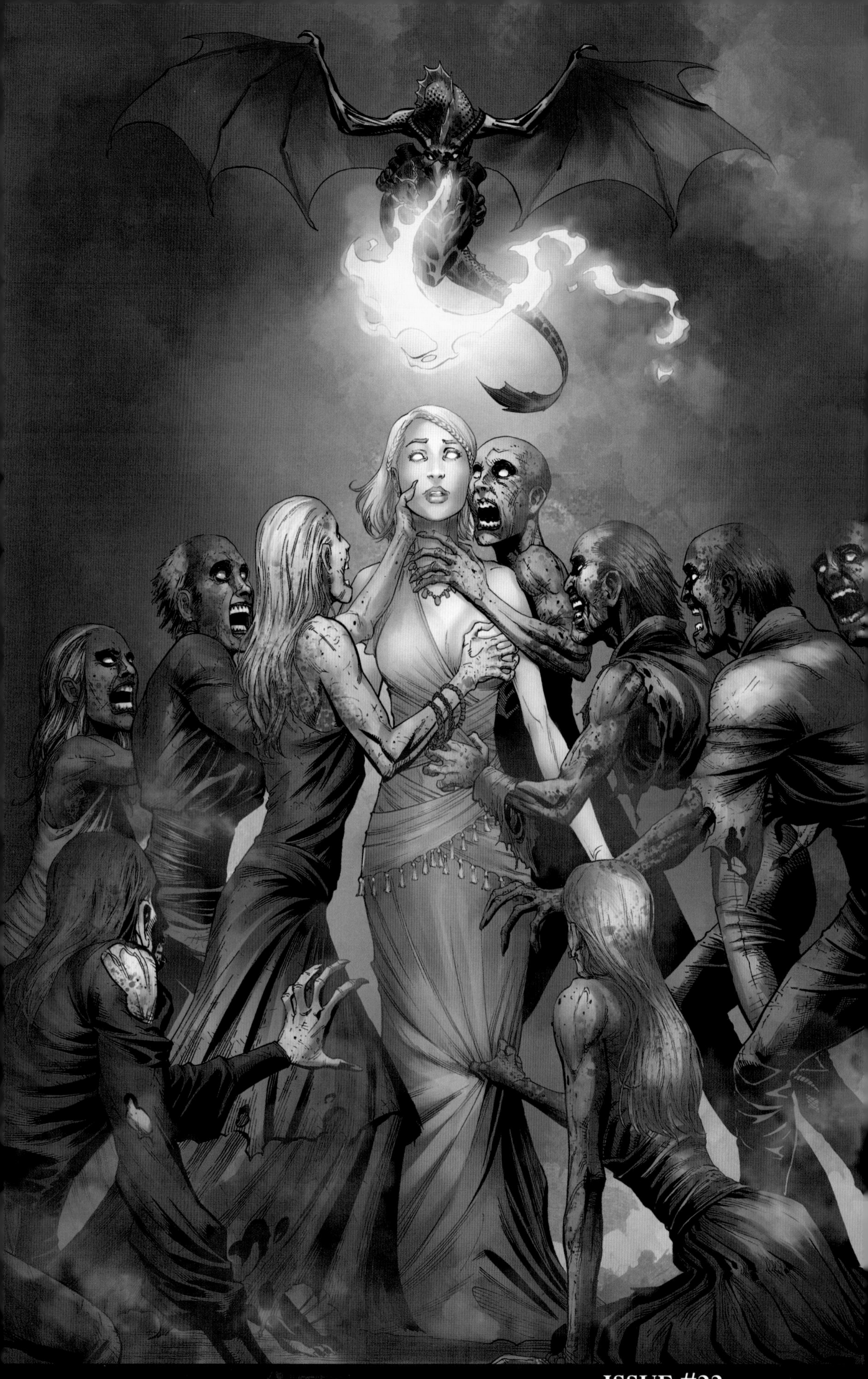

ISSUE #22

CATELYN

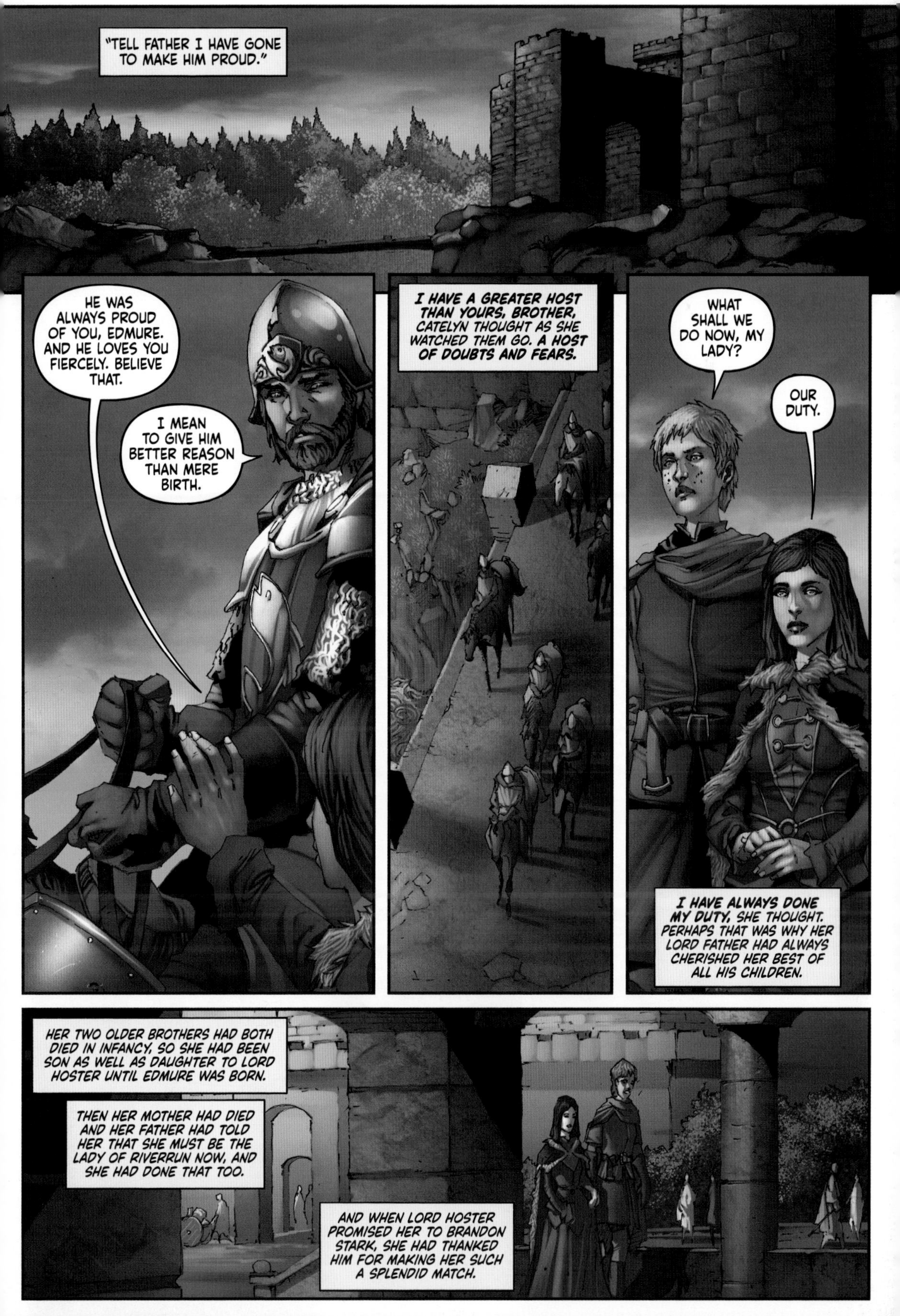
"TELL FATHER I HAVE GONE TO MAKE HIM PROUD."
HE WAS ALWAYS PROUD OF YOU, EDMURE. AND HE LOVES YOU FIERCELY. BELIEVE THAT.
I MEAN TO GIVE HIM BETTER REASON THAN MERE BIRTH.
I HAVE A GREATER HOST THAN YOURS, BROTHER, CATELYN THOUGHT AS SHE WATCHED THEM GO. A HOST OF DOUBTS AND FEARS.
WHAT SHALL WE DO NOW, MY LADY?
OUR DUTY.
I HAVE ALWAYS DONE MY DUTY, SHE THOUGHT. PERHAPS THAT WAS WHY HER LORD FATHER HAD ALWAYS CHERISHED HER BEST OF ALL HIS CHILDREN.
HER TWO OLDER BROTHERS HAD BOTH DIED IN INFANCY, SO SHE HAD BEEN SON AS WELL AS DAUGHTER TO LORD HOSTER UNTIL EDMURE WAS BORN.
THEN HER MOTHER HAD DIED AND HER FATHER HAD TOLD HER THAT SHE MUST BE THE LADY OF RIVERRUN NOW, AND SHE HAD DONE THAT TOO.
AND WHEN LORD HOSTER PROMISED HER TO BRANDON STARK, SHE HAD THANKED HIM FOR MAKING HER SUCH A SPLENDID MATCH.

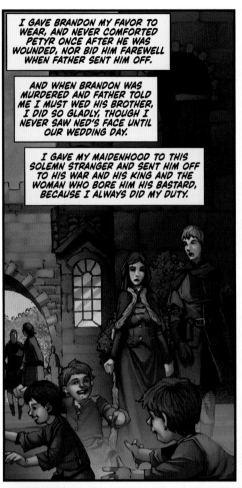

I GAVE BRANDON MY FAVOR TO WEAR, AND NEVER COMFORTED PETYR ONCE AFTER HE WAS WOUNDED, NOR BID HIM FAREWELL WHEN FATHER SENT HIM OFF.

AND WHEN BRANDON WAS MURDERED AND FATHER TOLD ME I MUST WED HIS BROTHER, I DID SO GLADLY, THOUGH I NEVER SAW NED'S FACE UNTIL OUR WEDDING DAY.

I GAVE MY MAIDENHOOD TO THIS SOLEMN STRANGER AND SENT HIM OFF TO HIS WAR AND HIS KING AND THE WOMAN WHO BORE HIM HIS BASTARD, BECAUSE I ALWAYS DID MY DUTY.

FIGHTING IS BETTER THAN THIS WAITING. YOU DON'T FEEL SO HELPLESS WHEN YOU FIGHT. WHEN YOU'RE ARMORED IT'S HARD FOR ANYONE TO HURT YOU.

KNIGHTS DIE IN BATTLE.

AS LADIES DIE IN CHILDBED. NO ONE SINGS SONGS ABOUT *THEM*.

CHILDREN ARE A BATTLE OF A DIFFERENT SORT.

A BATTLE WITHOUT BANNERS OR WARHORNS, BUT NO LESS FIERCE.

CARRYING A CHILD, BRINGING IT INTO THE WORLD...

PARDON, MY LADY, BUT THERE IS A LETTER.

THE MESSAGE WAS FROM ONE LORD MEADOWS, WHO NAMED HIMSELF CASTELLAN OF STORM'S END.

SER CORTNAY PENROSE WAS DEAD, THE MAN WROTE, AND STORM'S END HAD OPENED ITS GATE TO STANNIS BARATHEON, THE TRUEBORN AND RIGHTFUL HEIR.

THE CASTLE GARRISON HAD SWORN THEIR SWORDS TO HIS CAUSE, ONE AND ALL, AND NO MAN OF THEM HAD SUFFERED HARM.

SAVE CORTNAY PENROSE.

ROBB SHOULD KNOW OF THIS AT ONCE. DO WE KNOW WHERE HE IS?

AT LAST WORD HE WAS MARCHING TOWARD THE CRAG, THE SEAT OF HOUSE WESTERLING. IF I DISPATCHED A RAVEN TO ASHEMARK, IT MAY BE THAT THEY COULD SEND A RIDER AFTER HIM.

DO SO.

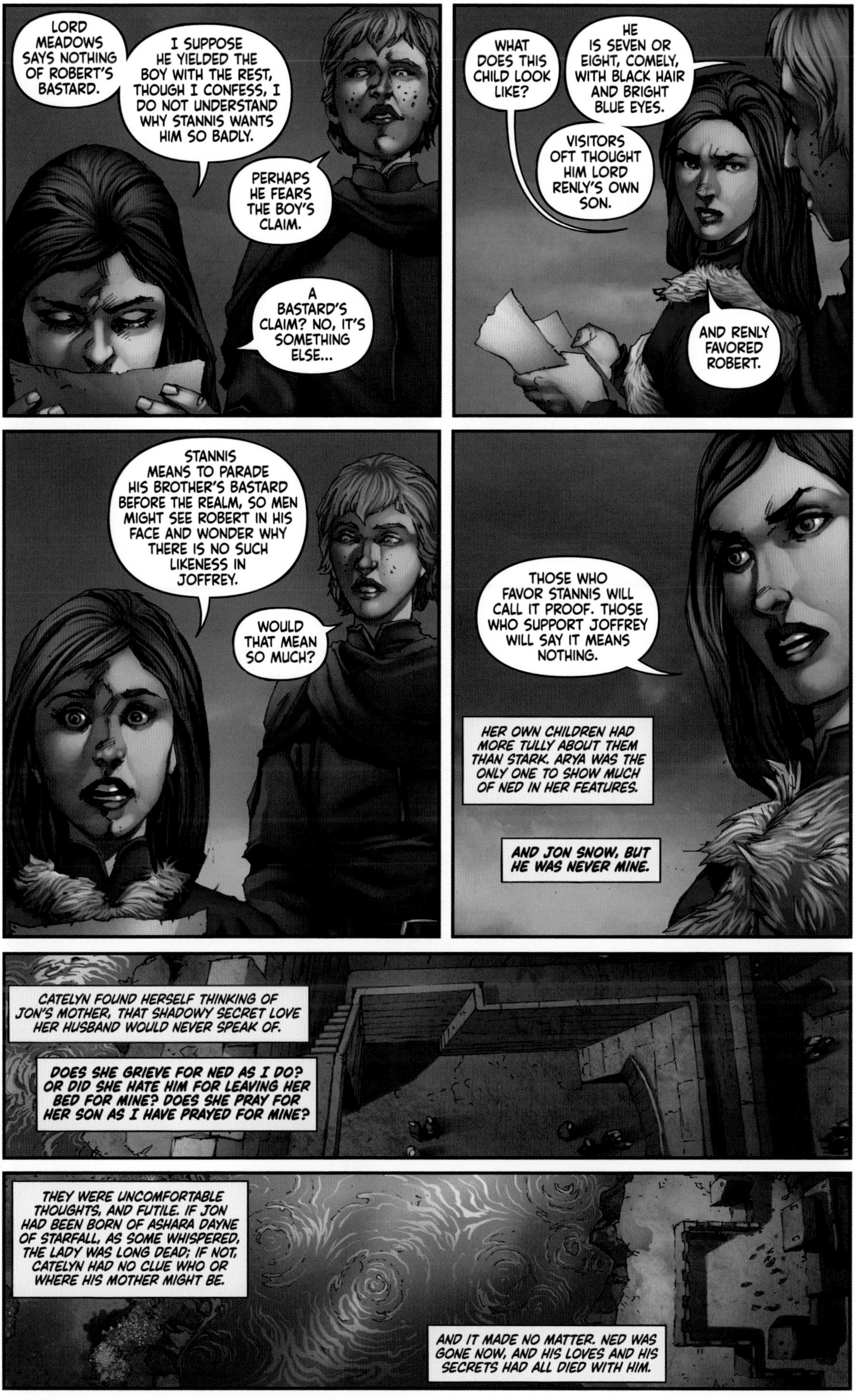
LORD MEADOWS SAYS NOTHING OF ROBERT'S BASTARD.
I SUPPOSE HE YIELDED THE BOY WITH THE REST, THOUGH I CONFESS, I DO NOT UNDERSTAND WHY STANNIS WANTS HIM SO BADLY.
PERHAPS HE FEARS THE BOY'S CLAIM.
A BASTARD'S CLAIM? NO, IT'S SOMETHING ELSE...
WHAT DOES THIS CHILD LOOK LIKE?
HE IS SEVEN OR EIGHT, COMELY, WITH BLACK HAIR AND BRIGHT BLUE EYES.
VISITORS OFT THOUGHT HIM LORD RENLY'S OWN SON.
AND RENLY FAVORED ROBERT.
STANNIS MEANS TO PARADE HIS BROTHER'S BASTARD BEFORE THE REALM, SO MEN MIGHT SEE ROBERT IN HIS FACE AND WONDER WHY THERE IS NO SUCH LIKENESS IN JOFFREY.
WOULD THAT MEAN SO MUCH?
THOSE WHO FAVOR STANNIS WILL CALL IT PROOF. THOSE WHO SUPPORT JOFFREY WILL SAY IT MEANS NOTHING.
HER OWN CHILDREN HAD MORE TULLY ABOUT THEM THAN STARK. ARYA WAS THE ONLY ONE TO SHOW MUCH OF NED IN HER FEATURES.
AND JON SNOW, BUT HE WAS NEVER MINE.
CATELYN FOUND HERSELF THINKING OF JON'S MOTHER, THAT SHADOWY SECRET LOVE HER HUSBAND WOULD NEVER SPEAK OF.
DOES SHE GRIEVE FOR NED AS I DO? OR DID SHE HATE HIM FOR LEAVING HER BED FOR MINE? DOES SHE PRAY FOR HER SON AS I HAVE PRAYED FOR MINE?
THEY WERE UNCOMFORTABLE THOUGHTS, AND FUTILE. IF JON HAD BEEN BORN OF ASHARA DAYNE OF STARFALL, AS SOME WHISPERED, THE LADY WAS LONG DEAD; IF NOT, CATELYN HAD NO CLUE WHO OR WHERE HIS MOTHER MIGHT BE.
AND IT MADE NO MATTER. NED WAS GONE NOW, AND HIS LOVES AND HIS SECRETS HAD ALL DIED WITH HIM.

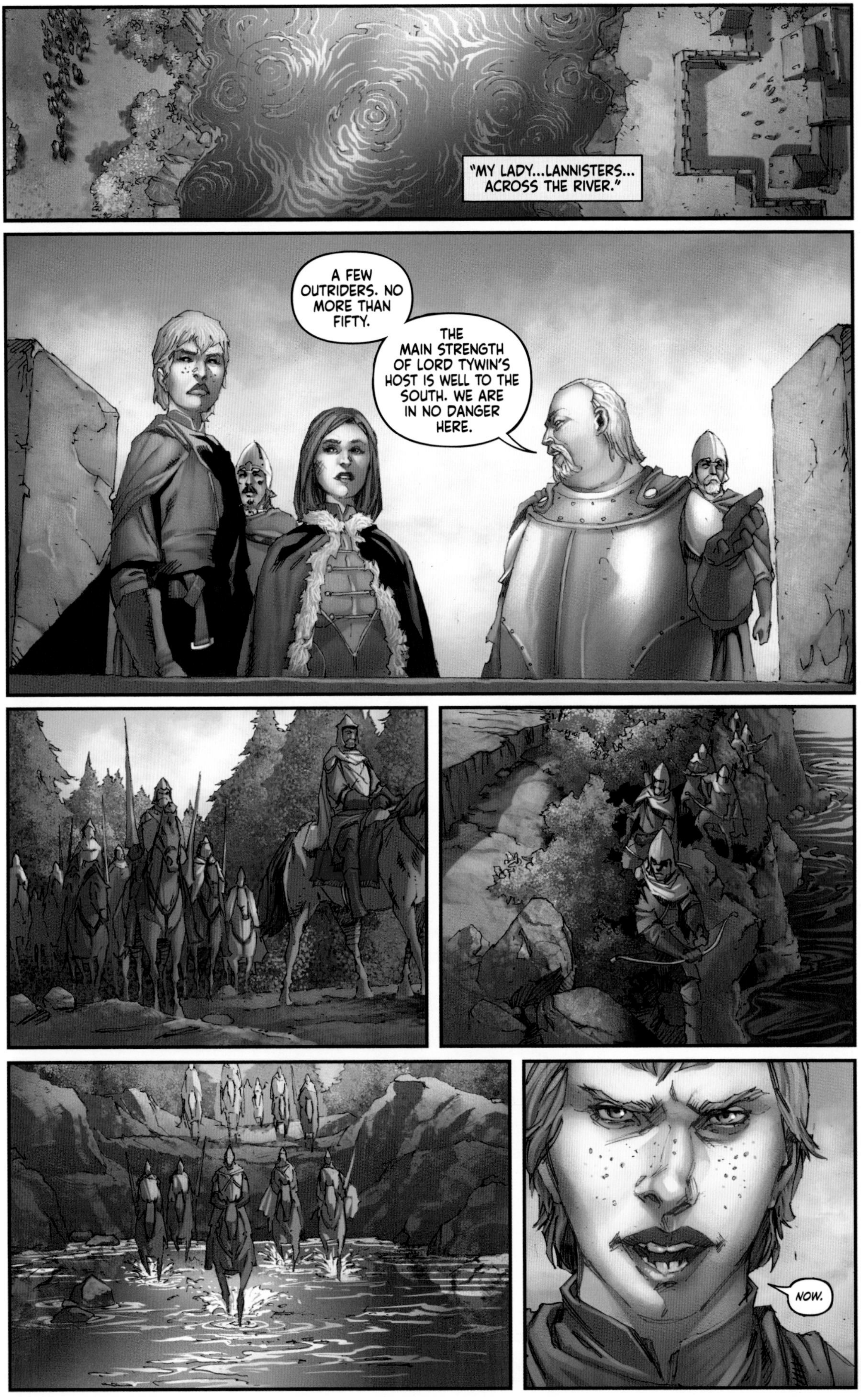
"MY LADY...LANNISTERS... ACROSS THE RIVER."
A FEW OUTRIDERS. NO MORE THAN FIFTY.
THE MAIN STRENGTH OF LORD TYWIN'S HOST IS WELL TO THE SOUTH. WE ARE IN NO DANGER HERE.
NOW.

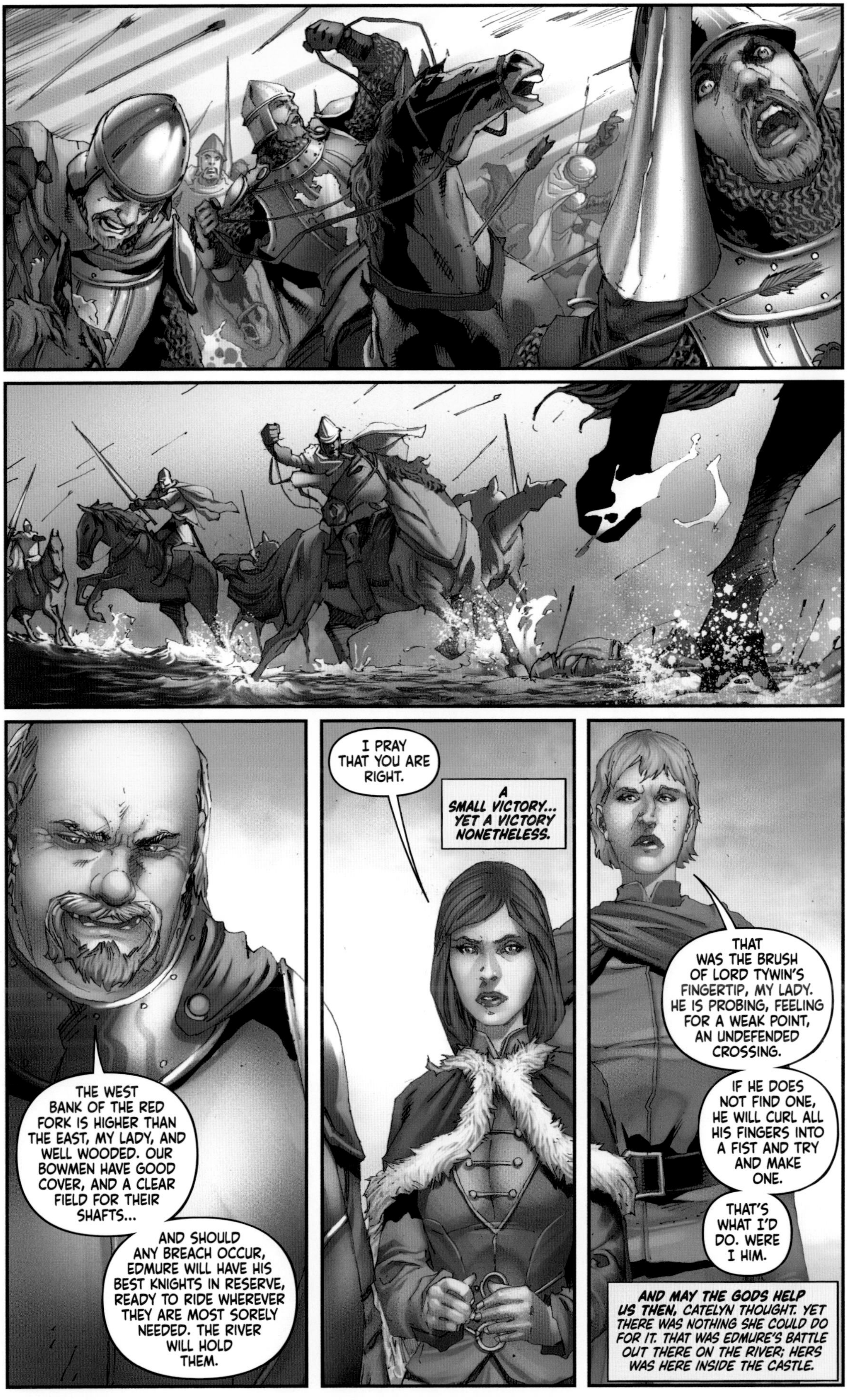
THE WEST BANK OF THE RED FORK IS HIGHER THAN THE EAST, MY LADY, AND WELL WOODED. OUR BOWMEN HAVE GOOD COVER, AND A CLEAR FIELD FOR THEIR SHAFTS...
AND SHOULD ANY BREACH OCCUR, EDMURE WILL HAVE HIS BEST KNIGHTS IN RESERVE, READY TO RIDE WHEREVER THEY ARE MOST SORELY NEEDED. THE RIVER WILL HOLD THEM.
I PRAY THAT YOU ARE RIGHT.
A SMALL VICTORY... YET A VICTORY NONETHELESS.
THAT WAS THE BRUSH OF LORD TYWIN'S FINGERTIP, MY LADY. HE IS PROBING, FEELING FOR A WEAK POINT, AN UNDEFENDED CROSSING.
IF HE DOES NOT FIND ONE, HE WILL CURL ALL HIS FINGERS INTO A FIST AND TRY AND MAKE ONE.
THAT'S WHAT I'D DO. WERE I HIM.
AND MAY THE GODS HELP US THEN, CATELYN THOUGHT. YET THERE WAS NOTHING SHE COULD DO FOR IT. THAT WAS EDMURE'S BATTLE OUT THERE ON THE RIVER; HERS WAS HERE INSIDE THE CASTLE.

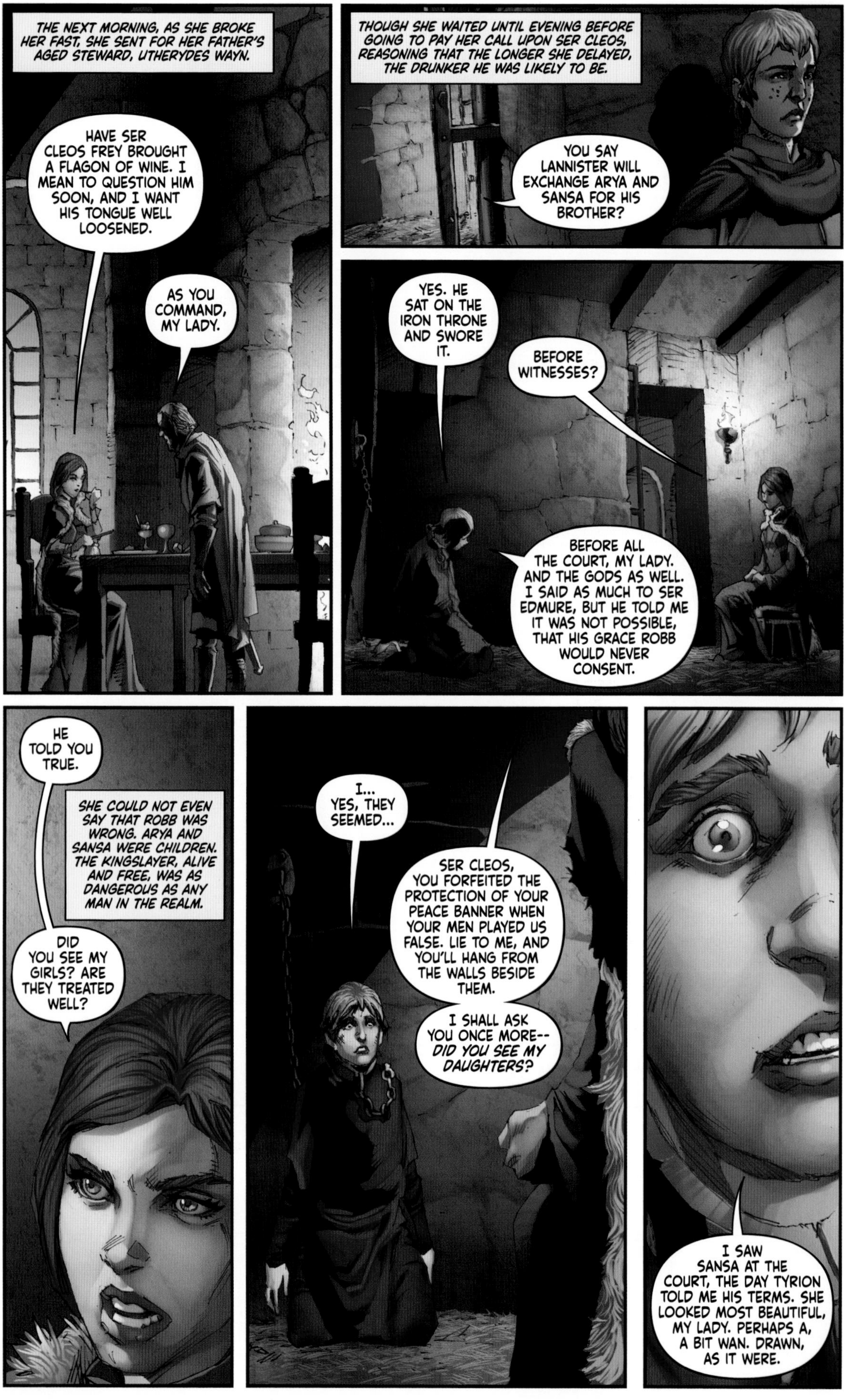
THE NEXT MORNING, AS SHE BROKE HER FAST, SHE SENT FOR HER FATHER'S AGED STEWARD, UTHERYDES WAYN.
HAVE SER CLEOS FREY BROUGHT A FLAGON OF WINE. I MEAN TO QUESTION HIM SOON, AND I WANT HIS TONGUE WELL LOOSENED.
AS YOU COMMAND, MY LADY.
THOUGH SHE WAITED UNTIL EVENING BEFORE GOING TO PAY HER CALL UPON SER CLEOS, REASONING THAT THE LONGER SHE DELAYED, THE DRUNKER HE WAS LIKELY TO BE.
YOU SAY LANNISTER WILL EXCHANGE ARYA AND SANSA FOR HIS BROTHER?
YES. HE SAT ON THE IRON THRONE AND SWORE IT.
BEFORE WITNESSES?
BEFORE ALL THE COURT, MY LADY. AND THE GODS AS WELL. I SAID AS MUCH TO SER EDMURE, BUT HE TOLD ME IT WAS NOT POSSIBLE, THAT HIS GRACE ROBB WOULD NEVER CONSENT.
HE TOLD YOU TRUE.
SHE COULD NOT EVEN SAY THAT ROBB WAS WRONG. ARYA AND SANSA WERE CHILDREN. THE KINGSLAYER, ALIVE AND FREE, WAS AS DANGEROUS AS ANY MAN IN THE REALM.
DID YOU SEE MY GIRLS? ARE THEY TREATED WELL?
I... YES, THEY SEEMED...
SER CLEOS, YOU FORFEITED THE PROTECTION OF YOUR PEACE BANNER WHEN YOUR MEN PLAYED US FALSE. LIE TO ME, AND YOU'LL HANG FROM THE WALLS BESIDE THEM.
I SHALL ASK YOU ONCE MORE-- DID YOU SEE MY DAUGHTERS?
I SAW SANSA AT THE COURT, THE DAY TYRION TOLD ME HIS TERMS. SHE LOOKED MOST BEAUTIFUL, MY LADY. PERHAPS A, A BIT WAN. DRAWN, AS IT WERE.

SANSA, BUT NOT ARYA. THAT MIGHT MEAN ANYTHING. ARYA HAD ALWAYS BEEN HARDER TO TAME.

PERHAPS CERSEI WAS RELUCTANT TO PARADE HER IN OPEN COURT FOR FEAR OF WHAT SHE MIGHT SAY OR DO.

THEY MIGHT HAVE HER LOCKED SAFELY OUT OF SIGHT.

OR THEY MIGHT HAVE KILLED HER.

CATELYN SHOVED THE THOUGHT AWAY.

HIS TERMS, YOU SAID...YET CERSEI IS QUEEN REGENT.

TYRION SPOKE FOR BOTH OF THEM. THE QUEEN WAS NOT THERE. SHE WAS INDISPOSED THAT DAY, I WAS TOLD.

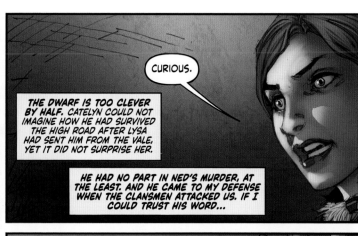

CURIOUS.

THE DWARF IS TOO CLEVER BY HALF. CATELYN COULD NOT IMAGINE HOW HE HAD SURVIVED THE HIGH ROAD AFTER LYSA HAD SENT HIM FROM THE VALE, YET IT DID NOT SURPRISE HER.

HE HAD NO PART IN NED'S MURDER, AT THE LEAST. AND HE CAME TO MY DEFENSE WHEN THE CLANSMEN ATTACKED US. IF I COULD TRUST HIS WORD...

HIS DAGGER'S MARKS, SHE REMINDED HERSELF. HIS DAGGER, IN THE HAND OF THE KILLER HE PAID TO OPEN BRAN'S THROAT.

THOUGH THE DWARF DENIED IT, TO BE SURE. EVEN AFTER LYSA LOCKED HIM IN ONE OF HER SKY CELLS AND THREATENED HIM WITH HER MOON DOOR, HE HAD STILL DENIED IT.

HE LIED. THE LANNISTERS ARE LIARS EVERY ONE, AND THE DWARF IS THE WORST OF THEM. THE KILLER WAS ARMED WITH HIS OWN KNIFE.

I KNOW NOTHING OF ANY--

YOU KNOW NOTHING.

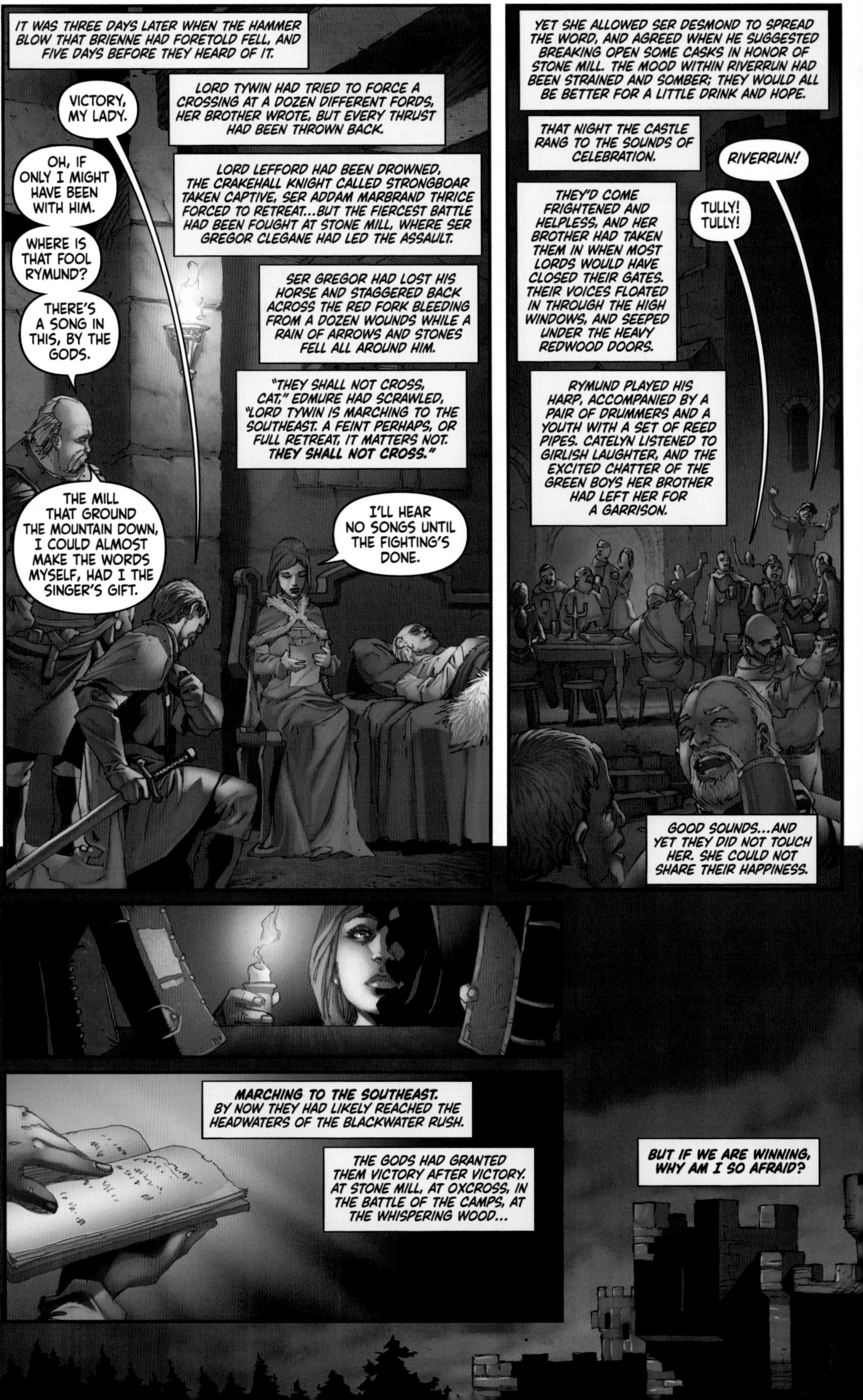
IT WAS THREE DAYS LATER WHEN THE HAMMER BLOW THAT BRIENNE HAD FORETOLD FELL, AND FIVE DAYS BEFORE THEY HEARD OF IT.
LORD TYWIN HAD TRIED TO FORCE A CROSSING AT A DOZEN DIFFERENT FORDS, HER BROTHER WROTE, BUT EVERY THRUST HAD BEEN THROWN BACK.
VICTORY, MY LADY.
LORD LEFFORD HAD BEEN DROWNED, THE CRAKEHALL KNIGHT CALLED STRONGBOAR TAKEN CAPTIVE, SER ADDAM MARBRAND THRICE FORCED TO RETREAT...BUT THE FIERCEST BATTLE HAD BEEN FOUGHT AT STONE MILL, WHERE SER GREGOR CLEGANE HAD LED THE ASSAULT.
OH, IF ONLY I MIGHT HAVE BEEN WITH HIM.
WHERE IS THAT FOOL RYMUND?
SER GREGOR HAD LOST HIS HORSE AND STAGGERED BACK ACROSS THE RED FORK BLEEDING FROM A DOZEN WOUNDS WHILE A RAIN OF ARROWS AND STONES FELL ALL AROUND HIM.
THERE'S A SONG IN THIS, BY THE GODS.
"THEY SHALL NOT CROSS, CAT," EDMURE HAD SCRAWLED, "LORD TYWIN IS MARCHING TO THE SOUTHEAST. A FEINT PERHAPS, OR FULL RETREAT, IT MATTERS NOT. THEY SHALL NOT CROSS."
THE MILL THAT GROUND THE MOUNTAIN DOWN, I COULD ALMOST MAKE THE WORDS MYSELF, HAD I THE SINGER'S GIFT.
I'LL HEAR NO SONGS UNTIL THE FIGHTING'S DONE.
YET SHE ALLOWED SER DESMOND TO SPREAD THE WORD, AND AGREED WHEN HE SUGGESTED BREAKING OPEN SOME CASKS IN HONOR OF STONE MILL. THE MOOD WITHIN RIVERRUN HAD BEEN STRAINED AND SOMBER; THEY WOULD ALL BE BETTER FOR A LITTLE DRINK AND HOPE.
THAT NIGHT THE CASTLE RANG TO THE SOUNDS OF CELEBRATION.
RIVERRUN!
THEY'D COME FRIGHTENED AND HELPLESS, AND HER BROTHER HAD TAKEN THEM IN WHEN MOST LORDS WOULD HAVE CLOSED THEIR GATES. THEIR VOICES FLOATED IN THROUGH THE HIGH WINDOWS, AND SEEPED UNDER THE HEAVY REDWOOD DOORS.
TULLY! TULLY!
RYMUND PLAYED HIS HARP, ACCOMPANIED BY A PAIR OF DRUMMERS AND A YOUTH WITH A SET OF REED PIPES. CATELYN LISTENED TO GIRLISH LAUGHTER, AND THE EXCITED CHATTER OF THE GREEN BOYS HER BROTHER HAD LEFT HER FOR A GARRISON.
GOOD SOUNDS...AND YET THEY DID NOT TOUCH HER. SHE COULD NOT SHARE THEIR HAPPINESS.
MARCHING TO THE SOUTHEAST. BY NOW THEY HAD LIKELY REACHED THE HEADWATERS OF THE BLACKWATER RUSH.
THE GODS HAD GRANTED THEM VICTORY AFTER VICTORY. AT STONE MILL, AT OXCROSS, IN THE BATTLE OF THE CAMPS, AT THE WHISPERING WOOD...
BUT IF WE ARE WINNING, WHY AM I SO AFRAID?

DAENERYS

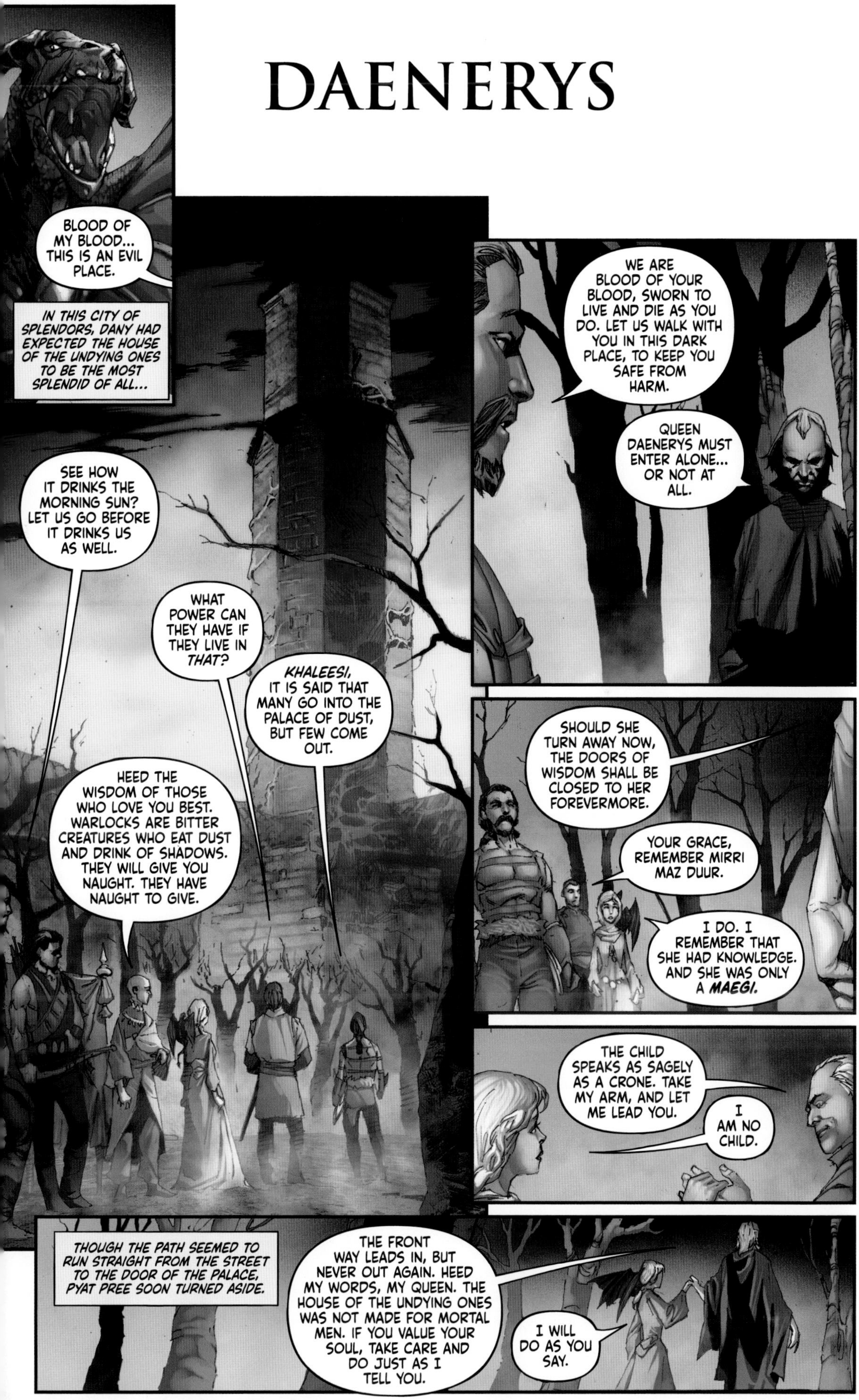
BLOOD OF MY BLOOD... THIS IS AN EVIL PLACE.
IN THIS CITY OF SPLENDORS, DANY HAD EXPECTED THE HOUSE OF THE UNDYING ONES TO BE THE MOST SPLENDID OF ALL...
SEE HOW IT DRINKS THE MORNING SUN? LET US GO BEFORE IT DRINKS US AS WELL.
WHAT POWER CAN THEY HAVE IF THEY LIVE IN *THAT?*
KHALEESI, IT IS SAID THAT MANY GO INTO THE PALACE OF DUST, BUT FEW COME OUT.
HEED THE WISDOM OF THOSE WHO LOVE YOU BEST. WARLOCKS ARE BITTER CREATURES WHO EAT DUST AND DRINK OF SHADOWS. THEY WILL GIVE YOU NAUGHT. THEY HAVE NAUGHT TO GIVE.
WE ARE BLOOD OF YOUR BLOOD, SWORN TO LIVE AND DIE AS YOU DO. LET US WALK WITH YOU IN THIS DARK PLACE, TO KEEP YOU SAFE FROM HARM.
QUEEN DAENERYS MUST ENTER ALONE... OR NOT AT ALL.
SHOULD SHE TURN AWAY NOW, THE DOORS OF WISDOM SHALL BE CLOSED TO HER FOREVERMORE.
YOUR GRACE, REMEMBER MIRRI MAZ DUUR.
I DO. I REMEMBER THAT SHE HAD KNOWLEDGE. AND SHE WAS ONLY A ***MAEGI.***
THE CHILD SPEAKS AS SAGELY AS A CRONE. TAKE MY ARM, AND LET ME LEAD YOU.
I AM NO CHILD.
THOUGH THE PATH SEEMED TO RUN STRAIGHT FROM THE STREET TO THE DOOR OF THE PALACE, PYAT PREE SOON TURNED ASIDE.
THE FRONT WAY LEADS IN, BUT NEVER OUT AGAIN. HEED MY WORDS, MY QUEEN. THE HOUSE OF THE UNDYING ONES WAS NOT MADE FOR MORTAL MEN. IF YOU VALUE YOUR SOUL, TAKE CARE AND DO JUST AS I TELL YOU.
I WILL DO AS YOU SAY.

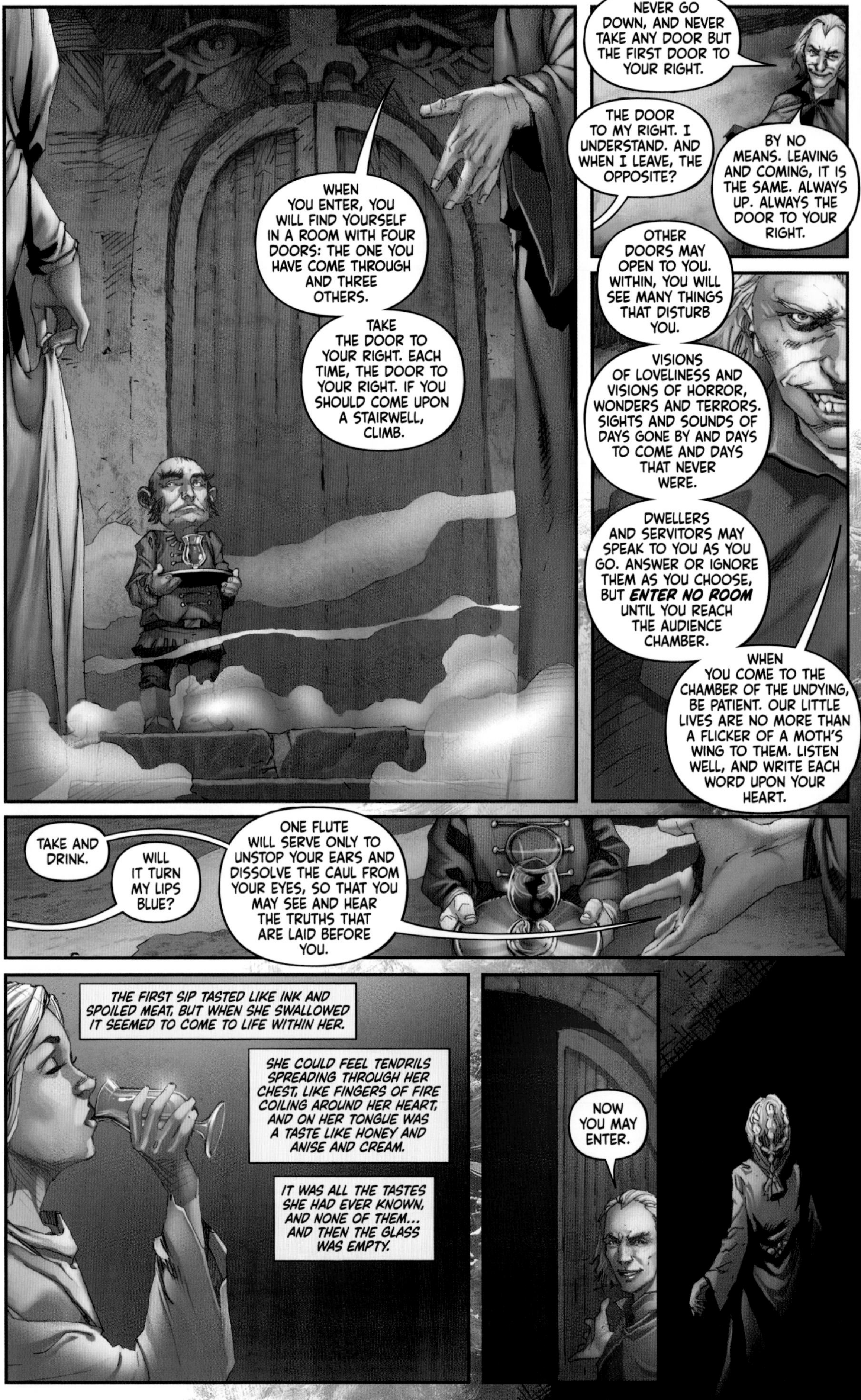
WHEN YOU ENTER, YOU WILL FIND YOURSELF IN A ROOM WITH FOUR DOORS: THE ONE YOU HAVE COME THROUGH AND THREE OTHERS.
TAKE THE DOOR TO YOUR RIGHT. EACH TIME, THE DOOR TO YOUR RIGHT. IF YOU SHOULD COME UPON A STAIRWELL, CLIMB.
NEVER GO DOWN, AND NEVER TAKE ANY DOOR BUT THE FIRST DOOR TO YOUR RIGHT.
THE DOOR TO MY RIGHT. I UNDERSTAND. AND WHEN I LEAVE, THE OPPOSITE?
BY NO MEANS. LEAVING AND COMING, IT IS THE SAME. ALWAYS UP. ALWAYS THE DOOR TO YOUR RIGHT.
OTHER DOORS MAY OPEN TO YOU. WITHIN, YOU WILL SEE MANY THINGS THAT DISTURB YOU.
VISIONS OF LOVELINESS AND VISIONS OF HORROR, WONDERS AND TERRORS. SIGHTS AND SOUNDS OF DAYS GONE BY AND DAYS TO COME AND DAYS THAT NEVER WERE.
DWELLERS AND SERVITORS MAY SPEAK TO YOU AS YOU GO. ANSWER OR IGNORE THEM AS YOU CHOOSE, BUT ***ENTER NO ROOM*** UNTIL YOU REACH THE AUDIENCE CHAMBER.
WHEN YOU COME TO THE CHAMBER OF THE UNDYING, BE PATIENT. OUR LITTLE LIVES ARE NO MORE THAN A FLICKER OF A MOTH'S WING TO THEM. LISTEN WELL, AND WRITE EACH WORD UPON YOUR HEART.
TAKE AND DRINK.
WILL IT TURN MY LIPS BLUE?
ONE FLUTE WILL SERVE ONLY TO UNSTOP YOUR EARS AND DISSOLVE THE CAUL FROM YOUR EYES, SO THAT YOU MAY SEE AND HEAR THE TRUTHS THAT ARE LAID BEFORE YOU.
THE FIRST SIP TASTED LIKE INK AND SPOILED MEAT, BUT WHEN SHE SWALLOWED IT SEEMED TO COME TO LIFE WITHIN HER.
SHE COULD FEEL TENDRILS SPREADING THROUGH HER CHEST, LIKE FINGERS OF FIRE COILING AROUND HER HEART, AND ON HER TONGUE WAS A TASTE LIKE HONEY AND ANISE AND CREAM.
IT WAS ALL THE TASTES SHE HAD EVER KNOWN, AND NONE OF THEM... AND THEN THE GLASS WAS EMPTY.
NOW YOU MAY ENTER.

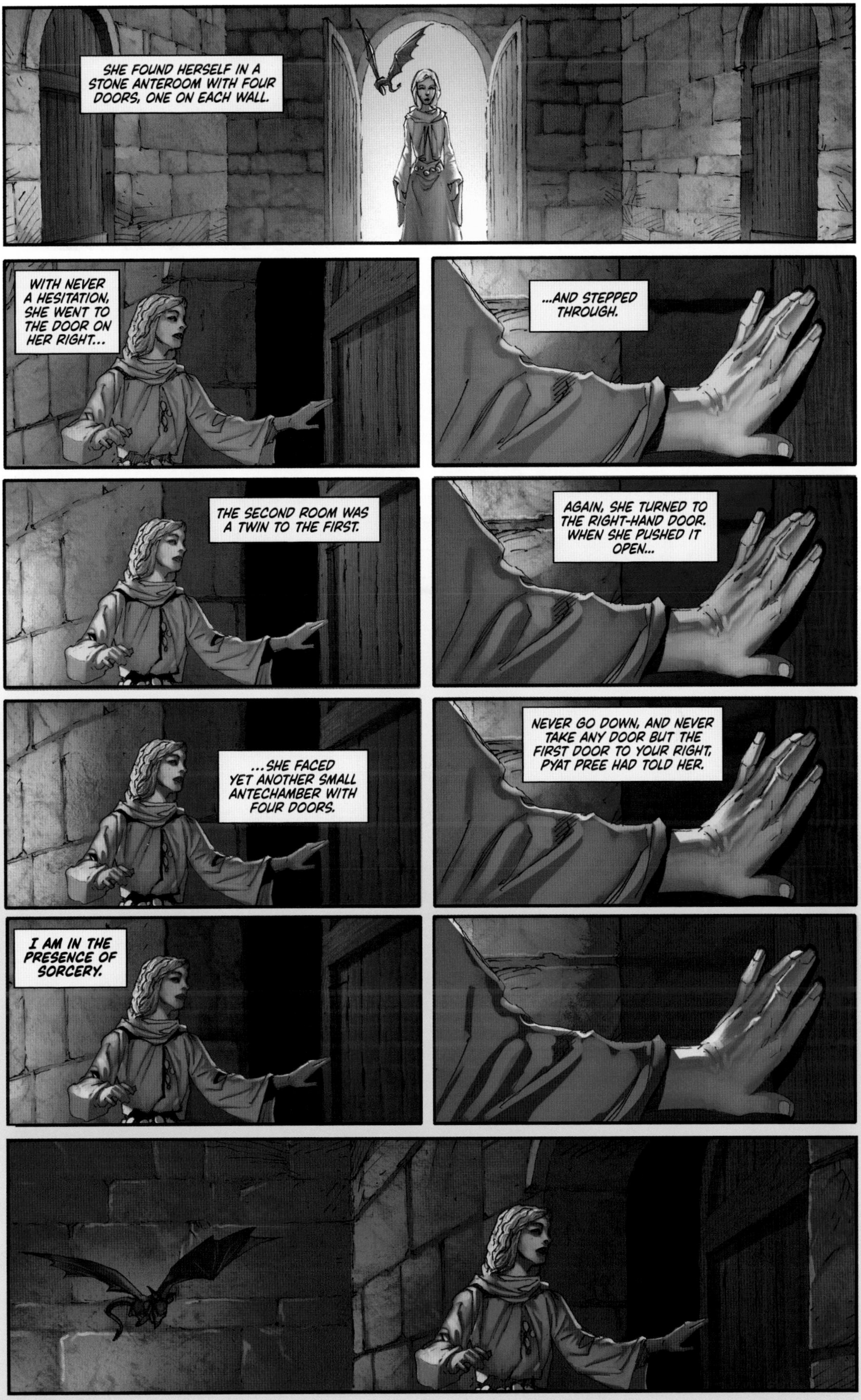
SHE FOUND HERSELF IN A STONE ANTEROOM WITH FOUR DOORS, ONE ON EACH WALL.
WITH NEVER A HESITATION, SHE WENT TO THE DOOR ON HER RIGHT...
...AND STEPPED THROUGH.
THE SECOND ROOM WAS A TWIN TO THE FIRST.
AGAIN, SHE TURNED TO THE RIGHT-HAND DOOR. WHEN SHE PUSHED IT OPEN...
...SHE FACED YET ANOTHER SMALL ANTECHAMBER WITH FOUR DOORS.
NEVER GO DOWN, AND NEVER TAKE ANY DOOR BUT THE FIRST DOOR TO YOUR RIGHT, PYAT PREE HAD TOLD HER.
I AM IN THE PRESENCE OF SORCERY.

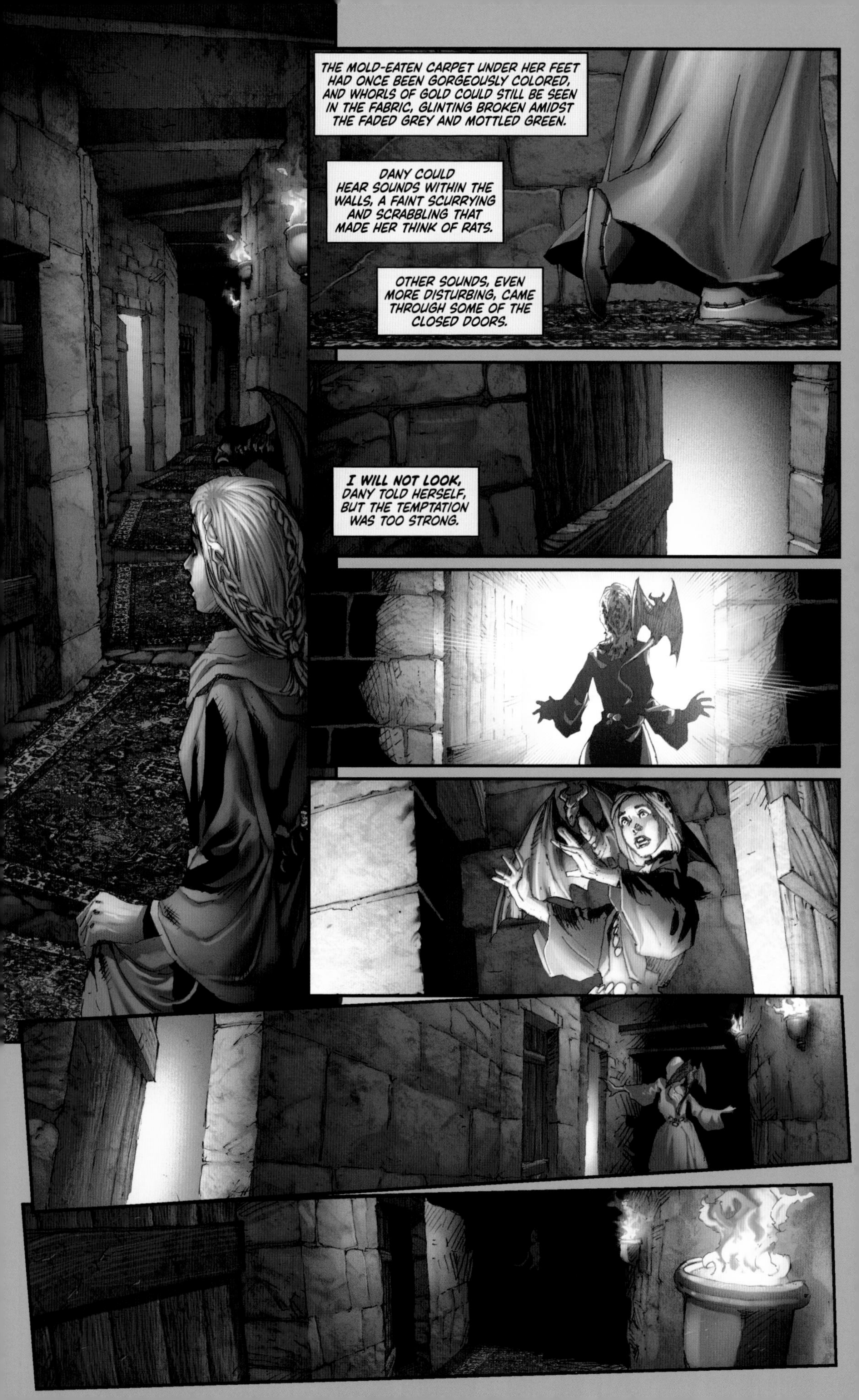
THE MOLD-EATEN CARPET UNDER HER FEET HAD ONCE BEEN GORGEOUSLY COLORED, AND WHORLS OF GOLD COULD STILL BE SEEN IN THE FABRIC, GLINTING BROKEN AMIDST THE FADED GREY AND MOTTLED GREEN.
DANY COULD HEAR SOUNDS WITHIN THE WALLS, A FAINT SCURRYING AND SCRABBLING THAT MADE HER THINK OF RATS.
OTHER SOUNDS, EVEN MORE DISTURBING, CAME THROUGH SOME OF THE CLOSED DOORS.
I WILL NOT LOOK, DANY TOLD HERSELF, BUT THE TEMPTATION WAS TOO STRONG.

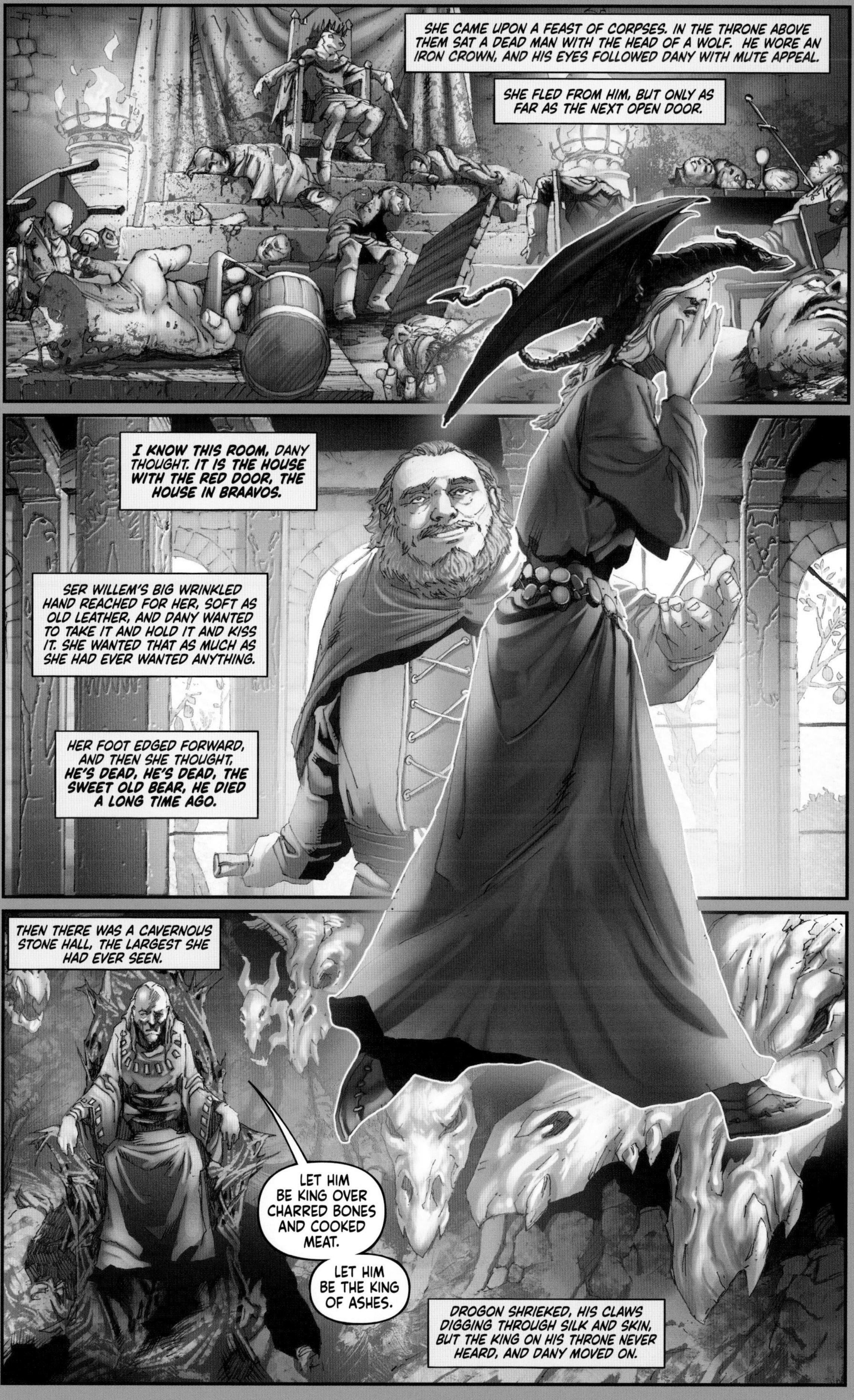
SHE CAME UPON A FEAST OF CORPSES. IN THE THRONE ABOVE THEM SAT A DEAD MAN WITH THE HEAD OF A WOLF. HE WORE AN IRON CROWN, AND HIS EYES FOLLOWED DANY WITH MUTE APPEAL.
SHE FLED FROM HIM, BUT ONLY AS FAR AS THE NEXT OPEN DOOR.
I KNOW THIS ROOM, DANY THOUGHT. IT IS THE HOUSE WITH THE RED DOOR, THE HOUSE IN BRAAVOS.
SER WILLEM'S BIG WRINKLED HAND REACHED FOR HER, SOFT AS OLD LEATHER, AND DANY WANTED TO TAKE IT AND HOLD IT AND KISS IT. SHE WANTED THAT AS MUCH AS SHE HAD EVER WANTED ANYTHING.
HER FOOT EDGED FORWARD, AND THEN SHE THOUGHT, HE'S DEAD, HE'S DEAD, THE SWEET OLD BEAR, HE DIED A LONG TIME AGO.
THEN THERE WAS A CAVERNOUS STONE HALL, THE LARGEST SHE HAD EVER SEEN.
LET HIM BE KING OVER CHARRED BONES AND COOKED MEAT.
LET HIM BE THE KING OF ASHES.
DROGON SHRIEKED, HIS CLAWS DIGGING THROUGH SILK AND SKIN, BUT THE KING ON HIS THRONE NEVER HEARD, AND DANY MOVED ON.

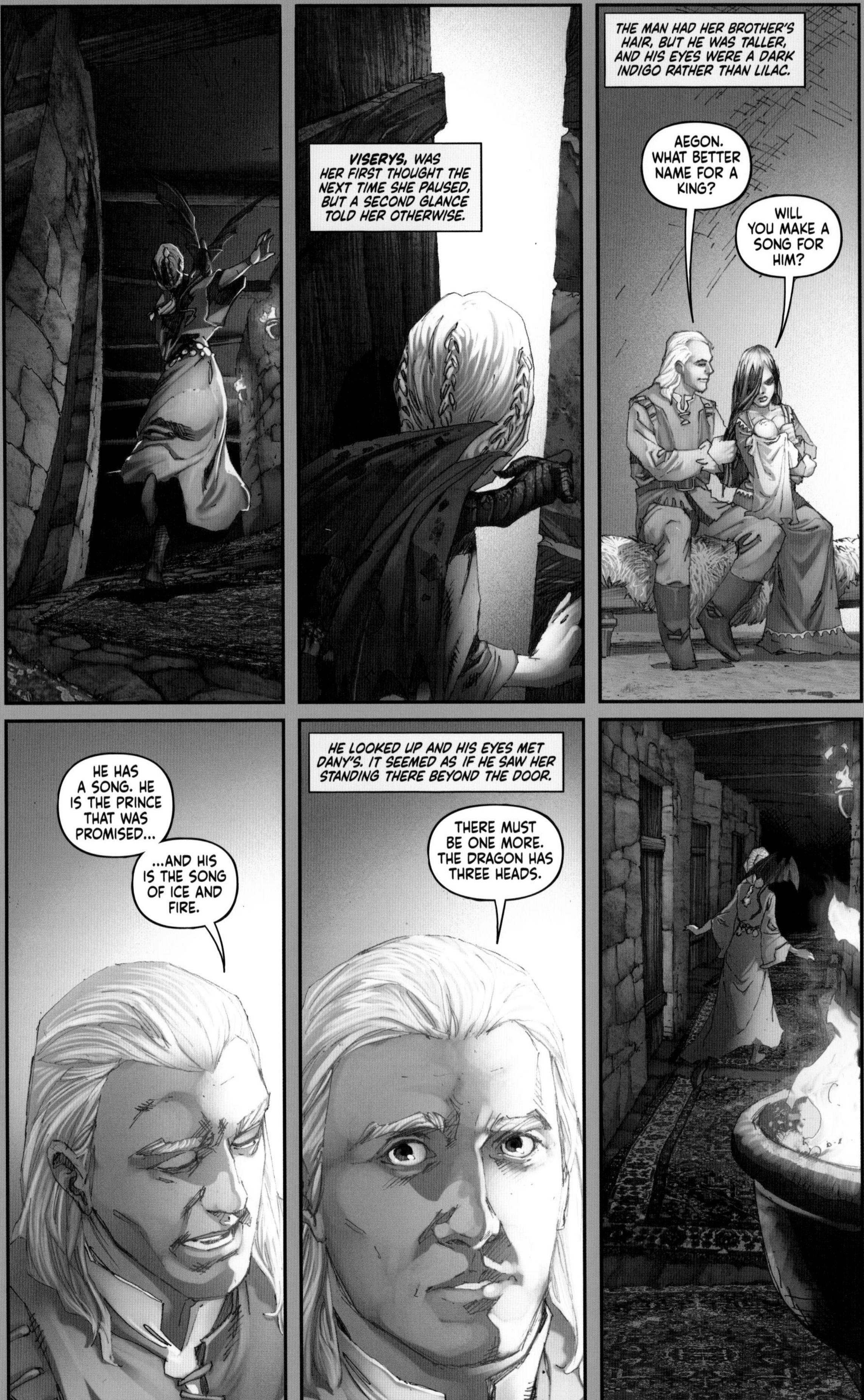
VISERYS, WAS HER FIRST THOUGHT THE NEXT TIME SHE PAUSED, BUT A SECOND GLANCE TOLD HER OTHERWISE.
THE MAN HAD HER BROTHER'S HAIR, BUT HE WAS TALLER, AND HIS EYES WERE A DARK INDIGO RATHER THAN LILAC.
AEGON. WHAT BETTER NAME FOR A KING?
WILL YOU MAKE A SONG FOR HIM?
HE HAS A SONG. HE IS THE PRINCE THAT WAS PROMISED...
...AND HIS IS THE SONG OF ICE AND FIRE.
HE LOOKED UP AND HIS EYES MET DANY'S. IT SEEMED AS IF HE SAW HER STANDING THERE BEYOND THE DOOR.
THERE MUST BE ONE MORE. THE DRAGON HAS THREE HEADS.

IT SEEMED AS THOUGH SHE WALKED FOR ANOTHER HOUR BEFORE THE LONG HALL FINALLY ENDED IN A STEEP STONE STAIR, DESCENDING INTO DARKNESS.

EVERY DOOR, OPEN OR CLOSED, HAD BEEN TO HER LEFT.

THE TORCHES WERE GOING OUT, SHE REALIZED WITH A START OF FEAR. PERHAPS TWENTY STILL BURNED. THIRTY AT MOST.

THE DARKNESS CAME CREEPING TOWARDS HER. AND IT SEEMED AS IF SHE HEARD SOMETHING ELSE COMING, SHUFFLING AND DRAGGING ITSELF SLOWLY ALONG THE FADED CARPET.

TERROR FILLED HER. SHE COULD NOT GO BACK AND SHE WAS AFRAID TO STAY HERE, BUT HOW COULD SHE GO ON? THERE WAS NO DOOR TO HER RIGHT, AND THE STEPS WENT DOWN, NOT UP.

COULD THERE BE A SECRET DOOR, A DOOR I CANNOT SEE?

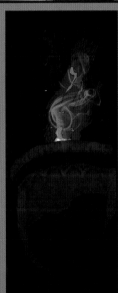

THE FIRST DOOR ON THE RIGHT, HE SAID, ALWAYS THE FIRST DOOR ON THE RIGHT. THE FIRST DOOR ON THE RIGHT...

...IS THE LAST DOOR ON THE LEFT!

THE BLOOD OF THE DRAGON MUST NOT BE AFRAID.

BEYOND THE DOORS WAS A GREAT HALL AND A SPLENDOR OF WIZARDS. SHAFTS OF SUNLIGHT SLANTED THROUGH WINDOWS OF STAINED GLASS, AND THE AIR WAS ALIVE WITH THE MOST BEAUTIFUL MUSIC SHE HAD EVER HEARD.

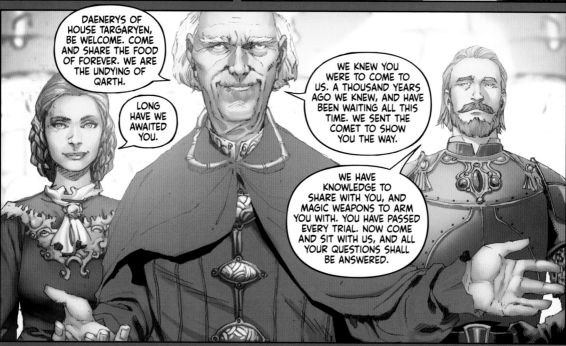

DAENERYS OF HOUSE TARGARYEN, BE WELCOME. COME AND SHARE THE FOOD OF FOREVER. WE ARE THE UNDYING OF QARTH.

LONG HAVE WE AWAITED YOU.

WE KNEW YOU WERE TO COME TO US. A THOUSAND YEARS AGO WE KNEW, AND HAVE BEEN WAITING ALL THIS TIME. WE SENT THE COMET TO SHOW YOU THE WAY.

WE HAVE KNOWLEDGE TO SHARE WITH YOU, AND MAGIC WEAPONS TO ARM YOU WITH. YOU HAVE PASSED EVERY TRIAL. NOW COME AND SIT WITH US, AND ALL YOUR QUESTIONS SHALL BE ANSWERED.

SKREEEEE

A WILLFUL BEAST. SHALL WE TEACH YOU THE SECRET SPEECH OF DRAGONKIND? COME, COME...

THE GREAT DOOR WAS SO HEAVY IT TOOK ALL OF DANY'S STRENGTH TO BUDGE IT, BUT FINALLY IT BEGAN TO MOVE.

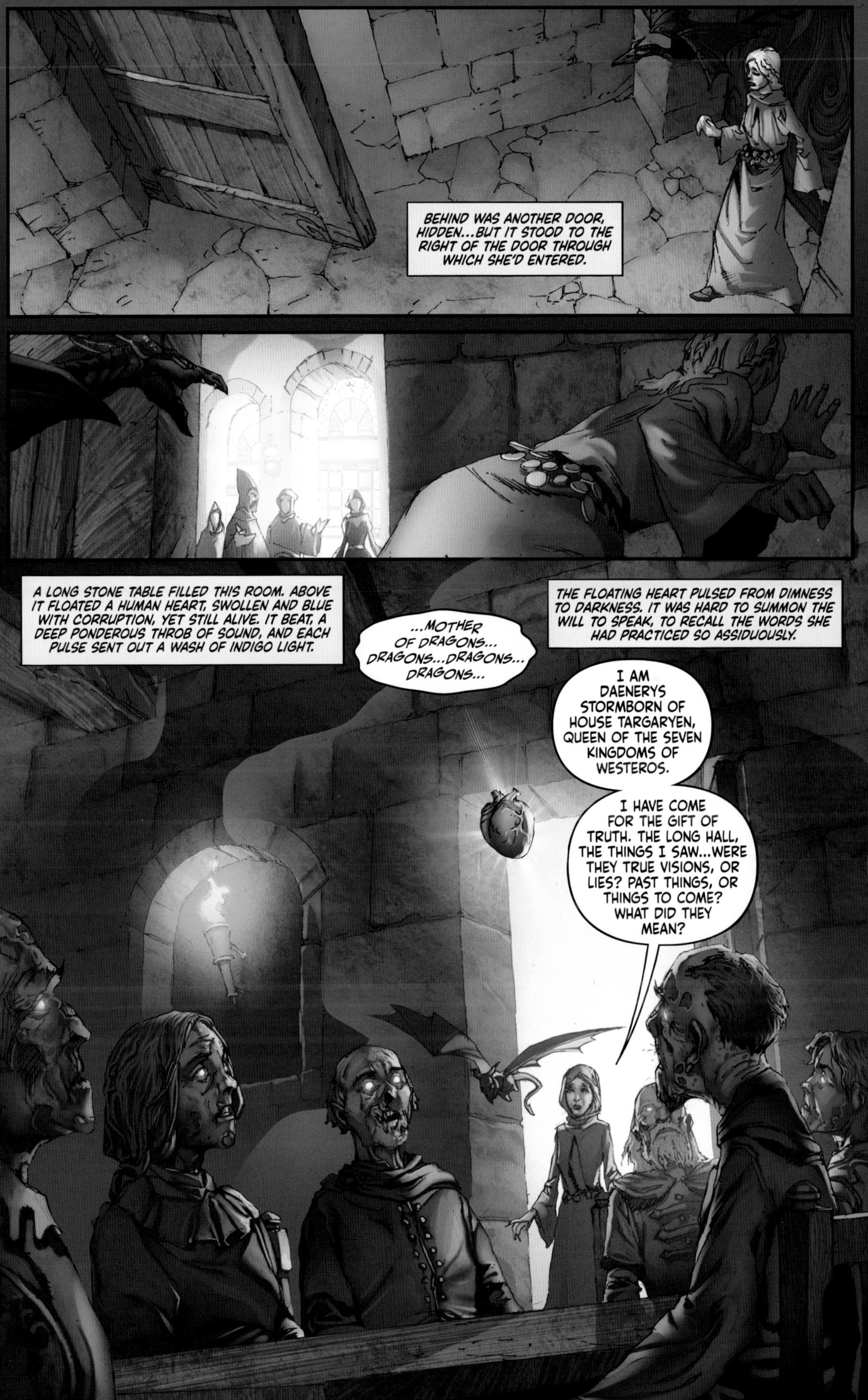
BEHIND WAS ANOTHER DOOR, HIDDEN...BUT IT STOOD TO THE RIGHT OF THE DOOR THROUGH WHICH SHE'D ENTERED.
A LONG STONE TABLE FILLED THIS ROOM. ABOVE IT FLOATED A HUMAN HEART, SWOLLEN AND BLUE WITH CORRUPTION, YET STILL ALIVE. IT BEAT, A DEEP PONDEROUS THROB OF SOUND, AND EACH PULSE SENT OUT A WASH OF INDIGO LIGHT.
...MOTHER OF DRAGONS... DRAGONS...DRAGONS... DRAGONS...
THE FLOATING HEART PULSED FROM DIMNESS TO DARKNESS. IT WAS HARD TO SUMMON THE WILL TO SPEAK, TO RECALL THE WORDS SHE HAD PRACTICED SO ASSIDUOUSLY.
I AM DAENERYS STORMBORN OF HOUSE TARGARYEN, QUEEN OF THE SEVEN KINGDOMS OF WESTEROS.
I HAVE COME FOR THE GIFT OF TRUTH. THE LONG HALL, THE THINGS I SAW...WERE THEY TRUE VISIONS, OR LIES? PAST THINGS, OR THINGS TO COME? WHAT DID THEY MEAN?

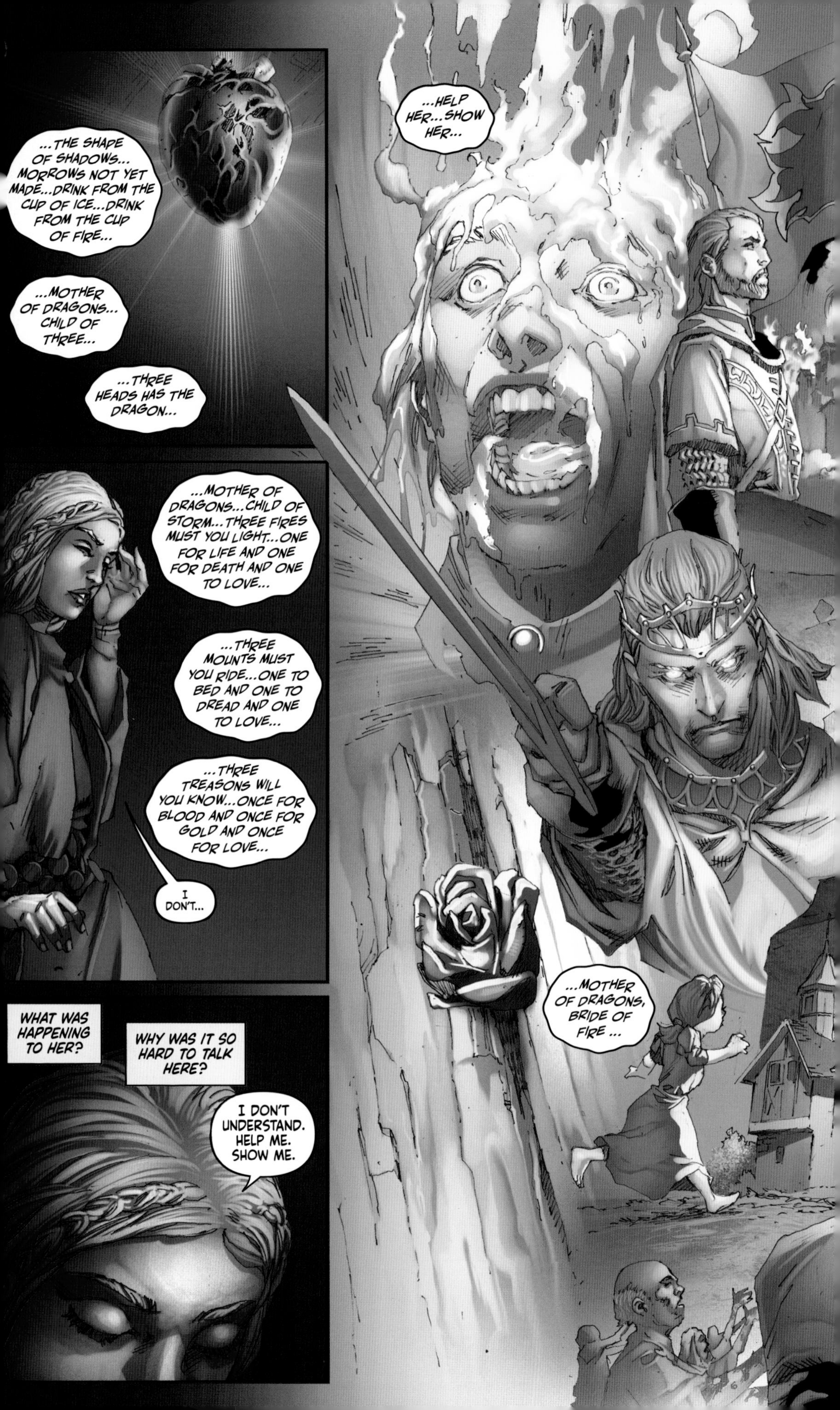
...THE SHAPE OF SHADOWS... MORROWS NOT YET MADE...DRINK FROM THE CUP OF ICE...DRINK FROM THE CUP OF FIRE...
...MOTHER OF DRAGONS... CHILD OF THREE...
...THREE HEADS HAS THE DRAGON...
...MOTHER OF DRAGONS...CHILD OF STORM...THREE FIRES MUST YOU LIGHT...ONE FOR LIFE AND ONE FOR DEATH AND ONE TO LOVE...
...THREE MOUNTS MUST YOU RIDE...ONE TO BED AND ONE TO DREAD AND ONE TO LOVE...
...THREE TREASONS WILL YOU KNOW...ONCE FOR BLOOD AND ONCE FOR GOLD AND ONCE FOR LOVE...
I DON'T...
WHAT WAS HAPPENING TO HER?
WHY WAS IT SO HARD TO TALK HERE?
I DON'T UNDERSTAND. HELP ME. SHOW ME.
...HELP HER...SHOW HER...
...MOTHER OF DRAGONS, BRIDE OF FIRE ...

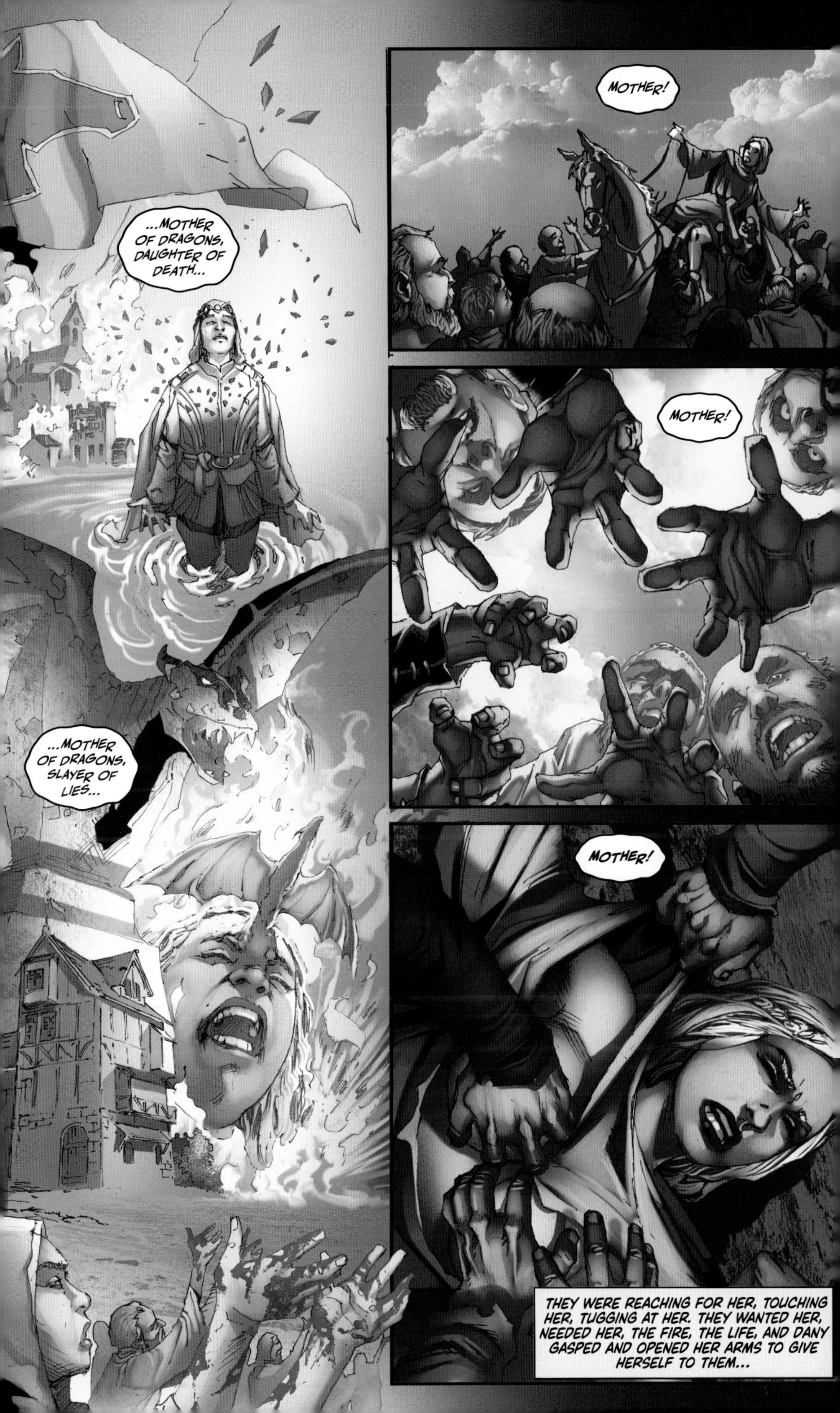

...MOTHER OF DRAGONS, DAUGHTER OF DEATH...
...MOTHER OF DRAGONS, SLAYER OF LIES...
MOTHER!
MOTHER!
MOTHER!
THEY WERE REACHING FOR HER, TOUCHING HER, TUGGING AT HER. THEY WANTED HER, NEEDED HER, THE FIRE, THE LIFE, AND DANY GASPED AND OPENED HER ARMS TO GIVE HERSELF TO THEM...

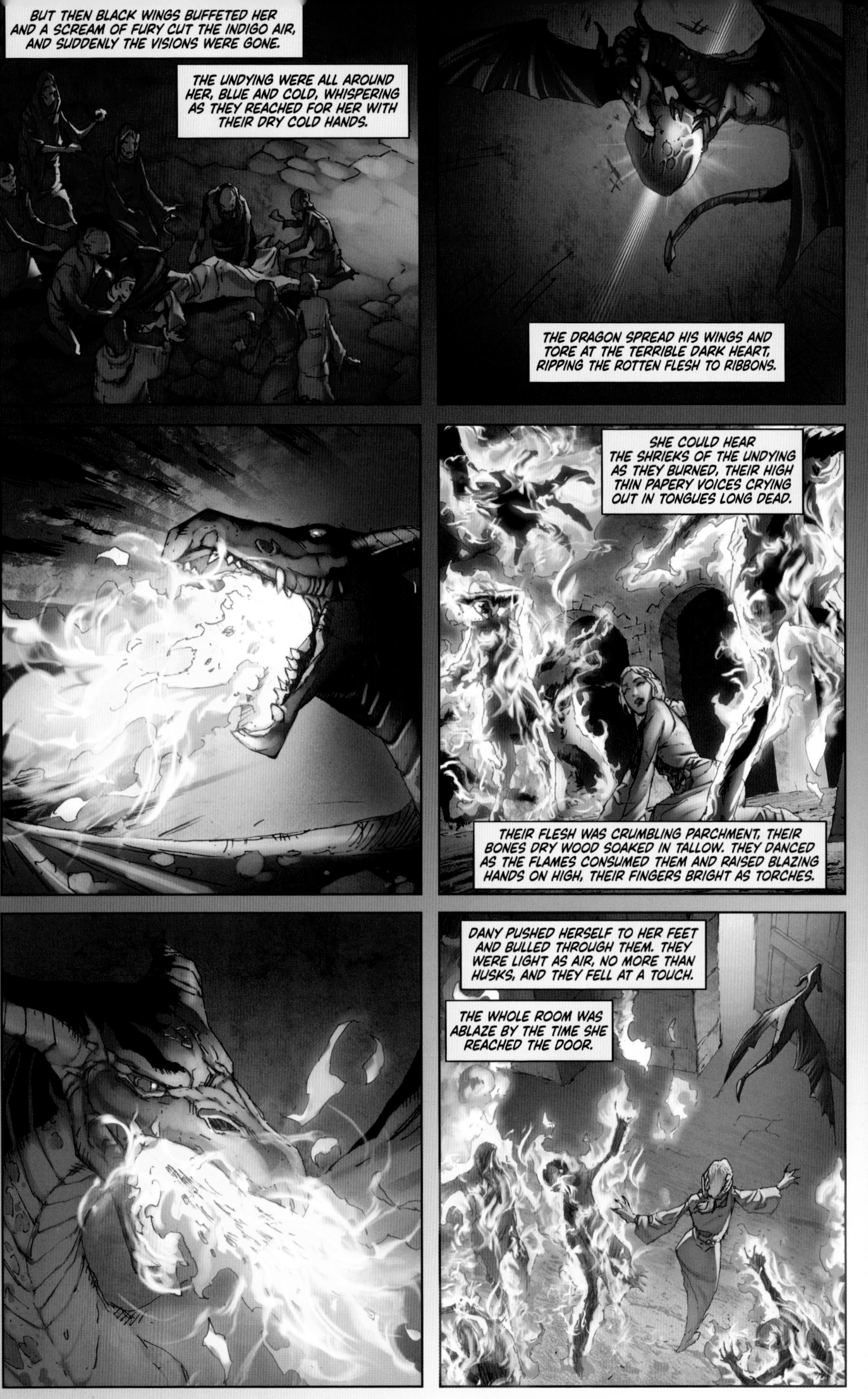
BUT THEN BLACK WINGS BUFFETED HER AND A SCREAM OF FURY CUT THE INDIGO AIR, AND SUDDENLY THE VISIONS WERE GONE.
THE UNDYING WERE ALL AROUND HER, BLUE AND COLD, WHISPERING AS THEY REACHED FOR HER WITH THEIR DRY COLD HANDS.
THE DRAGON SPREAD HIS WINGS AND TORE AT THE TERRIBLE DARK HEART, RIPPING THE ROTTEN FLESH TO RIBBONS.
SHE COULD HEAR THE SHRIEKS OF THE UNDYING AS THEY BURNED, THEIR HIGH THIN PAPERY VOICES CRYING OUT IN TONGUES LONG DEAD.
THEIR FLESH WAS CRUMBLING PARCHMENT, THEIR BONES DRY WOOD SOAKED IN TALLOW. THEY DANCED AS THE FLAMES CONSUMED THEM AND RAISED BLAZING HANDS ON HIGH, THEIR FINGERS BRIGHT AS TORCHES.
DANY PUSHED HERSELF TO HER FEET AND BULLED THROUGH THEM. THEY WERE LIGHT AS AIR, NO MORE THAN HUSKS, AND THEY FELL AT A TOUCH.
THE WHOLE ROOM WAS ABLAZE BY THE TIME SHE REACHED THE DOOR.

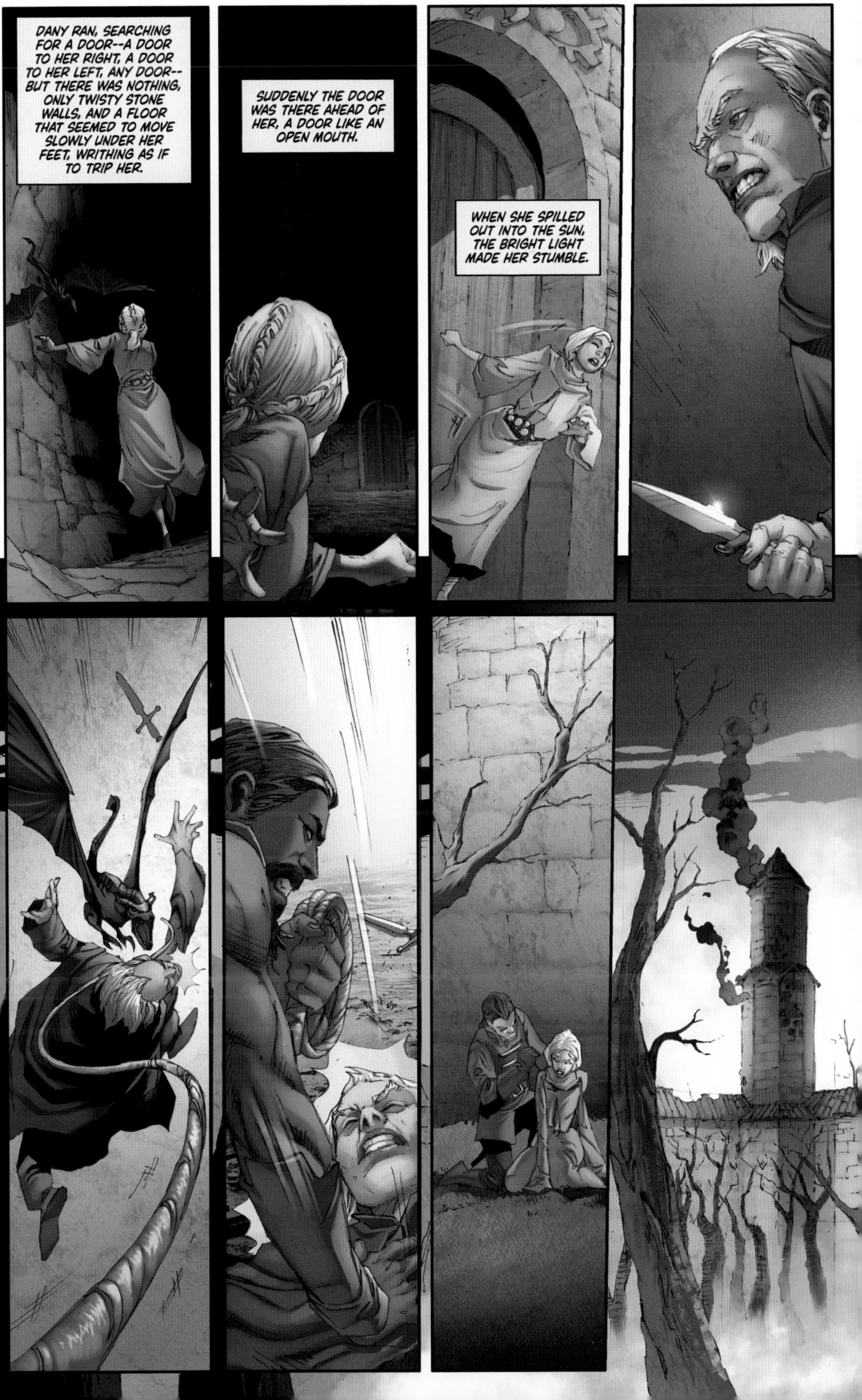
DANY RAN, SEARCHING FOR A DOOR--A DOOR TO HER RIGHT, A DOOR TO HER LEFT, ANY DOOR--BUT THERE WAS NOTHING, ONLY TWISTY STONE WALLS, AND A FLOOR THAT SEEMED TO MOVE SLOWLY UNDER HER FEET, WRITHING AS IF TO TRIP HER.
SUDDENLY THE DOOR WAS THERE AHEAD OF HER, A DOOR LIKE AN OPEN MOUTH.
WHEN SHE SPILLED OUT INTO THE SUN, THE BRIGHT LIGHT MADE HER STUMBLE.

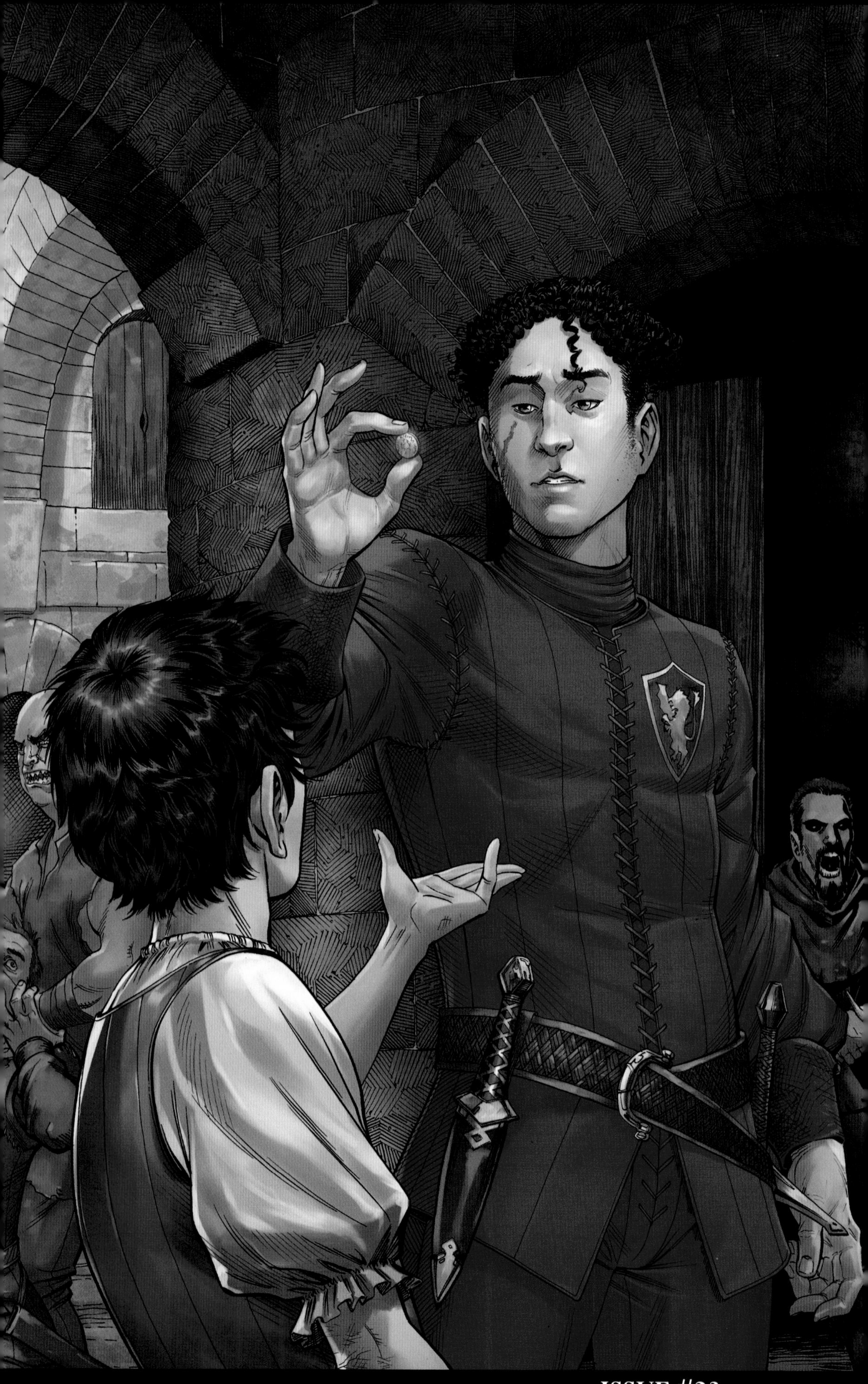

ISSUE #23

BRAN

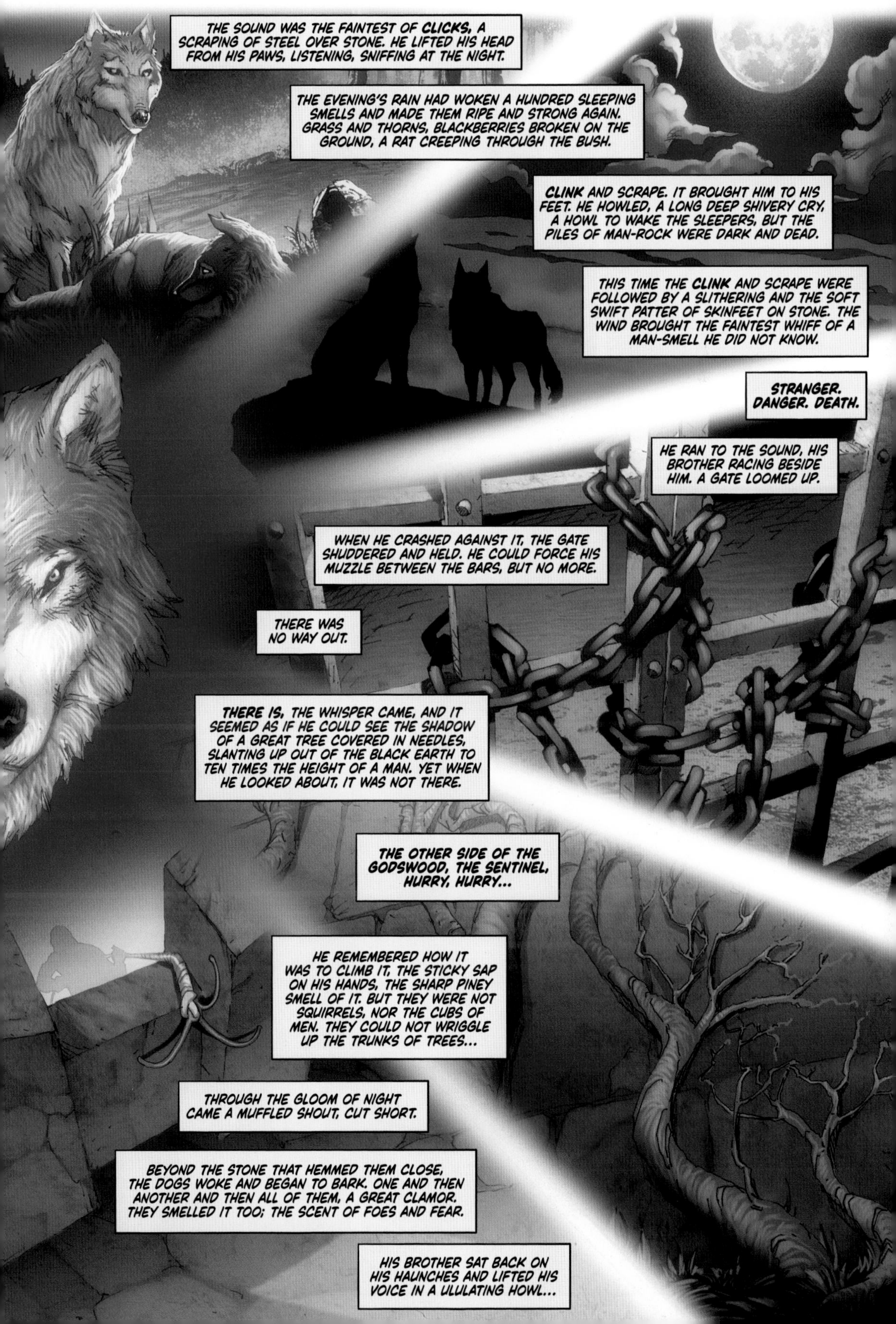
THE SOUND WAS THE FAINTEST OF **CLICKS**, A SCRAPING OF STEEL OVER STONE. HE LIFTED HIS HEAD FROM HIS PAWS, LISTENING, SNIFFING AT THE NIGHT.
THE EVENING'S RAIN HAD WOKEN A HUNDRED SLEEPING SMELLS AND MADE THEM RIPE AND STRONG AGAIN. GRASS AND THORNS, BLACKBERRIES BROKEN ON THE GROUND, A RAT CREEPING THROUGH THE BUSH.
CLINK AND SCRAPE. IT BROUGHT HIM TO HIS FEET. HE HOWLED, A LONG DEEP SHIVERY CRY, A HOWL TO WAKE THE SLEEPERS, BUT THE PILES OF MAN-ROCK WERE DARK AND DEAD.
THIS TIME THE **CLINK** AND SCRAPE WERE FOLLOWED BY A SLITHERING AND THE SOFT SWIFT PATTER OF SKINFEET ON STONE. THE WIND BROUGHT THE FAINTEST WHIFF OF A MAN-SMELL HE DID NOT KNOW.
STRANGER. DANGER. DEATH.
HE RAN TO THE SOUND, HIS BROTHER RACING BESIDE HIM. A GATE LOOMED UP.
WHEN HE CRASHED AGAINST IT, THE GATE SHUDDERED AND HELD. HE COULD FORCE HIS MUZZLE BETWEEN THE BARS, BUT NO MORE.
THERE WAS NO WAY OUT.
THERE IS, THE WHISPER CAME, AND IT SEEMED AS IF HE COULD SEE THE SHADOW OF A GREAT TREE COVERED IN NEEDLES, SLANTING UP OUT OF THE BLACK EARTH TO TEN TIMES THE HEIGHT OF A MAN. YET WHEN HE LOOKED ABOUT, IT WAS NOT THERE.
THE OTHER SIDE OF THE GODSWOOD, THE SENTINEL, HURRY, HURRY...
HE REMEMBERED HOW IT WAS TO CLIMB IT, THE STICKY SAP ON HIS HANDS, THE SHARP PINEY SMELL OF IT. BUT THEY WERE NOT SQUIRRELS, NOR THE CUBS OF MEN. THEY COULD NOT WRIGGLE UP THE TRUNKS OF TREES...
THROUGH THE GLOOM OF NIGHT CAME A MUFFLED SHOUT, CUT SHORT.
BEYOND THE STONE THAT HEMMED THEM CLOSE, THE DOGS WOKE AND BEGAN TO BARK. ONE AND THEN ANOTHER AND THEN ALL OF THEM, A GREAT CLAMOR. THEY SMELLED IT TOO; THE SCENT OF FOES AND FEAR.
HIS BROTHER SAT BACK ON HIS HAUNCHES AND LIFTED HIS VOICE IN A ULULATING HOWL...

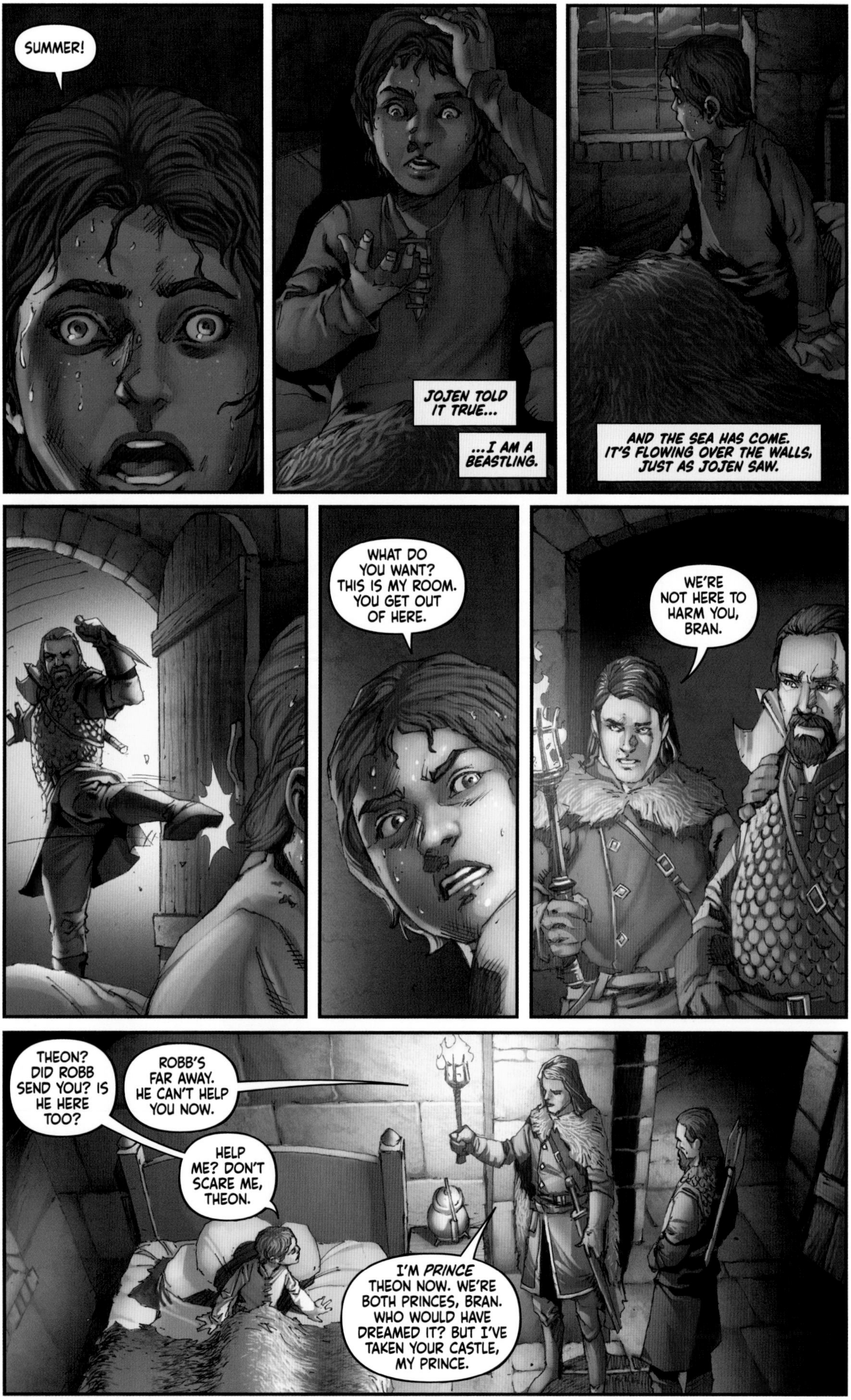
SUMMER!
JOJEN TOLD IT TRUE...
...I AM A BEASTLING.
AND THE SEA HAS COME. IT'S FLOWING OVER THE WALLS, JUST AS JOJEN SAW.
WHAT DO YOU WANT? THIS IS MY ROOM. YOU GET OUT OF HERE.
WE'RE NOT HERE TO HARM YOU, BRAN.
THEON? DID ROBB SEND YOU? IS HE HERE TOO?
ROBB'S FAR AWAY. HE CAN'T HELP YOU NOW.
HELP ME? DON'T SCARE ME, THEON.
I'M *PRINCE* THEON NOW. WE'RE BOTH PRINCES, BRAN. WHO WOULD HAVE DREAMED IT? BUT I'VE TAKEN YOUR CASTLE, MY PRINCE.

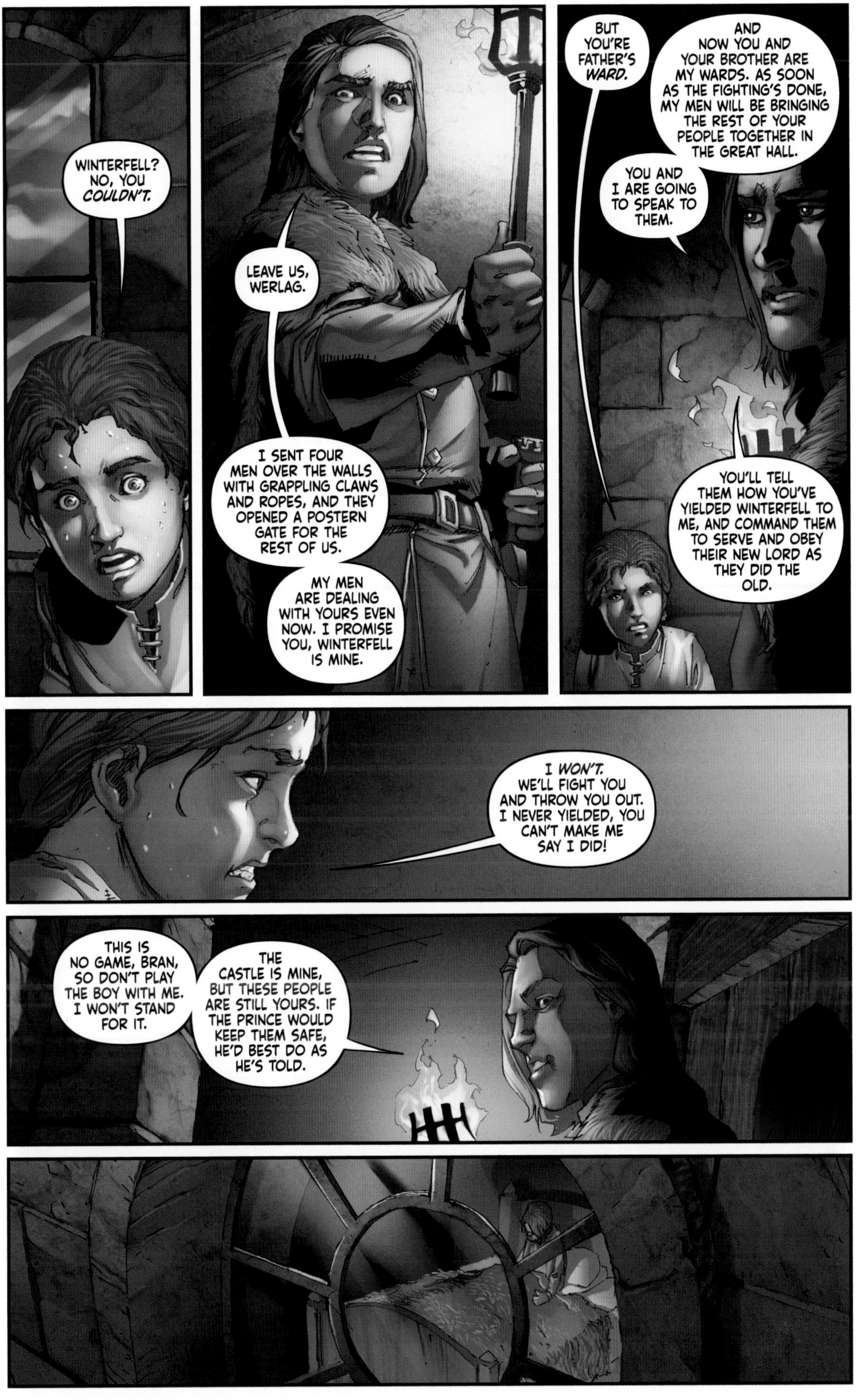
WINTERFELL? NO, YOU *COULDN'T.*
LEAVE US, WERLAG.
I SENT FOUR MEN OVER THE WALLS WITH GRAPPLING CLAWS AND ROPES, AND THEY OPENED A POSTERN GATE FOR THE REST OF US.
MY MEN ARE DEALING WITH YOURS EVEN NOW. I PROMISE YOU, WINTERFELL IS MINE.
BUT YOU'RE FATHER'S *WARD.*
AND NOW YOU AND YOUR BROTHER ARE MY WARDS. AS SOON AS THE FIGHTING'S DONE, MY MEN WILL BE BRINGING THE REST OF YOUR PEOPLE TOGETHER IN THE GREAT HALL.
YOU AND I ARE GOING TO SPEAK TO THEM.
YOU'LL TELL THEM HOW YOU'VE YIELDED WINTERFELL TO ME, AND COMMAND THEM TO SERVE AND OBEY THEIR NEW LORD AS THEY DID THE OLD.
I *WON'T.* WE'LL FIGHT YOU AND THROW YOU OUT. I NEVER YIELDED, YOU CAN'T MAKE ME SAY I DID!
THIS IS NO GAME, BRAN, SO DON'T PLAY THE BOY WITH ME. I WON'T STAND FOR IT.
THE CASTLE IS MINE, BUT THESE PEOPLE ARE STILL YOURS. IF THE PRINCE WOULD KEEP THEM SAFE, HE'D BEST DO AS HE'S TOLD.

BRAN...YOU... KNOW WHAT HAS HAPPENED? YOU HAVE BEEN TOLD?

THEON CAME. HE SAID WINTERFELL WAS HIS NOW.

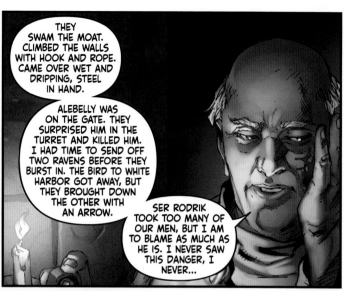

THEY SWAM THE MOAT. CLIMBED THE WALLS WITH HOOK AND ROPE. CAME OVER WET AND DRIPPING, STEEL IN HAND.

ALEBELLY WAS ON THE GATE. THEY SURPRISED HIM IN THE TURRET AND KILLED HIM. I HAD TIME TO SEND OFF TWO RAVENS BEFORE THEY BURST IN. THE BIRD TO WHITE HARBOR GOT AWAY, BUT THEY BROUGHT DOWN THE OTHER WITH AN ARROW.

SER RODRIK TOOK TOO MANY OF OUR MEN, BUT I AM TO BLAME AS MUCH AS HE IS. I NEVER SAW THIS DANGER, I NEVER...

JOJEN SAW IT, BRAN THOUGHT.

YOU BETTER HELP ME DRESS.

YES, THAT'S SO.

YOU ARE THE STARK IN WINTERFELL, AND ROBB'S HEIR. YOU MUST LOOK PRINCELY.

THEON WANTS ME TO YIELD THE CASTLE.

THERE IS NO SHAME IN THAT. A LORD MUST PROTECT HIS SMALLFOLK. CRUEL PLACES BREED CRUEL PEOPLES, BRAN, REMEMBER THAT AS YOU DEAL WITH THESE IRONMEN. YOUR LORD FATHER DID WHAT HE COULD TO GENTLE THEON, BUT I FEAR IT WAS TOO LITTLE AND TOO LATE.

I WANT MOTHER. I *WANT* HER. AND SHAGGYDOG TOO.

YOUR MOTHER IS FAR AWAY, MY PRINCE. BUT I'M HERE, AND BRAN.

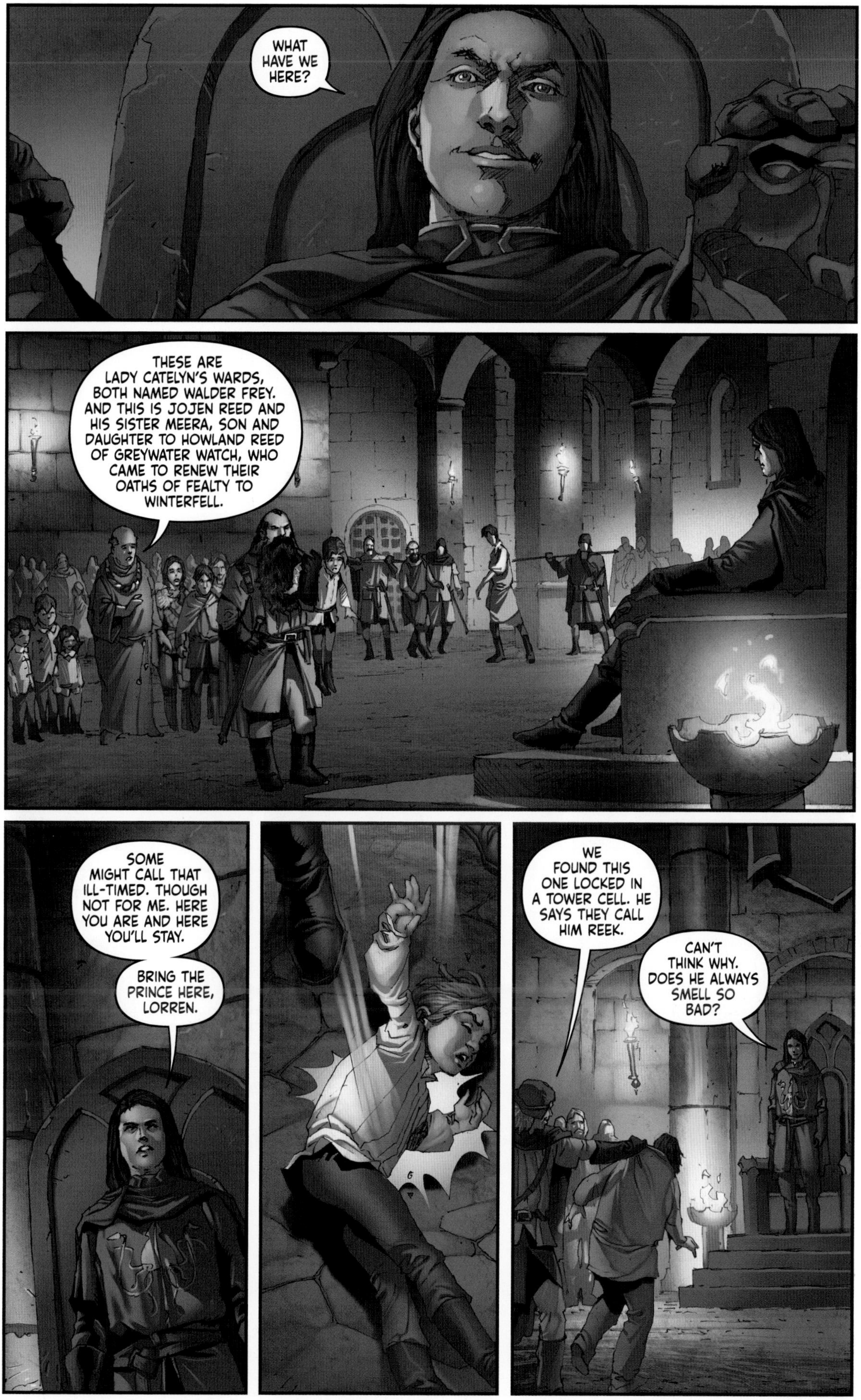
WHAT HAVE WE HERE?
THESE ARE LADY CATELYN'S WARDS, BOTH NAMED WALDER FREY. AND THIS IS JOJEN REED AND HIS SISTER MEERA, SON AND DAUGHTER TO HOWLAND REED OF GREYWATER WATCH, WHO CAME TO RENEW THEIR OATHS OF FEALTY TO WINTERFELL.
SOME MIGHT CALL THAT ILL-TIMED. THOUGH NOT FOR ME. HERE YOU ARE AND HERE YOU'LL STAY.
BRING THE PRINCE HERE, LORREN.
WE FOUND THIS ONE LOCKED IN A TOWER CELL. HE SAYS THEY CALL HIM REEK.
CAN'T THINK WHY. DOES HE ALWAYS SMELL SO BAD?

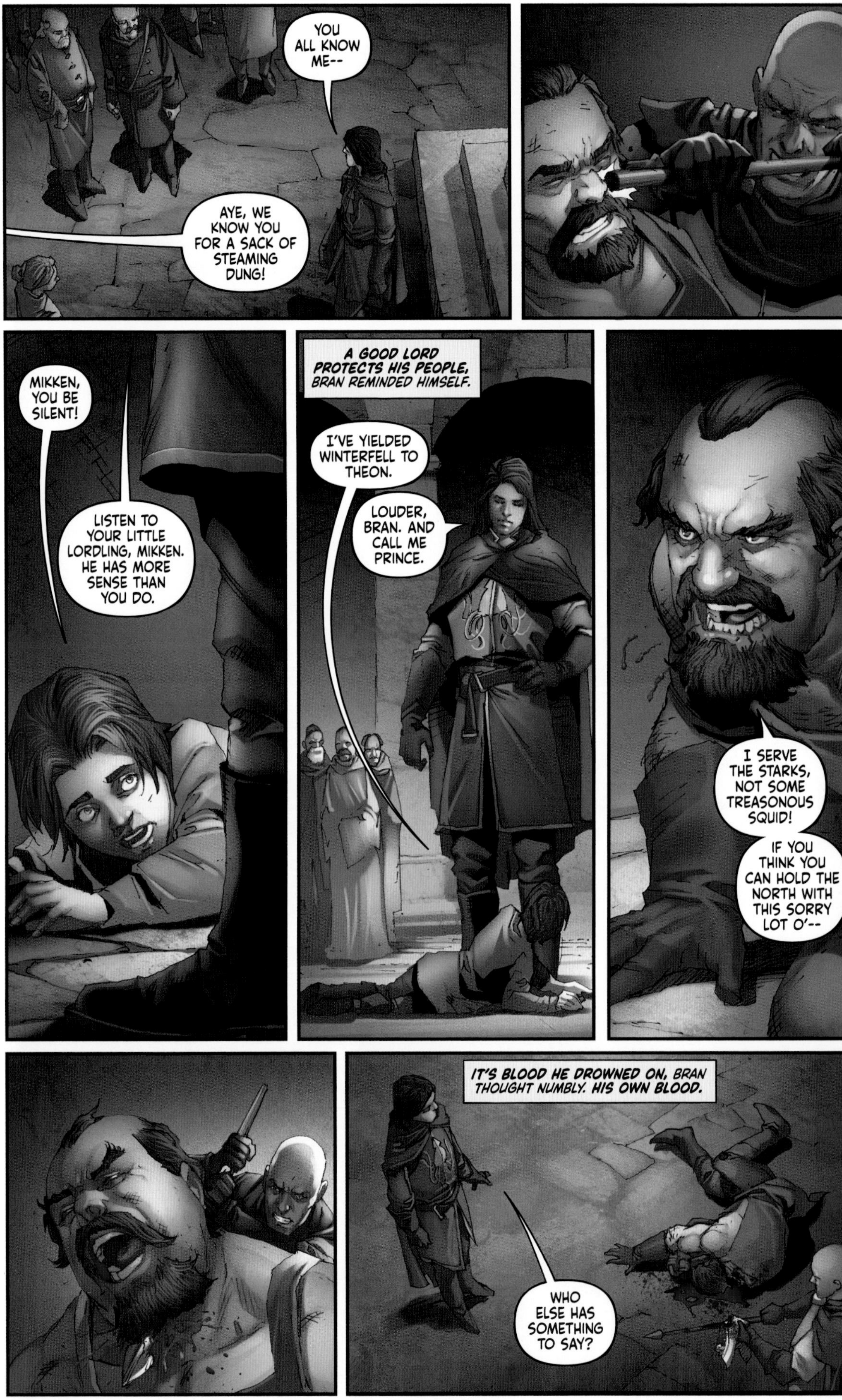
YOU ALL KNOW ME--
AYE, WE KNOW YOU FOR A SACK OF STEAMING DUNG!
MIKKEN, YOU BE SILENT!
LISTEN TO YOUR LITTLE LORDLING, MIKKEN. HE HAS MORE SENSE THAN YOU DO.
A GOOD LORD PROTECTS HIS PEOPLE, BRAN REMINDED HIMSELF.
I'VE YIELDED WINTERFELL TO THEON.
LOUDER, BRAN. AND CALL ME PRINCE.
I SERVE THE STARKS, NOT SOME TREASONOUS SQUID!
IF YOU THINK YOU CAN HOLD THE NORTH WITH THIS SORRY LOT O'--
IT'S BLOOD HE DROWNED ON, BRAN THOUGHT NUMBLY. HIS OWN BLOOD.
WHO ELSE HAS SOMETHING TO SAY?

HODOR HODOR HODOR HODOR!

SOMEONE KINDLY SHUT THAT HALFWIT UP.

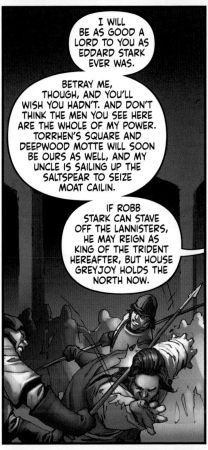

I WILL BE AS GOOD A LORD TO YOU AS EDDARD STARK EVER WAS.

BETRAY ME, THOUGH, AND YOU'LL WISH YOU HADN'T. AND DON'T THINK THE MEN YOU SEE HERE ARE THE WHOLE OF MY POWER. TORRHEN'S SQUARE AND DEEPWOOD MOTTE WILL SOON BE OURS AS WELL, AND MY UNCLE IS SAILING UP THE SALTSPEAR TO SEIZE MOAT CAILIN.

IF ROBB STARK CAN STAVE OFF THE LANNISTERS, HE MAY REIGN AS KING OF THE TRIDENT HEREAFTER, BUT HOUSE GREYJOY HOLDS THE NORTH NOW.

STARK'S LORDS WILL FIGHT YOU. THAT BLOATED PIG AT WHITE HARBOR FOR ONE, AND THEM UMBERS AND KARSTARKS TOO. YOU'LL NEED MEN. FREE ME AND I'M YOURS.

YOU'RE CLEVERER THAN YOU SMELL, BUT I COULD NOT SUFFER THAT STENCH.

WELL, I COULD WASH SOME. IF I WAS FREE.

A MAN OF RARE GOOD SENSE. BEND THE KNEE.

BRAN COULD NOT LOOK. THE GREEN DREAM WAS COMING TRUE.

M'LORD GREYJOY! I WAS BROUGHT HERE CAPTIVE TOO. YOU WERE THERE THE DAY I WAS TAKEN.

OSHA. I THOUGHT YOU WERE A FRIEND, BRAN THOUGHT, HURT.

I NEED FIGHTERS, NOT KITCHEN SLUTS.

IT WAS ROBB STARK PUT ME IN THE KITCHENS.

FOR THE BEST PART OF A YEAR, I'VE BEEN LEFT TO SCOUR KETTLES, SCRAPE GREASE, AND WARM THE STRAW FOR THIS ONE. I'VE HAD A BELLYFUL OF IT.

PUT A SPEAR IN MY HAND AGAIN.

I GOT A SPEAR FOR YOU RIGHT HERE--

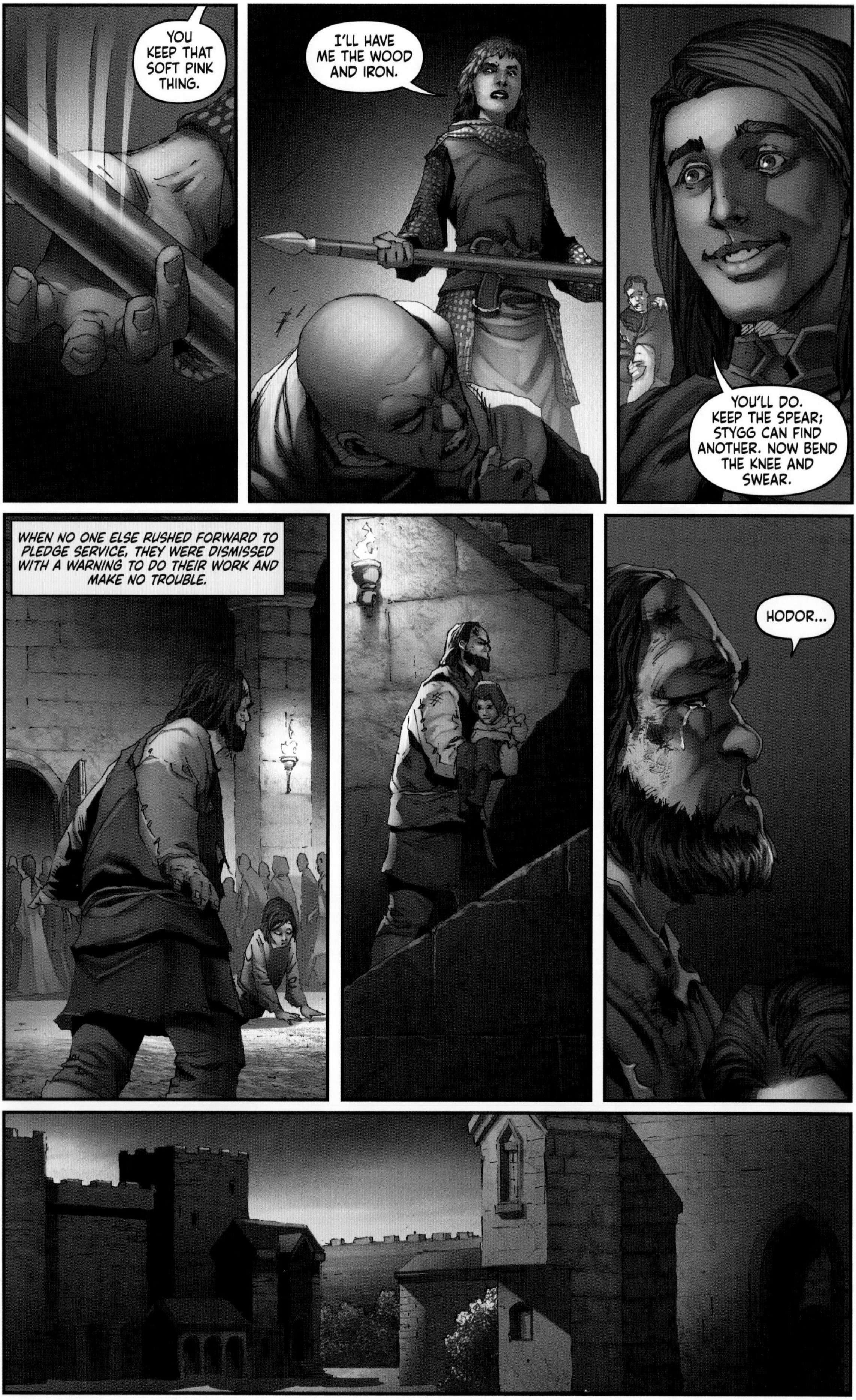
YOU KEEP THAT SOFT PINK THING.
I'LL HAVE ME THE WOOD AND IRON.
YOU'LL DO. KEEP THE SPEAR; STYGG CAN FIND ANOTHER. NOW BEND THE KNEE AND SWEAR.
WHEN NO ONE ELSE RUSHED FORWARD TO PLEDGE SERVICE, THEY WERE DISMISSED WITH A WARNING TO DO THEIR WORK AND MAKE NO TROUBLE.
HODOR...

ARYA

"CAN I HAVE A TART? YOU BAKED A WHOLE TRAY."

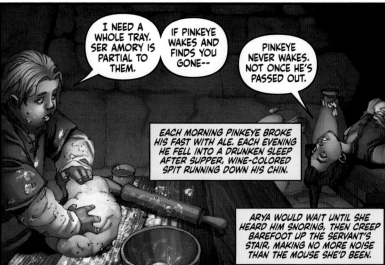

I NEED A WHOLE TRAY. SER AMORY IS PARTIAL TO THEM.

IF PINKEYE WAKES AND FINDS YOU GONE--

PINKEYE NEVER WAKES. NOT ONCE HE'S PASSED OUT.

EACH MORNING PINKEYE BROKE HIS FAST WITH ALE. EACH EVENING HE FELL INTO A DRUNKEN SLEEP AFTER SUPPER, WINE-COLORED SPIT RUNNING DOWN HIS CHIN.

ARYA WOULD WAIT UNTIL SHE HEARD HIM SNORING, THEN CREEP BAREFOOT UP THE SERVANT'S STAIR, MAKING NO MORE NOISE THAN THE MOUSE SHE'D BEEN.

SYRIO HAD TOLD HER ONCE THAT DARKNESS COULD BE HER FRIEND, AND HE WAS RIGHT. IF SHE HAD THE MOON AND THE STARS TO SEE BY, THAT WAS ENOUGH.

I BET WE COULD ESCAPE, AND PINKEYE WOULDN'T EVEN NOTICE I WAS GONE.

I DON'T WANT TO ESCAPE. IT'S BETTER HERE THAN IT WAS IN THEM WOODS. I DON'T WANT TO EAT NO WORMS. HERE, SPRINKLE SOME FLOUR ON THE BOARD.

WHAT'S THAT?

WHAT? I DON'T--

LISTEN WITH YOUR EARS, NOT YOUR MOUTH. THAT WAS A WARHORN. TWO BLASTS, DIDN'T YOU HEAR? AND THERE, THAT'S THE PORTCULLIS CHAINS. SOMEONE'S GOING OUT OR COMING IN.

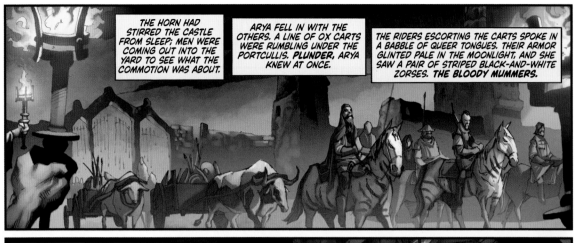

THE HORN HAD STIRRED THE CASTLE FROM SLEEP; MEN WERE COMING OUT INTO THE YARD TO SEE WHAT THE COMMOTION WAS ABOUT.

ARYA FELL IN WITH THE OTHERS. A LINE OF OX CARTS WERE RUMBLING UNDER THE PORTCULLIS. *PLUNDER*, ARYA KNEW AT ONCE.

THE RIDERS ESCORTING THE CARTS SPOKE IN A BABBLE OF QUEER TONGUES. THEIR ARMOR GLINTED PALE IN THE MOONLIGHT, AND SHE SAW A PAIR OF STRIPED BLACK-AND-WHITE ZORSES. *THE BLOODY MUMMERS.*

ARYA WITHDREW A LITTLE DEEPER INTO THE SHADOWS AND WATCHED AS A HUGE BLACK BEAR ROLLED BY, CAGED IN THE BACK OF A WAGON.

OTHER CARTS WERE LOADED DOWN WITH SILVER PLATE, WEAPONS AND SHIELDS, BAGS OF FLOUR, PENS OF SQUEALING HOGS AND SCRAWNY DOGS AND CHICKENS.

ARYA WAS THINKING HOW LONG IT HAD BEEN SINCE SHE'D HAD A SLICE OFF A PORK ROAST WHEN SHE SAW THE FIRST OF THE PRISONERS.

BY HIS BEARING AND THE PROUD WAY HE HELD HIS HEAD, HE MUST HAVE BEEN A LORD. SHE COULD SEE MAIL GLINTING BENEATH HIS TORN RED SURCOAT.

AT FIRST ARYA TOOK HIM FOR A LANNISTER, BUT WHEN HE PASSED NEAR A TORCH SHE SAW HIS DEVICE WAS A SILVER FIST, NOT A LION.

SHE TRIED TO JUDGE HOW MANY PRISONERS THERE WERE, BUT LOST COUNT BEFORE SHE GOT TO FIFTY. IN THE TORCHLIGHT IT WAS HARD TO MAKE OUT ALL THEIR BADGES AND SIGILS, BUT SOME SHE RECOGNIZED.

TWIN TOWERS. SUNBURST. BLOODY MAN. BATTLE-AXE. THE BATTLE-AXE IS FOR CERWYN, AND THE WHITE SUN ON BLACK IS KARSTARK.

THEY'RE NORTHMEN. MY FATHER'S MEN, AND ROBB'S. SHE DIDN'T LIKE TO THINK WHAT THAT MIGHT MEAN.

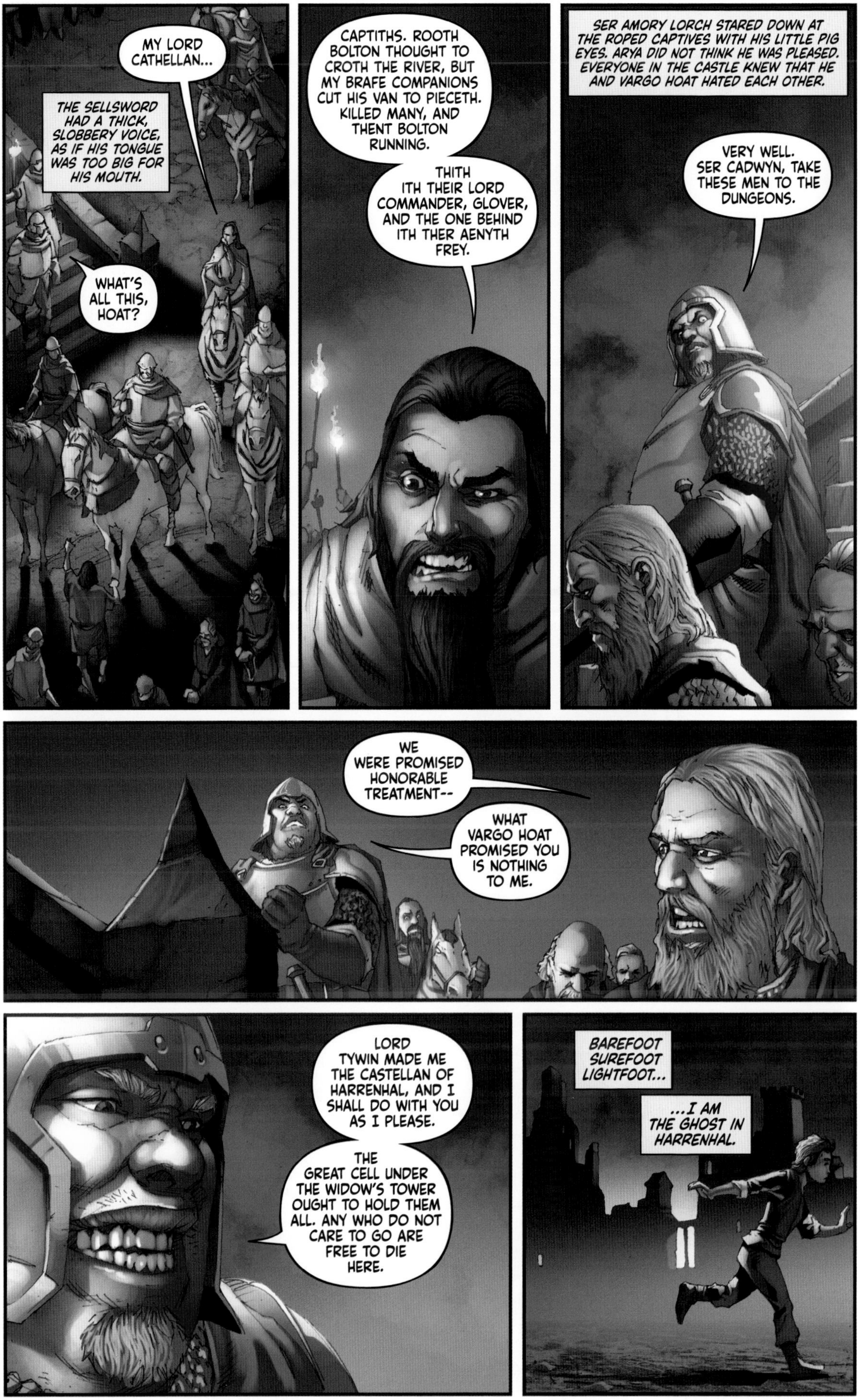
MY LORD CATHELLAN...
THE SELLSWORD HAD A THICK, SLOBBERY VOICE, AS IF HIS TONGUE WAS TOO BIG FOR HIS MOUTH.
WHAT'S ALL THIS, HOAT?
CAPTITHS. ROOTH BOLTON THOUGHT TO CROTH THE RIVER, BUT MY BRAFE COMPANIONS CUT HIS VAN TO PIECETH. KILLED MANY, AND THENT BOLTON RUNNING.
THITH ITH THEIR LORD COMMANDER, GLOVER, AND THE ONE BEHIND ITH THER AENYTH FREY.
SER AMORY LORCH STARED DOWN AT THE ROPED CAPTIVES WITH HIS LITTLE PIG EYES. ARYA DID NOT THINK HE WAS PLEASED. EVERYONE IN THE CASTLE KNEW THAT HE AND VARGO HOAT HATED EACH OTHER.
VERY WELL. SER CADWYN, TAKE THESE MEN TO THE DUNGEONS.
WE WERE PROMISED HONORABLE TREATMENT--
WHAT VARGO HOAT PROMISED YOU IS NOTHING TO ME.
LORD TYWIN MADE ME THE CASTELLAN OF HARRENHAL, AND I SHALL DO WITH YOU AS I PLEASE.
THE GREAT CELL UNDER THE WIDOW'S TOWER OUGHT TO HOLD THEM ALL. ANY WHO DO NOT CARE TO GO ARE FREE TO DIE HERE.
BAREFOOT SUREFOOT LIGHTFOOT...
...I AM THE GHOST IN HARRENHAL.

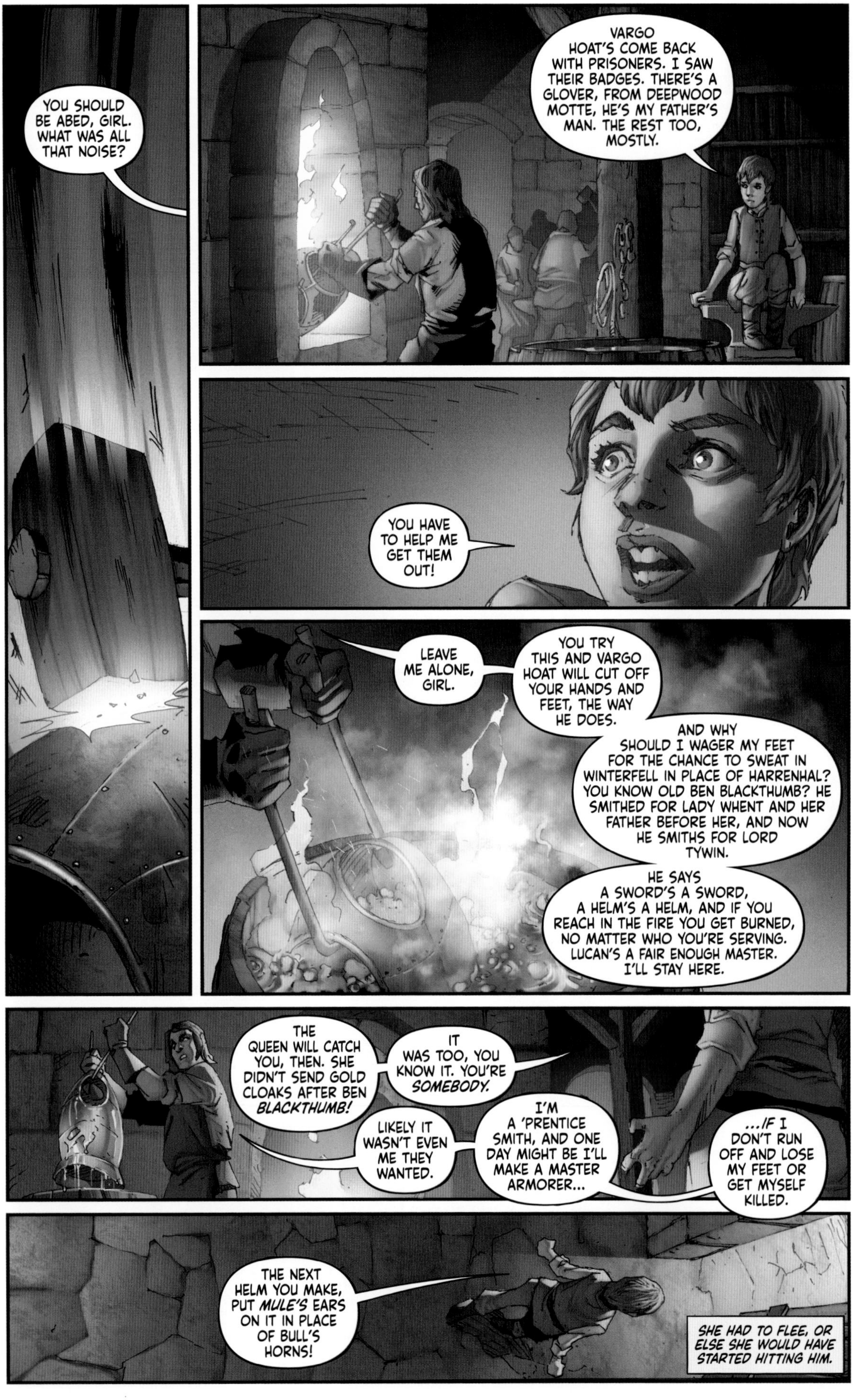

YOU SHOULD BE ABED, GIRL. WHAT WAS ALL THAT NOISE?
VARGO HOAT'S COME BACK WITH PRISONERS. I SAW THEIR BADGES. THERE'S A GLOVER, FROM DEEPWOOD MOTTE, HE'S MY FATHER'S MAN. THE REST TOO, MOSTLY.
YOU HAVE TO HELP ME GET THEM OUT!
LEAVE ME ALONE, GIRL.
YOU TRY THIS AND VARGO HOAT WILL CUT OFF YOUR HANDS AND FEET, THE WAY HE DOES.
AND WHY SHOULD I WAGER MY FEET FOR THE CHANCE TO SWEAT IN WINTERFELL IN PLACE OF HARRENHAL? YOU KNOW OLD BEN BLACKTHUMB? HE SMITHED FOR LADY WHENT AND HER FATHER BEFORE HER, AND NOW HE SMITHS FOR LORD TYWIN.
HE SAYS A SWORD'S A SWORD, A HELM'S A HELM, AND IF YOU REACH IN THE FIRE YOU GET BURNED, NO MATTER WHO YOU'RE SERVING. LUCAN'S A FAIR ENOUGH MASTER. I'LL STAY HERE.
THE QUEEN WILL CATCH YOU, THEN. SHE DIDN'T SEND GOLD CLOAKS AFTER BEN *BLACKTHUMB!*
IT WAS TOO, YOU KNOW IT. YOU'RE *SOMEBODY.*
LIKELY IT WASN'T EVEN ME THEY WANTED.
I'M A 'PRENTICE SMITH, AND ONE DAY MIGHT BE I'LL MAKE A MASTER ARMORER...
...*IF* I DON'T RUN OFF AND LOSE MY FEET OR GET MYSELF KILLED.
THE NEXT HELM YOU MAKE, PUT *MULE'S* EARS ON IT IN PLACE OF BULL'S HORNS!
SHE HAD TO FLEE, OR ELSE SHE WOULD HAVE STARTED HITTING HIM.

NOT KNOWING WHERE ELSE TO GO, SHE MADE FOR THE GODSWOOD.

I WAS A SHEEP, AND THEN I WAS A MOUSE, I COULDN'T DO ANYTHING BUT HIDE.

JAQEN MADE ME BRAVE AGAIN. HE MADE ME A GHOST INSTEAD OF A MOUSE.

JAQEN STILL OWED HER ONE DEATH...BUT ONCE SHE USED THAT UP, SHE WOULD ONLY BE A MOUSE AGAIN.

IT LOOKS JUST LIKE THE ONE IN WINTERFELL FROM HERE.

IS THAT WHAT A GOD LOOKED LIKE? COULD GODS BE HURT, THE SAME AS PEOPLE?

I SHOULD PRAY, SHE THOUGHT SUDDENLY.

HELP ME, YOU OLD GODS, SHE PRAYED SILENTLY. HELP ME GET THOSE MEN OUT OF THE DUNGEON SO WE CAN KILL SER AMORY, AND BRING ME HOME TO WINTERFELL.

MAKE ME A WATER DANCER AND A WOLF AND NOT AFRAID AGAIN, EVER.

WAS THAT ENOUGH? SOMETIMES HER FATHER HAD PRAYED A LONG TIME, BUT THE OLD GODS HAD NEVER HELPED HIM.

YOU SHOULD HAVE SAVED HIM! HE PRAYED TO YOU ALL THE TIME. I DON'T CARE IF YOU HELP ME OR NOT. I DON'T THINK YOU COULD EVEN IF YOU WANTED TO!

GODS ARE NOT MOCKED, GIRL.

A MAN COMES TO HEAR A NAME. ONE AND TWO AND THEN COMES THREE. A MAN WOULD HAVE DONE.

A MAN SEES. A MAN HEARS. A MAN KNOWS.

HOW DID YOU KNOW I WAS HERE?

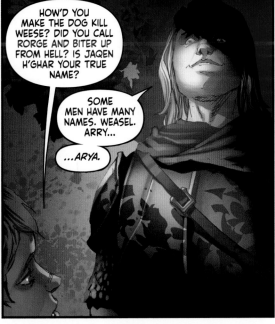

HOW'D YOU MAKE THE DOG KILL WEESE? DID YOU CALL RORGE AND BITER UP FROM HELL? IS JAQEN H'GHAR YOUR TRUE NAME?

SOME MEN HAVE MANY NAMES. WEASEL. ARRY...

...ARYA.

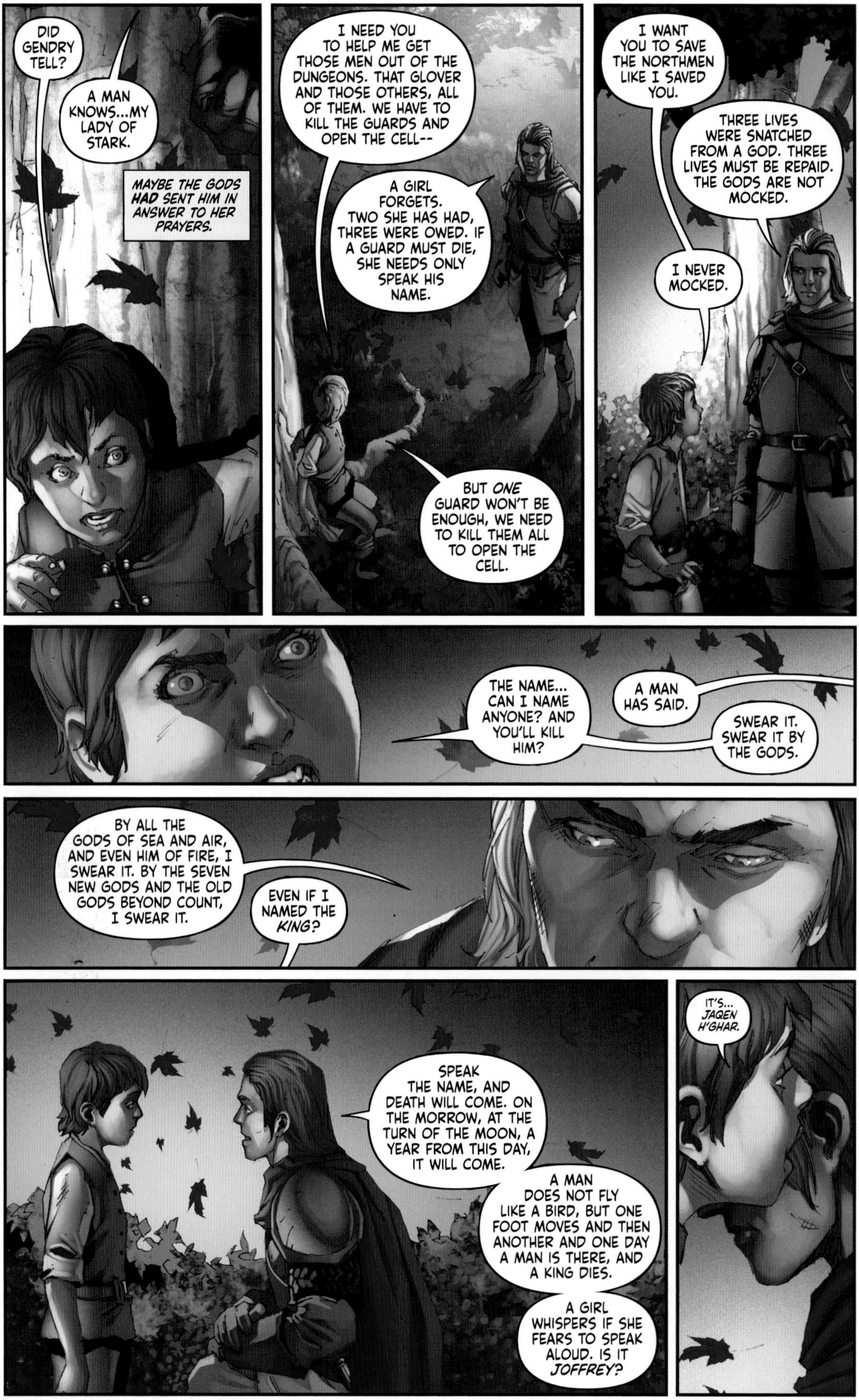
DID GENDRY TELL?
A MAN KNOWS...MY LADY OF STARK.
*MAYBE THE GODS **HAD** SENT HIM IN ANSWER TO HER PRAYERS.*
I NEED YOU TO HELP ME GET THOSE MEN OUT OF THE DUNGEONS. THAT GLOVER AND THOSE OTHERS, ALL OF THEM. WE HAVE TO KILL THE GUARDS AND OPEN THE CELL--
A GIRL FORGETS. TWO SHE HAS HAD, THREE WERE OWED. IF A GUARD MUST DIE, SHE NEEDS ONLY SPEAK HIS NAME.
BUT *ONE* GUARD WON'T BE ENOUGH, WE NEED TO KILL THEM ALL TO OPEN THE CELL.
I WANT YOU TO SAVE THE NORTHMEN LIKE I SAVED YOU.
THREE LIVES WERE SNATCHED FROM A GOD. THREE LIVES MUST BE REPAID. THE GODS ARE NOT MOCKED.
I NEVER MOCKED.
THE NAME... CAN I NAME ANYONE? AND YOU'LL KILL HIM?
A MAN HAS SAID.
SWEAR IT. SWEAR IT BY THE GODS.
BY ALL THE GODS OF SEA AND AIR, AND EVEN HIM OF FIRE, I SWEAR IT. BY THE SEVEN NEW GODS AND THE OLD GODS BEYOND COUNT, I SWEAR IT.
EVEN IF I NAMED THE *KING*?
SPEAK THE NAME, AND DEATH WILL COME. ON THE MORROW, AT THE TURN OF THE MOON, A YEAR FROM THIS DAY, IT WILL COME.
A MAN DOES NOT FLY LIKE A BIRD, BUT ONE FOOT MOVES AND THEN ANOTHER AND ONE DAY A MAN IS THERE, AND A KING DIES.
A GIRL WHISPERS IF SHE FEARS TO SPEAK ALOUD. IS IT *JOFFREY*?
IT'S... *JAQEN H'GHAR.*

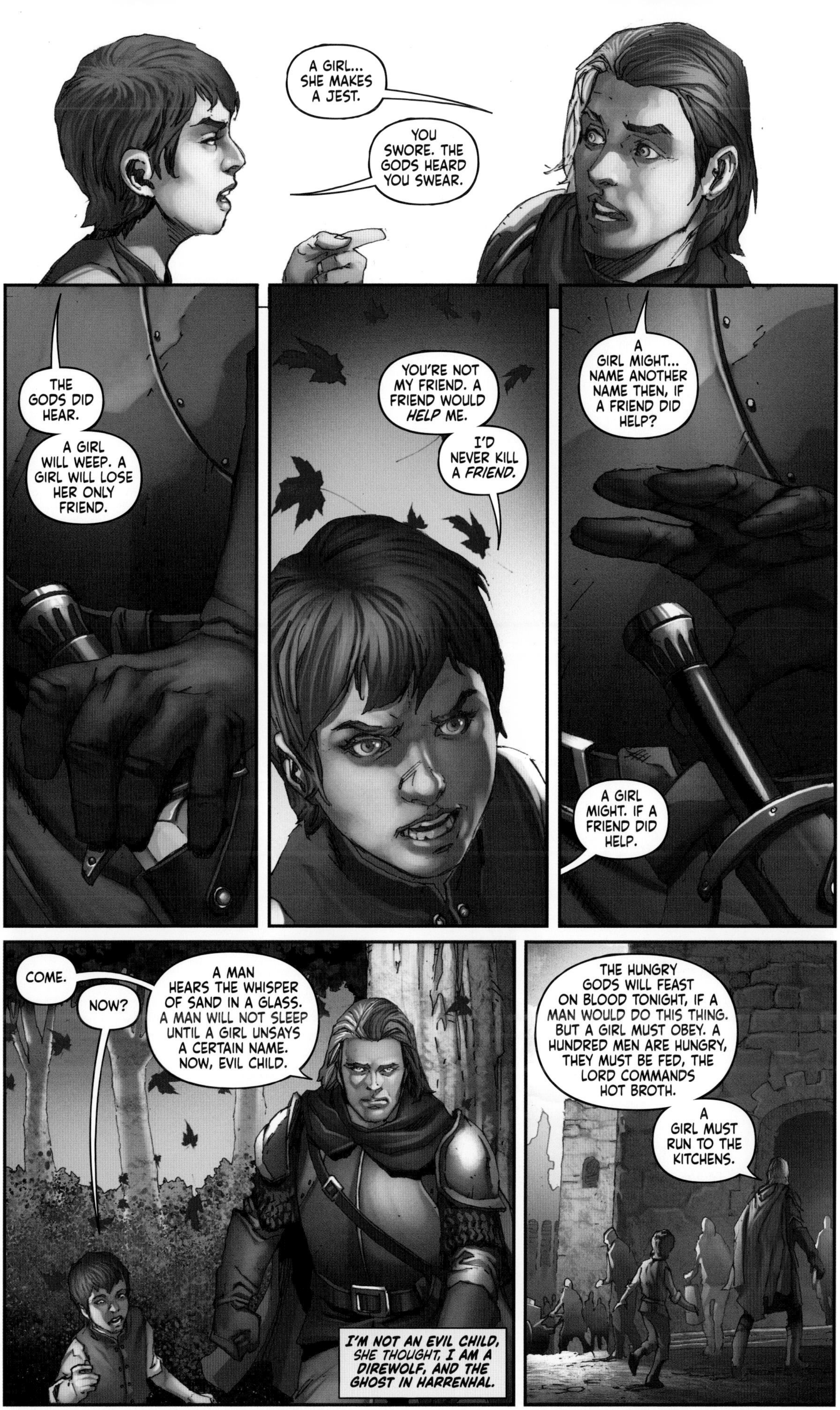
A GIRL... SHE MAKES A JEST.
YOU SWORE. THE GODS HEARD YOU SWEAR.
THE GODS DID HEAR.
A GIRL WILL WEEP. A GIRL WILL LOSE HER ONLY FRIEND.
YOU'RE NOT MY FRIEND. A FRIEND WOULD HELP ME.
I'D NEVER KILL A FRIEND.
A GIRL MIGHT... NAME ANOTHER NAME THEN, IF A FRIEND DID HELP?
A GIRL MIGHT. IF A FRIEND DID HELP.
COME.
NOW?
A MAN HEARS THE WHISPER OF SAND IN A GLASS. A MAN WILL NOT SLEEP UNTIL A GIRL UNSAYS A CERTAIN NAME. NOW, EVIL CHILD.
I'M NOT AN EVIL CHILD, SHE THOUGHT, I AM A DIREWOLF, AND THE GHOST IN HARRENHAL.
THE HUNGRY GODS WILL FEAST ON BLOOD TONIGHT, IF A MAN WOULD DO THIS THING. BUT A GIRL MUST OBEY. A HUNDRED MEN ARE HUNGRY, THEY MUST BE FED, THE LORD COMMANDS HOT BROTH.
A GIRL MUST RUN TO THE KITCHENS.

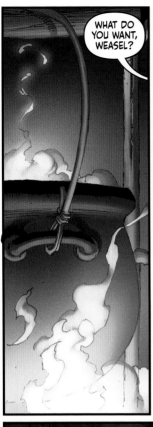

WHAT DO YOU WANT, WEASEL?

BROTH. MY LORD WANTS BROTH.

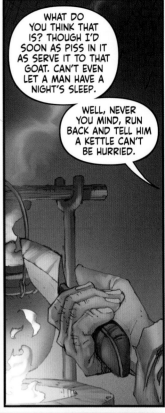

WHAT DO YOU THINK THAT IS? THOUGH I'D SOON AS PISS IN IT AS SERVE IT TO THAT GOAT. CAN'T EVEN LET A MAN HAVE A NIGHT'S SLEEP.

WELL, NEVER YOU MIND, RUN BACK AND TELL HIM A KETTLE CAN'T BE HURRIED.

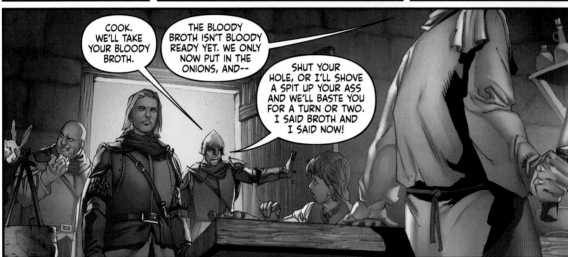

COOK. WE'LL TAKE YOUR BLOODY BROTH.

THE BLOODY BROTH ISN'T BLOODY READY YET. WE ONLY NOW PUT IN THE ONIONS, AND--

SHUT YOUR HOLE, OR I'LL SHOVE A SPIT UP YOUR ASS AND WE'LL BASTE YOU FOR A TURN OR TWO. I SAID BROTH AND I SAID NOW!

TAKE YOUR BLOODY BROTH, THEN, BUT IF THE GOAT ASKS WHY IT TASTES SO THIN, YOU TELL HIM.

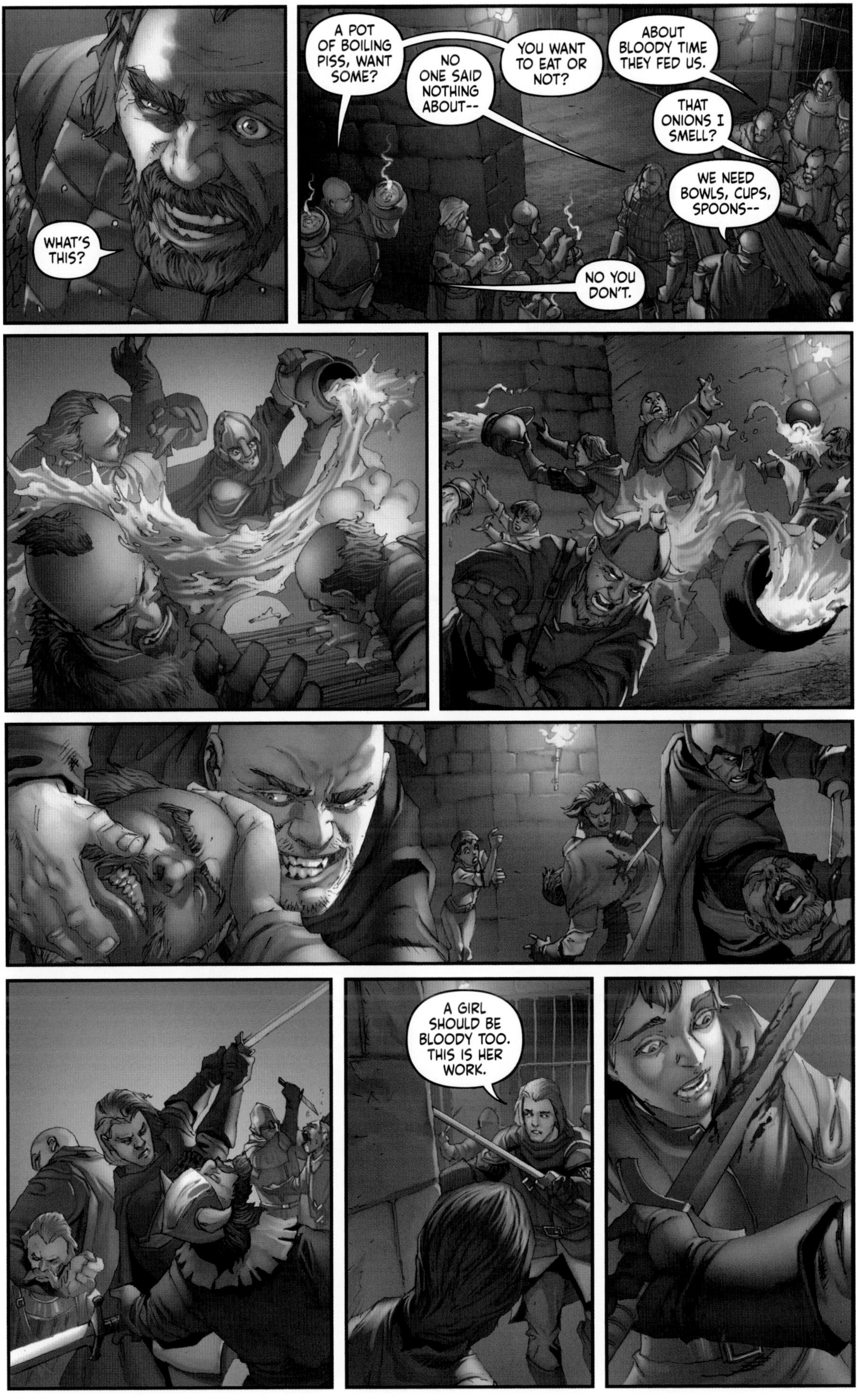
WHAT'S THIS?
A POT OF BOILING PISS, WANT SOME?
NO ONE SAID NOTHING ABOUT--
YOU WANT TO EAT OR NOT?
ABOUT BLOODY TIME THEY FED US.
THAT ONIONS I SMELL?
WE NEED BOWLS, CUPS, SPOONS--
NO YOU DON'T.
A GIRL SHOULD BE BLOODY TOO. THIS IS HER WORK.

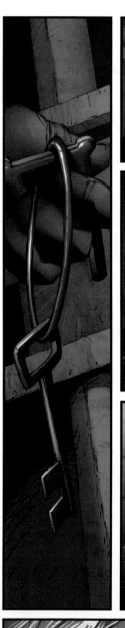

WELL DONE. I AM ROBETT GLOVER.

MY LORD.

WHO ARE YOU MEN? YOU WERE NOT WITH HOAT WHEN HE CAME TO LORD BOLTON'S ENCAMPMENT. ARE YOU OF THE BRAVE COMPANIONS?

WE ARE NOW.

VERY WELL. LET'S MAKE AN END TO THIS BLOODY BUSINESS.

A GIRL DOES NOT UNDERSTAND?

YES I DO.

THOUGH SHE DIDN'T, NOT TRULY.

A GOAT HAS NO LOYALTY. SOON A WOLF BANNER IS RAISED HERE, I THINK. BUT FIRST A MAN WOULD HEAR A CERTAIN NAME UNSAID.

I TAKE BACK THE NAME. DO I STILL HAVE A THIRD DEATH?

THE DEBT IS PAID.

A GOD HAS HIS DUE. AND NOW A MAN MUST DIE.

DIE? BUT I UNSAID THE NAME. YOU DON'T NEED TO DIE NOW!

I DO. MY TIME IS DONE.

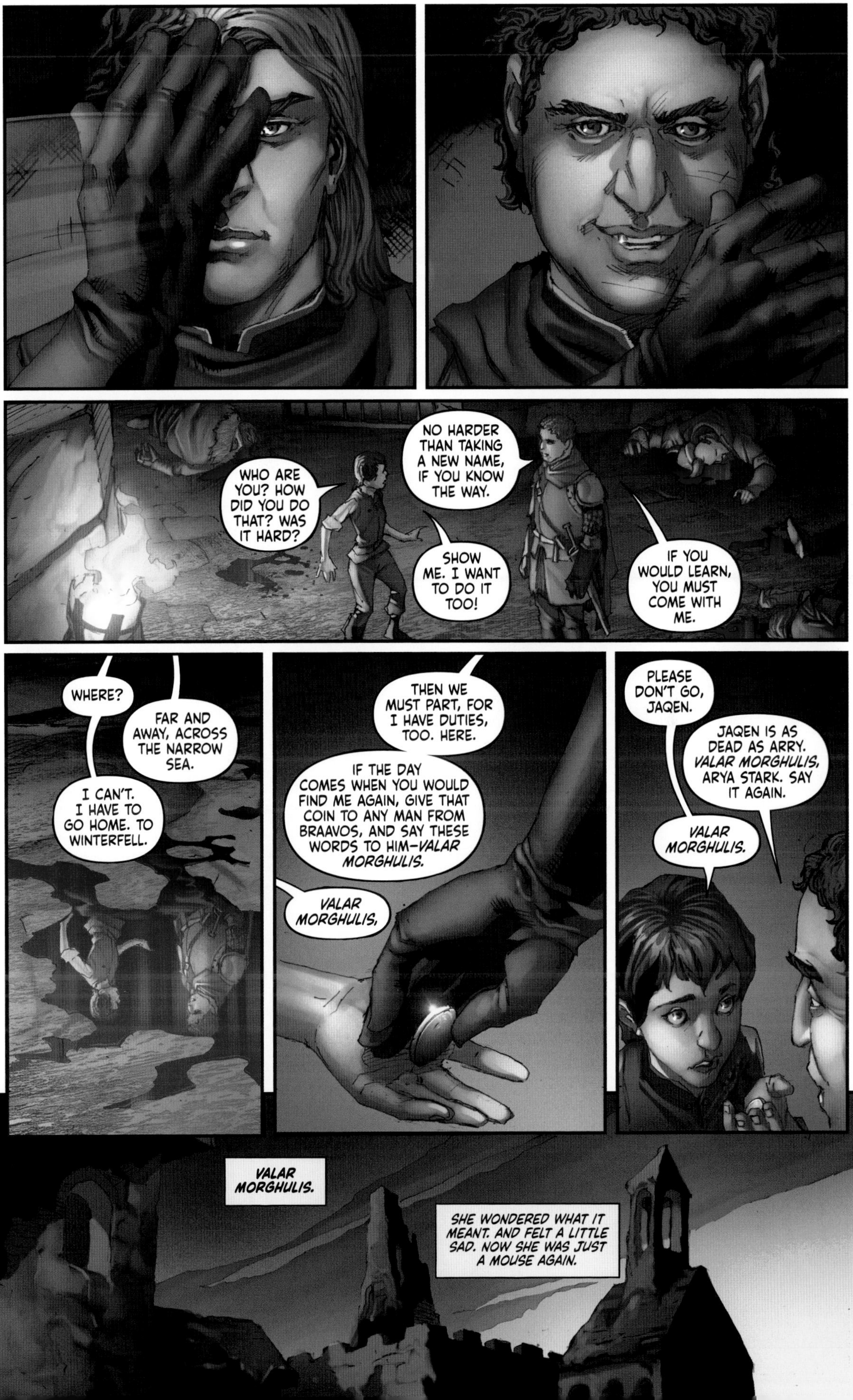
WHO ARE YOU? HOW DID YOU DO THAT? WAS IT HARD?
NO HARDER THAN TAKING A NEW NAME, IF YOU KNOW THE WAY.
SHOW ME. I WANT TO DO IT TOO!
IF YOU WOULD LEARN, YOU MUST COME WITH ME.
WHERE?
FAR AND AWAY, ACROSS THE NARROW SEA.
I CAN'T. I HAVE TO GO HOME. TO WINTERFELL.
THEN WE MUST PART, FOR I HAVE DUTIES, TOO. HERE.
IF THE DAY COMES WHEN YOU WOULD FIND ME AGAIN, GIVE THAT COIN TO ANY MAN FROM BRAAVOS, AND SAY THESE WORDS TO HIM—VALAR MORGHULIS.
VALAR MORGHULIS,
PLEASE DON'T GO, JAQEN.
JAQEN IS AS DEAD AS ARRY. VALAR MORGHULIS, ARYA STARK. SAY IT AGAIN.
VALAR MORGHULIS.
VALAR MORGHULIS.
SHE WONDERED WHAT IT MEANT. AND FELT A LITTLE SAD. NOW SHE WAS JUST A MOUSE AGAIN.

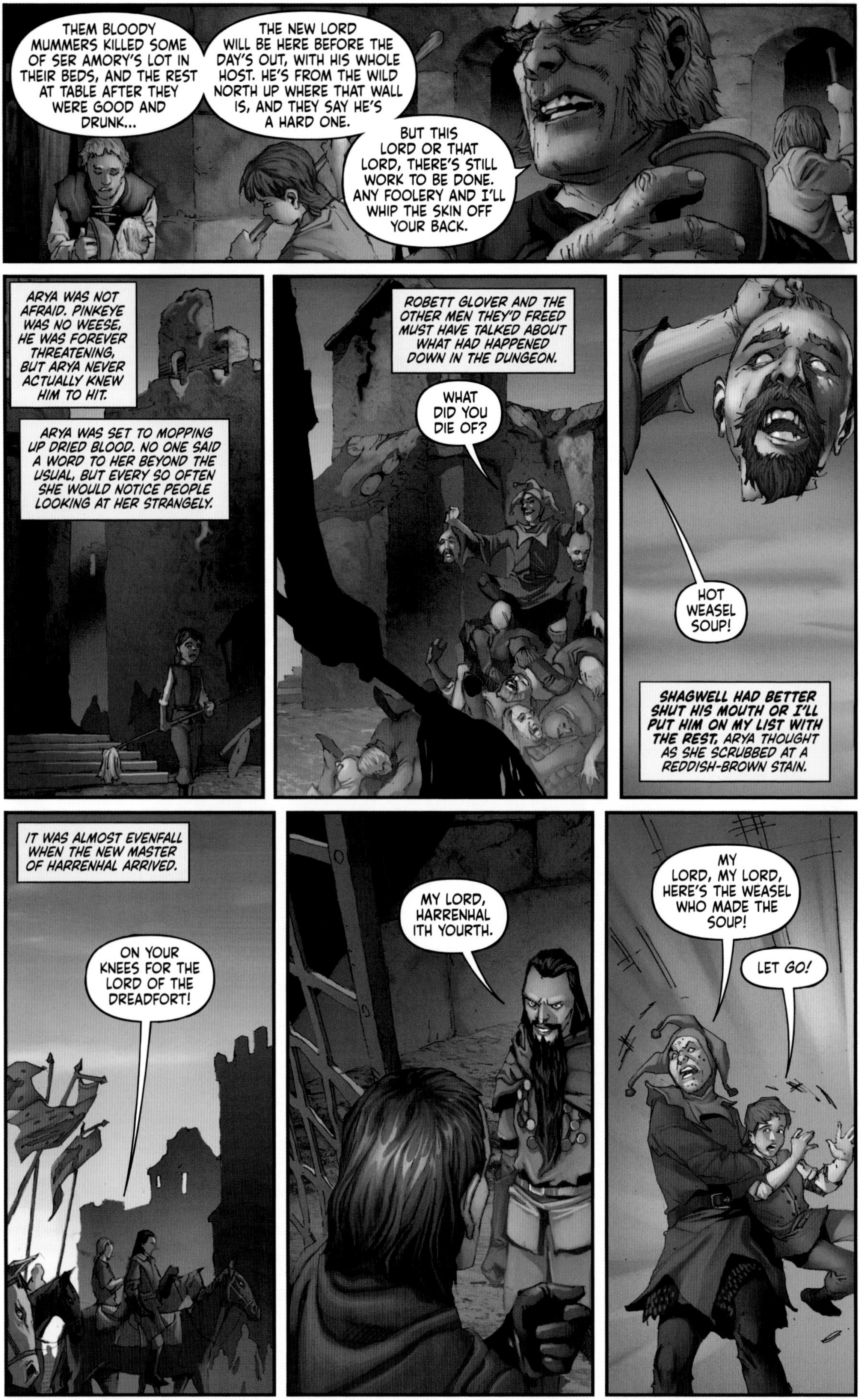
THEM BLOODY MUMMERS KILLED SOME OF SER AMORY'S LOT IN THEIR BEDS, AND THE REST AT TABLE AFTER THEY WERE GOOD AND DRUNK...
THE NEW LORD WILL BE HERE BEFORE THE DAY'S OUT, WITH HIS WHOLE HOST. HE'S FROM THE WILD NORTH UP WHERE THAT WALL IS, AND THEY SAY HE'S A HARD ONE.
BUT THIS LORD OR THAT LORD, THERE'S STILL WORK TO BE DONE. ANY FOOLERY AND I'LL WHIP THE SKIN OFF YOUR BACK.
ARYA WAS NOT AFRAID. PINKEYE WAS NO WEESE, HE WAS FOREVER THREATENING, BUT ARYA NEVER ACTUALLY KNEW HIM TO HIT.
ARYA WAS SET TO MOPPING UP DRIED BLOOD. NO ONE SAID A WORD TO HER BEYOND THE USUAL, BUT EVERY SO OFTEN SHE WOULD NOTICE PEOPLE LOOKING AT HER STRANGELY.
ROBETT GLOVER AND THE OTHER MEN THEY'D FREED MUST HAVE TALKED ABOUT WHAT HAD HAPPENED DOWN IN THE DUNGEON.
WHAT DID YOU DIE OF?
HOT WEASEL SOUP!
SHAGWELL HAD BETTER SHUT HIS MOUTH OR I'LL PUT HIM ON MY LIST WITH THE REST, ARYA THOUGHT AS SHE SCRUBBED AT A REDDISH-BROWN STAIN.
IT WAS ALMOST EVENFALL WHEN THE NEW MASTER OF HARRENHAL ARRIVED.
ON YOUR KNEES FOR THE LORD OF THE DREADFORT!
MY LORD, HARRENHAL ITH YOURTH.
MY LORD, MY LORD, HERE'S THE WEASEL WHO MADE THE SOUP!
LET GO!

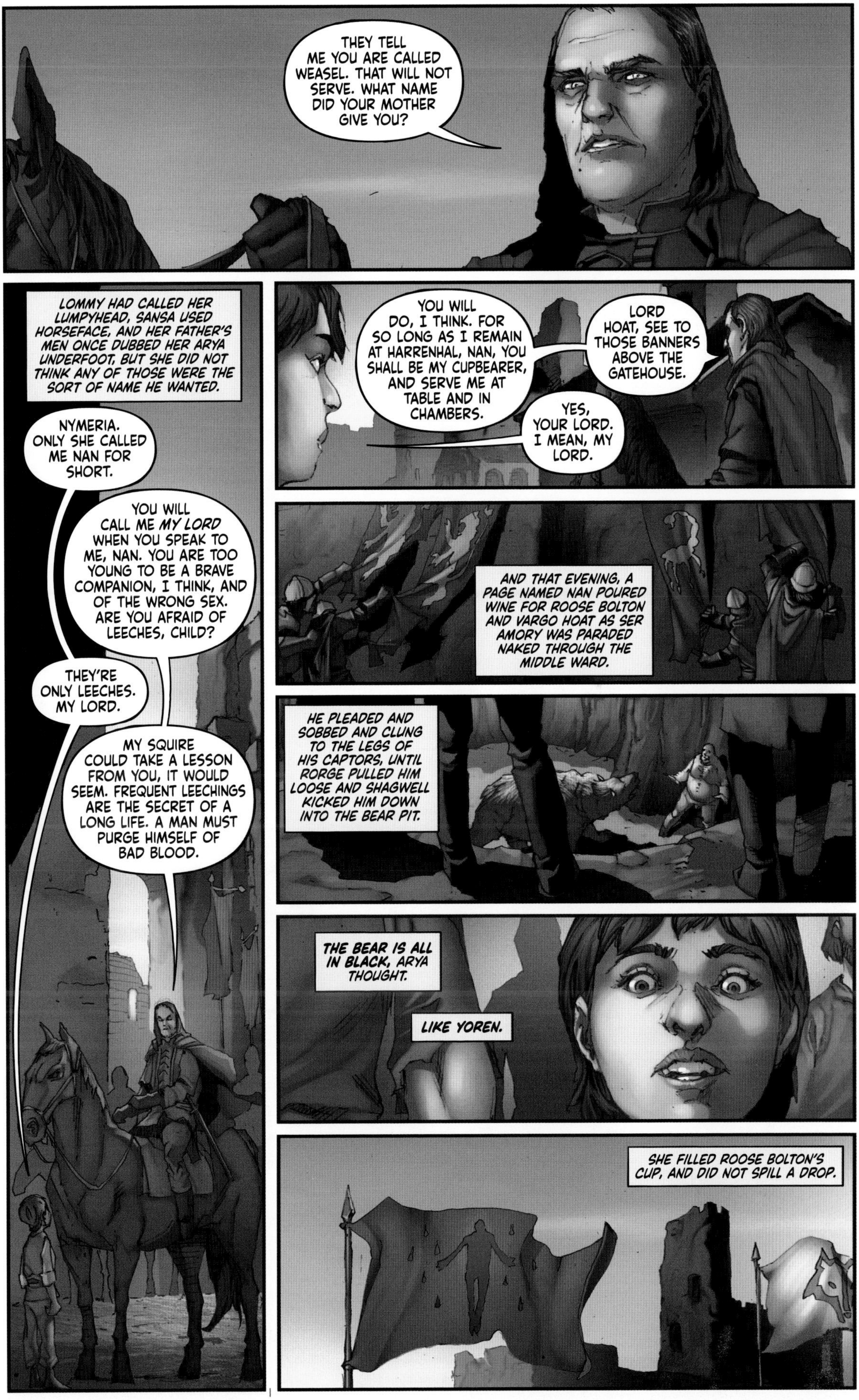
THEY TELL ME YOU ARE CALLED WEASEL. THAT WILL NOT SERVE. WHAT NAME DID YOUR MOTHER GIVE YOU?
LOMMY HAD CALLED HER LUMPYHEAD, SANSA USED HORSEFACE, AND HER FATHER'S MEN ONCE DUBBED HER ARYA UNDERFOOT, BUT SHE DID NOT THINK ANY OF THOSE WERE THE SORT OF NAME HE WANTED.
NYMERIA. ONLY SHE CALLED ME NAN FOR SHORT.
YOU WILL CALL ME *MY LORD* WHEN YOU SPEAK TO ME, NAN. YOU ARE TOO YOUNG TO BE A BRAVE COMPANION, I THINK, AND OF THE WRONG SEX. ARE YOU AFRAID OF LEECHES, CHILD?
THEY'RE ONLY LEECHES. MY LORD.
MY SQUIRE COULD TAKE A LESSON FROM YOU, IT WOULD SEEM. FREQUENT LEECHINGS ARE THE SECRET OF A LONG LIFE. A MAN MUST PURGE HIMSELF OF BAD BLOOD.
YOU WILL DO, I THINK. FOR SO LONG AS I REMAIN AT HARRENHAL, NAN, YOU SHALL BE MY CUPBEARER, AND SERVE ME AT TABLE AND IN CHAMBERS.
LORD HOAT, SEE TO THOSE BANNERS ABOVE THE GATEHOUSE.
YES, YOUR LORD. I MEAN, MY LORD.
AND THAT EVENING, A PAGE NAMED NAN POURED WINE FOR ROOSE BOLTON AND VARGO HOAT AS SER AMORY WAS PARADED NAKED THROUGH THE MIDDLE WARD.
HE PLEADED AND SOBBED AND CLUNG TO THE LEGS OF HIS CAPTORS, UNTIL RORGE PULLED HIM LOOSE AND SHAGWELL KICKED HIM DOWN INTO THE BEAR PIT.
THE BEAR IS ALL IN BLACK, ARYA THOUGHT.
LIKE YOREN.
SHE FILLED ROOSE BOLTON'S CUP, AND DID NOT SPILL A DROP.

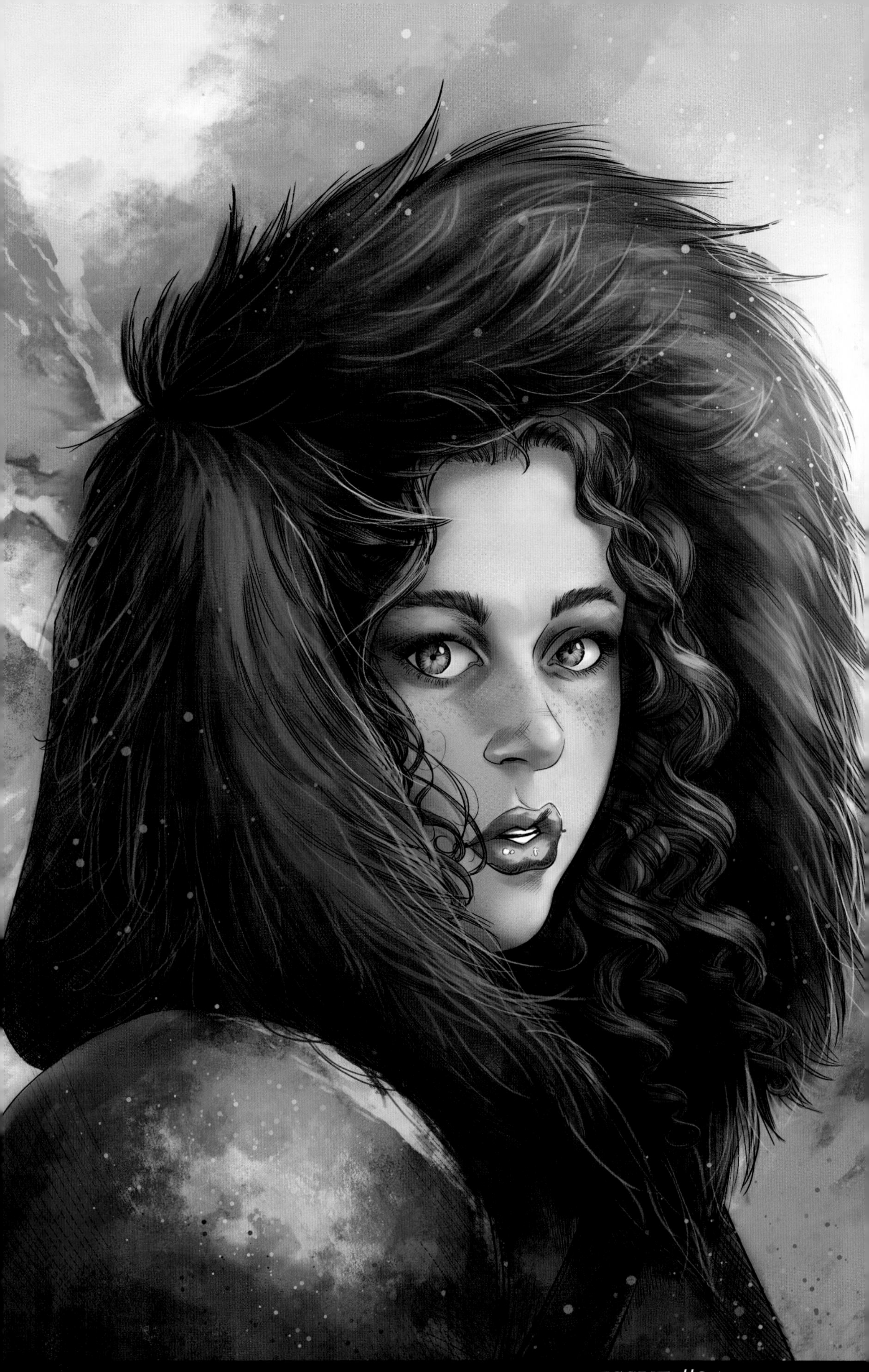

ISSUE #24

JON

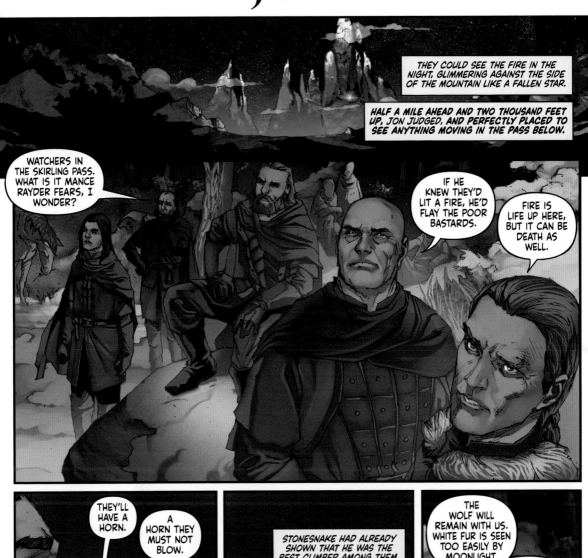

THEY COULD SEE THE FIRE IN THE NIGHT, GLIMMERING AGAINST THE SIDE OF THE MOUNTAIN LIKE A FALLEN STAR.

HALF A MILE AHEAD AND TWO THOUSAND FEET UP, JON JUDGED, AND PERFECTLY PLACED TO SEE ANYTHING MOVING IN THE PASS BELOW.

WATCHERS IN THE SKIRLING PASS. WHAT IS IT MANCE RAYDER FEARS, I WONDER?

IF HE KNEW THEY'D LIT A FIRE, HE'D FLAY THE POOR BASTARDS.

FIRE IS LIFE UP HERE, BUT IT CAN BE DEATH AS WELL.

THEY'LL HAVE A HORN.

A HORN THEY MUST NOT BLOW.

THAT'S A LONG CRUEL CLIMB BY NIGHT.

AND A LONGER FALL. TWO MEN, I THINK. THERE ARE LIKE TO BE TWO UP THERE, SHARING THE WATCH.

ME.

STONESNAKE HAD ALREADY SHOWN THAT HE WAS THE BEST CLIMBER AMONG THEM. IT WOULD HAVE TO BE HIM.

AND ME.

THE WOLF WILL REMAIN WITH US. WHITE FUR IS SEEN TOO EASILY BY MOONLIGHT.

WHEN IT'S DONE, THROW DOWN A BURNING BRAND. WE'LL COME WHEN WE SEE IT FALL.

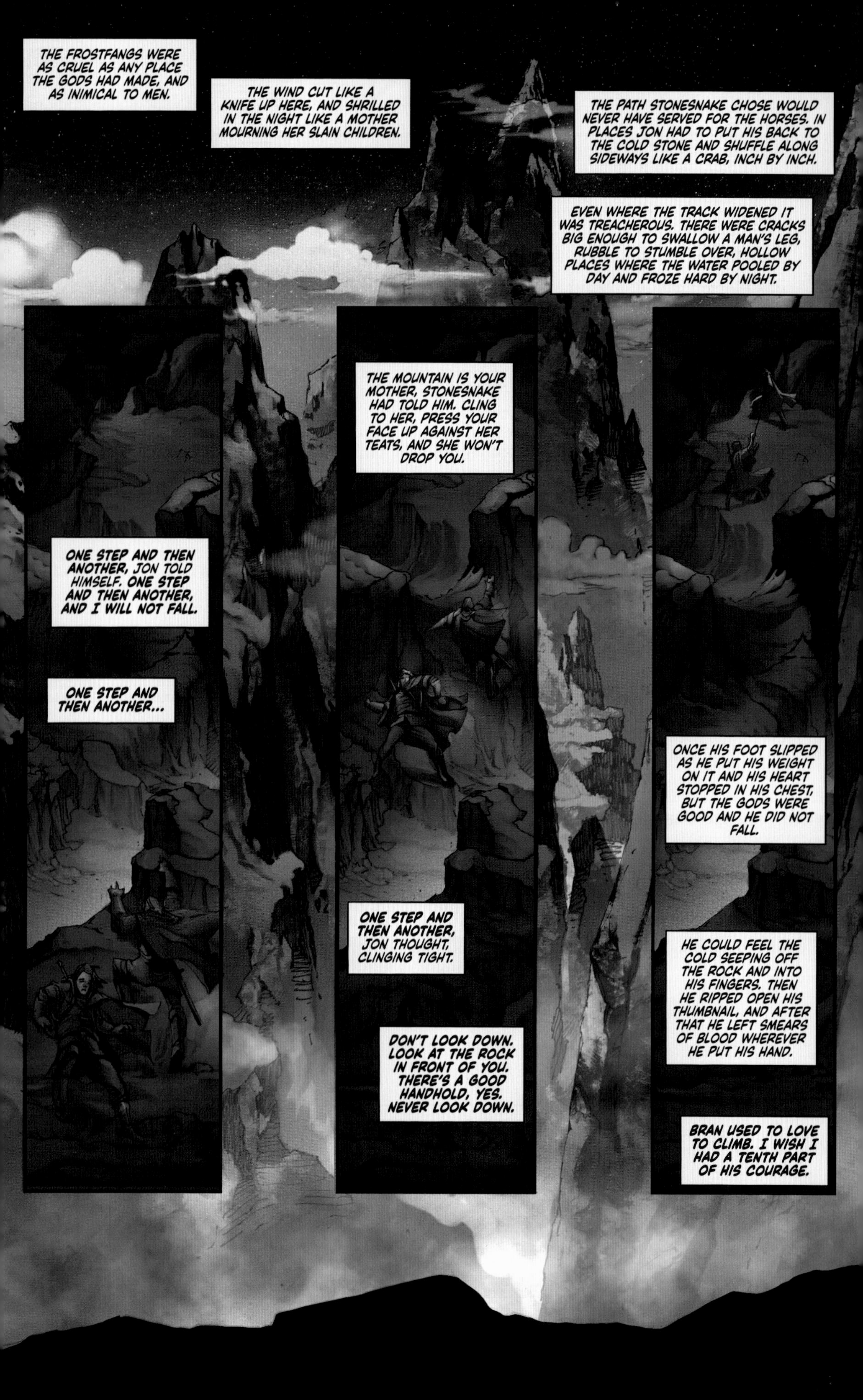
THE FROSTFANGS WERE AS CRUEL AS ANY PLACE THE GODS HAD MADE, AND AS INIMICAL TO MEN.
THE WIND CUT LIKE A KNIFE UP HERE, AND SHRILLED IN THE NIGHT LIKE A MOTHER MOURNING HER SLAIN CHILDREN.
THE PATH STONESNAKE CHOSE WOULD NEVER HAVE SERVED FOR THE HORSES. IN PLACES JON HAD TO PUT HIS BACK TO THE COLD STONE AND SHUFFLE ALONG SIDEWAYS LIKE A CRAB, INCH BY INCH.
EVEN WHERE THE TRACK WIDENED IT WAS TREACHEROUS. THERE WERE CRACKS BIG ENOUGH TO SWALLOW A MAN'S LEG, RUBBLE TO STUMBLE OVER, HOLLOW PLACES WHERE THE WATER POOLED BY DAY AND FROZE HARD BY NIGHT.
ONE STEP AND THEN ANOTHER, JON TOLD HIMSELF. ONE STEP AND THEN ANOTHER, AND I WILL NOT FALL.
ONE STEP AND THEN ANOTHER...
THE MOUNTAIN IS YOUR MOTHER, STONESNAKE HAD TOLD HIM. CLING TO HER, PRESS YOUR FACE UP AGAINST HER TEATS, AND SHE WON'T DROP YOU.
ONE STEP AND THEN ANOTHER, JON THOUGHT, CLINGING TIGHT.
DON'T LOOK DOWN. LOOK AT THE ROCK IN FRONT OF YOU. THERE'S A GOOD HANDHOLD, YES. NEVER LOOK DOWN.
ONCE HIS FOOT SLIPPED AS HE PUT HIS WEIGHT ON IT AND HIS HEART STOPPED IN HIS CHEST, BUT THE GODS WERE GOOD AND HE DID NOT FALL.
HE COULD FEEL THE COLD SEEPING OFF THE ROCK AND INTO HIS FINGERS. THEN HE RIPPED OPEN HIS THUMBNAIL, AND AFTER THAT HE LEFT SMEARS OF BLOOD WHEREVER HE PUT HIS HAND.
BRAN USED TO LOVE TO CLIMB. I WISH I HAD A TENTH PART OF HIS COURAGE.

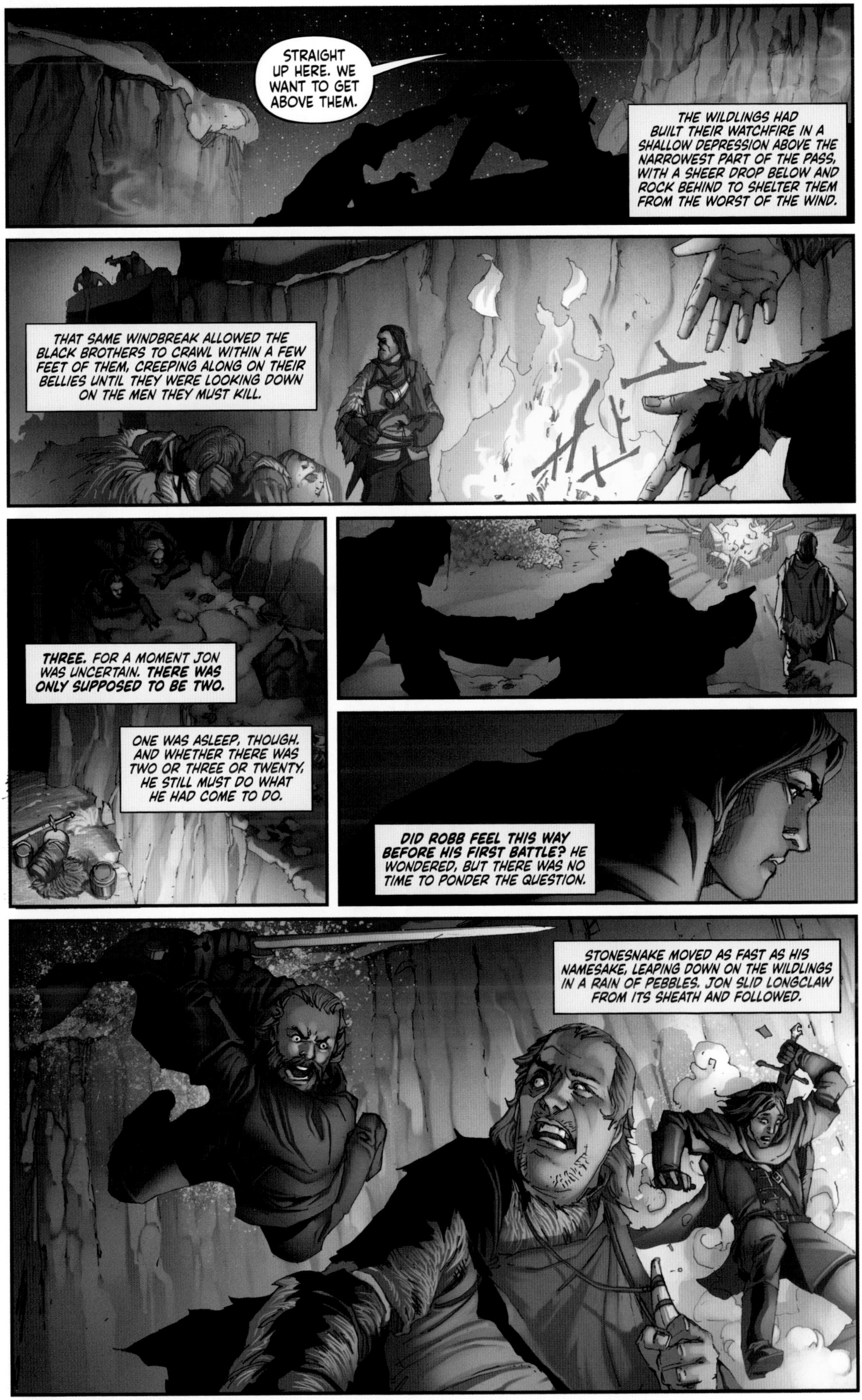
STRAIGHT UP HERE. WE WANT TO GET ABOVE THEM.
THE WILDLINGS HAD BUILT THEIR WATCHFIRE IN A SHALLOW DEPRESSION ABOVE THE NARROWEST PART OF THE PASS, WITH A SHEER DROP BELOW AND ROCK BEHIND TO SHELTER THEM FROM THE WORST OF THE WIND.
THAT SAME WINDBREAK ALLOWED THE BLACK BROTHERS TO CRAWL WITHIN A FEW FEET OF THEM, CREEPING ALONG ON THEIR BELLIES UNTIL THEY WERE LOOKING DOWN ON THE MEN THEY MUST KILL.
THREE. FOR A MOMENT JON WAS UNCERTAIN. THERE WAS ONLY SUPPOSED TO BE TWO.
ONE WAS ASLEEP, THOUGH. AND WHETHER THERE WAS TWO OR THREE OR TWENTY, HE STILL MUST DO WHAT HE HAD COME TO DO.
DID ROBB FEEL THIS WAY BEFORE HIS FIRST BATTLE? HE WONDERED, BUT THERE WAS NO TIME TO PONDER THE QUESTION.
STONESNAKE MOVED AS FAST AS HIS NAMESAKE, LEAPING DOWN ON THE WILDLINGS IN A RAIN OF PEBBLES. JON SLID LONGCLAW FROM ITS SHEATH AND FOLLOWED.

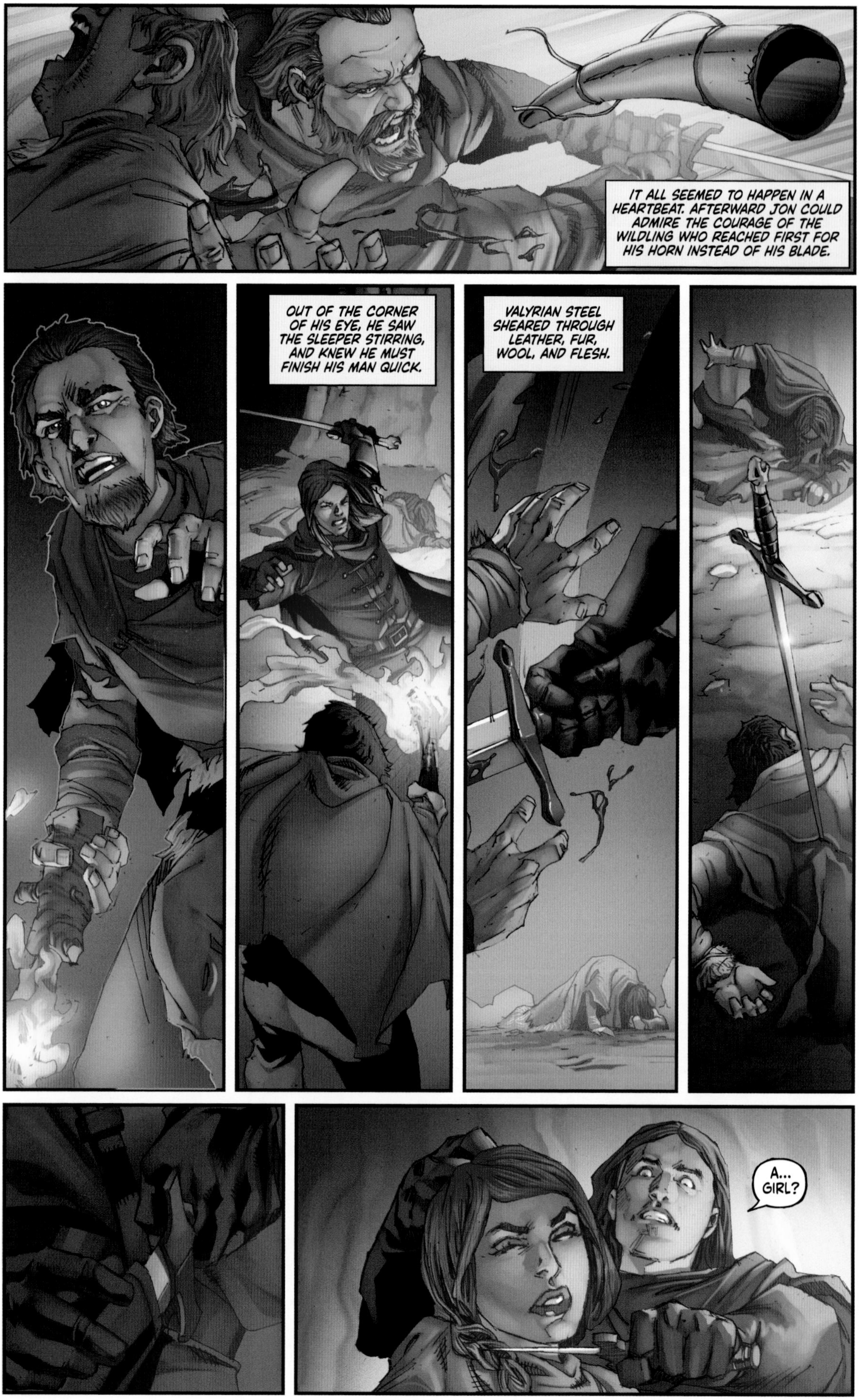
IT ALL SEEMED TO HAPPEN IN A HEARTBEAT. AFTERWARD JON COULD ADMIRE THE COURAGE OF THE WILDLING WHO REACHED FIRST FOR HIS HORN INSTEAD OF HIS BLADE.
OUT OF THE CORNER OF HIS EYE, HE SAW THE SLEEPER STIRRING, AND KNEW HE MUST FINISH HIS MAN QUICK.
VALYRIAN STEEL SHEARED THROUGH LEATHER, FUR, WOOL, AND FLESH.
A... GIRL?

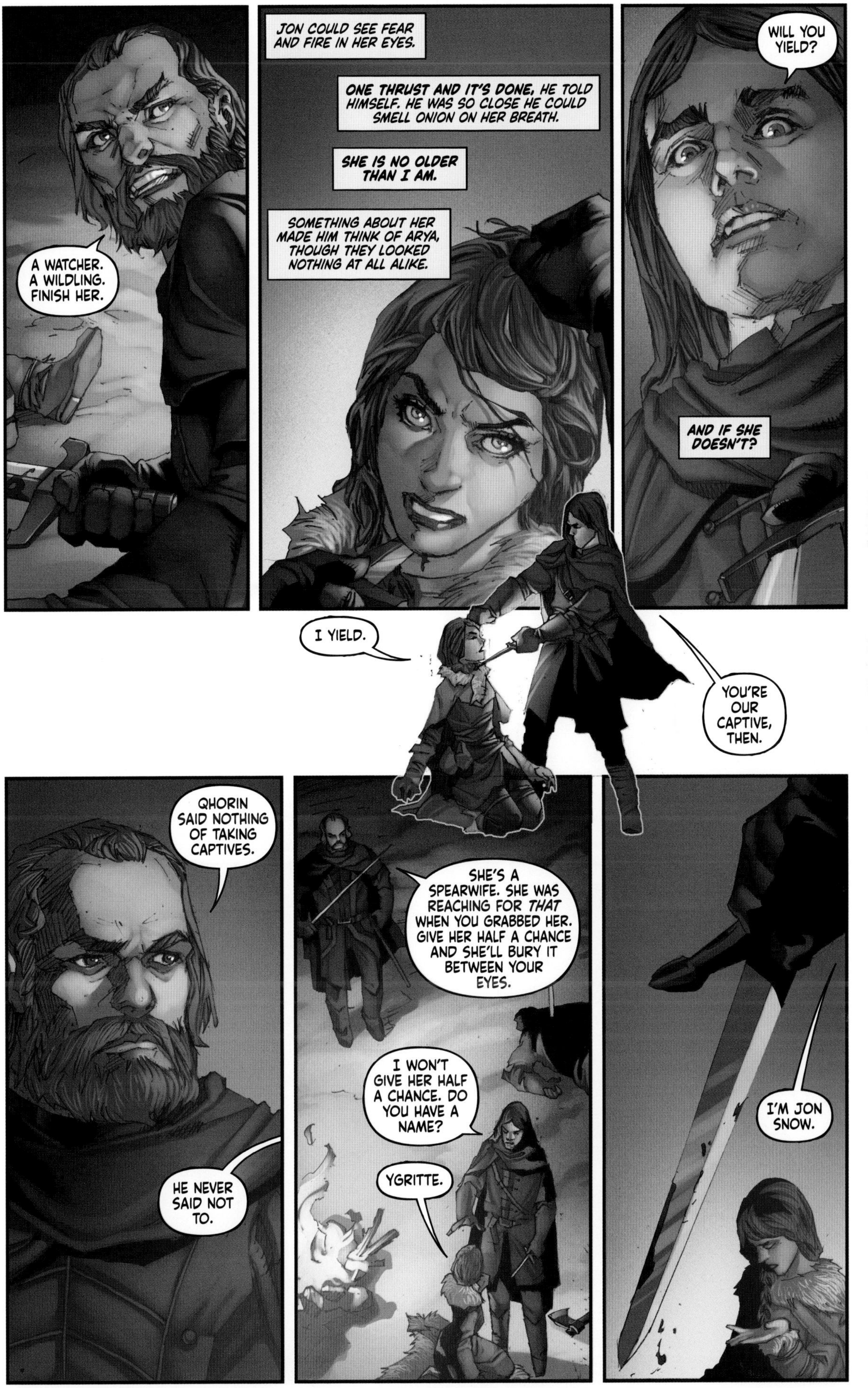
A WATCHER. A WILDLING. FINISH HER.
JON COULD SEE FEAR AND FIRE IN HER EYES.
ONE THRUST AND IT'S DONE, HE TOLD HIMSELF. HE WAS SO CLOSE HE COULD SMELL ONION ON HER BREATH.
SHE IS NO OLDER THAN I AM.
SOMETHING ABOUT HER MADE HIM THINK OF ARYA, THOUGH THEY LOOKED NOTHING AT ALL ALIKE.
WILL YOU YIELD?
AND IF SHE DOESN'T?
I YIELD.
YOU'RE OUR CAPTIVE, THEN.
QHORIN SAID NOTHING OF TAKING CAPTIVES.
HE NEVER SAID NOT TO.
SHE'S A SPEARWIFE. SHE WAS REACHING FOR THAT WHEN YOU GRABBED HER. GIVE HER HALF A CHANCE AND SHE'LL BURY IT BETWEEN YOUR EYES.
I WON'T GIVE HER HALF A CHANCE. DO YOU HAVE A NAME?
YGRITTE.
I'M JON SNOW.

AN EVIL NAME.

A BASTARD NAME. MY FATHER WAS LORD EDDARD STARK OF WINTERFELL.

IT'S THE CAPTIVE SUPPOSED TO TELL THINGS, REMEMBER?

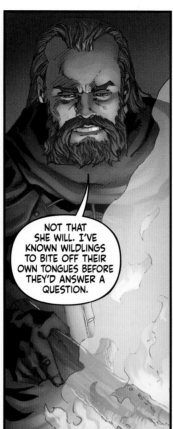

NOT THAT SHE WILL. I'VE KNOWN WILDLINGS TO BITE OFF THEIR OWN TONGUES BEFORE THEY'D ANSWER A QUESTION.

YOU OUGHT TO BURN THEM YOU KILLED.

NEED A BIGGER FIRE FOR THAT, AND BIG FIRES BURN BRIGHT. ARE THERE MORE WILDLINGS CLOSE BY, IS THAT IT?

BURN THEM, OR IT MIGHT BE YOU'LL NEED THEM SWORDS AGAIN.

MAYBE WE SHOULD DO AS SHE SAYS.

THERE ARE OTHER WAYS.

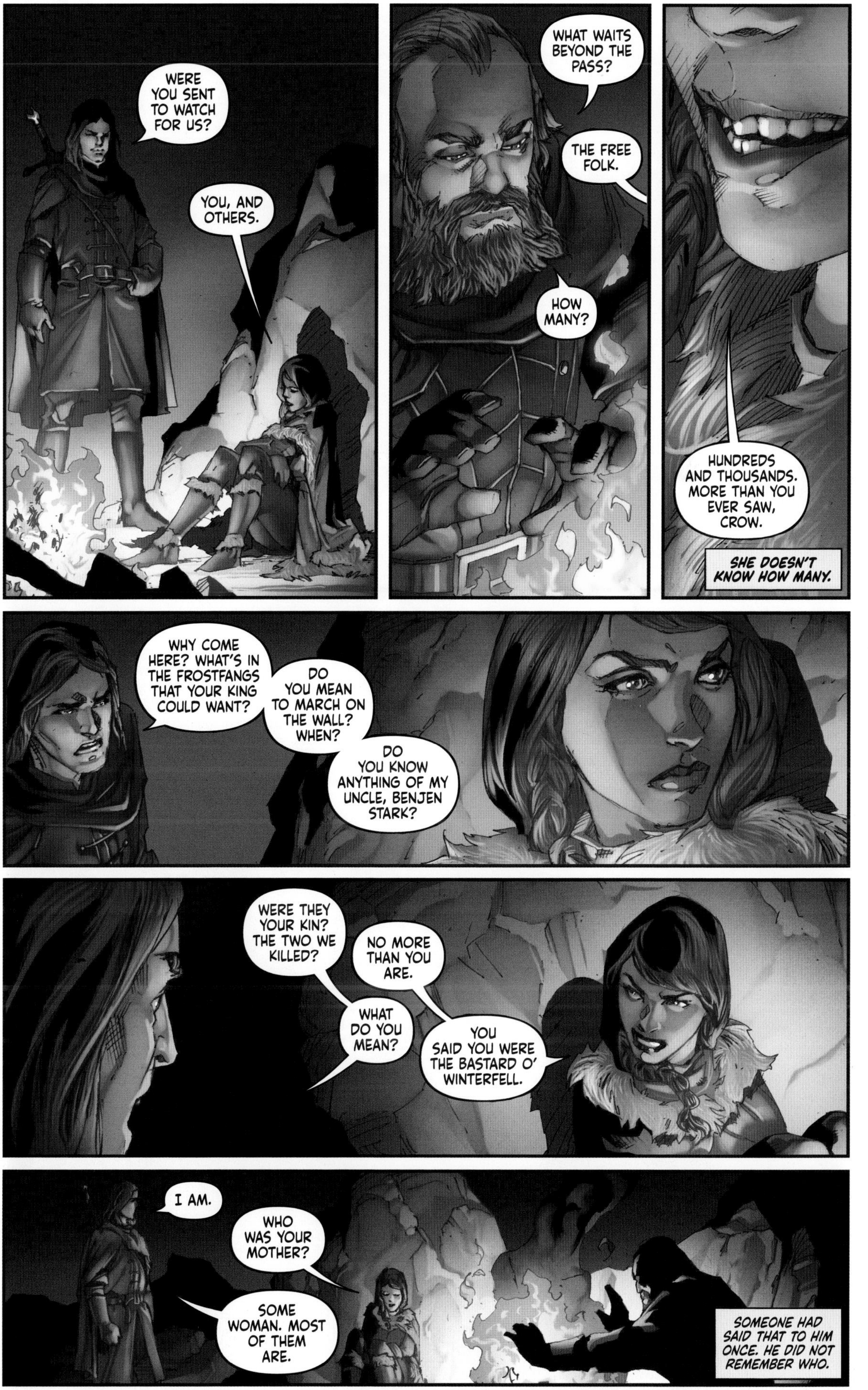
WERE YOU SENT TO WATCH FOR US?
YOU, AND OTHERS.
WHAT WAITS BEYOND THE PASS?
THE FREE FOLK.
HOW MANY?
HUNDREDS AND THOUSANDS. MORE THAN YOU EVER SAW, CROW.
SHE DOESN'T KNOW HOW MANY.
WHY COME HERE? WHAT'S IN THE FROSTFANGS THAT YOUR KING COULD WANT?
DO YOU MEAN TO MARCH ON THE WALL? WHEN?
DO YOU KNOW ANYTHING OF MY UNCLE, BENJEN STARK?
WERE THEY YOUR KIN? THE TWO WE KILLED?
NO MORE THAN YOU ARE.
WHAT DO YOU MEAN?
YOU SAID YOU WERE THE BASTARD O' WINTERFELL.
I AM.
WHO WAS YOUR MOTHER?
SOME WOMAN. MOST OF THEM ARE.
SOMEONE HAD SAID THAT TO HIM ONCE. HE DID NOT REMEMBER WHO.

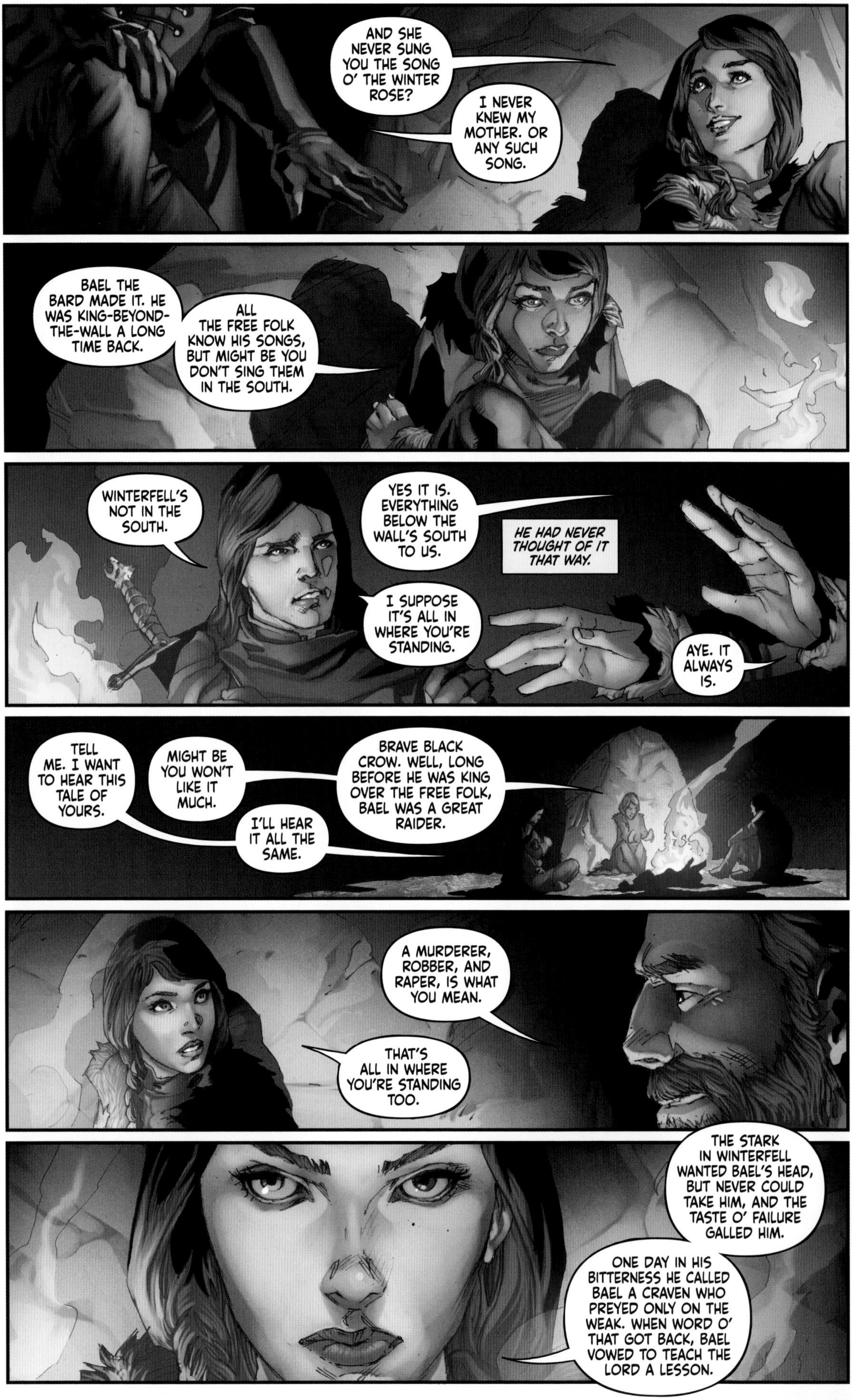

AND SHE NEVER SUNG YOU THE SONG O' THE WINTER ROSE?
I NEVER KNEW MY MOTHER. OR ANY SUCH SONG.
BAEL THE BARD MADE IT. HE WAS KING-BEYOND-THE-WALL A LONG TIME BACK.
ALL THE FREE FOLK KNOW HIS SONGS, BUT MIGHT BE YOU DON'T SING THEM IN THE SOUTH.
WINTERFELL'S NOT IN THE SOUTH.
YES IT IS. EVERYTHING BELOW THE WALL'S SOUTH TO US.
HE HAD NEVER THOUGHT OF IT THAT WAY.
I SUPPOSE IT'S ALL IN WHERE YOU'RE STANDING.
AYE. IT ALWAYS IS.
TELL ME. I WANT TO HEAR THIS TALE OF YOURS.
MIGHT BE YOU WON'T LIKE IT MUCH.
I'LL HEAR IT ALL THE SAME.
BRAVE BLACK CROW. WELL, LONG BEFORE HE WAS KING OVER THE FREE FOLK, BAEL WAS A GREAT RAIDER.
A MURDERER, ROBBER, AND RAPER, IS WHAT YOU MEAN.
THAT'S ALL IN WHERE YOU'RE STANDING TOO.
THE STARK IN WINTERFELL WANTED BAEL'S HEAD, BUT NEVER COULD TAKE HIM, AND THE TASTE O' FAILURE GALLED HIM.
ONE DAY IN HIS BITTERNESS HE CALLED BAEL A CRAVEN WHO PREYED ONLY ON THE WEAK. WHEN WORD O' THAT GOT BACK, BAEL VOWED TO TEACH THE LORD A LESSON.

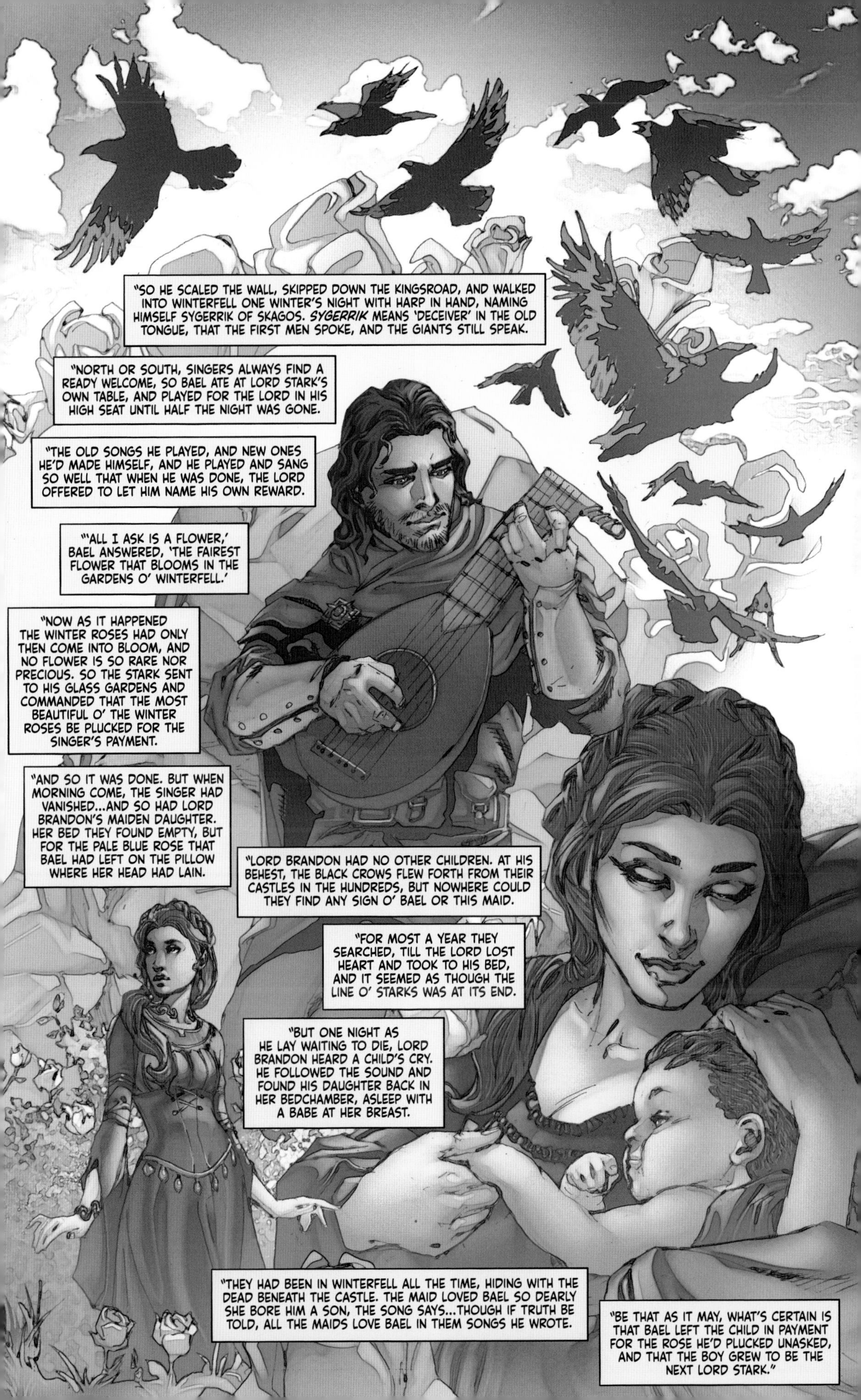
"SO HE SCALED THE WALL, SKIPPED DOWN THE KINGSROAD, AND WALKED INTO WINTERFELL ONE WINTER'S NIGHT WITH HARP IN HAND, NAMING HIMSELF SYGERRIK OF SKAGOS. *SYGERRIK* MEANS 'DECEIVER' IN THE OLD TONGUE, THAT THE FIRST MEN SPOKE, AND THE GIANTS STILL SPEAK.
"NORTH OR SOUTH, SINGERS ALWAYS FIND A READY WELCOME, SO BAEL ATE AT LORD STARK'S OWN TABLE, AND PLAYED FOR THE LORD IN HIS HIGH SEAT UNTIL HALF THE NIGHT WAS GONE.
"THE OLD SONGS HE PLAYED, AND NEW ONES HE'D MADE HIMSELF, AND HE PLAYED AND SANG SO WELL THAT WHEN HE WAS DONE, THE LORD OFFERED TO LET HIM NAME HIS OWN REWARD.
"'ALL I ASK IS A FLOWER,' BAEL ANSWERED, 'THE FAIREST FLOWER THAT BLOOMS IN THE GARDENS O' WINTERFELL.'
"NOW AS IT HAPPENED THE WINTER ROSES HAD ONLY THEN COME INTO BLOOM, AND NO FLOWER IS SO RARE NOR PRECIOUS. SO THE STARK SENT TO HIS GLASS GARDENS AND COMMANDED THAT THE MOST BEAUTIFUL O' THE WINTER ROSES BE PLUCKED FOR THE SINGER'S PAYMENT.
"AND SO IT WAS DONE. BUT WHEN MORNING COME, THE SINGER HAD VANISHED...AND SO HAD LORD BRANDON'S MAIDEN DAUGHTER. HER BED THEY FOUND EMPTY, BUT FOR THE PALE BLUE ROSE THAT BAEL HAD LEFT ON THE PILLOW WHERE HER HEAD HAD LAIN.
"LORD BRANDON HAD NO OTHER CHILDREN. AT HIS BEHEST, THE BLACK CROWS FLEW FORTH FROM THEIR CASTLES IN THE HUNDREDS, BUT NOWHERE COULD THEY FIND ANY SIGN O' BAEL OR THIS MAID.
"FOR MOST A YEAR THEY SEARCHED, TILL THE LORD LOST HEART AND TOOK TO HIS BED, AND IT SEEMED AS THOUGH THE LINE O' STARKS WAS AT ITS END.
"BUT ONE NIGHT AS HE LAY WAITING TO DIE, LORD BRANDON HEARD A CHILD'S CRY. HE FOLLOWED THE SOUND AND FOUND HIS DAUGHTER BACK IN HER BEDCHAMBER, ASLEEP WITH A BABE AT HER BREAST.
"THEY HAD BEEN IN WINTERFELL ALL THE TIME, HIDING WITH THE DEAD BENEATH THE CASTLE. THE MAID LOVED BAEL SO DEARLY SHE BORE HIM A SON, THE SONG SAYS...THOUGH IF TRUTH BE TOLD, ALL THE MAIDS LOVE BAEL IN THEM SONGS HE WROTE.
"BE THAT AS IT MAY, WHAT'S CERTAIN IS THAT BAEL LEFT THE CHILD IN PAYMENT FOR THE ROSE HE'D PLUCKED UNASKED, AND THAT THE BOY GREW TO BE THE NEXT LORD STARK."

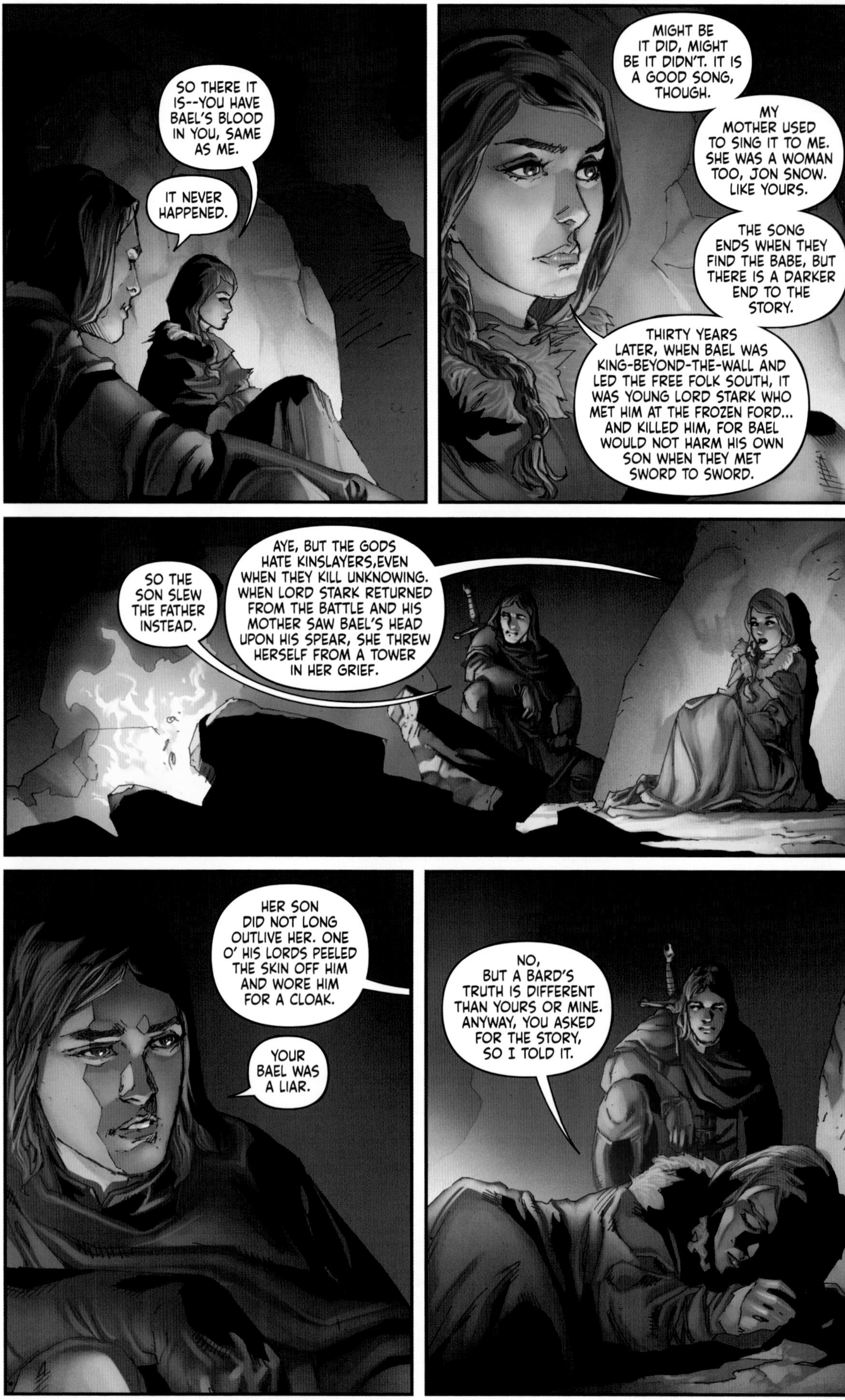
SO THERE IT IS--YOU HAVE BAEL'S BLOOD IN YOU, SAME AS ME.
IT NEVER HAPPENED.
MIGHT BE IT DID, MIGHT BE IT DIDN'T. IT IS A GOOD SONG, THOUGH.
MY MOTHER USED TO SING IT TO ME. SHE WAS A WOMAN TOO, JON SNOW. LIKE YOURS.
THE SONG ENDS WHEN THEY FIND THE BABE, BUT THERE IS A DARKER END TO THE STORY.
THIRTY YEARS LATER, WHEN BAEL WAS KING-BEYOND-THE-WALL AND LED THE FREE FOLK SOUTH, IT WAS YOUNG LORD STARK WHO MET HIM AT THE FROZEN FORD... AND KILLED HIM, FOR BAEL WOULD NOT HARM HIS OWN SON WHEN THEY MET SWORD TO SWORD.
SO THE SON SLEW THE FATHER INSTEAD.
AYE, BUT THE GODS HATE KINSLAYERS,EVEN WHEN THEY KILL UNKNOWING. WHEN LORD STARK RETURNED FROM THE BATTLE AND HIS MOTHER SAW BAEL'S HEAD UPON HIS SPEAR, SHE THREW HERSELF FROM A TOWER IN HER GRIEF.
HER SON DID NOT LONG OUTLIVE HER. ONE O' HIS LORDS PEELED THE SKIN OFF HIM AND WORE HIM FOR A CLOAK.
YOUR BAEL WAS A LIAR.
NO, BUT A BARD'S TRUTH IS DIFFERENT THAN YOURS OR MINE. ANYWAY, YOU ASKED FOR THE STORY, SO I TOLD IT.

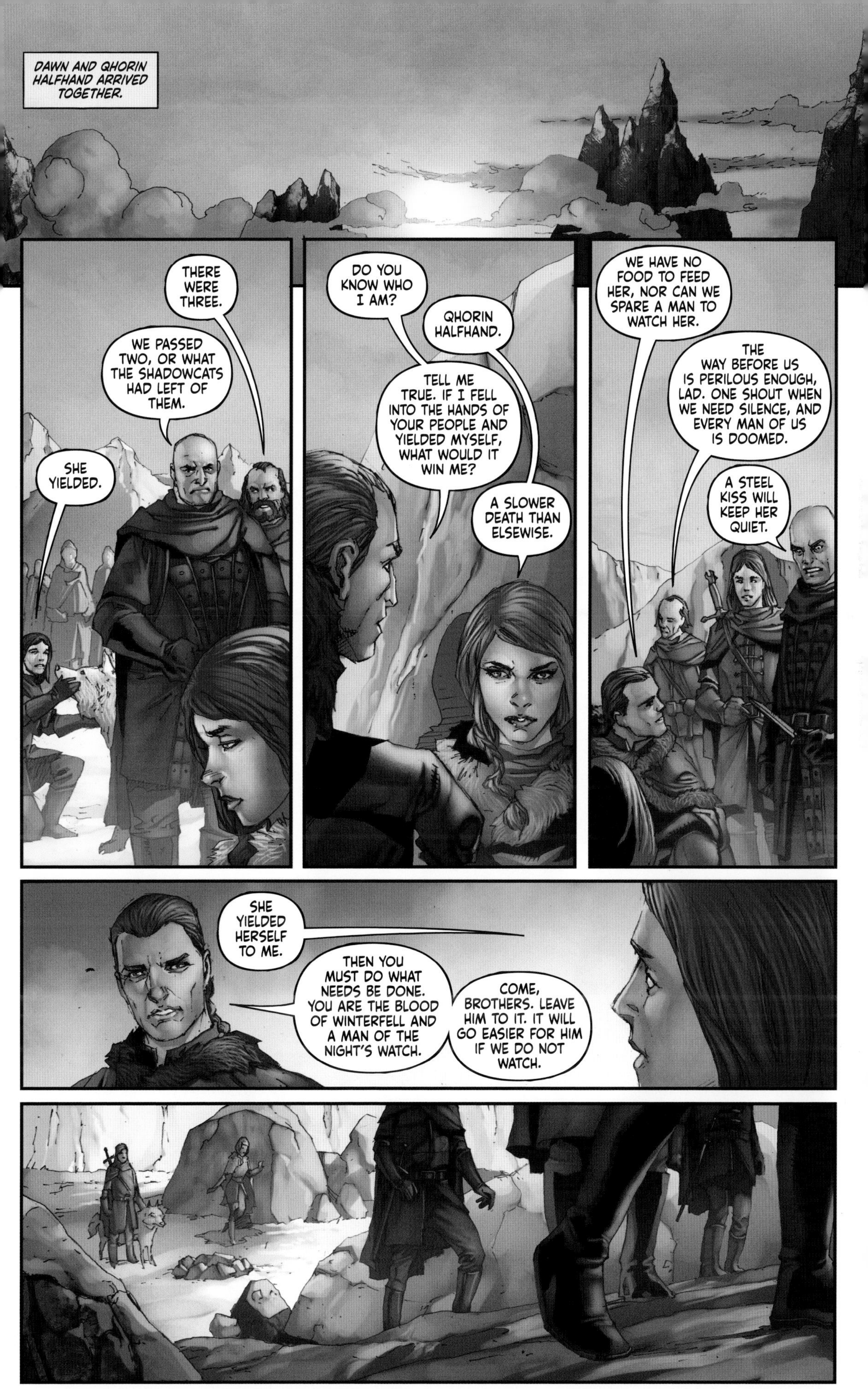
DAWN AND QHORIN HALFHAND ARRIVED TOGETHER.
THERE WERE THREE.
WE PASSED TWO, OR WHAT THE SHADOWCATS HAD LEFT OF THEM.
SHE YIELDED.
DO YOU KNOW WHO I AM?
QHORIN HALFHAND.
TELL ME TRUE. IF I FELL INTO THE HANDS OF YOUR PEOPLE AND YIELDED MYSELF, WHAT WOULD IT WIN ME?
A SLOWER DEATH THAN ELSEWISE.
WE HAVE NO FOOD TO FEED HER, NOR CAN WE SPARE A MAN TO WATCH HER.
THE WAY BEFORE US IS PERILOUS ENOUGH, LAD. ONE SHOUT WHEN WE NEED SILENCE, AND EVERY MAN OF US IS DOOMED.
A STEEL KISS WILL KEEP HER QUIET.
SHE YIELDED HERSELF TO ME.
THEN YOU MUST DO WHAT NEEDS BE DONE. YOU ARE THE BLOOD OF WINTERFELL AND A MAN OF THE NIGHT'S WATCH.
COME, BROTHERS. LEAVE HIM TO IT. IT WILL GO EASIER FOR HIM IF WE DO NOT WATCH.

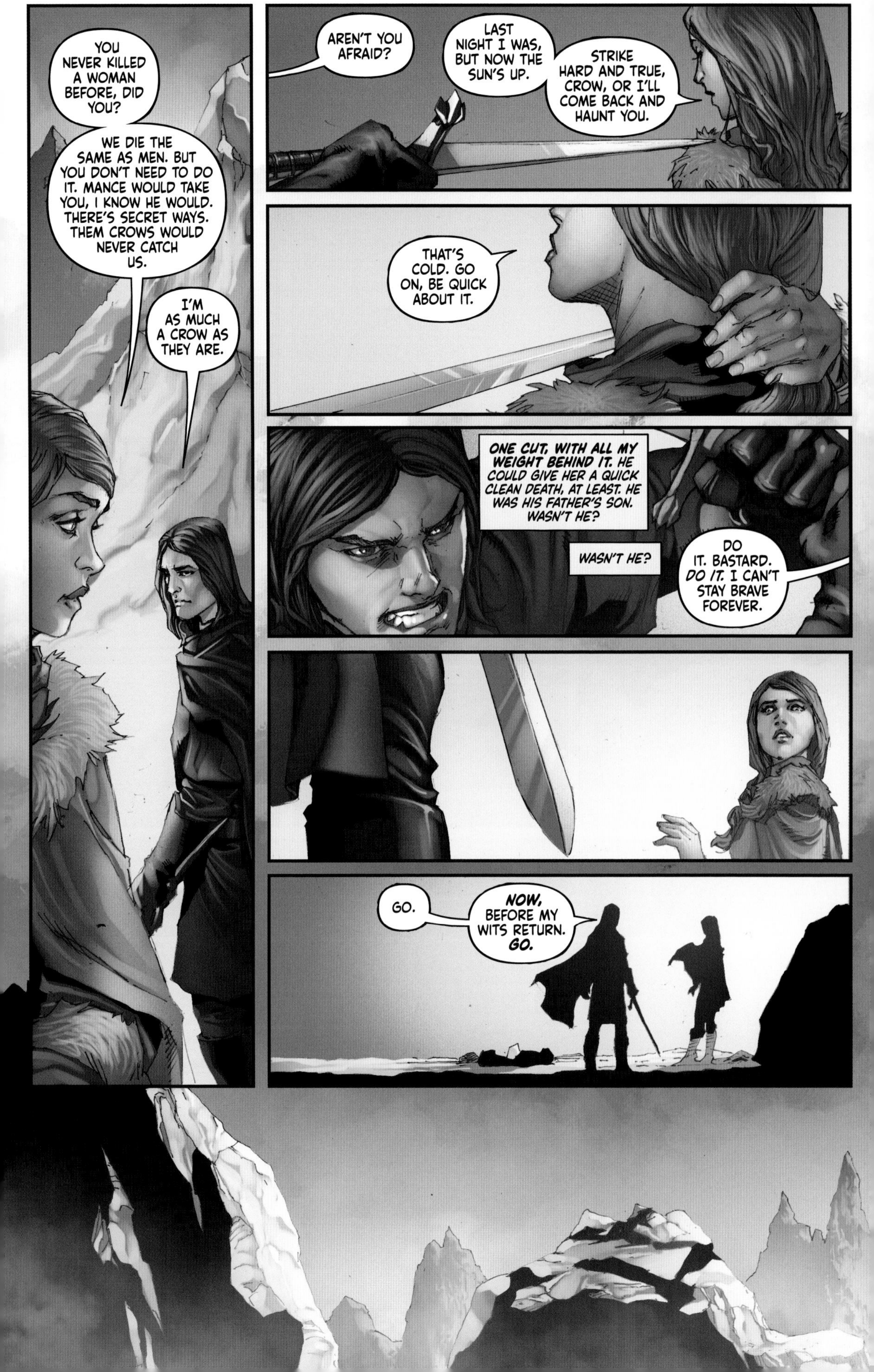
YOU NEVER KILLED A WOMAN BEFORE, DID YOU?
WE DIE THE SAME AS MEN. BUT YOU DON'T NEED TO DO IT. MANCE WOULD TAKE YOU, I KNOW HE WOULD. THERE'S SECRET WAYS. THEM CROWS WOULD NEVER CATCH US.
I'M AS MUCH A CROW AS THEY ARE.
AREN'T YOU AFRAID?
LAST NIGHT I WAS, BUT NOW THE SUN'S UP.
STRIKE HARD AND TRUE, CROW, OR I'LL COME BACK AND HAUNT YOU.
THAT'S COLD. GO ON, BE QUICK ABOUT IT.
ONE CUT, WITH ALL MY WEIGHT BEHIND IT. HE COULD GIVE HER A QUICK CLEAN DEATH, AT LEAST. HE WAS HIS FATHER'S SON. WASN'T HE?
WASN'T HE?
DO IT. BASTARD. *DO IT.* I CAN'T STAY BRAVE FOREVER.
GO.
NOW, BEFORE MY WITS RETURN. ***GO.***

THEON

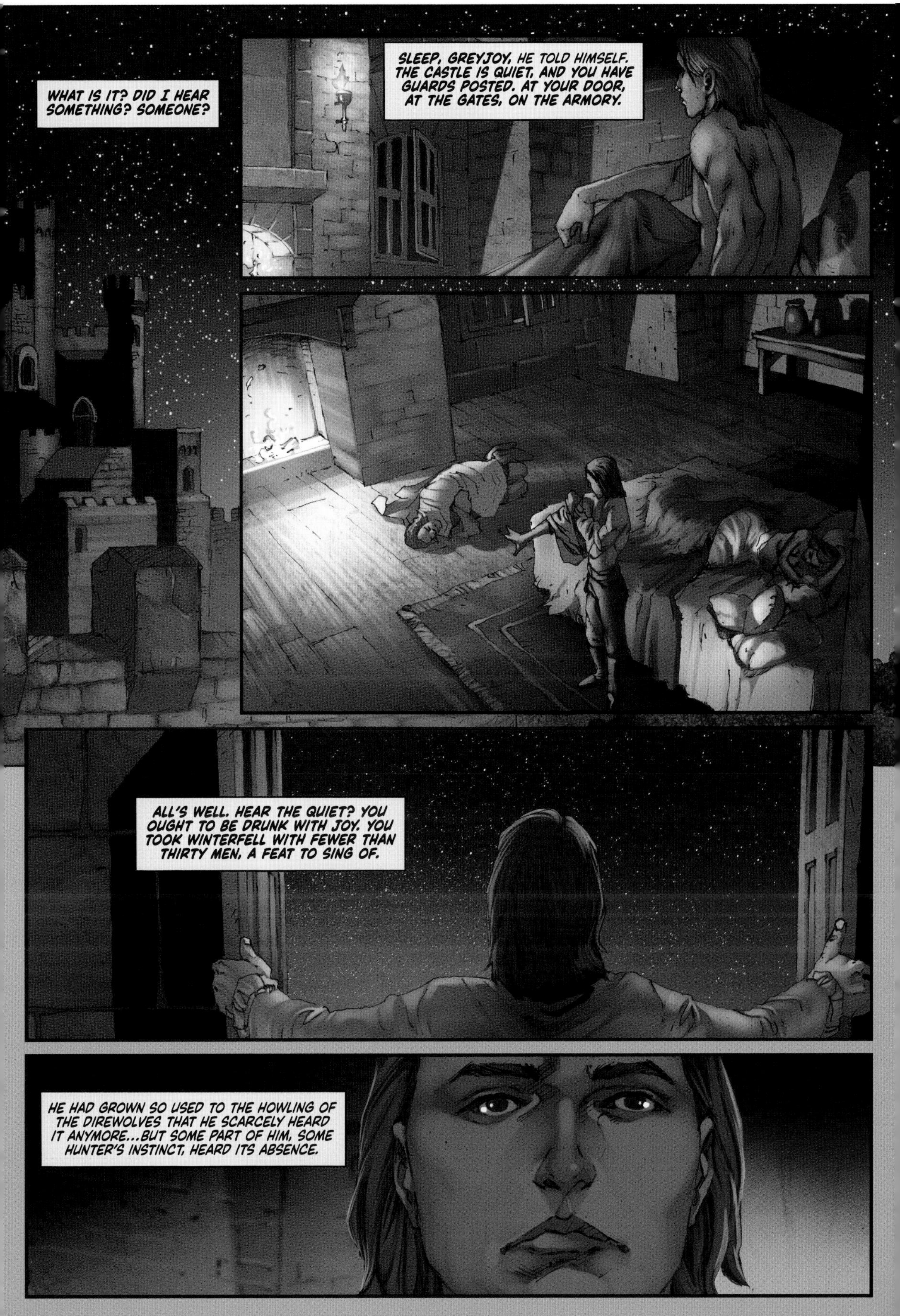
WHAT IS IT? DID I HEAR SOMETHING? SOMEONE?
SLEEP, GREYJOY, HE TOLD HIMSELF. THE CASTLE IS QUIET, AND YOU HAVE GUARDS POSTED. AT YOUR DOOR, AT THE GATES, ON THE ARMORY.
ALL'S WELL. HEAR THE QUIET? YOU OUGHT TO BE DRUNK WITH JOY. YOU TOOK WINTERFELL WITH FEWER THAN THIRTY MEN, A FEAT TO SING OF.
HE HAD GROWN SO USED TO THE HOWLING OF THE DIREWOLVES THAT HE SCARCELY HEARD IT ANYMORE...BUT SOME PART OF HIM, SOME HUNTER'S INSTINCT, HEARD ITS ABSENCE.

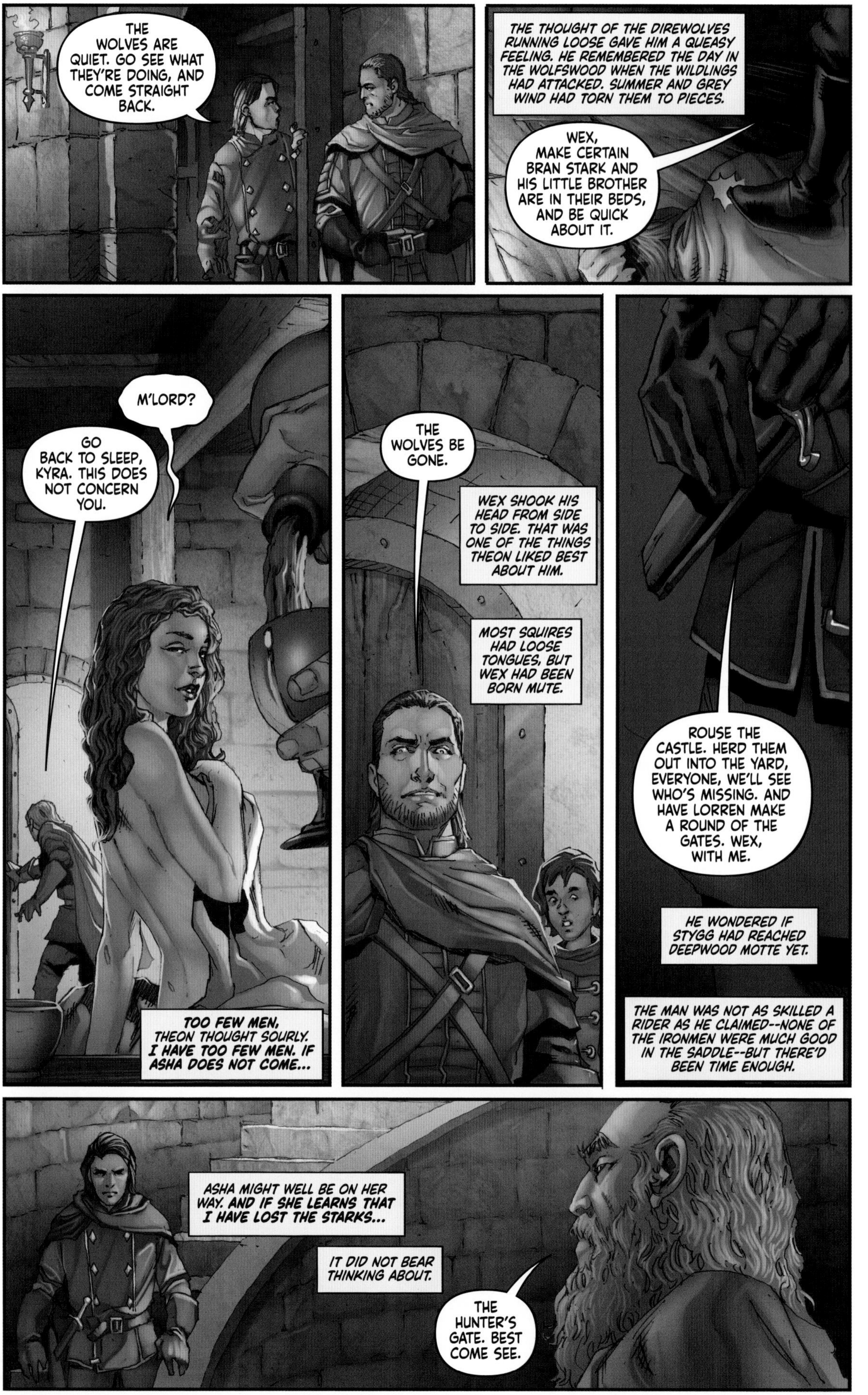
THE WOLVES ARE QUIET. GO SEE WHAT THEY'RE DOING, AND COME STRAIGHT BACK.
THE THOUGHT OF THE DIREWOLVES RUNNING LOOSE GAVE HIM A QUEASY FEELING. HE REMEMBERED THE DAY IN THE WOLFSWOOD WHEN THE WILDLINGS HAD ATTACKED. SUMMER AND GREY WIND HAD TORN THEM TO PIECES.
WEX, MAKE CERTAIN BRAN STARK AND HIS LITTLE BROTHER ARE IN THEIR BEDS, AND BE QUICK ABOUT IT.
M'LORD?
GO BACK TO SLEEP, KYRA. THIS DOES NOT CONCERN YOU.
TOO FEW MEN, THEON THOUGHT SOURLY. I HAVE TOO FEW MEN. IF ASHA DOES NOT COME...
THE WOLVES BE GONE.
WEX SHOOK HIS HEAD FROM SIDE TO SIDE. THAT WAS ONE OF THE THINGS THEON LIKED BEST ABOUT HIM.
MOST SQUIRES HAD LOOSE TONGUES, BUT WEX HAD BEEN BORN MUTE.
ROUSE THE CASTLE. HERD THEM OUT INTO THE YARD, EVERYONE, WE'LL SEE WHO'S MISSING. AND HAVE LORREN MAKE A ROUND OF THE GATES. WEX, WITH ME.
HE WONDERED IF STYGG HAD REACHED DEEPWOOD MOTTE YET.
THE MAN WAS NOT AS SKILLED A RIDER AS HE CLAIMED--NONE OF THE IRONMEN WERE MUCH GOOD IN THE SADDLE--BUT THERE'D BEEN TIME ENOUGH.
ASHA MIGHT WELL BE ON HER WAY. AND IF SHE LEARNS THAT I HAVE LOST THE STARKS...
IT DID NOT BEAR THINKING ABOUT.
THE HUNTER'S GATE. BEST COME SEE.

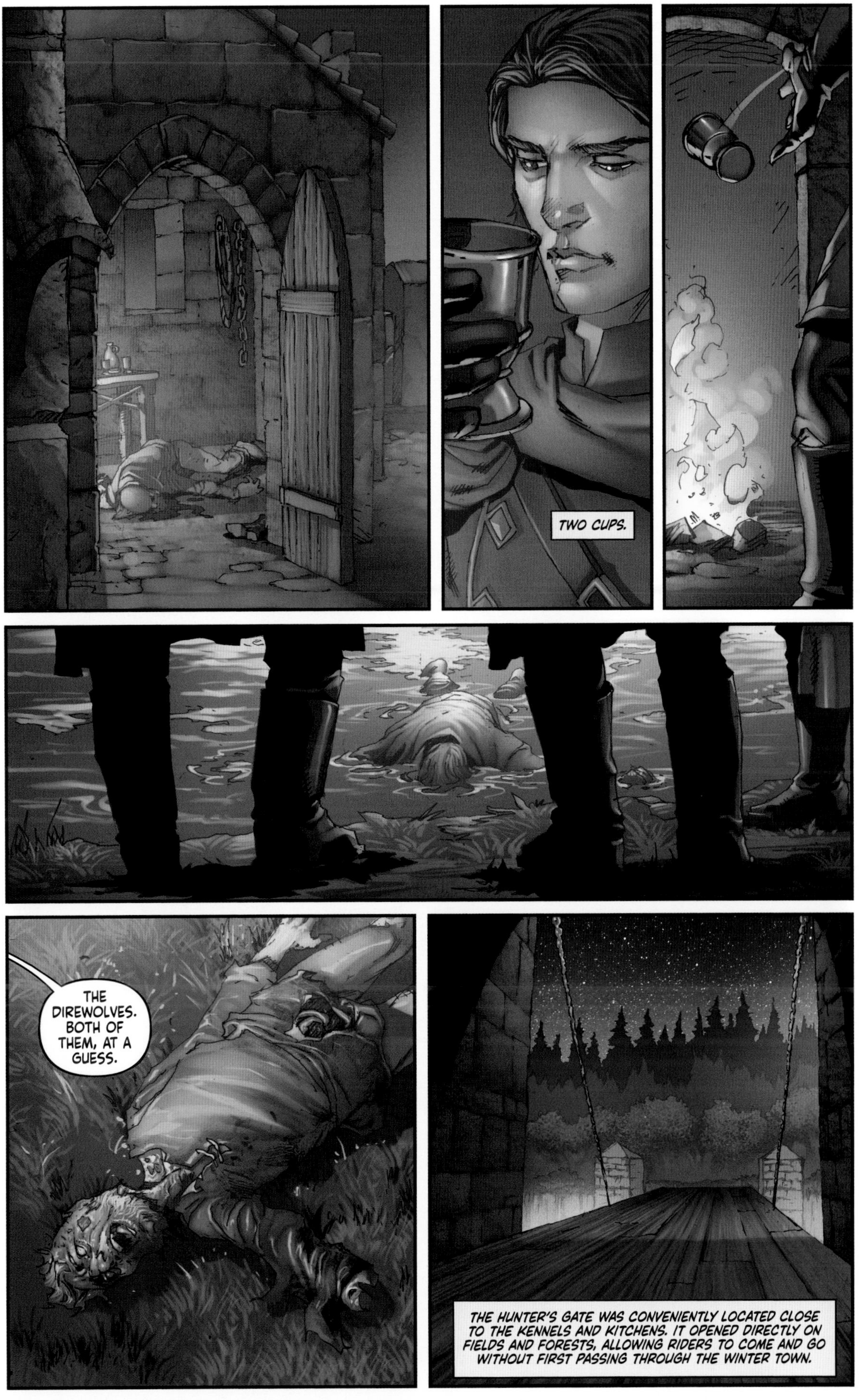
TWO CUPS.
THE DIREWOLVES. BOTH OF THEM, AT A GUESS.
THE HUNTER'S GATE WAS CONVENIENTLY LOCATED CLOSE TO THE KENNELS AND KITCHENS. IT OPENED DIRECTLY ON FIELDS AND FORESTS, ALLOWING RIDERS TO COME AND GO WITHOUT FIRST PASSING THROUGH THE WINTER TOWN.

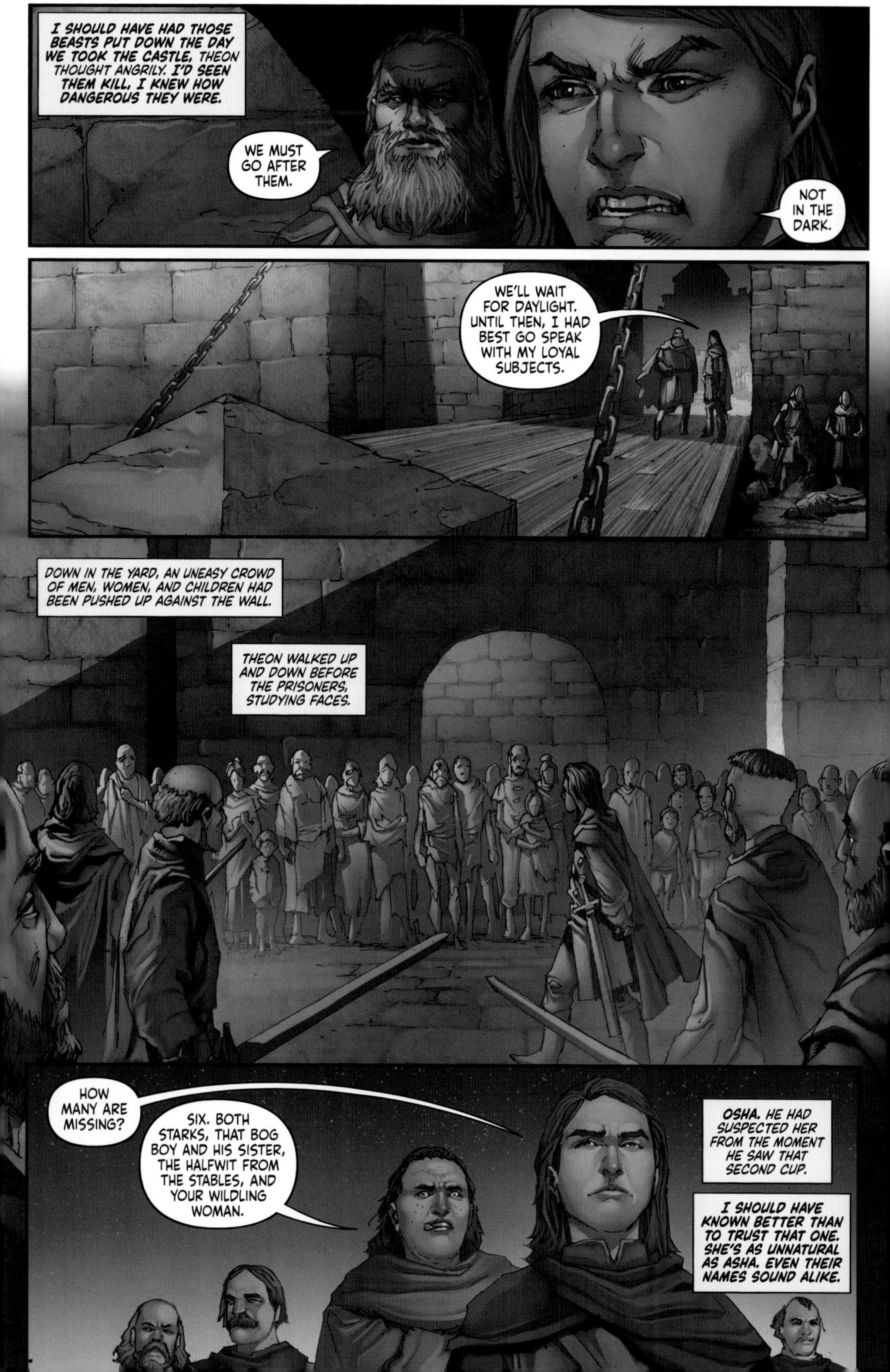
I SHOULD HAVE HAD THOSE BEASTS PUT DOWN THE DAY WE TOOK THE CASTLE, THEON THOUGHT ANGRILY. I'D SEEN THEM KILL, I KNEW HOW DANGEROUS THEY WERE.
WE MUST GO AFTER THEM.
NOT IN THE DARK.
WE'LL WAIT FOR DAYLIGHT. UNTIL THEN, I HAD BEST GO SPEAK WITH MY LOYAL SUBJECTS.
DOWN IN THE YARD, AN UNEASY CROWD OF MEN, WOMEN, AND CHILDREN HAD BEEN PUSHED UP AGAINST THE WALL.
THEON WALKED UP AND DOWN BEFORE THE PRISONERS, STUDYING FACES.
HOW MANY ARE MISSING?
SIX. BOTH STARKS, THAT BOG BOY AND HIS SISTER, THE HALFWIT FROM THE STABLES, AND YOUR WILDLING WOMAN.
OSHA. HE HAD SUSPECTED HER FROM THE MOMENT HE SAW THAT SECOND CUP.
I SHOULD HAVE KNOWN BETTER THAN TO TRUST THAT ONE. SHE'S AS UNNATURAL AS ASHA. EVEN THEIR NAMES SOUND ALIKE.

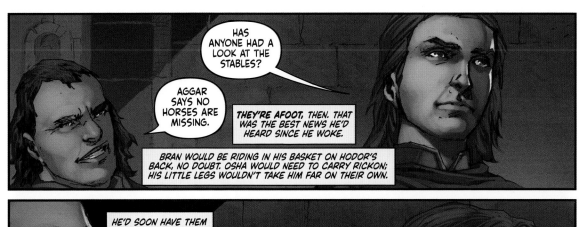

HAS ANYONE HAD A LOOK AT THE STABLES?

AGGAR SAYS NO HORSES ARE MISSING.

THEY'RE AFOOT, THEN. THAT WAS THE BEST NEWS HE'D HEARD SINCE HE WOKE.

BRAN WOULD BE RIDING IN HIS BASKET ON HODOR'S BACK, NO DOUBT. OSHA WOULD NEED TO CARRY RICKON; HIS LITTLE LEGS WOULDN'T TAKE HIM FAR ON THEIR OWN.

HE'D SOON HAVE THEM BACK IN HIS HANDS.

BRAN AND RICKON HAVE FLED. WHO KNOWS WHERE THEY'VE GONE?

THEY COULD NOT HAVE ESCAPED WITHOUT HELP. WITHOUT FOOD, CLOTHING, WEAPONS.

HE HAD LOCKED AWAY EVERY SWORD AND AXE IN WINTERFELL, BUT NO DOUBT SOME HAD BEEN HIDDEN FROM HIM.

I'LL HAVE THE NAMES OF ALL THOSE WHO AIDED THEM. ALL THOSE WHO TURNED A BLIND EYE.

I MIGHT HAVE KILLED EVERY MAN OF YOU AND GIVEN YOUR WOMEN TO MY SOLDIERS FOR THEIR PLEASURE, BUT INSTEAD I PROTECTED YOU. IS THIS THE THANKS YOU OFFER?

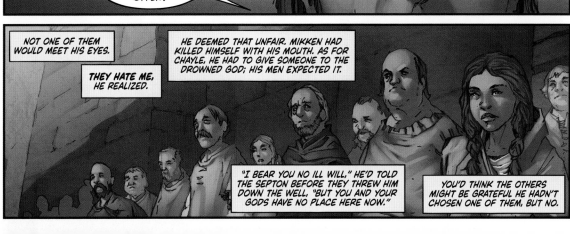

NOT ONE OF THEM WOULD MEET HIS EYES.

THEY HATE ME, HE REALIZED.

HE DEEMED THAT UNFAIR. MIKKEN HAD KILLED HIMSELF WITH HIS MOUTH. AS FOR CHAYLE, HE HAD TO GIVE SOMEONE TO THE DROWNED GOD; HIS MEN EXPECTED IT.

"I BEAR YOU NO ILL WILL," HE'D TOLD THE SEPTON BEFORE THEY THREW HIM DOWN THE WELL, "BUT YOU AND YOUR GODS HAVE NO PLACE HERE NOW."

YOU'D THINK THE OTHERS MIGHT BE GRATEFUL HE HADN'T CHOSEN ONE OF THEM, BUT NO.

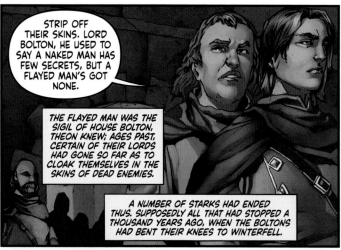

STRIP OFF THEIR SKINS. LORD BOLTON, HE USED TO SAY A NAKED MAN HAS FEW SECRETS, BUT A FLAYED MAN'S GOT NONE.

THE FLAYED MAN WAS THE SIGIL OF HOUSE BOLTON, THEON KNEW; AGES PAST, CERTAIN OF THEIR LORDS HAD GONE SO FAR AS TO CLOAK THEMSELVES IN THE SKINS OF DEAD ENEMIES.

A NUMBER OF STARKS HAD ENDED THUS. SUPPOSEDLY ALL THAT HAD STOPPED A THOUSAND YEARS AGO, WHEN THE BOLTONS HAD BENT THEIR KNEES TO WINTERFELL.

OR SO THEY SAY, BUT OLD WAYS DIE HARD, AS WELL I KNOW.

THERE WILL BE NO FLAYING IN THE NORTH SO LONG AS I RULE IN WINTERFELL.

I AM YOUR ONLY PROTECTION AGAINST THE LIKES OF HIM, HE WANTED TO SCREAM. HE COULD NOT BE THAT BLATANT, BUT PERHAPS SOME WERE CLEVER ENOUGH TO TAKE THE LESSON.

JOSETH, SADDLE SMILER AND A HORSE FOR YOURSELF. MURCH, GARISS, POXY TYM, YOU'LL COME AS WELL.

AND AGGAR, REDNOSE, GELMARR, REEK, WEX.

HE NEEDED HIS OWN TO WATCH HIS BACK.

FARLEN, I'LL WANT HOUNDS, AND YOU TO HANDLE THEM.

AND WHY WOULD I CARE TO HUNT DOWN MY OWN TRUEBORN LORDS, AND BABES AT THAT?

I AM YOUR TRUEBORN LORD NOW!

MAESTER LUWIN.

I KNOW NOTHING OF HUNTING.

NO, BUT I DON'T TRUST YOU IN THE CASTLE IN MY ABSENCE.

THEN IT'S PAST TIME YOU LEARNED.

LET ME COME TOO. I WANT A WOLFSKIN CLOAK.

COME IF YOU LIKE, BUT IF YOU CAN'T KEEP UP, DON'T THINK THAT I'LL NURSE YOU ALONG.

LORREN, WINTERFELL IS YOURS IN MY ABSENCE. IF WE DO NOT RETURN, DO WITH IT AS YOU WILL.

THAT BLOODY WELL OUGHT TO HAVE THEM PRAYING FOR MY SUCCESS.

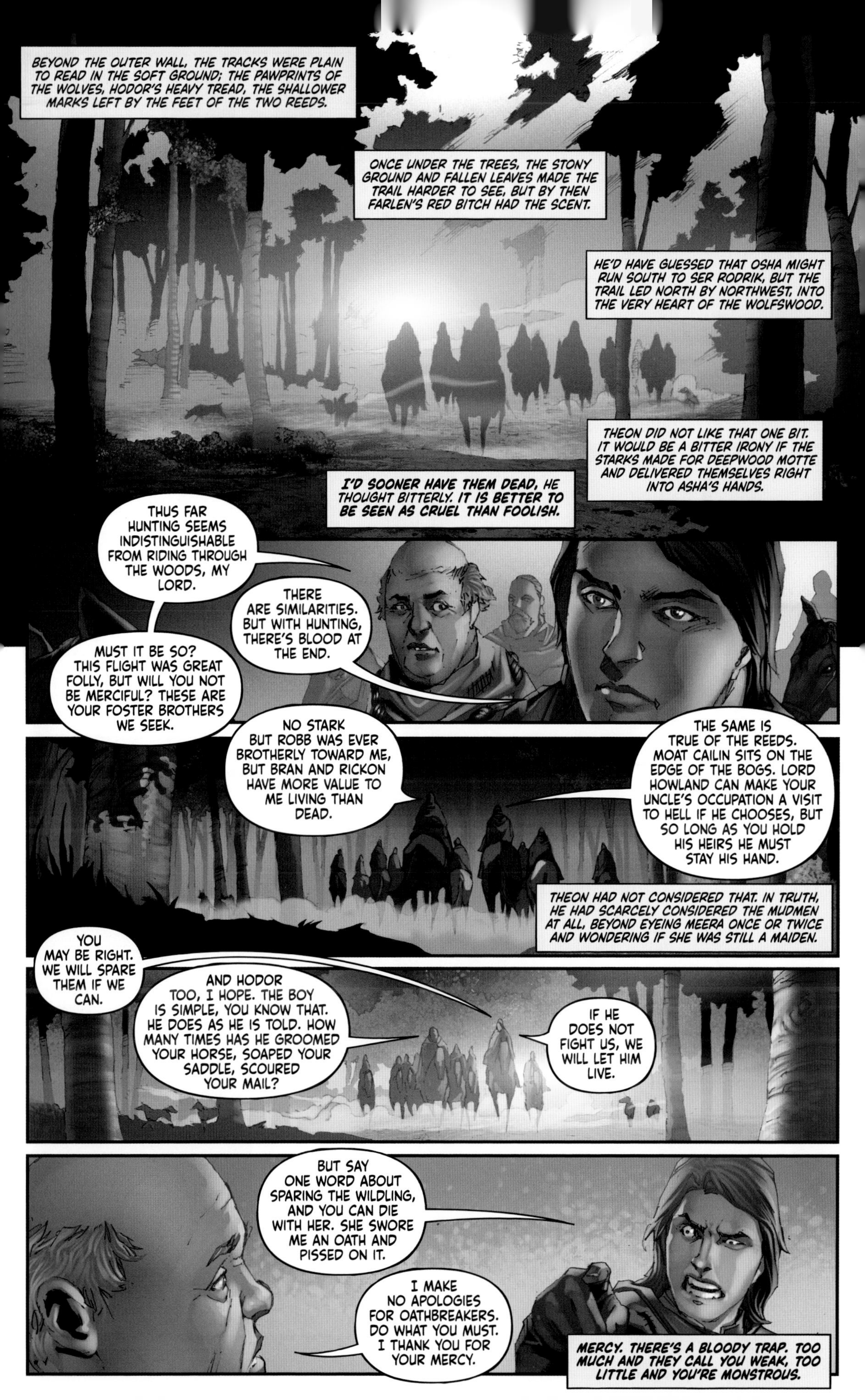
BEYOND THE OUTER WALL, THE TRACKS WERE PLAIN TO READ IN THE SOFT GROUND; THE PAWPRINTS OF THE WOLVES, HODOR'S HEAVY TREAD, THE SHALLOWER MARKS LEFT BY THE FEET OF THE TWO REEDS.
ONCE UNDER THE TREES, THE STONY GROUND AND FALLEN LEAVES MADE THE TRAIL HARDER TO SEE, BUT BY THEN FARLEN'S RED BITCH HAD THE SCENT.
HE'D HAVE GUESSED THAT OSHA MIGHT RUN SOUTH TO SER RODRIK, BUT THE TRAIL LED NORTH BY NORTHWEST, INTO THE VERY HEART OF THE WOLFSWOOD.
THEON DID NOT LIKE THAT ONE BIT. IT WOULD BE A BITTER IRONY IF THE STARKS MADE FOR DEEPWOOD MOTTE AND DELIVERED THEMSELVES RIGHT INTO ASHA'S HANDS.
I'D SOONER HAVE THEM DEAD, HE THOUGHT BITTERLY. IT IS BETTER TO BE SEEN AS CRUEL THAN FOOLISH.
THUS FAR HUNTING SEEMS INDISTINGUISHABLE FROM RIDING THROUGH THE WOODS, MY LORD.
THERE ARE SIMILARITIES. BUT WITH HUNTING, THERE'S BLOOD AT THE END.
MUST IT BE SO? THIS FLIGHT WAS GREAT FOLLY, BUT WILL YOU NOT BE MERCIFUL? THESE ARE YOUR FOSTER BROTHERS WE SEEK.
NO STARK BUT ROBB WAS EVER BROTHERLY TOWARD ME, BUT BRAN AND RICKON HAVE MORE VALUE TO ME LIVING THAN DEAD.
THE SAME IS TRUE OF THE REEDS. MOAT CAILIN SITS ON THE EDGE OF THE BOGS. LORD HOWLAND CAN MAKE YOUR UNCLE'S OCCUPATION A VISIT TO HELL IF HE CHOOSES, BUT SO LONG AS YOU HOLD HIS HEIRS HE MUST STAY HIS HAND.
THEON HAD NOT CONSIDERED THAT. IN TRUTH, HE HAD SCARCELY CONSIDERED THE MUDMEN AT ALL, BEYOND EYEING MEERA ONCE OR TWICE AND WONDERING IF SHE WAS STILL A MAIDEN.
YOU MAY BE RIGHT. WE WILL SPARE THEM IF WE CAN.
AND HODOR TOO, I HOPE. THE BOY IS SIMPLE, YOU KNOW THAT. HE DOES AS HE IS TOLD. HOW MANY TIMES HAS HE GROOMED YOUR HORSE, SOAPED YOUR SADDLE, SCOURED YOUR MAIL?
IF HE DOES NOT FIGHT US, WE WILL LET HIM LIVE.
BUT SAY ONE WORD ABOUT SPARING THE WILDLING, AND YOU CAN DIE WITH HER. SHE SWORE ME AN OATH AND PISSED ON IT.
I MAKE NO APOLOGIES FOR OATHBREAKERS. DO WHAT YOU MUST. I THANK YOU FOR YOUR MERCY.
MERCY. THERE'S A BLOODY TRAP. TOO MUCH AND THEY CALL YOU WEAK, TOO LITTLE AND YOU'RE MONSTROUS.

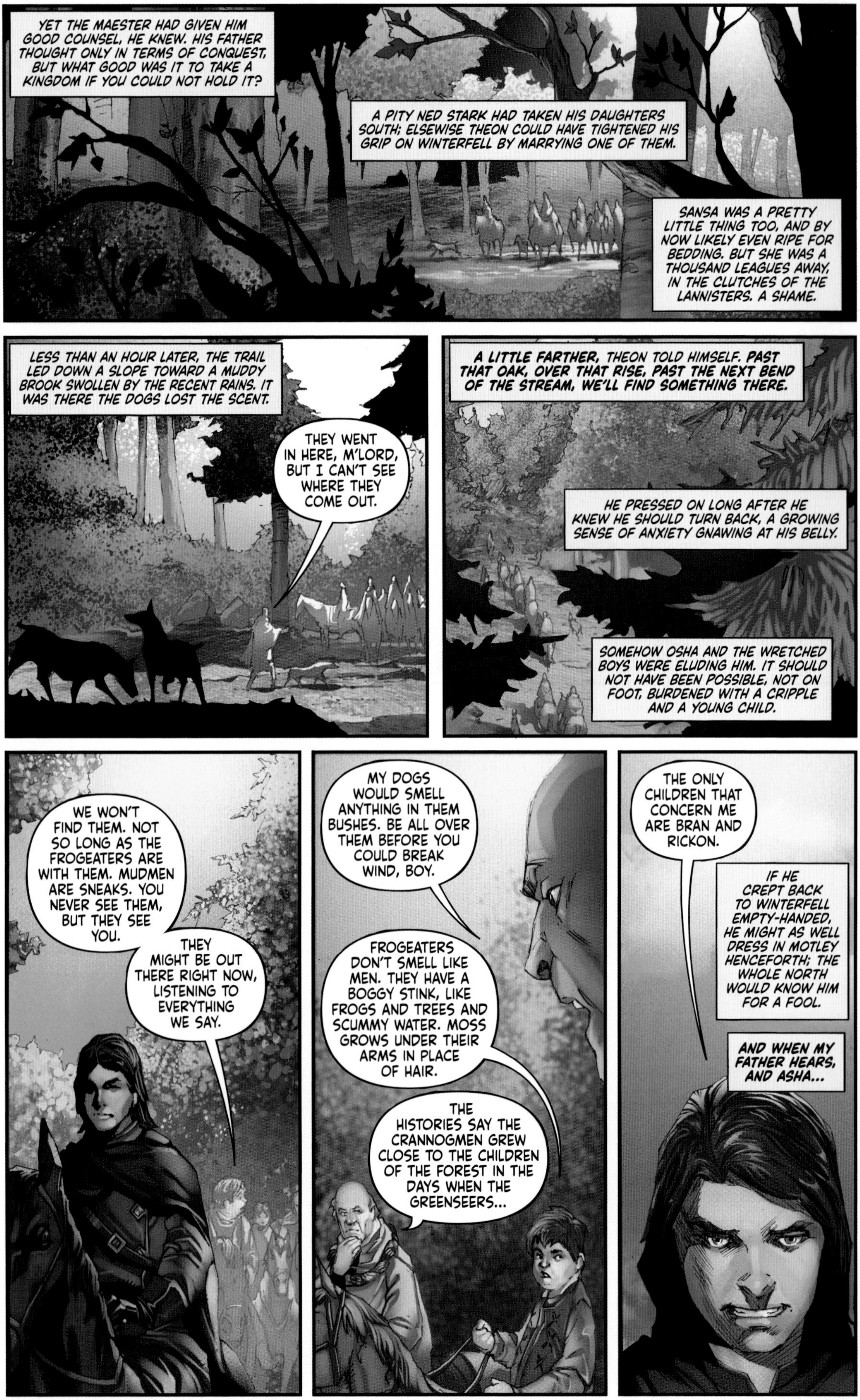
YET THE MAESTER HAD GIVEN HIM GOOD COUNSEL, HE KNEW. HIS FATHER THOUGHT ONLY IN TERMS OF CONQUEST, BUT WHAT GOOD WAS IT TO TAKE A KINGDOM IF YOU COULD NOT HOLD IT?
A PITY NED STARK HAD TAKEN HIS DAUGHTERS SOUTH; ELSEWISE THEON COULD HAVE TIGHTENED HIS GRIP ON WINTERFELL BY MARRYING ONE OF THEM.
SANSA WAS A PRETTY LITTLE THING TOO, AND BY NOW LIKELY EVEN RIPE FOR BEDDING. BUT SHE WAS A THOUSAND LEAGUES AWAY, IN THE CLUTCHES OF THE LANNISTERS. A SHAME.
LESS THAN AN HOUR LATER, THE TRAIL LED DOWN A SLOPE TOWARD A MUDDY BROOK SWOLLEN BY THE RECENT RAINS. IT WAS THERE THE DOGS LOST THE SCENT.
THEY WENT IN HERE, M'LORD, BUT I CAN'T SEE WHERE THEY COME OUT.
A LITTLE FARTHER, THEON TOLD HIMSELF. PAST THAT OAK, OVER THAT RISE, PAST THE NEXT BEND OF THE STREAM, WE'LL FIND SOMETHING THERE.
HE PRESSED ON LONG AFTER HE KNEW HE SHOULD TURN BACK, A GROWING SENSE OF ANXIETY GNAWING AT HIS BELLY.
SOMEHOW OSHA AND THE WRETCHED BOYS WERE ELUDING HIM. IT SHOULD NOT HAVE BEEN POSSIBLE, NOT ON FOOT, BURDENED WITH A CRIPPLE AND A YOUNG CHILD.
WE WON'T FIND THEM. NOT SO LONG AS THE FROGEATERS ARE WITH THEM. MUDMEN ARE SNEAKS. YOU NEVER SEE THEM, BUT THEY SEE YOU.
THEY MIGHT BE OUT THERE RIGHT NOW, LISTENING TO EVERYTHING WE SAY.
MY DOGS WOULD SMELL ANYTHING IN THEM BUSHES. BE ALL OVER THEM BEFORE YOU COULD BREAK WIND, BOY.
FROGEATERS DON'T SMELL LIKE MEN. THEY HAVE A BOGGY STINK, LIKE FROGS AND TREES AND SCUMMY WATER. MOSS GROWS UNDER THEIR ARMS IN PLACE OF HAIR.
THE HISTORIES SAY THE CRANNOGMEN GREW CLOSE TO THE CHILDREN OF THE FOREST IN THE DAYS WHEN THE GREENSEERS...
THE ONLY CHILDREN THAT CONCERN ME ARE BRAN AND RICKON.
IF HE CREPT BACK TO WINTERFELL EMPTY-HANDED, HE MIGHT AS WELL DRESS IN MOTLEY HENCEFORTH; THE WHOLE NORTH WOULD KNOW HIM FOR A FOOL.
AND WHEN MY FATHER HEARS, AND ASHA...

M'LORD PRINCE. MIGHT BE THE BOYS WILL SHELTER SOMEPLACE NEARER. MIGHT BE I KNOW WHERE.

TELL ME.

YOU KNOW THAT OLD MILL, SITTING LONELY ON THE ACORN WATER? WE STOPPED THERE WHEN I WAS BEING DRAGGED TO WINTERFELL A CAPTIVE.

THE MILLER'S WIFE SOLD US HAY FOR OUR HORSES WHILE THAT OLD KNIGHT CLUCKED OVER HER BRATS.

WHY THERE? THERE ARE A DOZEN VILLAGES AND HOLDFASTS JUST AS CLOSE.

WHAT ARE YOU SAYING? IF YOU'VE KEPT SOME KNOWLEDGE FROM ME--

WHY? NOW THAT'S PAST KNOWING. BUT THEY'RE THERE, I HAVE A FEELING.

M'LORD PRINCE?

HAVE A LOOK HERE.

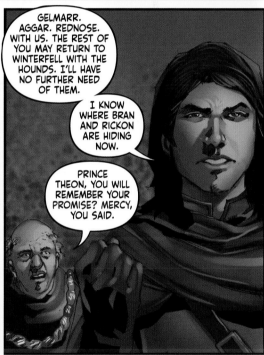

GELMARR. AGGAR. REDNOSE. WITH US. THE REST OF YOU MAY RETURN TO WINTERFELL WITH THE HOUNDS. I'LL HAVE NO FURTHER NEED OF THEM.

I KNOW WHERE BRAN AND RICKON ARE HIDING NOW.

PRINCE THEON, YOU WILL REMEMBER YOUR PROMISE? MERCY, YOU SAID.

MERCY WAS FOR THIS MORNING.

IT IS BETTER TO BE FEARED THAN LAUGHED AT.

"BEFORE THEY MADE ME ANGRY."

COVER GALLERY

PART II ISSUE #1 (Issue 17)
COVER B
Art by Mel Rubi
Colors by Ivan Nunes

PART II ISSUE #1 (Issue 17)
COVER C
Art by Stephen Segovia
Colors by Ivan Nunes

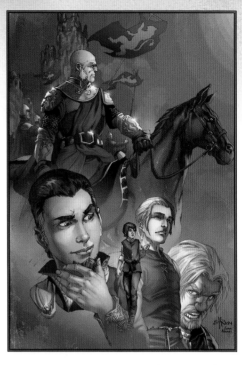

PART II ISSUE #1 (Issue 17)
COVER D
Art by Butch Guice
Colors by Dan Brown

PART II ISSUE #2 (Issue 18)
COVER B
Art by Mel Rubi
Colors by Ivan Nunes

PART II ISSUE #3 (Issue 19)
COVER B
Art by Mel Rubi
Colors by Ivan Nunes

PART II ISSUE #4 (Issue 20)
COVER B
Art by Mel Rubi
Colors by Ivan Nunes

PART II ISSUE #5 (Issue 21)
COVER B
Art by Mel Rubi
Colors by Ivan Nunes

PART II ISSUE #6 (Issue 22)
COVER B
Art by Mel Rubi
Colors by Ivan Nunes

PART II ISSUE #7 (Issue 23)
COVER B
Art by Mel Rubi
Colors by Ivan Nunes

PART II ISSUE #8 (Issue 24)
COVER B
Art by Mel Rubi
Colors by Ivan Nunes

GEORGE R. R. MARTIN is the #1 *New York Times* bestselling author of many novels, including those of the acclaimed series A Song of Ice and Fire—*A Game of Thrones, A Clash of Kings, A Storm of Swords, A Feast for Crows,* and *A Dance with Dragons*—as well as related works such as *Fire & Blood, A Knight of the Seven Kingdoms,* and *The World of Ice & Fire,* with Elio M. García, Jr., and Linda Antonsson. Other novels and collections include *Tuf Voyaging, Fevre Dream, The Armageddon Rag, Dying of the Light, Windhaven* (with Lisa Tuttle), and *Dreamsongs Volumes I* and *II.* As a writer-producer, he has worked on *The Twilight Zone, Beauty and the Beast,* and various feature films and pilots that were never made. He lives with his lovely wife, Parris, in Santa Fe, New Mexico.

georgerrmartin.com
Facebook.com/GeorgeRRMartinofficial
Twitter: @GRRMspeaking

LANDRY Q. WALKER is a *New York Times* bestselling author of comics and books. He lives with his cats and his wife, and he spends his days pushing buttons randomly on a keyboard until stories somehow happen.

MEL RUBI has been a professional artist since 1993, and enjoys challenging himself on every difficult task he takes on. He loves playing chess and is a family man.
Facebook.com/boundead

IVAN NUNES has been a professional colorist since 2006, having made approximately 200 comic books, mostly by Dynamite, and more than 900 covers. He is currently working on *A Clash of Kings* for Dynamite and *Action Comics* for DC Comics.
Facebook.com/ivan.nunes.73

TOM NAPOLITANO graduated from the School of Visual Arts in 2010, and has been working in the comics industry ever since. His talents have been used in design, prepress, and lettering. Tom's balloons and onomatopoeias have appeared in a plethora of titles for Andwold Design, Lion Forge, IDW, Dynamite, and DC Comics.

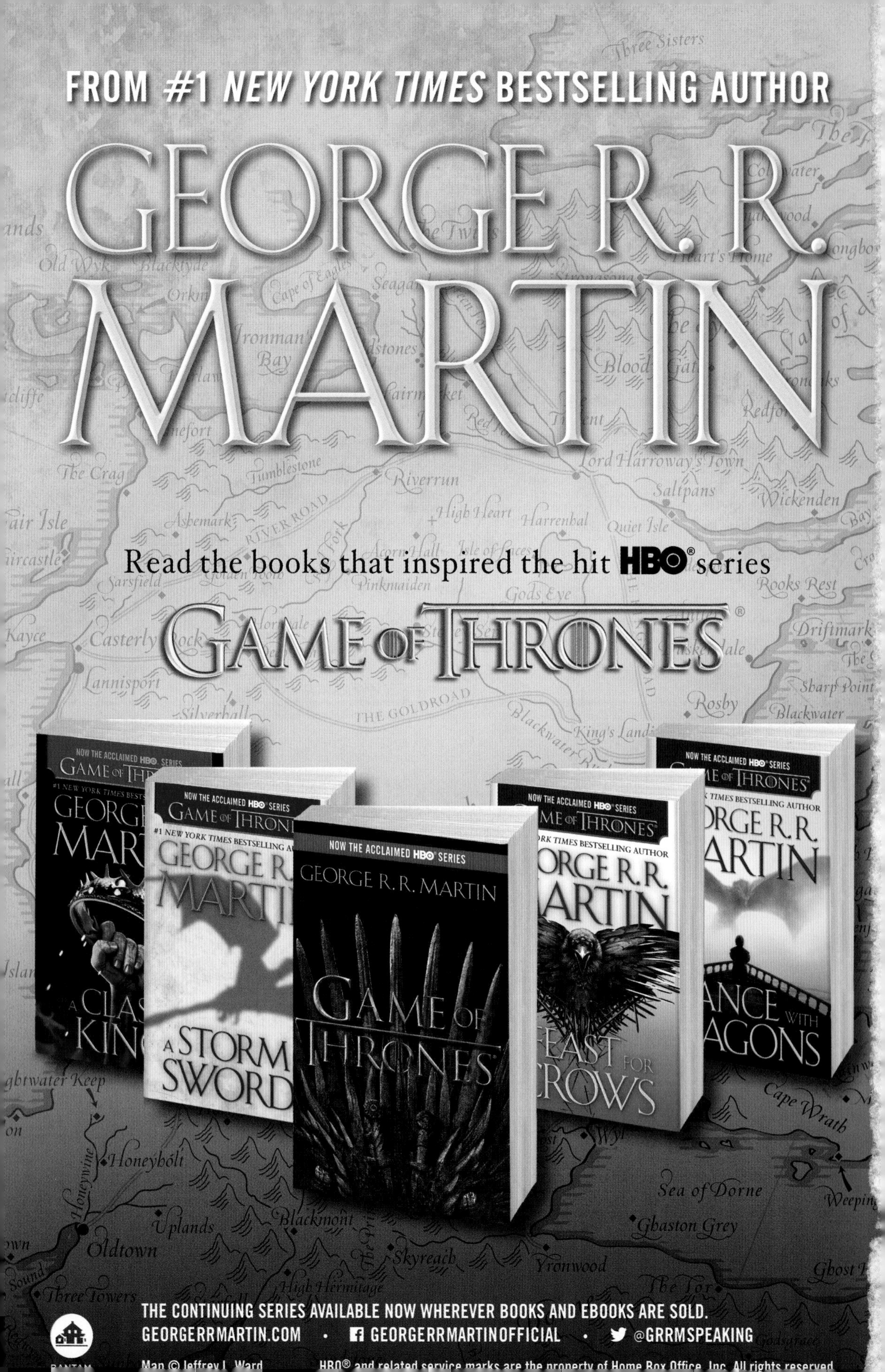
FROM #1 NEW YORK TIMES BESTSELLING AUTHOR
GEORGE R. R. MARTIN
Read the books that inspired the hit HBO® series
GAME OF THRONES®
NOW THE ACCLAIMED HBO® SERIES
GEORGE R. R. MARTIN
GAME OF THRONES
THE CONTINUING SERIES AVAILABLE NOW WHEREVER BOOKS AND EBOOKS ARE SOLD.
GEORGERRMARTIN.COM • GEORGERRMARTINOFFICIAL • @GRRMSPEAKING
Map © Jeffrey L. Ward
HBO® and related service marks are the property of Home Box Office, Inc. All rights reserved.

DATE DUE			